Lacey Smithsonian's School for Scandal

Right now, somewhere in Washington, D.C., a scandal is brewing. It hasn't happened yet, but it will. Tomorrow or the next day or the next. Somewhere a hapless victim is on the precipice of a fashion disaster. An unsuspecting woman will have her unsavory secrets exposed to the harsh light of day, the hot lights of television news, and the wisecracks of stand-up comedians everywhere.

When the scandal comes—and it will—this woman will be targeted for a full-scale assault on the way she acts, dresses, and looks, in addition to the salient details of her particular mess. Remember Linda, Paula, Monica, and now you.

Take it from a reporter. Whoever you are, we, the media, will excoriate you. Your old friends will rat on you. And it will be worse if your face isn't ready to face the music.

Killer Hair

A CRIME OF FASHION MYSTERY

Ellen Byerrum

A SIGNET BOOK

SIGNET
Published by New American Library, a division of
Penguin Group (USA) Inc., 375 Hudson Street,
New York, New York 10014, USA
Penguin Group (Canada), 10 Alcorn Avenue, Toronto,
Ontario M4V 3B2, Canada (a division of Pearson Penguin Canada Inc.)
Penguin Books Ltd., 80 Strand, London WC2R 0RL, England
Penguin Ireland, 25 St. Stephen's Green, Dublin 2,
Ireland (a division of Penguin Books Ltd.)
Penguin Group (Australia), 250 Camberwell Road, Camberwell, Victoria 3124,
Australia (a division of Pearson Australia Group Pty. Ltd.)
Penguin Books India Pvt. Ltd., 11 Community Centre, Panchsheel Park,
New Delhi - 110 017, India
Penguin Group (NZ), cnr Airborne and Rosedale Roads, Albany,
Auckland 1310, New Zealand (a division of Pearson New Zealand Ltd.)
Penguin Books (South Africa) (Pty.) Ltd., 24 Sturdee Avenue,
Rosebank, Johannesburg 2196, South Africa

Penguin Books Ltd., Registered Offices:
80 Strand, London WC2R 0RL, England

First published by Signet, an imprint of New American Library,
a division of Penguin Group (USA) Inc.

First Printing, August 2003
10 9 8 7 6 5

Printed in the United States of America

PUBLISHER'S NOTE
This is a work of fiction. Names, characters, places, and incidents either are the product of the author's imagination or are used fictitiously, and any resemblance to actual persons, living or dead, business establishments, events, or locales is entirely coincidental.

This book is dedicated to
my husband, Bob Williams,
first, last, and always.

ACKNOWLEDGMENTS

In the seemingly endless journey to publication, the following friends offered me their support, encouragement, and advice, and for that I will always be grateful: Guy Burdick Jennifer Combs, Joanne C. Duangmanee, Jay Farrell, Shantelle Fowler, Elaine and Ernie Joselovitz, Barbara McConagha, Mona Miller, Bernie Mower, Bob Swierczek, and Bob Williams.

For their specialized information and patience in answering my questions, I am indebted to Ann Geracimos, Robin Givhan, and especially Howard Miller.

Finally, I would like to thank my agent, Don Maass, and my editor, Genny Ostertag, for their part in guiding this book into print.

chapter 1

Lacey Smithsonian looked down at the unfortunate woman in the coffin and thought, *Oh my God, that is the worst haircut I've ever seen.*

And they say you can't die from a bad haircut. Even as that sentiment percolated through her brain, she added, *You are such a bitch, Lacey.* But she couldn't help it. It really was a bad haircut.

The haircut belonged to Angela Woods, "Angie" to her friends at Stylettos, the trendy Dupont Circle salon where she had worked until just a few days ago. Now Angie was the guest of honor in the polished maple casket at Evergreens Mortuary in the Nation's Capital.

At only twenty-five, Angie's sweet round face wasn't going to get any older. And that hairdo wasn't going to get any better. The deceased looked peaceful, if a little sad, laid to rest in the satin-lined box. She wore a dark rose silk jacquard dress with a lace collar that conflicted wildly with those strange short rainbow-colored clumps of hair sticking up in between patches of bruised bald scalp.

What on earth was she thinking?

Although Lacey had only known Angie casually, she remembered her as polite and demure. Her friends said Angie was committed to the proposition that every life could be improved with the help of a professional stylist. But there would be no more perms, colors, or highlights in Angie's attempt to make the world a prettier place.

At least the city didn't need any help that day. It was a beautiful Wednesday in April and there was a respite from the rain that had pounded the city into submission for the last two weeks. Cherry trees were exploding with blossoms, a pink snowstorm against a turquoise sky. On days like this, springtime in the Capital City is a wanton green feast that wraps itself around the heart. Days like this make Washingtonians forget that spring is usually a dreary, soggy endurance test that begins with endless drizzly fifty-degree days, then slams headlong into summer, drenching humidity, and ninety-degree heat, leaving psychic whiplash and a dull sinus headache.

Nevertheless, every spring D.C. is the scene of an invasion of curiously dressed tourists, Day-Glo families, busloads of polyester grandparents, and entire high-school classes wearing matching blue and orange neon T-shirts and baseball caps. They are nice, enthusiastic, and irritating as hell. The tourists hear the pumping heartbeat of spring. They answer unseen drums commanding them to swarm around the Tidal Basin in a yearly ritual as predictable as the swallows that return to Capistrano.

At least the tourist hordes Lacey had fought through to reach the mortuary, with their plastic cameras and camcorders, knew how to appreciate spring in Washington. A hundred thousand weak-eyed wonks would never see it, toiling in their anonymous beige and gray offices. The woman in the coffin would never again enjoy it.

Lacey wondered exactly what she was doing in a mortuary. But she'd rather be anywhere on a glorious spring day than back at her desk at the newspaper, opening stacks of press releases in search of something, anything, to write about.

"What did I tell you, Lacey? Is that not the worst razor job you ever saw?"

Lacey turned to see her own hairstylist, Stella Lake, standing behind her in the small viewing room.

Stella was the manager of Stylettos. She had an image to uphold, so she had dressed carefully for the occasion: her best black Lycra leggings, red leather bustier, and black leather bomber jacket. For Stella, this was uncharacteristically subdued, even with the fresh manicure—bold red nails inset with tiny lightning bolts. The leather dog collar set off an asymmetrical crew cut—burgundy this week—that spiked defiantly from Stella's perfectly round noggin. It was a disconcerting look for a petite thirty-five-year-old woman with the beginnings of crow's-feet and a whiskey voice, but attention getting nevertheless. Stella was small but managed to seem much larger.

The woman was a genius with a pair of scissors—on other people's heads. Yet Stella considered herself her own best work of art, one that changed with the moon or the tides or simply bad hair days that cried out to try something new.

"To be honest, Stella, now she looks like most of your stylists. Except for the bald spots. And the bruises."

"No way! The hand that did that was not professional. Besides, what I'm saying is, punk dominatrix isn't her style. Angie was more of a Guinevere type, you know?"

"Guinevere?" Lacey asked. Stella was the queen of stylistic shorthand.

"You know, romantic. Long hair, long dresses. Pink. Angie liked pink."

"Pink?" Lacey had complicated feelings about pink. She actually liked it, but it seemed out of place in this town. Washington, D.C., was the epitome of a taupe, bland, beige, oatmeal kind of town, and heavy on black and gray. Hairstylists and other artistic types preferred a wardrobe of stark black and white. Pink was considered far too perky, except among the preppier Republicans.

Stella shrugged and lifted her eyebrows. They both took another look at Angie.

An eight-by-ten photo of Angie was set up on a table near the casket. The Angie in the picture had long golden-blond hair that cascaded in soft waves to her waist. It was glorious hair, the kind of hair that poets write about, the kind that comes to mind when little girls read about Rapunzel.

Just a few days before, Lacey had nervously surrendered her own locks to Stella, who installed dazzling blond highlights in her honey-brown hair. Stella had dared her. "What? It's going to kill you to try something new? Trust me, Lacey, it'll work. Besides, you were probably blond as a kid. I'm right, aren't I?"

Angie had floated through the salon, a serene long-haired Madonna wearing a pink Stylettos smock in a sea of buzz-cut punkettes wearing black on black and enough eyeliner for a tree full of raccoons. She stopped to assure Lacey in her soft

Southern drawl that the highlights would be beautiful. Angie's chair-side manner was a good deal more soothing than Stella's.

Lacey looked back at Stella. "What happened to her?"

"What does it look like?"

"The paper's police log said suicide. But it didn't mention this monstrosity. Damn, Stella, it looks like she scalped herself in a fit of madness or was stone drunk or drugged out, came to her senses, took one look in the mirror, and killed herself. Is that *possible?*"

"That's what the police think." Stella pulled Lacey away from the casket as if the dead woman could hear them. The D.C. police had written off Angela Woods as a suicide, a "suicide blonde" as it were, and that was that.

Lacey knew the murder rate in the District of Columbia was astronomical, the rate of solved murders half the national average, the state of the morgue chaotic, and autopsy results as changeable as the weather. For years, the D.C. homicide squad had been a joke, and not even the funniest one in this town.

The cops thought they had it all wrapped up, Stella told her. The detectives concluded that hairstylist Angela Woods slit her wrists at Stylettos Salon in Dupont Circle, using a Colonel Conk straight razor, a common salon tool, then wrote *So Long* with her blood on the mirror—which they termed the "suicide note." She bled to death in the chair at her station sometime late Saturday night.

Sunday morning, with a gigantic hangover, Stella opened the salon, discovered the body, lost her breakfast, and called the police. Stella figured alerting the police was a bad idea, but she didn't have a better one at the time. It wasn't like she could call her psychic (who should have warned her in the first place) or her acupuncturist.

The body was collected, sent to the medical examiner's office, released, and laid out for viewing on Wednesday. The funeral was scheduled for Thursday morning at ten.

Stylettos never opened the day Stella found the body. It remained closed on Monday while a special crime-scene cleaning company removed the bloodstains. *Crime-scene cleaning crews: a growth industry in Washington,* Lacey thought. *Along with document shredding.*

"It must have been pretty awful finding her."

"I've had better days." Stella chewed at one lighting-bolted nail. "There was so much blood, Lacey. I never knew there could be so much blood. The cops told me she was probably doing drugs. I said 'Look at that haircut!' They said Angie must've been into self-mutilation. Assholes."

"Drugs? Did they order toxicology tests?"

"Who knows! They sent her body to the D.C. morgue! It's a miracle they even got the right body to the mortuary."

"So you don't know. What about an autopsy?"

Stella shook her head. According to the media, the morgue was another abyss you wouldn't wish on your worst enemy. The District was trying to clean it up and improve the office's image, but was fighting years of corruption and inefficiency, bad press, lack of money, bodies stacked in corners, and misidentified victims.

"I can't imagine her doing this. It's not her style, and frankly, it's a pretty piss-poor job," Stella concluded.

"The haircut or the suicide?"

"Either. Both."

"And why exactly did you want me to come here today?" Stella had been frantic on the phone: Lacey *had* to meet her at the mortuary. She stopped just short of threatening retribution on Lacey's head, or worse, on her hair, but it was implied that Lacey's freshly lightened locks would be in peril. "It's really awful, Stel, but what can I do?"

"I thought you'd be, you know, interested."

Lacey and Stella sank down on folding chairs and gazed at the flower arrangements. Lacey's eyes rested on a small basket of violets, sweet and sad, sent from the salon, and a showy arrangement of white roses, irises, and gladiolus, signed *Always, Boyd.* That would be Boyd Radford, owner of Stylettos, Stella's notorious boss. Sprays of pink carnations came from the Woods family. The subdued lighting made the coffin the focal point. The small room's dark wood paneling and deep burgundy carpeting were oppressive in spite of the bright flowers. Boxes of tissues were discreetly placed for the convenience of mourners.

" 'Interested'?" Lacey waited.

Stella sighed loudly. "Well, since you are an expert, I thought maybe, who knows—"

"An expert!" *What is she talking about?* Lacey was aghast. "Stella, I write a fashion column."

"Like I said."

"An expert on what?"

"Style. Nuances. Like you wrote last week. 'Nuances of style are clues to personality.' "

"Well, yes . . . Wait. You don't actually *read* my column."

" 'Crimes of Fashion'? Are you kidding? Like a Bible. Only more fun. And those 'Fashion Bites.' We love 'em. You should do them every day."

"Every day! It's hard enough to write 'Crimes' once a week. As for 'Fashion Bites,' they only bite when the spirit, or my editor, moves me."

Lacey did not want to believe anyone actually read her column, or *The Eye Street Observer*, the upstart daily newspaper in which it appeared. She thought of it as "The Little Paper That Couldn't," and she firmly believed the damn column would be the death of her. If not literally, then figuratively—the death of her dream of being a good reporter, a real reporter. Not a fashion reporter, or even an antifashion reporter, as she had decided to think of herself. She assumed her weekly sartorial diatribes were poured into the computer and then cast into the void. But as for people actually reading it, considering it, quoting it? *Oh my God.*

"And you thought that by just gazing at a dead woman, I could figure out what happened?"

Only in the District of Columbia could people actually believe that some random idiot off the street, or, yes, even a fashion reporter, could solve a murder before the cops.

"I am not an investigator, Stella." Lacey struggled for a way to escape her stylist's mad notion. "Why not call a private detective?"

"Like, for a hundred reasons. One, they cost money. Two, I don't know any. Three, I got you."

"Oh, Stella." Lacey sighed. "I don't know what to say."

"Four, nuances. Lacey, look at her. These are big nuances here. Like a neon sign. And you have a nose for nuances." Stella started chewing another nail. This whole mess was ruining her manicure and calling the cops hadn't solved anything. "Well, it was a thought. So sue me."

"It's very sweet, but . . . What kind of a thought, Stella?" *Leave now, Lacey. You don't want to know.*

"You know how you always write that the way people dress reveals who they really are, like it's a key to their personality or something? Their hair. Their grooming. Their clothes. Like it's a language, right, or a code? About how it's good to express yourself if you know what you're saying. Like you do that Forties thing with your clothes. It says, you know, Rosalind Russell meets Rosie the Riveter. Brains, beauty, and no bullshit. Something like that. Am I right?"

Lacey couldn't argue with Stella, but she was stopped cold at hearing her own fashion philosophy distilled into Stella's pungent vernacular. *Am I that transparent?*

Stella proudly indicated her own leather bondage outfit, heavy on the zippers. "Take me. What am I saying here? Come on. This is an easy one. 'Punk Goddess with a Heart of Gold.' Right?"

On acid, Lacey amended silently.

"It works on me because I *know* what I'm doing. I *know* what I'm saying with my clothes. I wear what I mean. I mean what I wear."

"I wrote that?"

"Not in so many words, but I knew what you meant, you know."

"Stella, my column is a joke. I have no business writing it. It was a fluke. I'm still trying to get out of it."

"No way. You should be proud of it, Lacey. We read 'Crimes of Fashion' aloud in the salon every Friday with our coffee. I just figured you could take a look at Angie and figure something out."

"I'm not psychic, Stella."

"She didn't kill herself, Lacey! Look at her. This look says, 'I wouldn't be caught dead looking this way.' Maybe you could just tell people that. In your column, where people she knew could read it. It would mean something to them. To her."

It occurred to Lacey that Stella was the only stylist in Washington who had found a way to cut her light brown locks into a style that always fell into place effortlessly and even evoked a hint of early Lauren Bacall. She had to admit the new highlights were stunning. The lightened waves skimmed her shoulders, framed her face, and made her blue-green eyes look enormous. And she liked Stella, who always made her laugh. *You're sunk, Lacey. She's got you by the roots.*

"She had plans for her life." Stella reached in the casket and gently ran her fingers over the short tufts of Angie's hair. She clicked her tongue. "If it was suicide, it was *assisted.* You know what I mean?"

Lacey sighed deeply and studied Angie. The woman in the picture. The corpse in the coffin. Stella was right. They didn't jive. "Nuances?"

Stella nodded. "Real big nuances."

But if Angie didn't kill herself . . . who did? Was it possible that some degenerate had spitefully hacked off her hair? Then what? Killed her? Or vice versa? Who wouldn't want to see her stylist dead at one time or another? Was it so far-fetched? Lacey's mind wandered back to notable hair disasters in her pre-Stella days. The perm that turned into a Brillo pad. The "trim" that rendered her a Joan of Arc look-alike. The highlights that turned green. *Mayhem maybe, but surely not—*

"Murder, Stella?" If the likelihood of a murder being solved in D.C. was merely remote, then the likelihood of a nice, neat suicide being reclassified as a murder, and *then* solved, was zilch. Stella shrugged. "But who would want to kill her? A client?" Lacey asked.

"Nah, everybody loved Angie. Unique, I know."

"What about a boyfriend?"

"None that I know of. She would have told me. You know how hard it is to find a decent male specimen here. Besides, Angie was totally choosy and completely into the career thing."

Lacey closed her eyes and tried to remember everything she knew about the dead woman.

Angela Woods was just coming into her own professionally. She had enjoyed a brief spurt of fame for magically transforming the latest fallen woman in a Capitol Hill scandal from a heifer into a fox—at least by D.C. standards. Angie was one of the few who had benefited from that ugly political potboiler.

Politics in Washington is like Muzak in elevators. It's everywhere, and for most Washingtonians it eventually just becomes background noise. But even the political junkies, the vampires of Washington, who eat, breathe, and live every little congressional stab in the back and read party-line votes like a fortuneteller reads tea leaves, need hairstylists. Which is how Angie Woods and politics intersected.

Congressional staffer Marcia Robinson needed a makeover—and a miracle. The town's latest scandal celebrity was the ideal grist for the media mill: young, naive, and far from innocent. Marcia believed a little too wholeheartedly in her First Amendment right to take it all off on the Web—and to recruit exhibitionistic underage Capitol Hill interns.

When she received her own invitation for a chat with the perennial special prosecutor, big-haired, toothy, would-be sexpot Marcia needed a new image fast. When a woman faces the TV cameras in a Washington scandal, Bad Hair means Bad News.

"It was a work of art what she did to that woman, that Marcia Robinson."

"More like a public service." Lacey had featured the makeover in a "Crimes of Fashion" column: "My Life Is a Mess, but I've Never Looked Better!"

Angela Woods' last worldly accomplishment was successfully repackaging a frumpy, frizzy-haired cyber-tart as a sadder-but-wiser naif with silky blow-dried locks, a doe-eyed innocent who was chastened by her media ordeal but bravely bearing up. And Angela reaped the benefits of her brief notoriety. For her efforts, she was featured in the LifeStyle sections of the various local newspapers, along with a few fashion dos and don'ts for looking your best in the media glare. As Lacey had summed up in her own column: "Tame the mane, emphasize the eyes, and keep the mouth glossy and *shut*." Always good advice in the District of Columbia.

Angie's client book was suddenly full and customers were waiting weeks for an appointment. Stylettos saved all the news clippings, which Stella posted on the front door of the salon. The attention was not without its downside, however. It created a ripple of resentment among the happy little crew at Stylettos. And now Angie was suddenly dead.

Stella interrupted Lacey's reverie. "How about it?"

"I can't write a column saying she was murdered. Not without the facts." *Unless no one reads it except Stella.*

"Investigate! You're a reporter. Reporters do it on TV all the time."

"Not fashion reporters."

"You'll be the first."

"Oh yeah, why not an investigative stylist?"

"Are you kidding? In this outfit? Besides, I got work to do." Stella whipped out hair spray, a comb, and a blond wig from her bag. "For Angie's mom, you know? She's flying in tonight."

"That's very considerate, Stel." Lacey's eyes started to tear. She grabbed a tissue.

"I get along really well with mothers, just not my own." Stella began to restyle the corpse for her last public appearance. "And Lacey, last week's column—'Never Wear Pink to Testify Before the Special Prosecutor'—was stellar. See you at the funeral."

"Hey, I didn't say yes! Funerals are depressing and I hardly knew her. Stella, are you listening?"

"You can start there. Your investigation. Killers always go to the funeral, don't they?"

"No, Stella. I said no. Besides, I have nothing to wear."

chapter 2

There's an old newspaper saying: If you're blind, they'll make you the art critic. If you're deaf, they'll make you the music critic. But if you're blind and deaf, they'll make you the drama critic.

By this logic, the fashion critic should be blind, deaf, and dressed in a burlap bag. Lacey didn't know what she had done to deserve being the fashion reporter—or antifashion reporter. She didn't dress badly. She knew a gore from a tuck and a ruffle from a pleat; she could use "ruching" in a sentence. Frankly, she loved good clothing. However, she didn't want to write about it. You didn't see Rosalind Russell in *His Girl Friday* shuffled off to the fashion beat, even though she was dressed like a million bucks. Rosalind Russell went right out in her best suit and found the killer. *Ooh, bad example.*

Lacey had never asked for the fashion beat. But then, life had never gone smoothly for her. She saw her friends climb the ladder of success and roar into high positions with acclaim and money. Meanwhile, her so-called career path was littered with potholes and detours.

She had finally made it back to D.C. after working for years on some of the worst small newspapers in Colorado. She had spent her college summers in D.C. with her favorite aunt, now deceased, Great-aunt Mimi. Those summers gave her the first full taste of freedom she had ever had. She had wound up in small Western towns, but always with her heart set on the East.

Now she was thirty-three years old and still trying to land a decent job at a decent paper. Instead, she was slinging words at

The Eye Street Observer like a waitress slinging hash at a roadside diner. She had been there three years.

The Eye, as employees and other media types tended to call it, was a feisty wannabe news sheet in the Nation's Capital. It was located on Eye Street between Sixteenth and Seventeenth streets in a granite and glass building facing Farragut Square, under the watchful eye of Admiral David "Damn the Torpedoes" Farragut in all his bronze glory. *The Observer*, as everyone else called it, was a daily broadsheet rag with a tabloid heart, the mutant offspring of a weekly alternative paper and a local dot-com millionaire with a *Citizen Kane* obsession, since departed.

It would never be top dog. Washingtonians clung to the established *Washington Post* with dismaying faithfulness. *The Washington Times* soldiered on to the right, spending bottomless Moonie money as if it were newsprint. *The Eye*, with no political bent except "throw the rascals out," got by on sheer nerve.

The paper's most popular feature was "The Daily Jam," a sarcastic and brutally accurate District traffic forecast that ran on the front page, below the fold. The new publisher was convinced that the single most important daily news story in Washington was the specific pothole, parade, detour, or demonstration that would make today's morning or evening commute a living hell. Features like "The Daily Jam" and "Crimes of Fashion" were winning *The Eye* an oddball niche in a tough media market, much to Lacey's chagrin.

But in a town glutted with journalists fighting for jobs, Lacey at least had a job on a real newspaper and was not stuck in one of the hundreds of trade associations, slapping together an in-house newsletter on the rubber industry or paper clip regulations.

On the other hand, she had to write about fashion, or what passed for it in the District of Columbia. The only upside was that other people thought it sounded glamorous. *And Stella thinks I'm the Sherlock Holmes of Style. The Philip Marlowe of Fashion. In the least fashionable city in America: The City That Fashion Forgot.*

* * *

Back at the overstuffed cubicle she called her office, Lacey couldn't get the images from the mortuary out of her mind. Angie with blond Guinevere tendrils in the photo. Angie almost bald in her polished coffin. Stella with her insane idea. A ghoulish rhyme thumped in Lacey's head. *A tisket, a tasket, a dead girl in a basket.*

Lacey was grateful that the evil food editor, Felicity Pickles, wasn't around. Instead, Felicity had left a dangerous batch of brownies at her desk, which was just across the aisle from Lacey's. The food editor was forever dieting and brought something fattening to the office every day. Today, the chocolate-iced fat bombs bore an elaborate handwritten note inviting everyone to *Eat Me.*

She has a gingerbread house in the forest somewhere. But she can't make me take one.

Lacey rubbed her temples and opened her eyes to see Tony Trujillo approaching. He grabbed a couple of brownies from Felicity's desk.

"Careful, they're poison," Lacey said.

"Don't I know it." He made a glutton of himself. She was, at that moment, in no mood for Tony, the police reporter extraordinaire. Tony's thick black hair, his smooth olive skin, his self-professed writing prowess, and his status as the cops writer, which entitled him to abuse the language in new and colorful ways, attracted women in droves.

Originally from Santa Fe, New Mexico, his Western nonchalance was a welcome change from uptight East Coast boys. He also appeared to like women, whereas most D.C. men seemed too busy, or too terrified. He wore his blue jeans and tight T-shirts so well that coming or going, Lacey had to admit, he was a feast for the eye.

Women on the staff who didn't know him called him "Tony Terrific." Although he had gone through a number of them, who later referred to him as "Terrible Tony," he was hard to dislike. He and Lacey started at the paper the same week. It galled her that his star rose, while she had been shanghaied to LifeStyle.

"Hey, Smithsonian. I hear blue is the new black. Or is beige the new white, green the new blue, purple the new brown?" He shoved some papers out of the way and perched on the end of her desk, licking brownie crumbs off his fingers. She looked up briefly.

"What's on your mind, Tony? New boots?"

Tony smiled, the corners of his cocoa-brown almond eyes crinkling. He propped one boot on her desk to show it off. He was the Imelda Marcos of the police beat.

"Pretty slick, huh, Lacey? Armadillo by Tony Lama. What do you think?"

"I suppose you think I'm jealous that your wardrobe is bigger than mine." Her eyes wandered up his leg.

"Just feel that leather. Smooth, huh? Last boots I bought, you said looked like roadkill."

"Ah. So these died of natural causes?"

Tony grinned. There was something about him. Something besides his smooth pecs. And his armadillo boots. *Time to change the subject, Lacey.*

The only subject that came to mind was a dead girl in a basket. Lacey figured that asking a few hypothetical questions of the police reporter wouldn't hurt. She didn't have to mention Angie specifically.

"Tony, if someone commits suicide in the District, who makes the official determination?"

He moved his boot off her copy. "Medical examiner. Why? Had a bad week?"

"Not as bad as those armadillos. So, if someone is ruled a suicide, how long do the cops investigate?"

"Not long. Suicide means case closed, move along to something else. And there's always something else here."

"Even if friends and family swear the victim was killed?"

"Police don't overrule the medical examiner."

"What if someone finds new evidence?"

"Better be good or the cops wouldn't care. What kind of evidence? You working on something I should know about?"

"Lower your radar, Boot Boy. Just a question."

"Interesting question, Smithsonian." Tony winked and strutted his armadillos toward the coffee machine.

As she watched him go, Lacey briefly wondered if the right guy would ever materialize or if she'd left her last best hope in the dead-end town of Sagebrush, Colorado. There'd been a man there once who'd looked even hotter in a pair of boots and jeans. . . . But she didn't have time to think about him.

Away from Stella, Lacey hoped she could reflect on Angie Woods' death more logically. But the waxy face of the young woman and the chilling silence of the mortuary were the only images she could fix on.

Unfortunately, "Crimes of Fashion" wouldn't wait. She had been toying with an idea not yet fully formed, after a D.C. city councilman introduced a new antiprostitution measure that would allow the police to arrest women for merely dressing provocatively, on the theory that "If you look like a hooker and quack like a hooker, you *are* a hooker." She had a couple of possible headlines: "This Look Is So Hot, It Got Me Arrested" or "Wear a Wonderbra, Go to Jail." But after that she was stuck.

Lacey wasn't in the mood to sit and stare out the window until the column fell into place. She grabbed her purse for a quick getaway. Luckily, the fashion beat and her process of generating ideas were a complete mystery to her editor, Mac. He didn't care as long as copy magically appeared at the appointed time and place. Out of the corner of her eye Lacey saw him sidling up to her desk. He glowered like a black G. Gordon Liddy.

From the moment he met her, Douglas MacArthur "Mac" Jones thought her name was hilarious.

"Smithsonian? That's not a name. That's a museum."

Lacey once made the mistake of telling Mac the family legend of how her great-grandfather, who emigrated from England, saw the Smithsonian Institution mentioned in a magazine and figured that if it was good enough for the Nation's Capital, it was good enough for him. "Smithsonian" would be much tonier than the original family name of "Smith," which was far too common for a Cockney shopkeeper. His Irish Catholic wife, Maura Kathleen O'Brian Smithsonian, laughed about it till the day he died.

"Just lucky you weren't named Lacey Airandspacemuseum," Mac had said.

Mac was now descending on her desk. She waited for the usual pleasantries. "Nice of you to grace us with your presence, Smithsonian."

Lacey decided not to tell him she'd been out viewing a

corpse. He'd just assume there was some style angle. And he'd say, as he often did when she suggested something new, "Well, you've offended everyone else, why not?"

Mac flourished a wad of letters. "Six for, eight against, and we got a call from the former First Lady's press secretary. Wants to know what your problem is. I bet you haven't even checked your e-mail yet."

"I haven't even peeked. So is this about the 'Never Wear Pink to Testify' column?" she asked. She tried to remember what she wrote. . . .

> . . . When accused of high crimes, Crimes of Fashion suggests you dress in high style. Meet your interrogator looking like a woman of substance, not an escapee from Mother Goose. When you're matching wits with the special prosecutor, we suggest that you dress with serious intent.
>
> Nevertheless, the former First Lady chose to make her appearance before the grand jury in a sweet little pink suit dress with baby-blue trim. She looked like Bo Peep had lost not only her sheep, but her mind as well. We hear she left the sunbonnet and lollipop in the limo at the last minute.
>
> Contrary to popular opinion, spun-sugar pastels do not signal a woman's innocence—merely a clumsy and obvious attempt to appear guileless. It screams manipulation and not sophistication. Get a new consultant. Get a clue. And plead guilty to a "Crime of Fashion."

With so many high-level officials called to testify in the Washington scandal of the week, "Never Wear Pink" was the kind of column that received a higher-than-average readership.

"My problem is that the former First Lady wears pastels every time she gets into trouble," Lacey said.

Mac wore the editorial I-don't-get-it look.

"She's trying to disarm people by—very obviously, I might add—looking like Little Miss Muffet. You copyedited it, Mac. Remember?"

"Sure, but I didn't exactly read it. It's like it's in a foreign language."

"Like sports?" she asked. He looked blank. "Tell her press secretary that if the FFL must take her inspiration from fairy tales, she should dress like the evil queen in *Snow White*. Blood reds, passionate purple, poison-apple green. Now, that was a dame with style."

Mac groaned. He had a soft spot for the FFL, the Dragon Lady, but Lacey couldn't care less. Left, right, or center, a Crime of Fashion was a crime against the senses. While Mac yammered on, Lacey cleared her desk, switched off the desk lamp, turned off the computer, and packed her buff-colored leather tote bag. She freshened her lipstick and switched into comfortable, yet still attractive, low-heeled shoes. So many women still clung to the worn-out cliché of suits and clunky athletic shoes, even though there were other choices. *A definite Washington look,* Lacey thought. *Maybe a column for next week.*

"Hey, where are you going?"

"I need inspiration, Mac. This beat is deadly."

"Murder? Wait a minute. Your hairstylist wants you to investigate a murder? I thought she wanted to give you highlights." Brooke Barton, a thin, blond, K Street lawyer driven by dreams of conspiracies, nursed a gin and tonic on Lacey's balcony, one of Lacey's favorite sources of inspiration.

"I already got the killer highlights. This is murder." Lacey sipped her own drink and felt the day finally slip away. After she escaped from the office, she fought her way through the cherry-blossom-crazed tourists and made it back to her apartment just in time to buzz in her best friend.

"Right." Brooke squinted at Lacey. "They look very nice. The highlights, I mean. My contacts are fuzzy. Or maybe it's the gin."

"She wants me to play detective. Follow the fashion clues to the killer." Lacey sighed and admired the view. A slight breeze rippled the air. It was understood that on lovely spring evenings Brooke was always invited. Lacey supplied the gin and the seventh-floor balcony overlooking the Potomac River in Old Town, Alexandria, Virginia. Brooke brought the tonic and limes. It was pleasant on the balcony, even though Lacey hadn't planted her petunias yet, the only flowers that would grow for her. She and Brooke had nursed more than a few drinks—and broken hearts—right here.

"So who's dead?" Brooke grabbed a handful of microwave popcorn.

Lacey's kitchen was always well stocked with liquid refreshment and popcorn. The vintage fridge contained two bottles of champagne, a few eggs, muffins, a variety of expensive cheeses, exotic olives, and open boxes of crackers. Low on balanced nutrition but high on instant gratification.

"Her name was Angela Woods. Another Stylettos stylist. She was a sweet kid. Blonde. I used to see her at the salon."

"One bad haircut too many, no doubt."

"Maybe. Who knows."

"I'm actually surprised that it doesn't happen more often." Brooke stopped, the popcorn halfway to her mouth. "Wait a minute. My God, not that stylist you wrote about, Marcia Robinson's stylist?" Her antennae were quivering. "Wow, that Robinson bimbo is really bad luck, isn't she?"

"Slow down, Brooke, I know what you're thinking, but there is no connection."

Although she could pass for the ultimate conservative poster model, nothing Brooke wore betrayed her love for clandestine political plotting, her belief that evildoers were around every corner, or her sheer delight in the drama of it all. Brooke embraced conspiracy theories like some women did their Jimmy Choo shoes.

"Six Hill staffers lost their jobs so far. More to come. Porno Web sites. Now this. Coincidence? Ha. And you're going to investigate? I love it."

"No, wait. I'm not. I'm just telling you about it."

"Great. So what did the stylist know and when did she know it?"

"Would you like to hear about it before you solve it?"

"Of course I would. The stylist obviously knew too much. Now she's dead. No connection? Bull. In this town everything is connected."

"The cops say it's suicide. Stella says no way." Lacey recapped the theory that someone else cut off Angie's hair, sliced her wrists, and made it look like a suicide, on Stella's unassailable logic that a stylist wouldn't be caught dead with that haircut. "Obviously I can't encourage her. I don't know anything about murder."

"No, but you know about killer style."

The hair rose on the back of Lacey's neck. "Not you too."

"It's because of your column. All that chat about fashion clues and deadly styles and you are what you wear. I see Stella's logic."

"So it's my column's fault that I'm suddenly a sleuth?" Lacey was appalled.

"It's entertaining," Brooke admitted. "And it tells the truth. So rare in journalism today."

"Gosh, Brooke, don't be so nice."

"I'm never nice. Your column is a great guilty pleasure. Hence, its popularity."

"I can't believe you actually read my column."

"You write it for real women. I'm a real woman."

"Yeah, but you don't need my help."

Brooke had flair that Lacey admired. Far from the stereotypical dumpy D.C. attorney, Ms. Barton, Esquire, knew how to wear a suit and still look feminine, adding touches like antique lace handkerchiefs and lace blouses that on another woman would look silly. Tonight she was wearing a cherry red sweater with jeans and pearls. All blondes think they look good in red, but Brooke really did. It made her eyes look more blue. More innocent. *Looks can be deceiving.*

In contrast, Lacey looked far from innocent. Her delicately arched brows gave her a knowing look she didn't feel. Tonight she wore comfortable old blue jeans, two or three washings away from ripping through, and a black V-neck sweater. You can never have too many black sweaters, according to Lacey. One of her rules for life, along with: Never let anyone take pictures of you naked. Never keep a diary you would not want published in a family newspaper. And never secretly tape-record your conversations, even in Virginia, where it is legal.

"I'll tell you one thing." Brooke broke into her thoughts. "It's just as well you don't get involved. You don't want to wind up dead, do you?"

"No one involved with Marcia Robinson has died."

"Until now."

"And that may have nothing to do with Marcia."

"That we know of."

"You have to keep in mind there could be jealous stylists,

unhappy clients, psycho boyfriends. And maybe it was suicide, after all."

"Point taken. Of course if you *do* look into it . . ."

"If I do?"

"Be interesting to see if Marcia has serious hair issues," Brooke suggested. "I wonder what she told her stylist. You know, 'Only her hairstylist knows for sure.' "

"Who knows? It's way too easy to blab away while someone is massaging your head," Lacey said. "Remind me to gag myself the next time I get my hair cut. You don't really think it's dangerous, do you?"

"Not really. But I'd like to think so."

"So tell me, Brooke, about that Marcia Robinson mess. Tell me why, instead of actually trying to talk to a real woman, men will spend hours on the Internet surfing Web sites where virtual women take off their clothes?"

"Pheromone jammers." It was Brooke's current favorite theory of why men and women in Washington, D.C., could not connect with each other. Obviously the Pentagon had installed pheromone jammers on its roof, beaming relationship-killing Romance Death Rays at every man within the Beltway. "It does something to their testosterone. Something weird. Turns it into decaf."

"Makes perfect sense to me," Lacey said. "My signals have been jammed for years."

"Romance Death Rays. We've been irradiated. You have to admit, it's pretty crazy purveying naughty photos of the Small Business Committee staff on the Internet. Good Lord! More of a horror show than erotica. Here in the Capital City of dweebs, geeks, and nerds."

"No one actually believed that was the attorney general wrestling nude with an alligator on Marcia's Web site," Lacey said. "Did they?"

"You had to buy the video for a better look. That was just a teaser. I was pulling for the alligator."

"Washington, D.C., the only place on earth where Henry Kissinger could be considered a sex symbol."

"There's a woman in my office who has a crush on James Carville," Brooke said, passing the popcorn.

"Oh please, the Human Snake Head? You just killed my appetite." Lacey swallowed her last handful and wiped off her hands.

"People think D.C. is full of sex scandals. The real scandal is that's all the sex there is," Brooke said. "I haven't had a date in two months. How's that cute cops reporter of yours?"

"Trujillo? Stomping on women's hearts with his new armadillo boots."

"Too bad." Brooke had only met Trujillo once, but the memory lingered. "So what about you, Lace? Any prospects?"

"Sorry. Long dry spell. No rain in sight."

"What about the one who got away?"

"He got away."

"I hate when that happens. At any rate, I think it's time for a new salon, Lacey. Crazy hairstylists. Crazy hair killers. You don't need the aggravation. And that Stella's a little strange."

"Yeah, but it's hard to get rid of your hairstylist. Especially when she knows where to find you."

Brooke fingered her own blond locks. She treasured her hair, which she wore in a long French braid when she went to court. "You know, if a crazy haircutting killer were out there, not only would you be dead—you'd be bald too!"

After Brooke left, Lacey lingered outside to admire the view. Gazing south down the Potomac, it was easy to forget the city and the noise. Spring was stealing over the landscape, creating a hush of green along the riverbanks. In just a week or two, the trees would be full and bushy, but she loved warm days like this when the first sign of green signaled that the long, dull winter was conquered at last.

Ah, spring in Washington—and pheromone jammers. It's such a good explanation, it should be true. Lacey wondered if she could still attract a man. *Maybe if I lived somewhere else.*

Lacey had a face that a man had once told her belonged on the cover of a pulp-fiction magazine. Pretty, but a little exaggerated, a little extreme for comfort. There were even men who had called her beautiful.

She didn't kid herself about her looks. She knew she was attractive, but she'd never be the most beautiful, the thinnest, or the most sought-after woman. She was five-foot-five with a curvy build that she fought to keep on the slim side. Her hair was good: thick, manageable, and slightly wavy. She wore it a couple of inches below the shoulder, long enough to wind into a French knot on bad-hair days. As a package deal, she figured she was pretty good. But the package was still on the shelf.

Her thoughts paused on one man from her past, but she told herself to forget him. After all, he was merely a footnote in her romantic history, a footnote that would take volumes to explain, even to Brooke. The last she heard, he had left Sagebrush, Colorado, but that's where the trail ended. Just another tumbleweed tumbling through. Like her.

Before she moved to Washington, Lacey was used to feeling strange, an outsider, an observer. When she was little, she had always considered herself a swan, and her family of ducks never knew what to make of her. Her mother often said she had no idea where Lacey came from, and she apparently was not implicating the mailman. Rose Smithsonian suggested that it was likely a caravan of gypsies had dropped in one night, stolen the real baby Smithsonian, and left Lacey as a little joke. The real baby Smithsonian would be perky and have cheerleading genes and wear what Mother wanted.

The real baby Smithsonian would have grown up and found a man by now. She'd be tied down to a house, kids, and meatloaf once a week.

Lacey let her eyes sail down the verdant Potomac. *My pheromones may be jammed,* she thought, *but at least I'm a swan on my own river.*

Chapter 3

It's probably a character flaw that I am more concerned at the moment with what to wear to the funeral than whether it was suicide or murder, Lacey thought. She figured she'd give herself time and some fragment of noble character would emerge. The darn job was turning her into a shallow caricature. She told herself that she had values. Somewhere.

Now that she wrote "Crimes of Fashion" everyone expected her to look totally put together all the time. Only Lacey knew how far below that ideal she fell. Like the memorial service: People always think they know what to wear to a funeral, but in fact they have no idea, and neither did Lacey. The "little black dress," for instance, is supposed to go everywhere. But showing up for a funeral in a little black cocktail dress simply does not demonstrate the proper respect. Unless the funeral is in a bar.

Wearing black seems appropriate, but it could be presumptuous if you're not a member of the immediate family, especially if none of them is wearing black. Your display then casts doubt on the family's grief—a breach of etiquette.

On the other hand, Stylettos' stylists almost always wore black and owned few clothes in anything remotely resembling a color. Lacey assumed they would look like true mourners anywhere, even at a picnic. Not that they would be caught dead at a picnic.

The April weather had taken a cool turn. Lacey selected a marine-blue wool crepe dress with princess lines and deep black cuffs, which she wore with dark stockings and black heels. She grabbed her favorite black wrap jacket, a vintage find from the Forties. She loved the clothes of that era. With vintage clothing, Lacey felt as if something of the original owner remained. There was a bravado about those clothes, a swagger that was both feminine and functional. They were classic. No matter how she tried, she could not rustle up the same feeling in a Lycra miniskirt and a tube top.

She always chose Forties clothes when she needed strength of character. The gabardine jacket had beautiful set-in shoulders and fine top stitching. It fit beautifully. Lacey considered it a work of art, and the union label attested to its creation by a member of the now-historic International Ladies Garment Workers Union, which had morphed into UNITE, the Union of Needletrades, Industrial and Textile Employees. Lacey wondered how much they paid a woman to make a work of art like this in 1945. Whatever it was, they couldn't have paid her enough. A vintage gold and pearl lapel pin finished the look. She tucked a lace hanky in the pocket, just in case she felt weepy. She got emotional at the worst times, reading sob stories in her own newspaper, for instance, or watching sappy commercials on television, especially during the holidays. Blubbering at the funeral of a near stranger was well within her realm of possibility.

Going to the funeral would merely encourage Stella's detective delusion. But she had already advised Lacey that she would be picking her up at nine-thirty, and there was no graceful way to back out. Lacey left a message at the paper that she would be in after lunch. She waited outside the front door of her apartment building. The dogwood buds were almost ready to pop open and scarlet tulips bloomed along the brick walkways.

Lacey's car was in the shop. Again. Her beautiful silver and burgundy Nissan 280ZX was deteriorating before her eyes, causing her pain and betraying her trust after she had poured thousands of dollars into the ungrateful hunk of steel. And it was starting to wear rusty accents around the doors and wheel wells, not a good sign in this humid swamp. But she loved driving it. The way it hugged the road and highway access ramps was a dream. It was not a car to scorn, even though it spent more time at Asian Engines than it did at home.

Paul, her mechanic, was intimately acquainted with the Z,

having laid his healing hands upon its every moving part. She had yet to meet the man who would understand her as well as Paul understood her Z.

A car that looked like a crazed windup toy pulled into the circle drive of her building, driven by the relentless Stella. Lacey prayed she wouldn't have to help pedal the stylist's new pride and joy, a tiny red-and-white BMW Mini Cooper with a giant American flag on the roof. Stella wore a black leather jacket and a black beret with a pin shaped like a broken heart. With a pair of sporty aviator sunglasses and a long red silk scarf, she looked like a bomber pilot on a mission of mercy. It was as if she belonged to some strange female army where they dressed with style and lived to break men's hearts. Maybe a French army: the French Fashion Legion. *Maybe I could join up too.*

"Hop in, Lacey!" They tore off at top speed. "One great thing about this car is that cops don't actually believe it can go fast. It's not even on their radar screen." Stella floored it and made it to the funeral home in twenty-five minutes. "What did I tell you? We're invisible!"

"In a red-and-white Mini with a flag on the roof? I don't think so."

Angela Woods' memorial service was the featured ten o'clock attraction at Evergreens, so named for the impressive trees surrounding the building in its Northwest Washington neighborhood. The casket had been moved and was now centrally located in the main chapel, accented by pastel flower arrangements.

Angie appeared serene after Stella's ministrations. The blond wig resembled her original hair, although it was considerably shorter. Angie's mother and two younger sisters were in the front row, dabbing at their red eyes and sniffling. Theirs was a family of women. The missing father occupied a spot in the family plot in Atlanta that Angie would soon join.

The bewildered Woods family was from the Deep South and apparently did not consider black a staple of their sunny wardrobes. They wore shades of blue, which were as somber as they could summon from their optimistic closets. Neither sister was as pretty as Angie, but the glorious hair was a family trademark, though not quite as glorious as Angie's. The sisters wore theirs pulled into long tails cascading down their backs, caught at the nape with blue velvet ribbons. Angie's mother wore a navy blue suit with pearls and a broad-brimmed navy hat that shadowed her light blond waves. The suit was summer and the hat was winter, but no one cared.

The stylists from the Dupont Circle salon were scrubbed clean in deference to Angie's family. *How sweet. They've left their usual pledge-night-at-the-coven look at home.* Lacey noticed several black cocktail dresses in attendance, looking a little too festive for the occasion and a little too bare for the weather.

Lacey and Stella were seated in the third row of the chapel, which accommodated about two hundred people and was nearly full. The entire Stylettos empire seemed to be present, all twenty-five salons. Lacey recognized a few other customers from the Dupont Circle salon, no doubt some of Angie's regulars. She scanned the room for the notorious Marcia Robinson, but the sullied congressional staffer failed to present her new glossy chestnut hairdo. Lacey realized that was a long shot. Marcia was being dogged by the media until she made her appearance before the special prosecutor to testify, presumably not in pink. Her attorney was keeping her under wraps. And so far, the mainstream press had not made the connection between the dead stylist and Ms. Robinson. If they had, it apparently didn't carry a large enough news hook.

Lacey leaned in to Stella and asked, "When was Marcia Robinson's last appointment with Angie?"

"A couple weeks ago. Marcia needed a blow-dry for some court appearance. Then she was supposed to see Angie last week, but she canceled."

"What day was that?"

"Saturday, I think."

"The day Angie died?"

"Yeah, I guess so."

"Why did she cancel?"

"I don't know. I didn't take the call. Is it important?" With the thought that it might be, Stella was now on full quivering alert.

An obviously distressed woman walked by. Stella made a

face. "That's Sherri Gold," she whispered. "She was Angie's last client, Saturday night. She's a trip."

"You mean, right before . . . ?"

"She's a total psycho. Wanna meet her?" She waved Sherri over. "Sherri, I want you to meet Lacey Smithsonian from *The Observer*."

"*The Eye Street Observer*? I never read it," Ms. Gold lied. The woman's lips curled with disdain. "I read *The Post*."

"Nice outfit."

"It's designer."

An inmate in a nineteenth-century women's prison would be dressed more attractively. Of course Lacey wasn't really sure what nineteenth-century prison garb looked like, but the woman's dirty gray outfit was punitive enough. The long, wrinkled skirt was gathered at the waist and would flatter no one. With it, the woman wore a matching oversized shapeless gray top, probably costing hundreds of dollars. Lacey hated gray. It was personal.

Sherri Gold was angular and muscular in an aggressively overtrained way that looked obsessive. She had medium brown hair and a bony face that some might call striking, even scary runway-model beautiful, but to Lacey the flaring nostrils and oversized mouth resembled a gargoyle. Sherri opened that mouth and wailed. "What am I going to do? No one can cut my hair like Angie." She pushed her hair away from her face with both hands. "It's so curly. Angie was the one who taught me how to blow-dry it straight."

So you, too, can achieve the Washington Helmet Head. Lacey shook herself. "It's tragic about Angie, don't you think?" Lacey glanced toward the coffin.

"My God, yes! Now I'll have to go to New York just to get my hair cut. And it costs a fortune in New York. You have no idea."

"Yeah, first you gotta take the Metroliner," Stella said.

"Did Angie seem depressed when you saw her last?" Lacey asked Sherri. "Suicidal?"

Sherri looked puzzled. Thinking about someone else apparently was a challenge. "I don't know. We talked about conditioners."

"Did she seem unhappy, or upset about anything?"

"Yes. She thought my ends were too dry. But she didn't have what I needed. Why?"

"Because she died that night," Lacey said.

"I know. Isn't it awful? What am I going to do?" Sherri wailed and stalked off, leaving Stella doing a slow burn.

"New York can have her."

"I'm with you, Stel," Michelle Wilson, Stella's assistant manager, said as she slipped in to sit on the other side of Stella. Michelle was a pretty black woman with skin the color of warm honey and striking amber eyes. Dark locks were coiled elaborately on her head. "Sherri's one of those clients who just wants a celebrity stylist. She switched to Angie as soon as Marcia's makeover was in the paper. With any luck she's out of our hair now."

"What does she do?" Lacey asked.

"I don't know. Something on the Hill."

"Like Marcia?"

"I guess."

"Did they know each other?"

"I don't know. But maybe, because Sherri was able to get Marcia's slot after she canceled. Maybe Marcia told her the time was open." Michelle picked up a memorial card and studied it.

"There's Ratboy." Stella nudged Lacey and indicated a man of about fifty seated two rows behind them and to the right. He caught Lacey's eye and winked. She turned back to Stella.

"Ratboy? Your boss?"

"Boyd Radford. The one and only."

Lacey turned back again and stared. From certain angles, the man did resemble a sleek, prosperous rodent. Radford must have been better looking when he was younger, she thought, but time was bringing out the rat in his DNA. Full-face he was almost handsome, in a high-school-jock-gone-to-seed way. But in profile, he had an elongated snout, a weak chin, mean little black bullet eyes, and slightly protruding teeth. His dark, slicked-back hair revealed a bald spot. The Rogaine wasn't working, Stella reported; he was considering plugs. Apparently every stylist he employed called him "Ratboy" behind his back. Nevertheless, in the tradition of rich creeps everywhere and despite all evidence to the contrary, he believed he was a babe magnet.

Boyd Radford was the owner of Stylettos, a growing chain of salons throughout Washington, Maryland, and Virginia. He was mean and feral, but he had managed to lock on to success in spite of himself. Boyd had inherited the salons from his uncle Maximilian, and with the genius of Boyd's former wife, Josephine Radford, had seen them grow from a chain of cheap chop shops to a reasonably well-respected group of salons with a sprinkling of star stylists.

It was Josephine who also changed the name from Chez Max to Stylettos, designed the Stylettos smocks, got rid of substandard stylists, and created training programs. Radford raised the prices, taking them out of the bottom of the shampoo bowl.

Like his uncle Max, Radford started out as a stylist. And although he hired many gay hairstylists, he was one of the straight men who become stylists because that was where the women were. He liked to have them at his mercy with dripping wet hair.

Ratboy's hobby was sleeping with the female stylists, and sometimes the customers too, according to Stella, whose number-one hobby was talking. Sexual harassment was not a well-understood concept at Stylettos, and the stylists were not on the cutting edge of political awareness. Some may have realized they could sue his pants off, but unemployed hairstylists can't afford legal counsel. And many found that sleeping with Ratboy enhanced their careers, if not their self-esteem. Most of his conquests wound up hating him, but oddly, Boyd was sentimental. He liked to keep them around. That's how Stella herself had become manager at the Dupont Circle salon.

"I can't believe you slept with him," Lacey whispered. She knew far too much about Stella from their salon chair sessions, and she suspected Stella knew too much about her as well. In self-defense, they had forged a friendship.

"It was five years ago," Stella whispered back.

"He's repulsive."

"I closed my eyes."

"It gives me hives just to look at him."

"You! He gave me a rash."

"Stella, please!"

"Nothing serious. I was younger. You know, lately the worm was trying to get into Angie's drawers."

"But he's way too old for her."

"Tell him that. He liked it that she was getting so hot in the newspapers. She wouldn't do it with him, though. Said he made her skin crawl."

Stella looked back at Ratboy and gave him the evil eye. He looked away.

A well-preserved woman on Ratboy's right side smacked his arm and glared first at Boyd and then at Lacey and at Stella, who smiled and waved in response.

"The bitch is Ratboy's ex-wife, Josephine," Stella whispered. "Mean as a snake and twice as deadly. Makes his life miserable. Couldn't have happened to a nicer guy."

"I thought you said they were divorced," Lacey said.

"A couple of years ago. She got half the business, but it's still not all settled. She likes to keep an eye on him. Partners till death do they part."

Lacey fished out a mirrored compact from her purse, opened it, and angled it just so to take a better look.

Josephine Radford was French and lived up to all the implied stereotypes. She was thin, stylish, and had a temper that could launch missiles, Stella said. She was great at small talk and fun to be around, if you didn't get too close. Josephine was not conventionally pretty, but she was dark and exotic. She was clad in a killer designer suit, royal purple trimmed with black grosgrain ribbon. Her glossy black hair was caught back in a chic chignon with a black bow at the nape. *Entirely too refined for Stylettos,* Lacey thought. *And how did she wind up with that crude animal Boyd?*

"How did she get along with Angie?" Lacey whispered.

"Actually, they had a fight a couple of weeks ago."

"What about?"

"I'm not sure, but Angie was crying, something about Marcia Robinson or maybe it was Ratboy. I tried to stay out of it."

It was common knowledge, Stella said, that Josephine hated all the women Boyd slept with. Although they hadn't lived together in years, neither could let go. In some weird way, they were still passionate about each other. Boyd enjoyed taunting Josephine about his other women, so she was able to keep an accurate running tally. He did the same with her conquests. Because they were divorced and civilized, they considered this good fun. They informed people they had a "cordial" relationship for the sake of the business and their family, which consisted of Beauregard Radford, or "Beau," a perennial college student. Wired together by recrimination and revenge. And Stylettos.

Beau, the heir apparent, was present and accounted for, sitting beside his mother. The stylists called him "Shampoo Boy," after the menial position he had held in the various salons when he was in high school. He looked slightly bored and somewhat less feral than Dad. He was neither as repulsive as his father, nor as exotic as his mother. It was as if the family genes had petered out by the time Shampoo Boy came along. His thin hair was nearly black and he wore it in a modified Prince Valiant that reached his shoulders. He had a smattering of freckles, the Radford nose, and an apparent inability to grow a beard. Beau was twenty-four years old, and had been sent home from another school in what seemed like an endless tour of colleges, due to his fondness for recreational drugs and naughty pranks. Beau wanted to go into the business as a stylist just like Dad, but Ratboy insisted he get a degree first. The son yearned to be like his father in the seduction category as well. Stella reported all this with relish.

"What kind of naughty pranks?"

"Don't know, Boyd doesn't broadcast Beau's crimes."

"Like you would."

"It's what you don't know, Lacey, that can kill you."

At fifteen minutes past ten, the short, pudgy minister cleared his throat and the room came to attention. There was a good deal of sniffling and teary eyes. A soloist sang "Bridge over Troubled Water," not quite hitting the high notes.

After the long wait, the service was short. The nondenominational preacher, squeamish about offering a eulogy for a suicide, and a stranger at that, gave a generic talk suitable for any candidate on his or her generic ride to a generic afterlife. Most of the mourners seemed willing to be generically comforted.

Not so Stella. "That's just not good enough," she growled to Lacey, who stared at her in alarm. "You call that a send-off?" Stella rose and strode purposefully to the podium, her beret bobbing. People turned to stare at her. Stella was not scheduled to speak, but the spirit moved her and there was no stopping her now. She cleared her throat and blew on the microphone. It squealed. "Is this thing on?" Stella's voice boomed over the speakers. Just to make sure no one slept, she scratched her long nails over the microphone, creating a shriek that opened every eye in the house. Except Angie's, of course.

"Excuse me, but I have something to say about this whole damn sorry mess." Stella took a deep breath, adjusted her black tam over her red crew cut, and flung a tail of the scarf over her right shoulder. "I was Angie's manager at Stylettos Dupont Circle salon. I know we're all feeling bad here because, well, Angie won't be with us anymore. And nobody feels worse than I do. She was a great kid who had a bright future as a star hairstylist. We all read about her in the papers. With all the sleazy politics and college-educated morons in this town, she could have had a steady gig improving their sorry asses." There were a few titters, but Stella soldiered on.

"But anyway, what happened to Angie should not have happened. Oh sure, the D.C. cops say it was suicide, and the coroner says it was suicide, and the newspapers say it was suicide. What do they know? Nothing!" The mike squealed again. The mourners had been drifting during the minister's soothing remarks, but they were fully awake now. Stella grabbed the mike and stalked the room like a TV preacher.

"Suicide my ass! Pardon my French. Angie Woods did not kill herself, and everyone who knows her knows she couldn't have done it. Now, I don't know much, but I do know hair. Angie had some of the prettiest hair I have ever seen. Like angel's hair. She was really proud of it too. She babied it, used the best conditioners, and never subjected it to harsh chemicals. She was good to her hair. You know what I'm saying?" One hundred and fifty stylists nodded in agreement and fought back tears.

"So the police tell me that last Saturday night she whacked off a good two feet of gorgeous hair, razored her scalp in patches, slapped some blue and orange and purple dye on her head, and then killed herself. Like hell she did! I'm the one who found her in the salon. Me, Stella Lake. It was not a pretty picture. It was pretty awful, the most awful thing I've ever seen. Honest to God, it was like Angie was almost scalped by some psycho barber before she died! I'm telling you, if I know one thing, I know this: This was not the work of a professional stylist."

There were shocked gasps from the family in the front row, but Stella's audience was rapt. "Well, I won't go into that, because her mother and sisters are here and this is painful enough for them. All you stylists know what I'm talking about. But I promise you that somebody, a professional that I know, is going to get to the bottom of this. And she is here today."

Stella paused and looked pointedly at Lacey, who froze like Bambi in a laser beam. *She didn't say what I think she said.* Stella aimed a lightning-bolted nail toward her. Lacey slumped down in her seat. "An expert," Stella emphasized. "Someone who knows crime and style and fashion clues. Someone who cares."

You know, Lacey, nuns don't need hairstylists, she told herself. *There are some lovely convents in upstate New York.*

"Somebody really smart, with really great investigative skills, is going to find out what really happened to Angela Woods so she can rest in peace and we can all sleep easier. She'll get to the bottom of this. She'll find the killer. I guarantee it. Okay, that's all I got to say. So long Angie, honey."

Stella wiped a tear from her cheek with one chewed fingernail and dropped the mike with a bone-rattling boom. Lacey noticed that Ratboy wiped his forehead and shifted in his seat. Josephine looked around the crowd, glaring. Son Beau had been stirred awake. His puzzled eyes followed Stella all the way back to her seat. Sherri Gold was twisting her fingers through her hair, a glazed look in her eyes. *No doubt taking the train to Manhattan in her mind. I'm joining her right now.*

Spontaneous applause erupted for Stella's proclamation. Angela's sisters beamed with approval and hugged each other, and her weeping mother fell upon Stella with a grateful hug.

"You answered our prayers, Stella, darlin'. I just know my angel could not ever take her own life. And her hair. That hair was her treasure. I . . ." Fighting tears, she took a breath. "She believed life was sacred. Thank you for telling that to all these people. For telling the world."

What a pair: the plump Southern matron and the crew-cut

rebel. Now bosom buddies, Mrs. Woods hugged Stella like she had found the Holy Grail. Locked in an endless embrace, Stella signaled Lacey frantically for help, but Lacey just smiled and waved, already mentally speeding through the Midtown Tunnel.

Chapter 4

The Radfords hosted a small catered reception at the Stylettos headquarters after the funeral. It was across the Potomac in Arlington, Virginia, in a nondescript building on Wilson Boulevard. The reception was set up in the stylist training center, a large room complete with wall-to-wall mirrors and shampoo bowls tucked away in a side nook.

Stylettos' inner sanctum doubled as a party room for company events, but it could be jarring to visitors. Lined up along a back counter were more than thirty disembodied wig heads with blond, brunette, black, and red wigs in varying textures, from straight to tightly curled. Under the circumstances, Lacey thought, the heads added a macabre touch and should have been removed. Like mute witnesses to unspeakable crimes, they all had bad haircuts. But they were invisible to the stylists.

This was the company mecca, where stylists learned about the latest hair products they were encouraged to push on customers, and all the up-to-the-minute styles. Up-to-the-minute in Washington, D.C., that is, which is not to be confused with up-to-the-minute anywhere else, particularly New York City, where a star stylist haircut, not including the train ride, might cost several hundred dollars.

For the reception, small café tables and chairs were set around the room. The tables were laid with black cloths and topped with white flower and candle centerpieces. Black crepe paper, somewhat out of place, but well meant, streamed down the mirrors, making it look more like Halloween than springtime in Washington.

A buffet and a bar were set up on a central platform in front of enormous black-and-white posters featuring haircuts and perms. Inside the door, a large photo of Angie was displayed next to a somber memorial wreath. Two chubby stylists were stationed there to make sure everyone signed the guest book. Stella and Lacey were seated at one of the tables, plates of hors d'oeuvres in front of them. Lacey eyed her plate without appetite.

"Stella, has anyone ever suggested that you might try a little subtlety? Just for shock value?"

"Oh sure, lots of times, but it doesn't work for me. Ah, don't be mad, Lacey, that sad-sack minister made it sound like she died of old age. I had to say something."

"Thanks to your theatrics, now everyone thinks I'm some kind of fashion detective. I am not, Stella. I am a reporter. Do you hear me?"

Stella was showing off Lacey like a celebrity, self-importantly introducing her to everyone in sight. The stylists seemed thrilled to meet her. They all wanted to be mentioned in "Crimes of Fashion." Not as one of the crimes, of course.

Okay, so maybe the least I can do is write a column about Angie. But that's it, positively it. If there were some mystery to Angie's death, Lacey had no hope of actually solving it. Even so, she reasoned, it wouldn't hurt to ask a few questions.

However, forming an opinion of the dead woman was hopeless. In death, Angie had taken on saintlike qualities. Later, a clearer picture might emerge, when there was a little distance from her death. Lacey figured she'd get out as quickly and gracefully as possible and ask questions later.

Josephine Radford approached. "Stella, an interesting little stunt. What would we do without you for excitement?"

"I have no idea," Stella said.

Josephine evaluated Lacey in a glance. "Ms. Smithsonian, the 'Crimes of Fashion' writer, of course. You must be so busy. So many crimes, so little time." Her eyes traveled critically up and down Lacey's outfit. She apparently was satisfied. "I'm so glad to meet you, even under such sad circumstances. Please don't let Stella's imagination lead you astray."

"Is it just her imagination?" Lacey asked.

"But of course it is. Perhaps we could go to lunch someday, Lacey." She pronounced it Lay-CEE. "I have lots of ideas for you." Before Lacey could respond, Josephine was distracted. "Oh, there is Boyd, stupid man. I'd better see what he wants now. Probably to meet you. He's dangerous. Don't let him charm you."

As if that were possible, Lacey thought. Josephine exited in a cloud of Chanel No. 5.

"Listen, Stella, one plate of canapés and a glass of punch and I'm out of here," Lacey said.

But Stella was paying no attention. The Stylettos heir apparent, Beau Radford, was working his way around the room. Stella leaned in close to Lacey.

"Did I warn you about Beau?"

"Now what?"

"He's kind of a Ratboy-in-training," Stella said.

"Meaning?"

"Just slap him if he hits on you. I'll back you up."

"But he's just a kid." Lacey looked at him. He was wearing a tight sports jacket that stretched over his thin shoulders, obviously left over from high school, a pair of baggy khaki pants, a blue work shirt, and a tie emblazoned with Bugs Bunny. A cowlick that would not be tamed stuck out at the back of his head.

"He doesn't have any jobs to dangle as bait. But he's persistent. Just smack him on the head and he'll go away," Stella said.

"Like father, like son?"

"Little rat like big rat."

"Stella, did Boyd dangle a manager's position for Angela?"

Stella dropped her voice. "I don't know. But he's opening another Stylettos in Virginia Beach. I hear there's a lot of interest." Stella stopped talking and started munching carrot sticks as Beau sidled up.

The young Radford introduced himself and held Lacey's hand a little too long. He wasn't so bad when he smiled, Lacey realized. A good orthodontist had ensured that when he grinned Beau had the impish look of a mischievous boy, not a rat.

"Is Smithsonian your real name?" he asked.

"Yes. No relation to the museum." Lacey noticed that Stella had grabbed her plate and headed back toward the buffet table, leaving her alone with this junior Lothario. *You'll pay for this, Stella.*

"I read your column," Beau purred.

"I'll bet you do." *He lies like a rug.*

"I'll be reading it now, I promise."

"Good. There'll be a pop quiz."

"By the way, you've got great hair, Lacey. Bedroom hair. All tousled like that."

"Maybe I should comb it." Lacey noticed that people in the hair business had no compunction whatever against commenting on your dark roots, split ends, bad cuts, perm damage or, apparently, bedroom hair. Turning the subject away from herself, Lacey asked about Angie.

"I knew she worked with Stella. I just got home on spring break." Beau explained that he wasn't going back to school, as he and the business school in Iowa had had a falling out.

"What did you do?"

"This and that. A little weed. You interested? I know a place."

"No, thanks, really. I'm trying to quit." *That was a joke, you little rat.*

He drew up a chair next to Lacey. "It's something the folks don't know yet," he confided to her. "So about what Stella said. Are you really going to look into Angie's death? I thought the cops said it was suicide."

Lacey shrugged and shook her head slightly. "Stella," she said, implying that, of course, Stella was nuts.

"Stella," he agreed. "Perhaps we could discuss Stella over dinner sometime." He was pushy, she had to give him that. But she was ready with her automatic excuse.

"Sorry, I'm seeing someone." *In my dreams, that is.* Beau excused himself and slunk off in search of the woman who would be his Mrs. Robinson.

Lacey picked up her untouched plate to find the trash, but as if on cue Boyd Radford popped over to flatter her and put in a bid for a few inches of newsprint about how great his salons were. He also told her she should write a profile about—who else?—Boyd Radford.

"We have a great story to tell, Lacey."

She wondered what that could be. *Maybe, "Rich Weasel Gets in Your Hair—and Your Pants!"*

"Call me. I'll take you to lunch, "Boyd said. "We'll talk about that article on me."

Aren't I the prom queen. Everyone wants to buy me lunch and dinner. Boyd spent too much time pressing a business card into her hand and trying to stare into her eyes, turning on all that imagined charm. People who insisted they would make great copy really irritated Lacey.

"By the way, you're not paying any attention to what Stella says about Angela Woods?"

"Stella's my stylist. We share all kinds of secrets." Lacey smiled.

"I didn't know Stella had any secrets," Boyd said.

"How well did you know Angie?"

"As well as any stylist who works for me."

"Did you think she was depressed lately?"

"How would I know? It was tragic about the girl, but nothing more. Just a terrible personal tragedy. Remember that," Radford said, turning away. Apparently he'd used up all his charm. And Lacey's patience.

She marched decisively toward the door. Unfortunately, Polly Parsons, Stylettos' promotion coordinator, blocked her way. Polly called Lacey at least once a week with some new promotional pitch and always spoke in a breathless rush. For example: "Have you heard? Short bobs with frosted highlights are in style! Isn't that great?" Today she was blathering on about some fashion show. "Lacey, have you heard? Stylettos is doing the hair for the Sizzle in the City fashion show! Isn't that great?"

Stella had reported that Polly was currently sleeping with Ratboy. Stella was also spreading the rumor that Polly was a charter member of the Condom of the Month Club. "They send a case of assorted rubbers in different sizes, shapes, and colors every month. I swear!"

Lacey edged around the towering woman: Six feet and thirty-one years of aggressively self-involved female. Polly had a great figure, but a weirdly androgynous face. She dressed in thigh-high skirts to keep attention focused on her legs. She was exquisitely lacquered, perfumed, and hair sprayed. However, in spite of all her efforts at exaggerated femininity, Polly managed to look like a man in drag.

"Send me a press release, Polly. Gotta go."

"It's a great cause, Lacey. The proceeds go to . . . umm, something to do with kids, but it's fantastic and totally politically correct, so you don't have to worry about anything. I mean, there's no fur in the show or child labor or sweatshops or anything like that. Nothing depressing. I don't think. I'm pretty sure."

"That's so interesting, Polly." Lacey was looking for an out. The hulking promo maven was crowding her against the wall.

"Lacey, I really want to know what you think of my hair. Should I cut it?" It would have been curious that Polly did not even allude to the deceased at the funeral reception, but Polly always managed to turn the conversation to her favorite subject: herself. She was busy flipping her locks hither and yon. She wore a long bob, a variation of the Washington Frosted Helmet Head, medium brown with silvery blond highlights. Lacey thought it was standard D.C. issue, although it looked thick and healthy.

"Do you think I should change it? Because I just don't know. And you are such an expert! I never know what to do with it." She asked Lacey the same thing every time she saw her. Thankfully, Stella arrived, carrying a refilled plate.

"It gives you so much grief, Polly, I think you should just shave your head," Stella said. Polly opened her eyes all the way. "Yeah, bald as a billiard ball. I'd be happy to wield the razor. My treat."

"Well, Stella, I guess you'd be the expert on bald heads, wouldn't you?" They glared at each other, Polly towering over the petite but pugnacious Stella. Lacey interrupted them.

"Polly, did you know Angie Woods? What do you think happened that night?"

"Happened? To Angie?" Polly seemed stumped. "When?"

"The night she died."

"Died? Oh, wow, I better talk to Boyd." Polly promised to send Lacey information on the fashion show and stomped off in her enormous red patent leather high heels. Stella guided Lacey back to the table.

"That bitch. I swear I'll deck her someday."

"Don't forget your slingshot, little David. Can we go now?" Lacey asked.

But they were joined by Jamie Towers, one of Stella's coworkers at the Dupont Circle salon. Jamie was all bouncy curls and perky personality, which couldn't be masked by too much black eyeliner and purple nails. She bubbled in spite of herself and seemed younger than her twenty-four years. It could have been the multicolored hair, light brown striped with shades of bright orange and clown red.

"Stella, you were so fabulous! It's like you think someone killed Angie and she so didn't do it to herself, but like the cops are too stupid to even notice, right? Wow!" She contemplated those thoughts while crunching a carrot. "That's so brave." Jamie stared at Lacey. "And you're going to, like, do something about it, right? That is so tremendous."

Lacey glared at Stella. "Actually, I'm not—"

A tall, slender man flung himself down in a chair next to Stella. "How much longer for this little drama, do you think?" Wire-framed glasses were perched on an aquiline nose. He pushed them up with his middle finger and gazed around the room. A dark auburn lock of hair drooped ever so piquantly over his forehead. Black slacks and a white linen poet's shirt completed the tormented-artist look. He was, Lacey concluded, not one of the straight male hairstylists. "Piled it on a little thick, didn't we, Stella?" he said. "You really think she was Little Miss I-Love-My-Hair-Too-Much-to-Die?"

"What do you think?" Stella said.

"I think the salon was closed for two whole days just to clean up the bloody mess she left. Simply destroyed my appointment book."

"Don't be a jerk. She didn't kill herself, Leo."

"Of course she did. Angela Woods was not important enough to murder."

Stella's eyes were daggers and her bloodred fingernails looked dangerous as she spread them on the table.

"Maybe not, Leo, but you are." He merely snorted. "Leo, this is Lacey Smithsonian. You know, 'Crimes of Fashion' Lacey Smithsonian. Lacey, this is Leonardo, *the* Leonardo. He worked next to Angie. Sometimes he's almost human."

"Dear sweet Angie. *C'est la vie.* She was so young and

naive. I shared what I could with her. My skills, my experience, my *je ne sais quoi.* My card."

Lacey took his offered business card. "Why would Angie kill herself when she was a rising star? Isn't that what she worked so hard for?"

"Because she couldn't handle all the attention. Besides, Marcia Robinson should have been mine."

Lacey had heard a lot about the temperamental Leonardo. No last name, just Leonardo. He had been the resident star stylist at Stylettos and "a royal pain in the butt," to quote Stella. He often left other stylists in tears during a tirade. He refused to see clients if they had been "unfaithful." He overbooked his schedule and made clients wait for hours, or he disappeared for days and made others cover for him.

Leonardo straightened up and gave his full attention to Lacey. "So you're the little style sniper at *The Eye*. I can't believe we haven't met before. But of course, Stella has told me all about you. We just adore your column. You know, you have great hair. You're wasted on Stella."

Leo grabbed a handful of Lacey's hair and ran his fingers through it, pulling gently and letting it fall into place. "Nice texture, good weight. Do make an appointment with me, doll, next time Stella's out of town. Don't tell Stella." He winked at Stella and squeezed Lacey's hand.

"You wouldn't like her, Leo," Stella snarled. "She's one of 'those.'"

"You mean she insists on having it *her* way? Naughty, naughty. You have to remember who the expert is, Lacey."

Yes. Me. It's my hair. I'm the expert. "Sorry, Leonardo," Lacey said. "Stella's my stylist. I'm afraid to ditch her."

He sighed. "Come in anyway, we'll talk about 'Crimes.' You know it's a crime what women in this town do to their hair. Can you believe they still want their hair frosted? Oh my God. With all the edgy alternatives available? It's ridiculous. Does it make you want to gag or what? You take a twenty-five-year-old woman and give her a frosted Helmet Head, what do you get? A woman who looks forty-five. Of course, D.C. is full of the prematurely matronly and geezerly. Forget the spandex, and bring on the sweatpants, honey." Leo's private mission was to break the hammerlock of the frosted Helmet Head look that was so popular in Washington.

"Tell me, Leo, did you know Angie very well?"

"Are you going to quote me?" Leonardo thought for a moment, weighing each word, calculating its effect. "We were close, so close. It's hard to talk about." He paused and didn't seem at all embarrassed by his previous comments.

Josephine swooped by and placed her hand on Leonardo's shoulder. "Come, *cherí*. I need you." Leonardo dragged himself away from the table, tossing "It's so tragic," over his shoulder. Lacey watched Josephine latch on to him and lead him away.

"Thick as thieves, those two," Stella said.

"What did he mean when he said Marcia should have been his?" Lacey asked.

"Marcia actually had an appointment with Leonardo the first time she came in," Jamie explained. "But he was sick with Virginia Beach fever." Jamie rolled her eyes. "He's the one who called in sick, but he wouldn't even speak to Angie after she gave Marcia that great makeover and got her picture in all the papers. He is so not funny."

"Whatever," Stella said. "Marcia's lawyer and her mother, who is a close friend of Josephine Radford's, told Miss Robinson not to show her face to the cameras until she tamed that mop and lost a few pounds. Josephine wanted her star Leo to take care of her. As a special favor. No one thought it would be a big deal, so he played hooky. Anyway, with Leo out I gave Marcia to Angie. The rest is in the newspapers. Leonardo never forgave Angie for getting a break."

Jamie nodded her agreement. "Or for being more talented than him. I thought it was totally cool that Angie was recognized for what she did, because all the big celebrity stylists are men." She made a face. "You ever notice that? That is so . . . you know?" The younger stylist leaned forward. "So, are you going to write something about the funeral, Lacey?"

"Of course she's going to write something," Stella said. "She just has to think about it first." Stella tapped her manicured fingers on the table. "So what do you think, Lacey?"

"I think it's time for me to go." Lacey picked up her purse and stood up. Jamie took a roll and tore it into little pieces.

"You know, it's kind of funny, but Angie's death was just

like that game we play, Stella. You know the one," Jamie whispered. "Salon of Death."

Stella sighed. "No, it's not."

"Excuse me?" Lacey perked up. "Salon of Death?"

"Yeah, it is, kind of. Of course we don't play Salon of Suicide. Just murder."

Lacey perched on the edge of the table and took a petit four off Stella's plate. "Tell me about the game, Jamie."

Stella jumped in. "It has nothing to do with anything."

"I want to hear it, especially if it has nothing to do with anything," Lacey insisted.

Stella shrugged. "If you think the wig heads are creepy, you'll love this."

Jamie picked up all the bread pieces and balled them together in her fist, then rolled the ball around in her fingers. "Sometimes it gets really boring, right? So one day we just sort of started talking and everything, about how easy it would be to kill someone in the salon. There's lots of ways. Mostly we talked about how—actually it's Ratboy we kill. Once in a while Josephine, or a real irritating client like Sherri Gold. But anyway, Salon of Death is our imaginary board game, like Clue. Clue has these cute little plastic murder weapons? In Salon of Death you could have cute little plastic scissors and blowdryers and shampoo bowls and stuff." Jamie paused for breath and took a sip of Coke.

"In Clue you guess whodunit, like, you know, Colonel Mustard in the kitchen with the candlestick? In Salon of Death, we guess, How would *you* kill Ratboy? For example, Leo at the shampoo bowl, poisoning him with solution."

"How would you do that?" Lacey asked.

"Hold him down and make him drink it," Stella said. "That would be a permanent solution."

Jamie played with a stray curl, wrapping it around her index finger, which had a nail bitten to the quick. "There are lots of chemical things, you know, relaxers, dyes, and highlights. All totally toxic. Lots of them are flammable too. And for electrocution there's actually a really old permanent wave machine in the warehouse. They rolled up your hair on these crazy rods that are connected to wires on this machine, and plugged you in. Like way long ago, in the Twenties or Fifties or something.

She's really spooky. We call her Medusa. There's one just like it in the Smithsonian Museum—just like your name! Wow, I never even thought of that before!"

"It's more inventive than just dropping the blow-dryer in the water," Stella said. "In Salon of Death, you get points for originality."

"What about hair spray and matches?" Lacey asked. "Like a blowtorch?"

"Exactly," Jamie said. She was obviously a budding games designer. *Or mass murderer.* "Everyone has a favorite method."

"Really? Stella, what's yours?" Lacey snagged a potato chip off Stella's plate, but ignored the little hot dog. *Who catered this thing anyway?*

Stella rolled her eyes and snapped a carrot stick.

"Oh, you'd break his bones? That's my stylist," Lacey said.

"Stella got grossed out by it. Now if we talk about it, she makes us fold all the towels."

"It's only a game, Lacey," Stella said. "But after Angie—"

"What did Angie think about the game? Did she have a favorite method? A razor maybe?" Lacey asked.

"She wasn't into it much. She was kind of antiviolence," Jamie said. She lowered her voice. "Leo said he'd use a razor and slit Ratboy's throat. 'Course, that's pretty obvious. But when I think about Angie . . ."

All of a sudden Jamie ran out of steam. Her eyes teared up and she started sobbing. Stella handed Jamie a fresh black Stylettos napkin to wipe her eyes. She took one look at Lacey and handed her a napkin too.

There was another teary interlude with Angie's mother. In spite of her red-rimmed eyes, Adrienne Woods was, at fifty, still a pretty woman in the Southern manner of perfection that demanded equal parts charm and good grooming. The family hung together as if fearing another violent separation. In a show of support, Adrienne was followed closely by her two nearly grown daughters, both brown-eyed blondes: seventeen-year-old Abigail, the middle child, and Allison, the youngest at fifteen. Every memory of Angela Woods brought fresh tears.

"All she ever wanted was to make people happy. She didn't deserve this," Adrienne sobbed.

Lacey wanted to know if Angie had been depressed recently. Adrienne said that everyone gets blue every now and then, but Angie had been nothing but smiles since landing her job at the Dupont Circle salon, and the recognition she gained from styling Marcia Robinson put her "over the moon."

The funeral and reception left Lacey exhausted. Intimacy with so many strangers made her uncomfortable and Salon of Death gave her the creeps. She wanted to dry off all the tears that fell during all the hugs she endured. Suddenly, a pathway seemed to open up in front of her. Stella would just have to catch up. Lacey willed herself to be invisible as she raced for the door.

Chapter 5

Funny, I didn't see him at the funeral. He was about six feet tall, broad shoulders and narrow hips, a nice pair of muscular arms. He had curly dark brown hair and, she supposed, brown eyes, if only she could get a look at his face.

Lacey was almost out the door, waving for Stella and on her way to freedom, when she glanced sideways at a mirror and caught a glimpse of this stranger. She turned on a dime. Sightings of an attractive male specimen seemed to be getting rarer.

The view from where she stood was compelling. She admired his physique for a moment, suddenly aware that other women were marking their territory around him with invisible welcome signs. The heady charge of testosterone was in the air. She could feel her blood pumping. *Where did he come from?*

Polly stood by preening, waiting for him to notice all six feet of her. She tossed her hair. A pro at hair tossing, Polly tried to look up flirtatiously, but it was difficult from her height. However, the man seemed preoccupied with the buffet. No doubt he was used to women gathering around his star quality. It gave Lacey a few extra moments to stare.

Angling for a better look, Lacey managed to move in closer to pick up a glass of wine. He turned around and bumped her. He had eyes the color of summer grass and long lashes under thick arched eyebrows. Not brown, they were merry leprechaun eyes. All too soon she realized she knew him.

Oh my God. It can't be Victor Donovan, the tumbling tumbleweed. She was knocked for a loop and nearly spilled her wine.

Donovan had still been chief of police in Sagebrush, Colorado, six years ago, when she fled her job as a reporter on the local rag there. He would be thirty-eight now. *Damn, he's still handsome. The jerk.* Donovan had spent two years flirting mercilessly with Lacey, who'd covered the cops beat for the *The Sagebrush Daily Press*. She always believed he did it at least partly to distract her from getting the news. Vic hit on her constantly until it became a joke all over town. Lacey hated being the butt of jokes. It was a small town, with a very small police station. It was difficult not to physically bump into each other, which occasionally they did. The sparks were palpable. She refused him for many reasons. Conflict of interest for one. For another, he was married, albeit separated, both legally and by about four hundred miles. Vic said he didn't care. But she did. It was very simple. She was Catholic.

All this was played out in front of the cops, witnesses with knowing looks and winks. Lacey wondered if they had bets on the odds of her saying yes to Vic. They probably had a pool going on when he would nail her. She wished she could go back and be more clever about the whole thing, more witty, instead of so painfully green. She took a deep breath. *Relax, Lacey. It was years ago. He'll never even remember me, let alone recognize me.*

He studied her. His eyebrows went up and his mouth curled into a grin. *Does he have to have such a nice jawline?* He'd been crossing her mind for no good reason: spring, drinks on the balcony, Tony's new boots. She glanced down. Donovan was wearing well-worn cowboy boots. She'd forgotten how awkward he always made her feel.

"Lacey, Lacey Smithsonian? Wow. It is you. What are you doing here?"

She looked around to see if anyone was staring. Only wide-eyed Stella and a few other stylists, who had all snapped to attention. It was understandable, with the sudden hormonal charge in the air. Estrogen was rising. Stella nodded her obvious approval. Jamie made a thumbs-up gesture. Leonardo looked bemused, while Polly looked offended. She hated it when a petite woman walked off with an available tall guy.

"Well, well, well. Victor Donovan. Nice seeing you." Lacey just wanted to get away from him. As far as she was concerned

Polly could have him. Lacey spun on her heels, but not quickly enough.

"Not so fast." He grabbed her arm and spun her around. "I haven't seen you in what—five years? Six years?" He glanced quickly at her left hand. "Let's catch up."

"Let's not." She removed his hand from her arm.

"What's wrong?"

"Nothing. Gotta go."

"You're not still mad at me?" He looked surprised. "Damn, I never could figure that one out."

"Me neither. Probably some kind of toxic reaction."

Vic laughed, showing strong white teeth. "I'm a changed man, Lacey. Older and wiser."

"A wise old wolf?"

"Wolf! I'm a puppy dog, Smithsonian." Lacey glanced at his left hand. It was still bare, but that didn't mean anything. "And I'm not married anymore, Lacey." It irritated her that he noticed her looking. "Don't worry. This time around we should just be friends."

"What do you mean, 'this time around'? What do you mean, 'friends'?"

Vic wasn't wearing a scent, but something was making her dizzy. She reached for a canapé to keep her strength up.

"I mean friends. Purely platonic. What do you say?"

"I'd say just what the hell are you doing here? Why aren't you in Colorado?" She didn't need a "friendship" with Vic Donovan. *Why aren't you back in some rattlesnake den where you belong?*

"Why aren't you?" He steered her to an empty table back by the wig heads. Every female eye—and a few others—followed them.

"I live here. What's your excuse?"

"I'm living here too. Sort of. I didn't realize I needed your permission, Smithsonian. Is there an application to fill out?"

"You're living here? Since when?"

Vic explained that he had moved back East in stages, first from Sagebrush to Steamboat Springs, Colorado, as chief of police for a three-year stint, and finally all the way back to Virginia. Now he was helping his dad run his security consulting business, which these days had way too much work, and Boyd

Radford was a brand-new client with a major employee theft problem. Vic's dad was slowing down and he wanted Vic to take over the company, but Vic was on the fence. He still had a house in Steamboat Springs. Lacey recalled vaguely that Vic was a military brat who had grown up all over the country: grade school in Colorado Springs when his dad was at NORAD, high school in Alexandria, Virginia, when Dad went to the Pentagon. Now he was staying out in McLean, near his folks' house, trying to decide whether to buy a place of his own here. He'd been in town all of two months.

"And you just hadn't gotten around to calling me yet." Lacey smirked. She regretted it the moment she said it.

"I didn't even know you were here! I thought you were still in Denver someplace, where your folks are. Besides, why should I call you? You don't even like me."

Lacey had spent an eventful two years covering Vic and his cops at very close range back in Sagebrush. She had followed him through homicides, suicides, scores of bar fights and drunken car wrecks, and even a case of stolen dynamite that drew a crowd of obnoxious federal agents. Vic had brought her along on the hunt, over the objections of the arrogant clods from the Bureau of Alcohol, Tobacco and Firearms. He was a natural as top cop, at dealing with people, the press, the crusty ranchers on the town council who couldn't see why he needed patrol cars newer than Fred Flintstone's. Lacey had developed her reporting skills in self-defense. She learned how to get Vic and his cops to tip her off on the dirt at the county sheriff's office, and she used the sheriff and his deputies to get the inside scoop on Vic and his boys. And she'd have scooped up Vic in a minute and quit the police beat, if he'd really been unattached. If he hadn't been such a roving lover boy. And if the whole town hadn't been watching them as if they were *Days of Our Lives*.

"I like you fine, you big jerk. So why'd they kick you out of Steamboat?"

Vic snorted in exasperation. "Steamboat and I are fine, thank you. But corporate security is where the money is, and to move up in law enforcement I'd have to tackle a bigger city with bigger headaches. Or else run for county sheriff. We still elect 'em in Colorado, you know. And you remember how much I love politics."

"Let me get this straight, Vic. You're moving to Washington, D.C., to get away from politics, and you're trading being chief of police for counting shampoo bottles in a rat-infested warehouse? Wow, good career move."

"Well, it looks like your career is booming too, Smithsonian. I suppose you're living in the District with your wacky old aunt, what's her name? Minnie? Mamie? And I see you gave up on the newspaper biz. I should have figured a stylish gal like you would end up being a hairstylist. I bet you're terrific at the old cut and curl."

Lacey felt hot blood rising to her cheeks. "I am not!" she said, much too loudly. Eyes that had drifted away snapped back to their table. "A hairstylist? Do I look like a hairstylist to you? I am a reporter! I have my own column! In a major daily Washington newspaper!"

Stella appeared at Lacey's shoulder, drawn like a magnet to the sound of righteous indignation.

"Yeah, you bet. Lacey's a hell of a reporter. She's the best thing that ever happened to *The Eye Street Observer*."

"Oh, *The Eye Street Observer*," Vic said grandly. "That's different. I guess you must be too big a talent for *The Washington Post*." Lacey steamed silently. "Isn't *The Observer* some sort of *Thrifty Nickel Super Shopper* kind of rag?"

Lacey opened her mouth, but it was Stella's voice she heard.

"No way! *The Eye* is totally like a real newspaper. And Lacey is the best fashion reporter in Washington, bar none."

"Stella, please—" she began.

"You write a fashion column?" Vic said. "About funerals? A little ghoulish, isn't it, Lacey, taking advantage of some poor kid who killed herself in a really messy way?"

"I invited her," Stella bellowed, shoving all her might into Vic's face. "And she is here to investigate a murder, not a suicide! It was murder, damn it, and Lacey is going to get to the bottom of it."

"Stella!" Lacey didn't know which of them made her angrier. Stella gave her a big wink just as Boyd Radford grabbed Stella's arm and pulled her away.

"Right." Vic was laughing now. "The fashion expert is going

to solve a murder. Remember to wear your high-heel gumshoes."

Lacey fixed Vic with a steely glare. "I'm a good reporter, Vic. You know I am. Stella may be right about this thing. And reporters investigate crime all the time, remember? You ever heard of an investigative reporter?"

"Yeah, I know how investigative reporters really investigate. Someone else does the dirty work. You pull a few quotes, a little rewrite, and presto! Instant Pulitzer."

"Hey, I've worked the cops beat. I know how to dig up my own—"

"Sure you do. You're the big-city fashion reporter now. So you can spot those killers—how, exactly? Because they have that killer look?"

"Who the hell do you think you're fooling, Vic Donovan? I know all about you. You were the top cop in a town where you practically had to buy your own bullets. Where a major crime wave was getting your skis ripped off, or kids chasing cows with a stolen tractor. Where the big sex scandal was when the massage parlor opened and the ministers shut it down. You only had one real first-degree murder the whole time I was there. But did you ever solve that one, Marshall Dillon? So don't you try to tell me how to investigate a murder!"

Lacey stood up. She wished she hadn't finished her wine; she would have loved to throw it at him. It would make a perfect moment. Just then the sound of a tray of canapés crashing to the floor distracted them. Jamie and Michelle were picking up the debris. Lacey followed Vic's gaze to see Radford yanking Stella behind the screen of the shampoo area. Boyd seemed to think the screen was soundproof, or else he assumed Vic and Lacey were keeping the house fully entertained.

"What kind of crap are you pulling now, Stella? You can't do this to me!"

"I'm just telling your new security expert the truth. It wasn't suicide."

"Don't be a moron."

"I am not a moron, you bully."

"The cops say she killed herself."

"For crying out loud, Boyd, you're taking the word of D.C. homicide cops? What do they know? What do they care about a lousy hairstylist? You know what they told me when I said, 'Look at that haircut'? 'All you chicks got bad haircuts.' Good God!"

"Get it through your thick crew cut. Angela killed herself. That's bad enough. Any more negative publicity will hurt Stylettos," Boyd said. "And me."

"Well, maybe you've got something to hide. I don't." A stinging slap was heard from behind the screen. Lacey jumped back on Vic's foot. "Sorry," she whispered. He steadied her, then let go.

A red-haired fireball stormed out and Boyd followed a moment later, rubbing the side of his face. He avoided Lacey's eyes and plowed his way to the bar.

Lacey pulled Stella to her side. "Stella? Are you okay?"

"I'm fine, but that jackass has got something to worry about, once you start asking questions." Stella was obviously energized by her little scene. "Lacey is going to investigate the hell out of Angie's death. She's the best damn fashion reporter in this sleazy town."

"I'm sure she is," Vic said.

"One thing about Lacey, she really understands nuance," Stella confided.

"Oh, she always did," Vic said.

Lacey had heard more than enough. She grabbed Stella's arm in one hand, her purse in the other.

Boyd Radford watched them steam toward the exit. He glared at Stella, still rubbing his jaw. "Now I suppose all our dirty laundry will be hung out to dry in that cheap rag of a paper. And she's *your* friend, Stella. You can have a friend or a job. You decide."

Lacey turned at the door just in time to see Josephine approaching Boyd with an evil smile on her face and a full wineglass in her hand. She looked him in the eye and threw it in his face.

"It just isn't an event without you causing a scene, is it, Boyd?"

Damn, I wanted to do that, Lacey thought. *Why is my glass always empty?*

Lacey Smithsonian's

FASHION BITES

Show a Little Respect: It's a Funeral, Not a Cocktail Party.

Stumped about what to wear to a funeral? You are not alone. Most of us would simply reach for something in black. For many women, that means the ubiquitous little black dress, the same one that got you through last night's cocktail party, last weekend's late-night clubbing, last month's charity ball, and last year's Christmas party. But a party dress is not appropriate for mourning. Unless, dingdong, the Wicked Witch is dead, and you're invited to the parade.

Give your little black dress a rest. Remember the black or navy or otherwise somber suit you had to buy for the job interview but you never wear because it is too depressing? That suit is suitable for a funeral. However, there are some people who are afraid to wear black to a funeral. Apparently they're too busy wearing black to weddings and the theatre and a double latte at Starbucks. But whatever you decide, it should not be too tight, too short, too revealing, or too festive. Maybe you're conflicted about your feelings for the deceased. Don't let it show. Here are a few guidelines:

- Veils covering one's face imply inconsolable grief, so please restrict them to close family members, who have a good excuse.
- It is inappropriate for mistresses to show up at the funeral wearing widow's weeds. That is the purview of the widow, and if she's smart, she's barred all the unsavory mourners.
- If you do choose that little black dress, please make sure it is not too bare, and consider pairing it with a silky cardigan or shapely jacket to add a serious note.
- Tennis togs and other sporting apparel are not advised,

nor are pastels, bright colors, Hawaiian shirts, halter tops, or strapless dresses.

Of course these tips don't cover the occasional wild and wacky send-off where the dearly departed has left instructions for everyone to party down till dawn and lift a cold one (or ten) in his or her name. In that case, you—and the little black dress—are on your own.

chapter 6

Some people have small rituals to help them find solace after a stressful week. A drink. A hot bath. A novel. A stranger in a two-bit dive.

On Friday night, Lacey went straight to Great-aunt Mimi's ancient steamer trunk.

She had dragged her butt to the office that morning, scanned her "Fashion Bite" on funeral attire she dashed off after the reception, read her column, "You're Not Going to Wear That, Are You?" in the morning edition, contemplated next week's column, discarded a stack of press releases, told Stella she was working out her strategy, and realized that enlightening women on their style options against the tyranny of money-hungry designers and big business would all have to wait. She had to get away.

At home she donned comfort clothes, jeans and a vintage emerald-green sweater. She cleared a stack of magazines off the top of the old trunk, which also served as her coffee table. Inside were Great-aunt Mimi's patterns, dating from the late 1930s and '40s.

It was a trunk full of dreams. As she fingered the illustrated envelopes, she could see the fantasies that Mimi had seen. The trunk held everything from slacks and suits to evening gowns. Mimi had kept every pattern she ever bought, carefully matched with cut-out pictures of movie stars wearing something similar that she hoped to re-create. Katharine Hepburn dressed for the country in slacks and a blouse, à la *Adam's Rib,* 1949. Barbara Stanwyck, the ultimate temptress, in an exquisite gown by Edith Head for *Double Indemnity*, 1944. And Joan

Crawford, the quintessential businesswoman in a no-nonsense suit in *Mildred Pierce*, 1945. Mimi celebrated a flair for the dramatic.

Mimi Smith had a bad rep in the family as a dotty old lady in the habit of starting projects she never finished. Her trunk was filled with patterns she had bought but never opened, or had half finished or barely begun. Some patterns were still pinned to materials partially cut out. Mimi was a fickle seamstress; the evidence lay in the trunk. Portions of some garments were just basted together. Outfits were dropped as quickly as if Pompeii had erupted between stitches, a sleeve finished, the buttonholes completed, but the hem unpinned and buttons left off. For every five projects she started, perhaps one was completed. But she couldn't discard them. She had merely packed them away, wrapped in tissue with the materials she planned to use, crepes, wools, cotton. Her intention clearly was to return again and pick up the jilted pieces. Lacey often wondered why so many were unfinished; perhaps Mimi had run out of thread and while buying more had fallen in love with another gown? They left a record frozen in a time when women were urged to sew. Mimi had good intentions and great style, but a short attention span. At the end of the Forties, the collection stopped for unknown reasons. No more patterns, projects, and movie-star photos. She had closed the trunk and left Lacey an accidental time capsule. It never failed to transport her into a more elegant era.

Many things divide the sexes, but none quite like a simple shopping trip for clothes. Men see clothes, they think size. Shirts, pants, jackets, shoes: They fit, they buy them. They go home, they watch the game. *Mmmm, clothes good! Now Tarzan not naked. Tarzan want Jane naked.*

Women see a dress and imagine a mood, a moment, a scenario. *This dress would be perfect on the beach at sunset, a barefoot walk along the water with waves lapping at my feet. I'll carry a pair of slim-strapped sandals to slip on later. Pair it with a broad-brimmed straw hat, tied with a light blue ribbon around the crown, pinned with an antique cameo. It's just right for a candlelight dinner on the deck of an elegant restaurant overlooking the Mediterranean. And then, perhaps a dance in the moonlight . . .*

The fact that the scenario is wildly unlikely, no beach vacation is planned, no romantic walks along the water's edge at dusk are on the horizon, does not deter a woman in the clutches of the perfect dress. Usually she'll get ahold of herself and let out a sigh. She won't buy it, because after all, it is impractical, but she'll feel better, because for a moment, she was on that beach and smelled the salt air. Someone was waiting for her at that restaurant and she looked perfect.

Aunt Mimi's patterns did that for Lacey.

"My aunt was a crazy old dame," her father always said. But Lacey never thought of Mimi that way. She had a formal portrait of Mimi at twenty-five, taken in 1945 at the end of the war. Hollywood's effect was evident in her sultry look and come-hither hair. The hand-tinted portrait revealed a beauty with high cheeks, green eyes, and deep chestnut-red hair. Mimi gazed out at the world with a look of happy expectation and a hint of her legendary "strangeness." Lacey always felt closer to Mimi than to anyone else in her family.

Under the influence of the 1939 Jimmy Stewart movie, *Mr. Smith Goes to Washington*, Mimi changed her name back to Smith. Her family was aghast. "Nobody changes their name to Smith! Only a criminal would want to be called Smith." But Mimi was undeterred. Smith it was and Smith it remained.

She left home to go to Washington at the start of the war, looking to be an adventuress, not a happy homemaker. She was the Smithsonian family's equivalent of Miss Haversham. "Nutty as a fruitcake," Lacey's father said. Steven Smithsonian seldom spoke except to state the obvious or repeat others' opinions. Generally, he was wrong. "Mimi Smith never finished a damn thing in her life," he always said.

Actually, Mimi had, on occasion, finished a project or two. There was the time during World War II, in a patriotic frenzy to make over old clothes—encouraged by the government to save fabric needed for the military—when Mimi took up the challenge. While her brother, Lacey's grandfather, was in the U.S. Army and missing in action on some battlefront, Mimi retrieved his best blue serge suit from his closet and had it remade into a suit for her. The pattern, adapted from the popular *Make and Mend for Victory* booklet, was still in the trunk, along with the ancient publication. When her brother turned up alive after all and anxious to change out of uniform into his snappy blue suit, he was furious to find Mimi wearing it. He remained sore about it for decades, no matter how many times Mimi tried to explain that they all assumed he was dead and that this was her memorial to him.

Lacey felt comfortable with the old woman and her dark furnishings and rich colors. Her college summers spent at Mimi Smith's Georgetown town house were comforting after the riot of orange and lime and cheap pine furniture that her mother had inflicted on the family—and Mimi had her own library.

Lacey discovered the trunk when she was fifteen, while visiting Mimi by herself. It was large and black and banded with thick leather straps, as exciting as a pirate's treasure chest. And it was in the attic, which Lacey also loved. Her parents' one-story ranch-style house in Denver had no secret corners, no nooks and crannies to explore. No dungeon, no attic, no treasure.

"Well, open it up, Lacey, if you're so curious."

Lacey was almost afraid it wouldn't live up to her expectations. The buckle was stiff and the lid creaked as she opened it. She wasn't disappointed with Mimi's whole cache of patterns and materials and dreams. It was a cabinet of wonders. Full of vintage linens, wools, velvets, and that exciting new fabric of the Thirties, rayon. The materials, kept for years in the dry, well-insulated attic, were still good, only a little musty. Miraculously, the patterns were Lacey's size. "I could never part with them," Mimi said. "I don't know why. Maybe I kept them for you." It was more than Lacey had ever hoped for.

Every time she visited Mimi she asked to see the trunk. Mimi, the old lady pirate, was Lacey's guide. They never quite reached the bottom. Together they would explore it and Mimi would tell Lacey stories about dates and dances and music and movie stars that the clothes would evoke. Even more wonderful, Lacey could see that these clothes were designed for real women, women with figures. Women with curves. Women who were strong and feminine. Women with wiles. Women with breasts and hips and a waist that they weren't afraid to show. Women like her. "Well, they wouldn't fit that beanpole sister of yours, now would they?" Mimi commented.

When Great-aunt Mimi died, she left the trunk to Lacey, as well as her books, her overstuffed velvet sofa, and her cherry dining room suite. Her parents found it hilarious that Lacey seemed to think these things were worth more than the old china and kitchenware Mimi had left to her younger, taller, skinnier sister, Cherise, who sold her inheritance in a garage sale.

"What on earth," her mother wanted to know, "are you going to do with that depressing old stuff?"

"I'm going to restore it, love it, and treasure it."

"Maybe some nice bright yellow and orange polka dots would brighten it up," her mother—who loved fast-food restaurant decor—suggested for the sofa. She was horrified when Lacey chose a rich sapphire blue velvet for the sofa and a striped rose and navy damask for the dining room chairs. "Well, with you in Washington, at least I won't have to look at it," Mother said.

Alas, Mimi's sewing skills had not been passed on with the trunk. But Lacey had found a seamstress in Arlington who finished and tailored several of the patterns for her. Alma Lopez had a way of subtly adjusting some of the more obvious period quirks, such as gigantic shoulders, to a more natural fit, making the clothes distinctive yet up-to-date at the same time. Lacey started with a black fitted dress and emerald-green bolero with black piping from the late Thirties. It featured a long green and black silk sash wrapped around the midriff. It was a classic look, with irony sewn into the details. The fact that having Mimi's clothes finished horrified her mother, who preferred matching sweat suits in neons, was a bonus.

"Lacey, what will people think of you in all those funny old clothes?"

"They'll think I'm something special, Mother." *Or they may think I'm a freaking loon, I don't care.*

As much as she desired it, Lacey couldn't afford to have more than a few of Mimi's clothes finished each year. But whenever she needed a lift, she'd wander through the patterns and select something promising. Little by little she was making a dent in the trunk and creating a unique and offbeat wardrobe.

After the week's disorienting events, Lacey found herself considering an evening gown with a fitted midriff, a V neck, and full sleeves. Mimi had attached a photo of Rita Hayworth in the spotlight, circa 1939. It was terribly glamorous and Lacey was imagining a promising scenario.

A cozy little club just off the beaten path. The band begins to play an old song with a bluesy beat, when suddenly a handsome rascal . . .

A knock on her apartment door interrupted her reverie. Probably a neighbor with mail. It was a rare day that the postal carriers got everything in all the right boxes. *Too many transient residents, or just dyslexic?* Lacey wondered. She peered out the tiny peephole to see a visitor waiting outside in the hallway. She sucked in a deep breath. *I don't believe this. Who does he think he is?*

Lacey opened the door but blocked the opening with her arm. He looked good, too good, wearing jeans that had faded in all the right places, comfortably scuffed boots, a black turtleneck, and a black leather jacket slung casually over his shoulder. Men in black sweaters, particularly turtlenecks, were a weakness of hers. She thought almost any breathing male specimen looked good in one. And Vic Donovan wasn't just any specimen. The sleeves were casually pushed up on his forearms, showing curly dark hair above the wrists, which only reminded her that she'd also like to know what his chest looked like uncovered. She was rooting for dark and curly. However, the reality of Donovan showing up on her doorstep was alarming.

"Yikes," she said.

"You could drop that right eyebrow and invite me in." Vic grinned. He offered her a six-pack of Dos Equis.

"How'd you get past our crackerjack security system?"

Her World War II–era building featured an intercom at the front door that rang the telephone when guests arrived. Nevertheless, friendly residents coming and going would politely hold the door for complete strangers. This was low-crime Old Town, of course.

"I just followed the pizza boy. I was hoping he was coming here."

She didn't bother asking how he found out where she lived. Considering his line of work it would be an insult. And in the old days he was not above giving Lacey a detailed rundown of where she and her car had been seen at any time, night or day.

"Sorry, wrong apartment. You can follow the pizza boy out."

"Lacey, let me in." She didn't budge. "Look, I'm really sorry if I insulted you yesterday. I didn't mean to. I was just—surprised."

"I don't like surprises either."

"How about letting me in?"

"What if I'm busy?"

"In that case, I'll just wait until your date comes by. We've got things to talk about."

Date? In that case you might be here until Christmas.

"Stylettos?"

"Among other topics of mutual interest."

Curiosity got the better of her. It always did and she was forever listening to crazy people with strange stories. Lacey thought if she had one thing going for her as a reporter, it was her passion for knowing how a story ended. She cursed herself.

"All right."

"You could discourage a guy, you know." He stepped into the kitchen, opened a beer, and offered Lacey one. He put the rest in the fridge and paused to examine its paltry contents. "I should have robbed the pizza boy. I think it was pepperoni."

"I can cook. I just don't care to. Shall I offer you some popcorn to go with the beer?"

"Popcorn is not an entrée."

He took the beer out of her hand and put it back in the fridge. "I have a better idea. I'll buy you dinner. It's chilly out. I'd grab a jacket if I were you."

She stood there looking at him.

"Yes? No? Next Wednesday?" he inquired. Vic wandered around the room. She suspected he was looking for telltale clues of a male presence. He made himself at home on Aunt Mimi's dark blue velvet sofa. "This is nice."

"Don't get too comfortable."

"Hey, what's in the trunk?"

"Pandora's box." She quickly gathered up her patterns, slipped them inside, and shut the trunk. She buckled the belt on the lid, put on her shoes, and wrapped her black jacket around her as armor. She hesitated. "What do you want, Vic?"

He stood up. "Dinner. And a truce."

"Actually, I am a little hungry."

"After looking at your fridge, I can believe it."

"You said something about being friends."

"Is that a new concept for you?"

Lacey shoved him out the door into the hall, pulled the door shut behind her, and locked it.

"It is when it comes to you. How about getting those boots in gear? I'm starved."

Of course he had a Jeep parked behind her building, still sporting Colorado plates. Somehow she knew he'd still be a Jeep Wrangler kind of guy. And she knew it would be mechanically perfect, but not too clean. "A dirty Jeep is a happy Jeep," she remembered him telling her. It had the right amount of clutter: a few maps, a water bottle. In the back, a metal box of tools was locked up, along with a small bag packed in case of emergency. Vic was the proverbial Boy Scout. The Jeep was also equipped with a good sound system and they listened quietly to an old Tom Waits CD, breaking-the-law kind of blues. They didn't need to fill the car with chat.

The last time she'd seen Vic Donovan was New Year's Eve at the Golden Slipper in Sagebrush, Colorado, six years ago. It was the biggest bar in town with a dance floor. Her boyfriend of the moment was highly peeved because she was leaving town and she had turned down his proposal of marriage. The man had surprised her with a diamond ring to convince her to stay, but it didn't work; it merely scared her off. She canceled their New Year's Eve plans and trooped along with the other three unattached *Daily Press* reporters to the Golden Slipper's New Year's blowout.

Lacey didn't remember much about the evening—except one unforgettable moment. Somehow, at the stroke of midnight, Chief Donovan was suddenly standing in front of her. He had one arm around her, his hand circling her waist; he drew her close and used the other hand to tip her face up toward his. He bent down and kissed her. He didn't give her any time to think about it. Vic's ambush took her by surprise, but she kissed him back. It was no use denying the electrical charge that she felt. Finally he let her go.

"I couldn't let you leave town before I got the chance to say good-bye. So long, Lacey. Good luck." And then he was gone, into the rollicking mass of cowboys, good-time gals, and coal miners.

He won't remember that in a million years. He was probably drunk. She didn't remember ever seeing him drunk. It always bothered her that she remembered Donovan's kiss, but she could barely remember the other man, the one she might have married, whose kisses left no impression at all.

Donovan took her to a steak house down the river, south of Alexandria, with walls of knotty pine, decorated with elk heads and moose heads. Her mouth watered as they entered and the aroma of grilled meat greeted her. Vic was met by a curly-haired brunette in a fringed miniskirt and cowboy boots, a look that definitely said, "Welcome, cowboy." She directed them to a cozy booth in Nonsmoking, tucked under a giant buffalo head. They ordered beer and steaks, medium rare with all the trimmings.

Lacey dove into her steak, savoring each bite. She rarely ate a big meal, but as a Colorado native, loving a good steak was her birthright. She closed her eyes in bliss, only to open them to find him watching her. He did this thing that made his eyes twinkle.

"You're making little sounds." He lifted his glass and indicated to the waitress to bring two more.

"I am not."

"Are too. Little 'umm' sounds. So I guess you haven't eaten in a week or two. Is that right?"

"You're a beast, you know that, Vic?"

"A diet of popcorn makes a woman pretty cranky, I see."

"I am not cranky."

"She said, crankily." Two more Dos Equis arrived.

"Does it make you happy to push my buttons?"

"It always did. You have cute buttons." He grinned and took a slug of cold beer. "It's not a bad thing, enjoying your food. A man likes a woman with a healthy appetite. Yours looks pretty healthy."

She didn't know what to say. Was he commenting on her weight? She ignored him and continued to savor the morsels left on her plate. But she tried to keep the sound effects to a minimum.

Vic finished his steak and was in the mood to talk. Their blowup at the funeral was definitely out of bounds. They danced around several light topics. Colorado. Virginia. Lacey even confessed that she loved the cherry blossoms in the District and would like to go to the Tidal Basin sometime to see them early in the morning before the crowds descended. She wanted to see the sun rise and drink coffee on the steps of the Jefferson Memorial, but she wanted it all to herself. Vic nodded. He hadn't seen them since high school.

Eventually, they got around to old times. "So, whatever happened to that boyfriend of yours?"

"He married someone else." She paused. "What happened to your wife?"

"She married somebody else. After the divorce. Someone who'll stay put, right under her thumb."

"Smart woman. What about girlfriends?"

"No one steady. And you?"

"Stella didn't tell you?"

He laughed. "She says you're pretty particular." After he sated Lacey with beef and beer, Vic decided it was time to utter the forbidden word: Stylettos. "About your investigation. Tell me more about your theory. What do you plan to do?

"I see. You come on all wine-'em-and-dine-'em and all you want is information."

"That's all I said I wanted."

Lacey did a slow burn. *Even if I don't want you, you could have the courtesy to want me.* "Actually, you said dinner and a truce. Information is a two-way street."

"We'll switch drivers later, Lacey." He ordered coffee. "Stella strikes me as a bit high-strung, to say the least. Do you think she's out on a limb with this murder theory?"

"She's always out on a limb, but I don't disbelieve her."

"She really rattled Radford."

"Don't you mean really slapped him? Ratboy is just afraid the customers will be spooked if they think someone's actually been killed in the salon. Suicide is bad enough," Lacey said.

"'Ratboy'?"

"Stylists' pet name for their boss." Lacey found herself defending Stella to Vic. Stella went from the spike-haired harpy who bugged Lacey to distraction to a noble, singular voice crying out for justice. It wasn't so crazy, Lacey told Vic. "The death looks suspicious. Angie had no history of depression or self-mutilation."

"According to Stella?"

"Yes. I know she talks a lot, but I don't think she lies. You've seen suicides, Vic. So why would Angela Woods do that to herself?"

"I didn't see this one."

"Okay, pal," Lacey said. "Your turn."

Vic confided that he had reservations about working for Radford, who had already gone through several security companies, making ridiculous demands on their time and personnel. But the money was too good to pass up. And it was his dad's contract. A murder, if it was murder, would complicate matters even more.

"Who do you think is stealing shampoo?"

"I just got here. Who are your suspects, Lacey?"

"It's not my problem, Vic." *I'll have to ask Stella.*

"Radford says our job is to clamp down on the shrinkage problem and not to trip over any dead bodies. That's okay by me. But he *kept* warning me off. Could be a little too much protesting going on. He told me not to listen to 'that nut Stella'—or you. You're just 'the crazy reporter.' Of course, I already knew that."

"That Ratboy, he's a charmer."

"Warn your friend to watch her step."

"Stella?"

"He's itching for the chance to fire her. In fact, he turned blue every time Stella's name came up."

"Sounds like high blood pressure, but he can't fire her. She knows where all the bodies are buried."

"Meaning?"

"She slept with him once and she knows others who tumbled for the promise of a management position. If he tries anything, she'll scream bloody murder, and file a sexual harassment lawsuit."

Vic had learned from Radford that the publicity surrounding Angie's magical makeover on Marcia Robinson was a huge boost to Stylettos' business. But as rapidly as the gods of public whim had smiled on Stylettos, they could just as easily fade. The less people knew about Angie Woods' death the better, Radford told Vic.

"He's terrified of what you'll write in that, quote, crummy little rag of yours." Vic lifted his glass to her. "I had no idea you had such power, Lacey."

"I am the fashion queen, Vic." She rolled her eyes. "The mighty tremble at my words."

"Yes, ma'am. But if you find out anything I should know, I want you to tell me. Got it?"

"Aren't you going back to Steamboat?"

"Haven't decided yet."

"You're not top cop anymore."

He sighed. "This account means a lot to my dad. He has a reputation to live up to. I'd appreciate any information you could pass along. Please."

"Please" wasn't a word she associated with Vic, but she didn't show her surprise. "Sure thing, cowboy, but remember it works both ways."

Lacey ordered a very expensive dessert, very chocolate, very bad. She knew she'd pay for it later with extra exercise. Vic could pay now. He didn't order his own dessert, but he picked up his fork and dug into hers.

They drove back in silence, listening to some sweet country swing music. Vic walked her to the door of her building and made sure she was safely in. It crossed her mind he might kiss her good night. But of course he didn't. She was relieved, puzzled, and irritated.

It was gone, she was convinced. Whatever she used to have that attracted men to her was gone. Washington—and time—had taken it away.

chapter 7

Arguing with her stylist was only slightly less pointless than bashing her head against a wall, Lacey decided.

"Stella, I don't like being told what to do. Do you get that? Do you understand?"

Stella was unperturbed. "I told you to get highlights and you did."

"Highlights! Do I really have to point out that getting highlights and investigating murder are two different things?"

"The highlights look great, and now you're investigating a murder."

"If I'm going to look into Angie's death, I'm doing it my way. As a reporter, not a detective. Anything I do has got to end up in a story I can sell my editor. Are we agreed?"

"Absolutely."

Lacey had agreed to meet Stella for coffee Saturday morning. As usual, it was a matter of life and death. So Lacey had insisted on the Mud Hut, a shabby but sweet little coffee shop just off King Street in Old Town, full of writers tapping on laptops. She had a habit of popping in on Saturday mornings, and she acknowledged a few other people she recognized.

The Mud Hut's shabbiness was refreshing. Old Town Alexandria generally is aggressively Colonial, heavy on Virginia's Founding Fathers and all things George Washington. Many Old Town homes of distinction keep their front drapes open so people walking by may gaze in reverence at the genuine period furnishings and illuminated portraits of illustrious Colonial ancestors.

Stella might raise eyebrows in the snooty part of town, but

here no one would look twice at her crew cut, double-digit earrings, and leather-lass look. Today she was wearing a purple leather halter dress that laced up her cleavage to a dramatic swelling, like a Valkyrie's Wagnerian WunderBra. Stella paired it with a cropped black jacket with gold leather lightning bolts stitched on the back and down the sleeves.

Lacey was wearing high-waisted, loose-fitting khaki slacks with a light blue fitted blouse. Her clothes were comfortable and attractive, but lacked the one-two punch that Stella mastered.

"Where *do* you get your clothes?" Lacey asked.

Stella beamed down at her purple laced bust. "Great dress, huh? Picked it up at this leather shop in Georgetown. I'm kind of a regular, so they call me when they get something special in my size. You should come with me sometime."

The brave, noble Stella of last night's discussion with Vic was once again Lacey's personal pain in the neck. Featuring Angie's death in "Crimes of Fashion" was only the beginning of Stella's plan. But Stella didn't count on extra help, which appeared in the shape of Brooke Barton.

The blond intruder, looking fresh in jogging shorts and a hooded navy sweatshirt even though she'd been out on a run, padded into the shop and spotted Lacey. "Aha! I thought I'd catch you here," she said.

Lacey was confused. "Did we have plans, Brooke?"

"No, it's just that you're a creature of habit and if it's ten a.m. on a Saturday morning, you're swilling down a mocha latte at the Mud Hut. So, catch me up." She grabbed a chair and sat down.

Stella and Brooke eyed each other doubtfully. Lacey introduced them. "So you're the famous Stella of the highlights. Nice to meet you."

"Likewise." Stella looked none too pleased, but Brooke ignored her. She got right to the point: conspiracy, as usual.

"Did Marcia Robinson show up at the funeral?" Lacey shook her head. "Too bad. Maybe it's not true that murderers go to the funerals of their victims."

Stella was horrified. "You think Marcia killed Angie?"

"My number-one suspect."

"You are so wrong. Why would she kill Angie? She owed Angie for that miraculous makeover."

"Who knows what terrible secrets about the Senate Small Business Committee Marcia may have spread? And to whom?"

"Brooke has a point," Lacey interjected as Stella's cleavage puffed up alarmingly. "Marcia is the subject of a congressional investigation."

"You agree with her? You think Marcia offed Angie?"

"I didn't say that. I said she has a point."

"And Marcia had pornographic clips of some of the most unlikely people," Brooke said. "Nobody even knows the whole list or how many. Maybe your Angela Woods was among them."

Stella was finally stunned speechless. But she had nerves of steel. Her genius was that she could outwait anyone, just like a cat, and she was waiting for Brooke to leave. A silence descended on the table that Brooke finally broke. Glancing at her watch, she said to Lacey, "Look, I have to take a deposition this afternoon, so I should be going. Call me later. Be careful. There are serious nuts out there." She looked at Stella. "I'd watch what Lacey tells you, Stella. It could be dangerous." She was kidding, but Stella didn't think it was funny. Brooke exited the Mud Hut, her blond braid bouncing as she jogged down the street.

"She could use a haircut," Stella said.

"What, are you offering?"

"No, I'd give her to Leo." Stella wore an evil grin. "Okay, now that Snooty Two Shoes is gone, we can talk about your investigation. And Angie was no porno pinup. Trust me. She was pure, in a nice way."

Lacey had decided to write something about the young stylist and her tragic death. More troubling was Stella's insistence that she also play gumshoe. As glamorous as it sounded and even with the interesting wardrobe challenges that it might present, the idea was absurd. She was a reporter. In any event, it would mean running down inevitable blind alleys and risking Vic's derision. *Vic again.* Her mind kept drifting back to him. *I have no idea how I feel about Vic,* she realized. People did not pop in and out of Lacey's life. When they were out, they stayed out.

"I'll write a column, Stella, but what have I got to say? That the corpse had a really bad hair day? That a dead hair day means murder?"

Lacey retrieved two Advils from her bag to quell the pounding in her head. It wasn't fair. She'd had only a couple of beers last night. She hadn't slept well. She was alternately angry at Vic for being high-handed, showing up on her doorstep and merely assuming she would be home alone on a Friday night; and confused, remembering that long-ago New Year's Eve kiss.

"Okay, Stella, let's suppose we play detective. I just want to know one thing. What happened to her hair?"

"The hair? What hair?"

"Angie's. What happened to the hair?"

"The hair?" A smoky Southern voice with a distinctive cadence interrupted them. "The hair is gone. Long gone. It *was* long, wasn't it?"

Impressive purple talons scooted a shockingly pink flyer in front of Lacey. She could read PSYCHIC over the large imposing Eye of Horus. It seemed to be her logo.

"Hey, y'all. I don't mean to interrupt, but I read cards, palms, faces, whatever y'all got. I'm Marie Largesse. Just opened up a little shop around the corner. The Little Shop of Horus. We sell crystals, oils, books on meditation. Tarot."

"Clever name," Lacey said. "What did you say about hair?"

"Hair? Oh, it just popped out. I don't know. I've lost it now. Maybe I meant hers," she said, smiling at Stella. "Gone, right?"

The large woman had sailed into the coffee shop as if she were the Queen Mary, creating invisible waves as she floated by. A black sundress that dipped low in the back exposed her shoulders and her arms, which were as round and white as birch logs. It also revealed a flock of tattoos, including two great eyes, one on each shoulder blade: the Eyes of Horus, the all-seeing, the eye of the mind, from Egyptian mythology. Over one arm, the woman had flung a black shawl with pink and crimson roses embroidered on it. She looked like a plump gypsy matriarch. Bountiful, not fat.

Stella wanted to know more; her own psychic had been falling down on the job. Lacey was polite. She took Marie's card and gave her one of her own.

"You're the one. Of course, 'Crimes of Fashion.' I read it all the time. I'm thinking about that column on nuances. It had a psychic strain to it, I thought."

"That's what I keep telling her," Stella said. "Nuances."

"Could be. I'm feeling a lot of vibes in here," Marie declared. "Y'all feel them too?"

Lacey looked at Stella, one hundred and ten pounds of quivering vibrations. "Oh yes, I can feel them," Lacey said.

"Y'all should really focus on your spiritual plane," Marie said to Lacey. Stella lifted her eyebrows and nodded.

"I am curious about the Eyes of Horus," Lacey said.

Marie beamed. "I thought y'all'd never ask."

"Watching your back, I bet," Stella said.

"Exactly, sugar. Some psychics receive impressions in their chest or their stomach or the head, in the third eye. With me it's always been the shoulders. Don't ask me why. Just vibrations hitting me in the shoulder blades, first the right, then the left. Like someone tapping my shoulder to get my attention. The Eyes of Horus are always watching for incoming pulsations."

Marie made her way to the counter and ordered a large latte and a gooey chocolate brownie. She was an impressive work in progress on her way to becoming the Illustrated Woman. *A story behind every little picture.*

"Maybe she'd be good for a column," Lacey said.

"You already have something to write about." Stella swirled the coffee in her cup. "This coffee tastes kind of like a rubber retread that you see on the highway."

"You don't like it?"

"I usually get a Coke. You know, 'Coking and smoking.'" That was what stylists called break time, though it sounded sinister and illegal to Lacey.

"You're trying to quit anyway," Lacey said.

"Listen, about Angie, I don't even know where to start. Stella, are you listening to me?"

Stella was ogling a guy who had just ambled in the door. He was Stella's type all right: long blond curls, five-day beard, motorcycle jacket and helmet, about thirty, on the thin side. A beautiful Cupid gone bad. He had a slow lazy smile that he directed past Lacey to Stella, who sent back a suggestive smile of her own and a wink.

"You'll think of something, Lacey. You're basically a good, decent human being," Stella said. "In spite of yourself."

Lacey jerked the table and slopped her coffee onto the marble top. "I am not. I need to be left alone."

"You don't mean that." Stella stood. "You want a refill?" She followed the silent mating call of the bad-boy blond to the counter. "I bet he's got a nice bike."

"You're only interested in his pistons."

"You see right through me, Lacey. You'd make a great detective."

A few minutes later, Stella came back with a bagel and refills. She announced that she and one Bobby Saratoga, he of the motorcycle, would be meeting the following day to take in a bluegrass concert at Glen Echo Park. Lacey was dumbfounded. *Damn those Pentagon pheromone jammers,* she thought.

"How do you do that? My God." Lacey could see that Stella, punk goddess that she was, had a kind of elfin charm, the crew cut notwithstanding. And her collection of leather bustiers reeled men in like fish waiting to be hooked.

"Easy, Lacey. I leave my signals on. I don't turn everything off like you do. You just need a wake-up call. Besides, how often do you see a guy like that up at the Circle?"

Dupont Circle's large and visible gay population was not the best place for a woman to look for an eligible man. Even Stella could experience the Washington man shortage. But Stella was taking matters into her own hands. Or her cleavage.

Stella poured three packets of sugar into her coffee, tasted it, and put in two more. "So tell me, since we're talking men, are you going to sleep with that guy? Or have you already?"

"What guy? Who are you talking about?" Lacey's voice rose and several writers turned around to stare.

"Don't pretend you don't know who I'm talking about. Mr. Curly-Lashes-and-Cute-Buns at the funeral reception."

"Not a chance. We drive each other nuts. Besides, I barely know him."

"That's not what he said. I gather you two have, like, a history." Stella clicked her fingernails on the table.

"Don't be silly, Stella."

"You *are* going to sleep with him."

"Shows what you know. What did he say about me?"

“Just that you’re old friends.”

“Don’t believe anything he says. The snake.” The Advil had not yet kicked in. She dropped her aching head to the table. Marie stopped on her way out the door and tapped Lacey on the shoulder. She lifted her head blearily.

“Come see me at The Little Shop of Horus. I’ll give y’all the special introductory offer. And Lacey, about that dark-haired man. He really is attracted to you.”

Lacey spilled her coffee again. “What man?” *Good heavens, is Vic written all over me?*

“With the green eyes.” Marie winked and continued to hand out cards to other coffee drinkers on her way out.

Stella sat there like the cat who swallowed the canary, cage and all. “You *are* going to sleep with him! All right!”

“Shut up, Stella.”

A familiar gleam lit Stella’s narrowed eyes. “You know, Lacey. You’re pretty particular about that hair of yours. Where do you think you could ever find another stylist who can make it do every perfect little thing that you want?”

“Blackmail will not work on me, Stella.”

“It’s not blackmail; it’s hairmail. It always works.” Stella dangled a key ring in front of Lacey. “And I know where you can start on Angie. At her apartment. I told her mom I’d go over.”

“Her apartment?” Lacey softened. “You can’t face it by yourself, can you?”

“It’s really hard. Kind of spooky, you know. Now that she’s dead and all.” Stella’s eyes suddenly glittered with tears.

Please don’t cry. If you cry, I’ll cry. “It’s okay. You don’t have to go alone.” Lacey grabbed Angie’s keys. “Lead the way, oh Leather Lass.”

Chapter 8

Adrienne Woods could not face the prospect of going to her dead daughter's apartment and rummaging through her possessions. She had asked Stella to collect a few personal items and give the rest to charity. Stella was presented with a modest list of things to retrieve: some jewelry, letters, photographs, a stuffed teddy bear, a decorative teapot, and a few other odds and ends. And of course, it was another chance for Lacey to find the crucial fashion clue and wrap up the case, just like that, according to the stylist-who-knew-everything.

"Another ride in the Barbie mobile?" Lacey asked, eyeing Stella's little red racer.

"Everyone knows Barbie drives a pink Corvette. I should be so lucky. You should be so lucky. I, at least, have wheels. Cute little wheels, too." Stella had her there.

In Stella's new Barbie toy of a car, Lacey secured the shoulder harness tightly and prayed. The prospect of another speed-of-light trip in the Mini Cooper made Lacey long for her 280ZX. It was supposed to be ready on Monday and would only set her back another three hundred dollars. Something about the fuel injectors.

After a few moments of quiet that she wasn't sure she wanted to break, Lacey asked, "I still want to know one thing, Stella. What happened to the hair? There must have been two feet of thick blond hair. Where did it all go?" The question kept nagging at her. "Did it fall on the floor? Was it swept up into the trash? It would have made a huge pile at the base of the chair. Unless it was cut in one long ponytail or braid and saved. Could it be hidden away in a drawer?"

"I don't know. Last time I saw her alive, she wore her hair French braided with a blue ribbon wound through it." Stella swerved to miss a white Honda that had the audacity to slow down in front of her.

"You found the body. Don't you remember?"

"God, Lacey, I don't want to remember that. I mean, all I see is red. Only it wasn't red. It was horrible-dried-blood color; dark, ugly brown." She sucked in a deep breath and stared straight ahead. "Okay. I'm thinking. The hair. I just see her head, that butcher job. I don't see the hair. You think it's important?" The Mini was lurching to a stop behind a huge gray Mercedes. Lacey closed her eyes and jammed her feet into the floor to supply additional braking power.

"It has to be. If she didn't cut it herself, someone else did. So what did they do with it? Take it with them? What?"

"I'm trying, Lacey. I can see what she wore. Her smock. The pink one. Nobody liked the pink ones but Angie. The bloody razor on the counter, the mirror, the blood. I don't see the hair."

"Someone has to know. And where's the razor?"

"The cops took it, I guess. It's not there now."

Someone had to take the hair. If the hair is really gone, it has to be murder. Was it some pervert? Or someone who wanted it to look like a pervert did it?

"Do you have the name and number of the company that cleaned up the crime scene?"

"Crime scene? Sure. I can get it for you," Stella said. "Yeah, the crime scene. Damn right, the crime scene!"

"I just want to know if they saw the hair. They could have cleaned it up. That would explain it. That's all."

A stillness descended on the car, each woman lost in her thoughts. Stella broke the silence. "You know what's spooky? Picking out clothes for a dead woman. That's what. I had to go over to her place before the funeral 'cause there wasn't anyone else to do it. Her mother asked me to take care of it and I have no idea why I said yes. It's a huge responsibility. I mean this is it—forever. Her last outfit. I thought the clothes should be pretty 'cause Angie liked pretty things, and sort of comfortable, not too tight, but special, you know?"

"You don't care about fashion when you're dead. Unless you're an ancient Egyptian."

"So I decided when I die, I got a special outfit in mind."

"Please, Stella. I can't handle a last-wardrobe request right now."

"Leather, Lacey. Just remember: Leather is forever. There's no one else I'd trust to take care of it."

"You're not going to die."

"I'm scared, Lacey."

"You're certainly not going to die and leave me to clean up the mess."

"Just so we understand each other. Leather. Red maybe, or black. No. Red is more cheerful. And a bustier. A timeless look. What do you think?"

"I think you're awfully proud of that body."

"It's a temple."

The Mini screeched to a halt in front of a small redbrick apartment building in Del Ray, a once-depressed neighborhood in Alexandria that was rapidly rising in price and upward mobility. As Lacey exited the tiny vehicle, she informed Stella she would drive next time.

"Ha! You really plan on seeing that Z-car again? I figure your bloodsucking mechanic is just selling you a new one piece by piece."

"His name is Paul. He's very nice."

"First-name basis with your mechanic. What does that tell you?" Stella locked the Club on the Mini's steering wheel. "You're never gonna get that car back. Face it. Paul probably had it towed to a hospice. Maybe it could be an organ donor. So that other Zs may live."

"Very funny, Stel."

"The paper must be paying you enough money. Why don't you just buy a new car? I got a great deal on this little baby. Although the flag cost extra."

"Look, most people treat their cars like appliances. Like refrigerators or toasters. You plug it in, it makes toast. One day you wake up, it doesn't make toast, you pull the plug and buy another toaster. My Z is not a toaster, Stella. It's got style. It's got personality. Nobody understands about my car. And besides, I don't have any payments."

Stella looked disgusted. "Ha! Sure you do—unless your mechanic works for free. My car's got lots of personality and it's a great little toaster too. You ought to take that car of yours to the Kevorkian Motor Works. You got to learn to let go."

Lacey didn't care. She wanted her Z back.

Angie's efficiency apartment was at the top of three flights of stairs. Stella opened the door and flipped on the light. The tiny foyer looked inviting. The afternoon sun streaming through the large window lit dust motes floating in the air. Angie had painted the walls a soft rose color and the trim white. "I told you she liked pink."

Beyond the pink foyer was a disaster. The small kitchenette was dusted with broken crockery. In the main room, large and square, the bed was overturned and bookshelves were toppled. From the walk-in closet, clothes had been ripped off hangers and strewn everywhere. A television was turned upside down and a VCR lay beside it. The entire floor was covered with Angie's possessions. Lacey gasped. For a moment, Stella was speechless.

"Oh my God, Lacey. I didn't leave it like this, I swear." Stella had selected Angie's funeral outfit on Tuesday. It was the only time she'd been in the apartment, the only time she'd visited the tidy little neighborhood with small apartment buildings and neatly painted frame houses with front porches. "I locked the door and everything was in its place. Honest to God."

Stella remembered that Angie's clothes were arranged in the closet by season and color, which greatly impressed her; she always wanted to be that organized. "Maybe we got the wrong apartment by mistake."

"Stella, the key fit. That's how we know we're in the right place," Lacey reasoned. "We have to call the police."

"The police? Again? What, are you crazy?"

"Stella?" Lacey had never seen Stella on the verge of tears so often. She had been completely in control at the funeral. *More or less.*

"I don't do well around cops. I mean, I'm really getting tired of this whole cops thing. They make me kind of anxious. I just don't do so good . . ." Tears overflowed their mascara borders. Lacey was so dumbfounded she actually put her arm around Stella's shoulder. Stella sobbed. Lacey handed her a handkerchief. She couldn't bear to see the brave petite punkette fall apart.

"Maybe we should call her family and see if someone can come over and decide what to do. After all, Stella, we can't even be sure of what might be missing." Stella wiped her tears.

Lacey borrowed Stella's cell phone and made the call to Mrs. Woods, who said she would send her older daughter over. Stella locked the apartment, sat with Lacey on the steps outside, and waited. Stella managed to pull herself together before Lacey joined in the crying jag. Half an hour later, seventeen-year-old Abigail Woods drove up in a rental car.

Lacey opened the door this time. Abigail took one look at the chaos inside and burst into tears. Stella provided an encore performance. There were too many volatile emotions for Lacey and she was running out of handkerchiefs. "Okay, ladies, I'm calling the police. But it will be all right. I promise."

The young Alexandria police officer with sandy hair and pale eyes took pity on Abigail. "It's my sister's apartment, Officer." Abigail tried hard to be brave, but her voice was shaky. He seemed less taken with Lacey and Stella, though he obviously enjoyed the view down Stella's leather-laced bodice. However, with Abigail's assurance, he accepted that they were there at the family's request.

Officer Mark Lincoln conscientiously conducted a search of the apartment and tried to establish from the women what, if anything, was taken. All Stella could do was go through her list and see if the items were there. Although the jewelry was scattered across the floor near a broken jewelry box, Abigail found all the baubles on her mother's list: a pearl necklace, a gold chain with a heart, an opal ring, and a few pairs of earrings. It seemed to Lacey that they were simple pieces but real, not junk, and well worth stealing. The teddy bear lay forlornly on the floor, and the teapot was smashed. A broken videotape: *Legally Blonde*. Nothing on Adrienne's list was missing.

Still hung up on the "where is the hair?" question, Lacey looked for signs that Angie's haircut could have taken place in the apartment before she returned to the salon. But there were no telltale long locks or short snippets of freshly cut hair, though there was something lacking about the bathroom.

Wouldn't someone with waist-length hair need a comb or a brush? All the blow-dryers, combs, brushes, and curling implements Lacey had bought over the years lay in a small graveyard of accessories in the hall closet by her bathroom door.

"Stella, isn't something missing in here? Combs, brushes? Styling paraphernalia?"

"God, it didn't even hit me. You're right, Lacey." Stella nodded approvingly. "Nuances. Style clues. See, you are good at this stuff."

Officer Lincoln gazed at the bathroom. He looked puzzled. "Ma'am? If you ladies could be more specific—"

"It's what you don't see," Lacey said.

Soft-spoken Abigail explained in her honeysuckle tones. "My sister Angela kept that cork bulletin board decorated with all her little treasures. They weren't much, but they meant something to her: brocaded ribbons, small jeweled butterfly clips, beaded headbands, and combs. Everything she used for her hair. Such beautiful hair, Officer Lincoln."

The board now hung empty, caught diagonally on a single nail, the other nail ripped from the wall. "And a small white wicker basket full of pretty hair sticks, maybe a dozen or so. To tie up her hair." The basket and contents were missing. "They always looked real elegant." Abigail sighed and leaned against the wall.

"Angie's a hairstylist, like me," Stella jumped in. "Stylists have tons of that stuff. We get free samples all the time: brushes, scrunchies, you name it. And we get a discount on blow-dryers and scissors and things."

For someone who was distrustful of cops, Stella was singing like the proverbial canary, Lacey thought. Officer Lincoln looked up from his notebook to surreptitiously stare at Stella's bosom.

Abigail gazed around the bathroom. "There isn't anything left." She was at a loss for an explanation.

Lacey kept her thoughts to herself. Without a doubt, Angie had been murdered and the dirty creep had taken not only the missing hair, but all the ornaments she used to gild the lily. *But there must be something else he was after,* Lacey thought. *Something pretty valuable.*

Stella seemed perplexed. "You see, Angie and me, we worked together," she continued. "I'm the manager of Stylettos' Dupont Circle salon and I found the body. But I don't see much stylist stuff here. Look—one blow-dryer, one curling iron. But the brushes and combs are missing. Jeez, who'd break in to steal a comb?"

"Whoa. Whoa. Whoa. Back up to 'found the body,' would you please, ma'am?" Officer Lincoln was getting that distrustful look again. He had been under the impression that the apartment's resident was on vacation or something, and her friends and family were just looking after it. Abigail burst into tears once more and Officer Lincoln thought about calling for backup.

"Oh, jeez, you didn't know. Angie . . ." Stella teared up and didn't know what to say. Lacey explained to the policeman that in the previous week, Angela Woods had died in a Washington hair salon, Stella had found the body, and the D.C. police had determined that the young woman committed suicide in the salon.

"And now look, someone's tossed her place," Stella said. Stella liked the sound of "tossed." It seemed more knowing than "burglarized."

Officer Lincoln took a deep breath and looked at Abigail. She was gazing at him with a look of complete trust through eyes shining with tears. "I'm sorry for your loss, miss. Sometimes burglars read obituaries and break in during the funeral," he said by way of explanation.

"But the TV and VCR are still here," Lacey said.

"I'm taking that into account, ma'am."

She wished he wouldn't call her ma'am. Officer Lincoln dutifully wrote down that the missing items included "hair sticks." The value was low. They weren't the kinds of things that detectives would comb through pawnshops for. The officer informed the women there would be a neighborhood canvass, but because it was impossible to pinpoint or even narrow the time of the burglary within the last three days, it didn't look good.

He addressed Abigail. "I know this is hard for you, miss, but I have to ask: Was your sister into drugs? Could someone be looking for her stash?" The young woman was so shocked she couldn't speak, but that didn't stop Stella.

"She never even drank. She was the last person on earth who'd be into drugs!" Stella looked like she might be an expert on the subject.

Officer Lincoln put away his pen. He also offered his insight that the door did not look forced and that whoever got in must have had a key, or that someone had left the door open. "Be sure to lock up when you leave."

"I locked up before!" Stella said.

Lacey held Stella back from going after Officer Lincoln and setting him straight. "It's okay, Stella. No one is blaming you."

No one said anything. They listened to his footsteps echo down the stairs and out the door. A car door opened, an engine turned over, and they heard the car drive away. Within a minute, the landlord came by to see what the police wanted. He was a young guy with a beer belly covered by a stretched-out T-shirt.

Angie had rented the apartment furnished, which meant it contained one double bed, a pine dresser, a set of cheap bookshelves, and a small kitchen table with two chairs. She had added a few pictures and an inexpensive red Oriental carpet on the scarred wood parquet floor.

The landlord figured he could file an insurance claim for the old broken furniture. He showed no emotion, but he told Abigail there were a couple of weeks remaining on the rent, so she could take her time getting things out. He belched, rubbed his stomach, and rubbed his hands through his hair as he surveyed the premises. "Be sure and lock up when you leave. Can't be too careful, you know." Stella glared at his retreating figure.

The Woods family was returning to Atlanta the following day, so the extra couple of weeks didn't help. Abigail collected personal items. Lacey and Stella folded clothes to donate to a battered-women's shelter. They sorted things into three piles, yes, no, maybe, with Abigail as final arbiter. It was depressing business.

It's a good thing I'm not a detective, Lacey thought. *I'd be destroying evidence right now. But if the real evidence is missing, who knows what I'm doing?*

Stella ordered pizza to keep their strength up. They depleted the refrigerator of all its diet soda and tossed the rest of the contents. They rolled up the Oriental rug. Abigail insisted that Stella take it; it filled the back of the red Mini. By the end of the day the three women were sweat stained and filthy. They moved bags to the cars and the trash and Abigail hugged them both good-bye. Stella drove Lacey home. This time she was grateful for a ride in the Mini.

"Thanks, Lacey," Stella said. Her face bore streaks of dirt and tears. The makeup she had carefully applied that morning had lost the battle. Lacey assumed she looked about the same.

"I didn't have anything better going on." Lacey thought of a dozen things she could have done. Saturday was shot.

"Yeah, me neither," Stella said.

"Whoever got into that apartment wanted something desperately. More than ribbons and brushes and pretty long hair." Irrationally, she thought of Sherri Gold. But she figured that the woman was merely unpleasant. There was no reason to convict her of murder—although she may have been the last person to see Angie alive.

"What? Like drugs? You mean some drug-crazed thief must've thought she had something? It'd have to be some crackhead to think that."

"Who's stealing products at Stylettos?"

"Who isn't? You think there's a connection?"

"I don't think anything. My mind is jumping like a jackrabbit on speed."

"Jeez, Lacey, I don't know. Everyone's pinched a perm or two in their time. 'Course, managers don't snitch anything. Anymore. If they ever did. Besides, the only one I ever knew who got in trouble for stealing, you know, quantities of stuff, was Leo, and that wasn't even at Stylettos."

"What did he steal? Where was it? How do you know this?"

"I don't know. We had a drink one night, or maybe we shut down the bar. He was around twenty, kid stuff. He's at least thirty now. It was some kind of burglary rap. He told me he got probation and went to beauty school."

"Maybe he kept it up as a sideline."

"No way. Leo doesn't need to steal shampoo. He's a star. I mean, you should see his car. He has a yellow Corvette."

"He must make some pretty impressive tips. Stella, you're the manager and you drive a Mini? He drives Barbie's dream car."

Stella looked over at Lacey and just missed hitting a curb. "Damn. I never thought of it that way."

It was dark and damp when Lacey got home. She didn't

even check for messages on the phone machine. One more thing would put her over the edge. She stripped, dropping her soiled clothes on the floor.

Lacey wondered who would paw through her things if anything happened to her. Would her treasures be thrown out as easily as Angie's? No one would know how valuable Aunt Mimi's patterns were, or how many nights she had snuggled up on Aunt Mimi's old velvet sofa with a handmade quilt.

Would her mother and sister toss her own lovely things in a ragbag, set aside for Goodwill? Had she unknowingly thrown away some treasure of Angie's, something as simple as a nightgown?

She opened her drawer and fingered her nightgowns and lingerie. They made lovely pools of silken color in her dresser drawers, not to mention what they did for her confidence. No one would know what they meant to her.

Lacey wasn't the pajama type. Once she turned ten, she insisted on nightgowns, just like Aunt Mimi. Her mother believed there was something salacious about nightgowns, especially on little girls, even if they were flannel. When she first visited Mimi on her own at age fifteen, Lacey discovered that nightgowns and lingerie also came in silk and satin. Now she slipped on her favorite black silk nightgown.

She finally felt strong enough to check her messages: nothing. Brooke's deposition must have run long. Vic's business card lay near the phone. He hadn't given her his home number. Lacey debated whether to let him know about the break-in. Maybe she could trade it for inside information, if he had any. She picked up the phone and dialed.

"Donovan, it's Lacey Smithsonian." *So formal? How many Laceys could he know?* "Somebody broke into Angie Woods' apartment and trashed the place. It doesn't look like anything valuable was taken. Just some odd personal items. I'm only calling to let you know. Umm. Thanks for dinner. So, what's up on your end? Call me. Good-bye."

She checked the door again and relocked it, tugged at the chain to make sure it was secure. It was only ten o'clock on a Saturday night and she was ready for bed. *This is pathetic,* Lacey thought. *He's probably out on the town with that steak house hostess and I'm living like a nun. . . . At least I'm a nun in a silk nightgown.*

Chapter 9

The phone jangled her out of bed at five-thirty, out of a dead sleep. She knocked it off the nightstand and fumbled around before finding it and picking it up. She refused to turn the light on. She yawned into the receiver.

"Did I wake you?" The voice was male, and even in her fog she could tell he was amused.

"Yes! Who is this?"

"It's Vic."

Who? Oh yeah. "It's five-thirty in the morning!" She crept over to the window, carrying the phone in her hand, and peered out through the venetian blinds. "It's still dark."

"Many's the morning in Sagebrush I'd see you sneaking home this early."

Lacey fell back on the bed. She groaned into the phone. "I did not sneak. I sauntered. What do you want?"

"You left me a message. I think we should talk. About the 'odd personal things' that were taken. A quote, by the way."

"At this hour? Are you nuts?"

"What's the matter, Lacey?" His voice was deep and teasing. "Aren't you alone?"

"Vic, I'm hanging up—"

"I'll be over in twenty minutes. Get dressed."

"Don't you order me around—" She heard him click off. She was determined that he wasn't going to catch her in her nightgown and looking like a rumpled mess, although possibly a rather inviting mess. She threw on black slacks and a black turtleneck sweater, shoes and socks. There was barely enough time to wash her face and dash some makeup on. *Good thing*

I'm a wizard with a mascara wand. A little foundation, blush, a bit of shadow, and pencil eyeliner. Vic's phone call had supplied her with unusual energy.

The phone rang again. She picked it up. "Now what?"

"I'm downstairs. Buzz me up."

"What, the security expert can't break in?"

"No pizza delivery at this hour. Buzz me in. Please, Lacey."

Lacey hit the number on the phone to release the door in the lobby, just so she could throw something at him when he got to her apartment. She had two minutes to drag a comb through her alarmingly out-of-control hair and fashion a quick French twist. She managed to stick the last hairpin in as the knock came on the door.

Taking a deep breath and composing her face, she opened the door. His eyes took her in. She noticed he needed a shave.

"Wow. You're already dressed. And I thought you'd be one of those women who take hours getting ready."

"I'm ready to shoot you."

"For complimenting you? You're a hard woman, Smithsonian."

"You have no idea."

"You're going to have to do something about that eyebrow, though. It shoots up every time you lay eyes on me." She uttered a sound deep in her throat. "You know you're sexy when you growl. Go on and get your coat."

"Stop giving me orders." The man was exasperating.

"Lacey, please go get your coat. I want to show you something. Please."

She informed him that on Sunday mornings she liked to sleep in and this had better be a matter of life and death. He listened politely.

"You wanted to talk about Angie?"

She grabbed a small bag and her black coat. It matched her mood as well as her ensemble. "Where are you taking me?"

He held the door open for her, then started down the hall while she locked the dead bolt.

"We're going to the Jefferson Memorial. I thought you wanted to see the cherry blossoms at dawn, didn't you?"

She looked at him, trying to control her eyebrow. "Theoretically, yes."

"You'll like this. Trust me."

Lacey didn't say another word until they were at the Jeep. She climbed in. Vic pulled onto South Washington Street and headed up the parkway as the sky lightened. Lacey closed her eyes and only opened them after he pulled into the parking lot, stopped the car, got out, and tapped on her window. *Why does he look good with a five o'clock shadow?* she wondered. *I guess it actually is a five o'clock shadow.* He waited for her to climb out. He had a paper bag in his hand. He offered her coffee and a lemon-poppy muffin the size of a small Frisbee.

"Breakfast, Smithsonian."

She smiled in spite of herself. The hot coffee was welcome in the nippy morning air. She sipped it as they headed to the front of the memorial overlooking the Tidal Basin. He grinned at her like a little boy presenting a frog to a princess.

"Tell me, Vic, don't you oversized Boy Scouts ever sleep?"

"That's a personal question, Lacey."

"Just curious."

"I was on surveillance."

"Anything juicy?"

"No, and I couldn't tell you if there was."

"Thanks for the vote of confidence."

"Nothing personal," he said. "But I was up and . . ."

"And you thought of me. Gee thanks."

Light was spilling over the water as the sun rose. There was no sign of the renegade beavers who had been attacking the historic pride of Washington, gnawing away at the priceless cherry trees and destroying several of them, much to the chagrin of the Park Service, who had pulled their own overnight surveillance on the water rodents. However, the cherry blossoms were picture-perfect, and right on cue, photographers arrived in their annual search for just the right flowers, to enshrine the exact background, the once-in-a-season moment.

"So, who discovered the burglary at the dead woman's apartment?"

"Stella and I."

"You got a knack for walking into these situations, Lacey." They argued for a few moments over whether this was a true statement. But they ended in a stalemate. He wanted to know more about the "personal items" Lacey mentioned. She told him that only hair ribbons and ornaments, brushes and combs, were gone.

"Anything valuable?" he asked.

"Not that we could tell. Whoever it was left the television and VCR."

"So the burglar only takes personal items, items that touched her body. Or her hair."

"It sounds even creepier when you say it like that."

"If it helps, it sounds creepy to me too."

They sat down on the cold cement steps beyond the statue of Thomas Jefferson observing the city, golden in the dawn. Lacey went through her story once, then twice on Vic's insistence, but balked when he began the same questions again. It was a cop routine she'd used herself, but she couldn't stand having it used on her.

"Cut it out, Vic. I didn't rob the place. I don't deserve the third degree."

"Sorry. Force of habit." They discussed the possibility that it was just a burglary, unrelated to Angie's death. They also admitted it was still in the realm of possibility that her death was a suicide, even if the probability had shifted.

"But you think there's a connection between the two?" Vic asked. "Could be an unrelated theft, someone who read the obits."

"That's what the cop said. But why not take the TV? I thought that was burglar bait."

"And if it's not a coincidence?"

"Then someone cut off her hair, killed her, and took her personal hair paraphernalia," Lacey said. "He also took her hair."

"A trophy? Or maybe the cleanup crew took it. And what about sexual assault?"

"They don't think so. She was fully dressed. And if she had been assaulted, they couldn't have ruled it a suicide, could they?"

He finished his muffin. "I've heard tales about D.C. police work. They've got suicides with two slugs in the back of the head. And they can't even find a missing intern's body in Rock Creek Park till the foxes toss the bones out of their burrow." He snorted. "So, was there an autopsy or just an examination?"

"I don't know. It was an open-casket funeral."

"Probably no autopsy. Cause of death must have seemed pretty obvious. My guess is the M.E. might have jumped to a conclusion about the circumstances. Women are mostly murdered by men. And if the killer has the time and the privacy, odds are rape or assault is part of the picture."

"So, without the assault, the suicide picture fits?"

"Right. And if it all fits, why look any deeper?" Vic sighed. "Some cops figure if it ain't got a bullet in it, it ain't their problem. They got plenty of bodies with bullets in 'em."

"Now it's your turn. Give *me* some information," Lacey said. "You must have heard something, being Stylettos' new watchdog."

"I've been instructed to stay away from it, remember? You stumbled onto the crime scene."

Jerk, Lacey thought. "I forgot. How's shampoo patrol?"

"Glamorous as hell. But it's a cash cow." She stared him down. "Okay, I'll tell you what I think. If Angie Woods was murdered, your chances of finding the killer could dance on the head of a pin."

"You're consistent, Chief. The first thing you ever told me in Sagebrush is if a murderer isn't caught in the first forty-eight hours, chances drop to almost nothing."

"Something like that. And once they call it a suicide, you don't even have a crime scene or a police investigation. In this case, seems you've got bad police work, followed by no police work, followed by a crime-scene cleanup crew. What a mess. Any evidence is probably long gone. You've got no crime-scene forensics, no suspect list, no interviews, no alibi checks, no neighborhood canvass, no blood work, no DNA, no fingerprints. There's no way for you to do all that now. And if the death is connected to the burglary, you helped clean up the secondary crime scene yourself."

"What else could I do?" She felt awful.

"Nothing. Don't beat yourself up. There probably wasn't a lot there to begin with. You'd have to tackle the angle the cops hate the most, that they try not to mess with, 'cause it's usually the hardest and the least productive: motive. And what if there's no motive, or none that makes any sense, like some druggie pervert off the street who just liked her pretty hair?"

"You really know how to cheer me up, don't you?"

"It's a heck of a lot of work, Lacey. Some cops get obsessed with a case, and it sticks with 'em for years. Are you going to do that?"

"Where do I start?"

Vic sighed again. "With the victim's basics. What did she do that last day? Who did she know? Did she have any enemies? Is there a connection to the salon?"

"I don't know. It seems to me that Stylettos has a thief. So, did Angie, a Stylettos stylist, know too much about the thief?"

"The connection is pretty far-fetched, Lacey."

"Then why did you call me? Tell me about your thief. What do you have?" It was his turn to stare her down. "Come on. I am not going to ruin your purloined shampoo investigation, Vic."

"I don't have much. Honestly. The thief is no amateur, but not a master criminal either. She'll make a mistake sooner or later."

"She? You think the thief is a woman?"

"Or he. But ninety percent of the employees are women."

"Even at the warehouse? That's where I heard the problem was." Vic just sipped his coffee. "So, you haven't caught her yet and the problem is bigger than the warehouse. More than shampoo? Is she stealing cash from the salons? Embezzling? Blackmail? Drugs?"

He laughed. "Keep those theories coming, Lacey. Maybe I could learn something. But I've got nothing else right now. Once I get all the surveillance cameras in, it'll be a piece of cake."

Lacey stood up and stretched. She gathered her trash and tossed it in a can. She had enough of death and its desolate aftermath. She ambled off to look at the perfect blossoms. Vic caught up with her and they walked in silence. The caffeine had kicked in and Lacey felt uncommonly awake for this ungodly hour. Dew-kissed buds delicately scented the air and the sun was warm on her face. A few early-morning joggers wearing headphones and sunglasses thumped past in their own world.

Vic and Lacey strolled around the Tidal Basin, something that few Washingtonians manage to do during D.C.'s brief, intoxicating spring fling with Mother Nature. They didn't even argue. Lacey began to feel contrite for her irritation at his early-morning call.

"It's very pretty and I do appreciate it, Vic."

"Anytime, Lacey."

"You should know, however, that I really hate surprises."

"That's what you say *now*."

She was stumped. On the one hand, waking her at the crack of dawn seemed like a sweet gesture, even romantic. On the other hand, he just wanted information to make his own job easier.

After circling the Tidal Basin, Vic said he was beat and took her home. He dropped her at the front of her building, not even turning off the engine. She turned around at the front door and glanced back. With no other options, she decided to face the apparent truth. Maybe they were destined to be friends after all and that was all it would be. And maybe that would be okay.

The rest of the day was filled with errands, laundry, and shopping. Later she tried to take a nap, but the phone began ringing. She knew it was Brooke, but she picked it up anyway.

"Hey, did you forget about me?"

"Hi, Brooke."

"How did you manage to ditch Stella the Spark Plug?"

"There was a little problem. . . ." Lacey recapped the previous day for Brooke's benefit.

"Yikes. I know I said you should investigate, but this is sounding very freaky."

"We didn't find anything."

"You wouldn't. Evidence in this town disappears like dew in the morn. It gets shredded, torched, or buried in a deep, deep hole." She paused. "Unless you're fishing for a big book deal."

"That's cynical. Any suggestions?"

"Just one. Back off now before it gets dangerous. I hate to say it, Lacey. But you'd be safer if you worked for *The Washington Post*. Working for *The Eye*, which I personally think is a beacon of truth in a town full of media swill, isn't going to stop these people."

"Who are 'these people' you're always talking about?"

"There are so many, they are legion."

"You think it's some kind of conspiracy, don't you?" Lacey closed her eyes and listened. Attributing these tawdry little crimes to a massive Washington conspiracy gave it a wacky cosmic weight she appreciated. Brooke rattled on.

"Now, if we could just figure out what kind of conspiracy—government, big business, left wing, right wing or international terrorists—maybe we could determine whether you're in a lot of danger. Of course, Marcia Robinson's involvement pretty much assures it's government, unless that porno Web site thing involved the Mob—"

"I gotta go, Brooke."

"Better be careful. Someone could always tamper with your car."

"If they did, they'd accidentally repair something. Besides, I'm still on foot."

Lacey eventually hung up and took the Metro to Arlington to a final fitting at Alma's. Her seamstress was stitching up a light wool crepe suit for Lacey from Mimi's *Vogue* pattern, circa 1942. The wine-colored jacket would be accented with navy velvet trim around the lapels and pockets, which of course were mandatory. It was almost too late to wear it, but there would be a few cool days left before summer attacked the city.

Lacey gazed in the full-length mirror as Alma Lopez sat on the floor, mouth full of pins, marking where the hem would go.

"Turn. Stand up straight. That's it," Alma said. Lacey was always afraid that the best seamstress in Arlington would swallow a pin while talking and it would be Lacey's fault. But, somehow, that never happened.

The jacket's strong shoulders and nipped-in waist and the long slightly flaring skirt said this was a suit that meant business, yet was all woman. *If I were investigating anything, this is definitely the look for it. Tough but seductive. Central casting sends in the lady detective. Yeah, right.* She made a mental note to remember to get ahold of the crime-scene cleaning crew. It seemed to be her only real lead in a hopeless case.

"What do you think, Alma?"

Alma shrugged. "*Vogue* says suits are out. No?"

"This is Washington. Suits will never be out."

"*Vogue* says twin sets are in."

"But do you think it's pretty?" Lacey insisted.

"Oh, *sí*. Very pretty, but pretty isn't in this year. Ugly is the new pretty. That's what *Vogue* says."

Chapter 10

Monday. The Sisyphean task that was "Crimes of Fashion" awaited her. The deadline was Wednesday afternoon for her column to appear in the Friday LifeStyle section. Lacey also had to write features on trends, the occasional brief what-to-wear tips she called "Fashion Bites," seasonal style whims, and profiles of local fashion personalities. And now there was Angie's death. *Where do I begin? Vic says it's impossible anyway.*

True to her word, Polly Parsons mailed a package of information on Stylettos' role in the upcoming Sizzle in the City fashion show. Lacey tossed it aside and tried to do the same with Angie Woods, but her growing belief that Angie was murdered kept bumping into the rationalization that Lacey could do little about it. *I'll just write the column and leave it up to the readers to decide.*

On a normal day, if Lacey could get any message across in her column, it would be that women deserved to look attractive in spite of all the forces at work against them: the forces of out-of-control hairstylists, demented designers, indifferent department stores, and that great American equalizer, ready-to-wear. Women didn't have to be left in the ragbag because they weren't wealthy. They needed only to believe they deserved better.

Unfortunately, the subtext of an authentic Washington power look, for the second tier beneath the political and cultural leaders, is to look "serious." To select a flattering color or cut on purpose marks you as frivolous and shames you as shallow.

This is why in Washington thick spectacles are favored over contact lenses. Why keeping your grad-school haircut for decades is not only acceptable, but lauded. Why so many women choose the dumpy jacket that dusts the knuckles, the oxford cloth shirt that camouflages your charms, the clunky short-heeled black pumps. Why thirty extra pounds declare you're too busy and important to exercise (unless you're the President), and your work is vital, even though you're but a tiny cog in a forgotten machine.

Lacey tried to write "Crimes of Fashion" for the regular woman who deserved better than to look prematurely serious. But she also wrote it for snobs and people who got a lift from a cheap laugh. This week, however, the column would be for Angie. It was risky because levity would be inappropriate for the subject, and Mac demanded levity. Lacey planned to spring it on Mac at the last minute on Wednesday so he would have no recourse but to run it, humor impaired as he was.

"Crimes of Fashion" weighed heavily on Lacey, especially on spring days like this, when everyone else at *The Eye* was gloriously scandal-drunk over Marcia Robinson. Brooke Barton wasn't the only person who loved the dish. The cyber-porn peccadilloes of the congressional staffers and White House interns sent delicious shock waves rippling through the newsroom. Rumors, factoids, and dirty jokes swirled around the newsroom in a heady whorefest, and Lacey was jealous. Each new turn in the contretemps was seasoned with mirth and derision. But Lacey was stuck with fashion. There had to be a way to weave the two together. After all, Marcia Robinson, the scandal ringleader, had been Angie's ticket to stylist stardom. Lacey had already covered Marcia's miraculous makeover. *How can I find a new angle?*

After playing dodge ball with the special prosecutor for months, Marcia was scheduled to testify at the federal court on Tuesday. But Lacey wanted to know why she had canceled her appointment the day Angie died and when they had spoken last. Maybe it would lead somewhere. Lacey reached for the phone and discovered that Marcia wasn't taking phone calls, and her lawyer had stopped taking phone calls. There was really only one way to reach her. Lacey would have to join the crowds of hard-news print reporters, broadcast journalists, and other media hangers-on perched like vultures outside the federal courthouse. "Marcia Beach," they were calling it.

The upside of waiting for Marcia was the possibility of ducking into a show of French Impressionists at the National Gallery of Art—*yes, a Smithsonian Institution*—right across the street. Lacey had been wanting to see the Monets and Renoirs.

The only problem was how to sell the story to Mac. She glanced over at his glassed-in office. He looked grumpy, but then Mac always looked grumpy. She made up her cover story as she approached his desk. She assumed he basically wouldn't care. He didn't understand what she wrote. He understood column inches and circulation numbers, and Lacey was good for both.

Marcia's appearance was good for a column, she told Mac. He glanced at her under the twin caterpillars he called eyebrows. Lacey always refrained from telling him to trim the eyebrows, because, after all, they were very distinctive. They were as bushy as his mustache.

"You already did the other thing, the fashion thing, the whatchamacallit."

"The makeover, right. But now I've got a new angle, Mac." It would be a good sign if he nodded. Marcia's makeover was a pretty good story, and scandal fever was still hot. Mac lived for scandal. And Lacey's column on the former First Lady had gotten everybody riled up.

"What are you thinking?"

"Well, I could write this column like a sports story, as if I were judging a skating competition, just as an example." Lacey didn't have a clue how they were judged, but she thought it sounded good. She reasoned that men like sports. *Sports good. Fashion like sports? Fashion good.* "Headline something like 'Robinson Wows Judges: Scores 8.2 on Style at Federal Court.' " Mac was nodding. *Just say yes and let me go.*

"See, if she arrives in a limo instead of a cab, she gets extra points. Exiting from the limo gracefully without her skirt riding up is a bonus. More points. If she hasn't stuck to her diet, that's a penalty. Lose points. Makeup, hair, clothes, the usual things all carry points. If she smiles at the press, two bonus points. If she waves, even better. If she scowls, we dock her." Mac's eyebrows did a jig. He was interested. *Uh-oh. Don't be too interested.*

"We'll need photos! Maybe a series, run them each a column wide across the top of the page. Top half, front page of the Sunday Style section."

"But Mac, wait, this is just a column." *I just want to ask about Angie, not write an epic.* "I didn't plan on—"

"You'll pull it together. You always do. Great idea. This takes care of Sunday for me." He favored her with a happy smile. "Get Hansen for the photos. He's a sports guy. He'll get it."

At least she'd have a shot at talking to Marcia. *But damn! A huge spread for Sunday? What have I done? I still have to write Friday's column about Angie.*

"Oh, and don't step on Johnson's toes." Peter Johnson was one of the Capitol Hill reporters. The Marcia Robinson story was his. He wouldn't take kindly to the lowly LifeStyle reporter getting in the way. Lacey thought the preening self-important Johnson was an idiot.

"Peter Johnson, the king of Capitol Hill, doesn't even know I exist. I could puke on his shoes and he wouldn't know it was me." Mac shrugged. She was dismissed.

"Just concentrate on your job, Lacey. And the photos. We need great photos."

Lacey Smithsonian had never asked to be shut away in the LifeStyle ghetto of the paper. She was relatively happy working on a city beat under her byline, "L. B. Smithsonian," when Mariah "The Pariah" Morgan, the late *Observer* fashion editor, dropped dead of heart failure at the office. Mariah simply petered out at her keyboard while dithering away on a story about Washington "style setters." *Bored herself to death,* Lacey thought.

Dead at fifty-eight, Mariah was discovered slumped over her desk, her signature black beret slipping off her silver pageboy. When it came to her own look, Mariah was a copycat. Her hair was smooth, parted on the side, and cut to the jawbone, the favorite of broadcast newswomen everywhere. Yet another version of the Washington Helmet Head.

But Mariah was a trouper. She finished the last sentence and typed *The End,* a weird little quirk of hers, before everything faded to black, though it was several hours before anyone got close enough to notice she wasn't napping. Rigor mortis had set in, and Mariah had to be wheeled out in her chair under a sheet. At *The Eye*, this passed for going out in style.

To his credit, Mac exhibited genuine human feelings as the corpse was escorted from her corner of the newsroom. "Damn it all, Mariah, we've got a fashion supplement to get out!" Mariah thoughtlessly did not respond.

There were copy editors and news editors, assignment editors and section editors, but Mac reigned supreme over the newsroom, including the sneered-at LifeStyle section—where there were news holes to fill. But Mariah had been a solitary queen in her little fashion kingdom, leaving no protégé lined up to take her place. Mac's mind went into red alert. Adrenaline pumped. He glared around the newsroom, bushy black brows raised over golden-brown eyes in a search-and-destroy mission.

Unfortunately for Lacey, she was the first person in Mac's line of vision. Like a baby chick that imprints on the first thing it sees, Mac imprinted on Lacey. He didn't see a hardworking reporter breaking stories, a woman cultivating sources, ferreting out the truth, and championing justice. Mac saw the only reporter at *The Eye* who dressed well, who could put two colors together without nauseating passersby on the street. The one with the funny name.

"Smithsonian!"

From her first day, Mac sensed a kindred spirit of sorts in Lacey Smithsonian. Mac was at ease yelling at her or prodding her with faint praise, such as, "Hey, this sucks less."

"Lacey Smithsonian." He always smiled when he uttered her name. "Get over here." She didn't like the way he said it. She looked at him, a squat tyrant with a bullet head and bristling mustache. Mac wasn't an ogre, but he was not a jolly old elf either.

Some intuition made Lacey glance at the empty desk that had been Mariah's. *He wouldn't dare.* She moved slowly, deliberately, fixing a glare on him, trying to send brain waves. *No. No. No.* Mac returned the glare in kind. Two word slingers facing each other at high noon over the corpse of a fallen comrade.

Mac pointed out that there was an unexpected opening. It would be a promotion, he lied. It would be temporary, he lied.

"A few weeks. How hard could it be? Just until I can find a replacement."

"No! It's a dead-end job. And I emphasize the dead. It killed Mariah, Mac." Lacey knew it would never be temporary. The dead-end beats never were. Was working night cops ever temporary? Was writing obits ever temporary?

"Lacey Smithsonian, Fashion Beat." He chuckled. "They go together." Mac studied her. She looked like she had stepped out of a Cary Grant movie. Lacey seemed perfect for the job, at least to him. Most reporters at *The Eye* looked like they dressed out of a rummage sale at the congressional cloakroom.

"It's L.B., Mac, not Lacey."

"Not anymore." The editorial sneer was back. "You've got a fashion column to write. For women. Besides, you do that 'matching' thing. You know, with your clothes. You're practically an expert."

"Mac, just because I don't wear plaids with stripes does not mean I'm qualified to write about fashion. I wouldn't even know where to begin."

"Qualified? For God's sake, it's just clothes! You don't need a Ph.D."

"But no one reads it! You could really improve the paper by just killing it, Mac. Bury it with Mariah."

No one told Mac how to improve *The Eye Street Observer* without suffering.

"You're breaking my heart. 'Lacey Smithsonian, Style Maven. Fashion Newshound.'" He laughed. She didn't.

She knew she shouldn't do it, but she couldn't help herself. Her soapbox beckoned.

"Fashion is ephemeral, Mac. *Style* is forever, but Mariah's column isn't about style," she proclaimed. "Fashion is commercial. It's tawdry and tacky and it's calculated to sell junk, not to flatter women. It has nothing to do with style. *Style* is what counts, Mac. Fashion today is about power-crazed designers who hate women. They design clothes for drag queens and little boys and mutant aliens. They know nothing about real women with breasts and hips and waists! They design for models who look like the emaciated skeletal remains of women.

Designers paint them up like women from Mars, spray their hair into ungodly sculptures, and they call that fashion. I can't write about that crap."

Mac leaned back in his chair. People were staring. Reporters looked up from their stories in midsentence.

"I don't know, Smithsonian. You sound pretty passionate about it to me."

The warning sign was lit up in neon, but she missed it.

"Male designers give us idiocies like sheer blouses and slips for dresses. They don't give women pockets: Why not? Men get pockets. Take your jacket." Lacey grabbed it off his chair. "You've got pockets on the outside, pockets on the inside. You don't have to drag a purse around. What about women?" She threw his jacket back at him. "Don't real women deserve pockets? They say it would destroy the lines. That would be fine if there *were* good lines. Women get no respect, no consideration—and no pockets! I want pockets!"

Lacey took a breath. "And what about shoes? Don't get me started. Most real women's clothes are not comfortable, they're not attractive, and they're not affordable. We should be writing about style, Mac. Face it—fashion news is ridiculous. It's obsolete."

"Like hell it is," Mac growled. "Fashion news is indispensable. Call it style if you like. It's what we string around the department-store ads. And did you hear yourself? You just wrote your first column! Give me twenty inches."

"Washingtonians wouldn't know style if it bit 'em on the butt."

Mac had turned back to his newspaper and snatched a half-eaten donut that rested on a paper towel on top of a tower of press releases and *Federal Registers.*

"So bite 'em hard, Lacey. The fashion beat: Beat 'em up with it. It's your oyster. Sink your teeth into it. Write it for those *real women.*"

To add insult to injury, Mac made her move to Mariah's old desk. *The dead woman's desk.* It was still haunted by Mariah's personal effects and had the extra stigma of being known as the "blue-hair zone," for Mariah's readers. Lacey wheeled her own chair over to the condemned area. "You better not try to give me the Death Chair, Mac. It's not even ergonomic."

"Fashion in Washington? It's Howdy *Dowdy* Time!" was the headline of Lacey's first column. She slammed everyone—the designers, the industry, and the frumps who inhabited the District and the burbs, from the blue-blooded to the blue collared.

As she keyed her copy, she longed for the days when reporters had typewriters. At least they could vent their feelings pounding on the keys, beating a tune to the savage anger in their hearts. Lacey figured she could sabotage this assignment, get it pulled, and return to the city beat in no time. She figured wrong. She failed to count on a fistful of letters to the editor cheering her on in the first week, and another dozen that hated her guts. Mariah had never gotten mail. Never. Lacey's fate was sealed.

The more outrageous she tried to be, the more her readers liked it. She went after known Washingtonians, sacred and not-so-sacred cows and bulls. "Gray Is Not a Color; It's a Tropical Depression." "Look for the Union Label, but Don't Wear It on Your Sleeve." "You Can Wear What You Want, but You Can't Stop People From Laughing."

"Crimes of Fashion" was born and refused to die.

The fashion beat wasn't the worst fit for Lacey Smithsonian, but she would never admit it. "Crimes of Fashion" was soon firmly entrenched. Lacey railed on about Washington's lack of style and stood up for the common woman, the one who couldn't afford designer clothing or even designer knockoffs. Readers loved her and hated her. She proved a particular thorn in the side of the FFL, the former First Lady. *The Eye Street Observer* didn't care, as long as there was a reaction.

And now she was after the truth about a killer haircut in the middle of a media mob scene.

Chapter 11

Lacey stopped by Stylettos at lunch to collect the number of the crime-scene cleanup company and let Stella know that Angela Woods would be this week's fashion crime. Lacey had composed most of the column in her head. Angela Woods would not fade from memory without a few more column inches. But she hadn't exactly told Mac about Angela, the dead hairstylist, and had managed only to give herself more work with Marcia's Sunday feature. *Bloodsuckers. No matter how much you give, editors only want more.*

Stylettos was about ten blocks from the office, a short cab ride or a nice walk. She decided to walk. But Lacey did a double take when she got there. The familiar lilac interior was freshly painted over in cream with black trim. The stations had been moved around and everything was now in a different location. New black-and-white posters adorned the walls, and a glass brick partition divided the reception area from the stylists' stations.

Stella was ringing up a customer's haircut, shampoo, and conditioner. She waved at Lacey. When she was finished with the sale, she led Lacey to the small back room. It was warmer than the rest of the shop; a load of towels was spinning in the dryer. Bottles of shampoos and chemicals lined shelves against the back wall. Stella grabbed a Coke and sat down at a small plastic table. She reached under her smock and rubbed vigorously. She sighed.

"Is something wrong?" Lacey asked. "You keep scratching your stomach."

"Oh no. I just got my navel pierced. It's really cool, but it itches. Want to see?"

"No!" Too late, the smock was hiked up and Stella proudly displayed the new gold ring hanging off the top of her belly button. She actually pulled on the shiny ornament in case Lacey hadn't noticed. "Thanks for sharing these intensely personal tidbits that I do not need to know."

Stella grinned. "Bobby loves it."

Lacey recalled the scene at the Mud Hut: Stella the Man Magnet and her overaged delinquent. "Bobby? Oh yeah, bad-boy-Cupid-on-a-motorcycle Bobby?"

"The curly-headed one. You know those are natural curls? And he's a real blond." She winked. "Anyway, he talked me into it. I was thinking about it anyway. I was like the last holdout in the whole salon. Guess what Bobby wants me to pierce next?" Stella raised both eyebrows.

"That's enough personal information for one day, Stella. Stop now or I'm out of here."

"Prude."

"So sue me. I am a prude."

"Yeah, that's what Vic said."

Oh he did, did he? She could feel the heat rise in her face. "He's dead. I ought to pierce his big fat . . . ego." With an urgent need to change the subject, Lacey asked, "So, what happened here? New colors?" The smell of fresh paint lingered under the salon's normal chemical aromas.

"Makeover for the salon. Looks good, doesn't it? The lilac was definitely passé," Stella said.

"But where's Angie's station? I don't see it."

"Gone." Stella moved an ashtray out of the way, fighting the urge for a cigarette.

"Gone where? I wanted to look at it."

Stella looked at her as if she were an idiot. "Well, no one was going to use it. Jeez. You can't expect that. Not after Angie died there, Lacey. For God's sake!"

Lacey had forgotten how superstitious Stella was. After all, Lacey was working at a desk where someone had died. *Reporters. We're nothing but a bunch of hard-hearted ghouls,* Lacey concluded. *Of course, I won't use that chair.* The Death Chair was wheeled right back up to the newsroom as soon as the former fashion writer's body had been put on a gurney. Empty but still afloat, like a ghost ship found abandoned.

"Everyone was pretty freaked out," Stella continued. "Even after they scrubbed the station down. Bad vibes and all that. Anyway, Ratboy had it hauled away, along with her chair. They're all modular units, the stand, counter, and mirror, all attached. And then he decided to redecorate. You know, drive out the evil spirits. Even had it done after hours. That must have cost him something."

"He got rid of the whole crime scene? In one fell swoop? Pretty darned efficient, I'd say. Very suspicious."

"Crime scene? Oh God, when you put it that way . . . I guess Ratboy put it in the warehouse. I mean, a couple guys from the warehouse came and got it."

Lacey had counted on seeing it. She thought the atmosphere might help her start the column, as trite as that seemed now. She was disappointed as well as disoriented by the sudden changes at Stylettos. Lacey assumed Stella would let her come back after closing so she could examine the place where Angie had spent her last moments. Somehow, in some alternate universe, she would get ahold of a spray bottle of luminol to raise the bloodstains and figure out what happened that night. Smears. Spatters. Bloody footprints. *Just like on TV.* Maybe she'd comb through the drawers for clues and just happen to find the hair. *Yeah, right.* The idea was preposterous, and anyway, fate had taken away that option. Now she was stymied. She wondered how she could get into the warehouse. In the dark, with luminol and a camera. No plan emerged.

"Stella, how come Angie was here alone that night? I thought you told me there were supposed to be two stylists to lock up every night." After one too many assaults on lone stylists closing up in deserted shopping centers, a company-wide edict had gone out detailing safety procedures. Never letting a stylist work alone was one of them.

"Yeah, well, you know, Lacey. Things happen." Stella averted her eyes.

"You weren't supposed to be here that night, were you?"

Stella pulled a load of towels out of the dryer and started folding them rapidly. "I got Michelle to cover for me. She was supposed to lock up with Angie. But her mother got sick and she had to leave early. Angie told her not to worry. It was a slow night. Oh shit, Lacey. I had a date, and Michelle and I cover for each other all the time. But it's probably all my fault." Her voice broke and she turned away.

"No, Stel, it wasn't your fault," Lacey said. There was no use in saying anything more.

"There are supposed to be two people to lock up. If an emergency comes up, you call someone else in, or you close early and catch hell the next day. But either way, you don't leave a stylist alone."

"Everyone in the salon thinks Angie was killed, right? Except maybe Leonardo."

Stella put a fresh load of towels in the washing machine and glanced out the door into the salon. She lowered her voice. "No one really buys suicide, except Ratboy. And who really knows what Leo thinks about anything?"

Stella picked up a pack of cigarettes from the debris on the table.

"I thought you were trying to quit."

"Right, at least in front of witnesses." She tossed the pack back on the table. "Anyway, after the funeral, Ratboy held a special salon meeting. He warned us not to talk about it or we could lose our jobs. He doesn't want to spook the clients. We've already lost a couple who only wanted Angie and don't think Leo is star enough for them. After all, Leo didn't do Marcia."

"What do you think?"

"I think everybody's acting screwy, including me." She gulped the rest of her Coke.

Lacey closed her eyes for a moment and stretched. She peered out the supply-room door. Across the salon the rhythm of a rapidly moving hand caught Lacey's eye.

"What the hell is Leonardo doing to that woman?" she asked. The woman looked stricken while Leonardo created a surrealistic rat's nest out of her hair.

Leonardo was flailing both arms like the conductor of a demented symphony. Instead of a baton, he wielded a comb in one hand, a straight razor in the other, which he slashed up and down with a great flourish, slicing off locks of hair as if they were strips of julienned carrots. Fine beads of sweat appeared on his forehead.

Leonardo's styling victim had plain brown hair, stick straight, medium length, somewhere between a Washington Bob and a Helmet Head. Leo obviously had a different look for her in mind. "It looks like wild animals chewed the ends off," Lacey said.

"Leo's in a bad mood," Stella said. "Besides, it'll grow. That's our secret motto here at Stylettos. And don't quote me."

"Not so much on top," the woman squeaked. Her French-manicured hands fluttered up ineffectually.

"Don't be ridiculous," Leonardo said. "Now it will have some style!"

"I just wanted a trim," she wailed.

The woman was one of Leonardo's regular customers who had made the mistake of going to another salon down the street for her last color and cut because Stylettos' temperamental maestro couldn't fit her in. "So she deserves to be tortured, according to Leo," Stella said. Even after this atrocity, the woman would no doubt return. After all, it was the work of the great Leonardo.

"But that looks awful," Lacey said.

"You want to be the one to tell him that?"

"Stella, look at him. He's very scary with that razor." She thought Angie's final haircut slightly resembled the weasel-chewed look that Leonardo was bestowing on this woman. His hand sliced through the air again and again. If Leonardo could do this with plain fine hair, what could he do with two feet of soft blond waves? She began, then stopped, a mental scene of Leonardo with Angela. She could imagine it far too well.

With a flourish he set down his razor and squirted mousse into both hands. For a final indignity, he rubbed the woman's hair so that the razored spikes stood at attention. She glanced up fearfully into the mirror and burst into tears. Everyone stopped talking, blow-dryers switched off, and clients and stylists alike stared.

"Stella, that man is never coming near my hair."

"You don't think Leo could have—" Stella managed to look shocked and offended at the same time.

"Was he really in Virginia Beach that day?"

"That's what Jamie thinks. He called in sick, swore he had the flu. It was a really beautiful Saturday. And he likes the beach. He says he'd like to live there."

"I want you to remember something the way I say it," Lacey said. "I am just a reporter, not an investigator. I will ask a few questions about Angie. I'll write a column. But simply asking questions could uncover things you don't want known. Like why Angie was the only one here that night when there were supposed to be two of you."

"You're not going to write that, are you? I mean *someone* could get in trouble."

"That's exactly what I'm saying, Stella."

"But you believe she was murdered, don't you?"

Lacey took a deep breath. "Yes, I believe someone murdered Angela Woods. But that doesn't mean I can find the killer. If I write the column, however, people might get interested and force the cops to reopen the case." Lacey picked up her bag and stood up to leave. "I'm going to have to talk to people, like Angie's last customer, and I'll have to know where Leonardo really was that night. It might even mean looking at Angie's station at the warehouse."

"But all the blood was cleaned up."

"I need that number for the cleanup company."

Stella leaned over the washer and examined a bulletin board covered with old notices and miscellaneous papers. She retrieved a card. "Here, I don't plan on using it again. If I ever have to look at another dead body, it better be mine."

Lacey glanced at the card: NOT-A-TRACE CRIME SCENE CLEANERS. "Who's in charge of the warehouse?"

"Ratboy's half-wit third cousin. But you know who's in charge of security now. Your friend Vic. He could get you in."

Vic. I was afraid of that.

On the way home, Lacey picked up the Z and depleted her bank account. Paul assured her the car had many miles to go before the junk gods would demand it back. It was the most rewarding moment of her day.

Lacey Smithsonian's

FASHION BITES

Bad Photographs Live Forever— Or, Pudgy Nude Photos on Page 3!

If a good picture is worth a thousand words, then one wretched photograph can spell your disaster. If you happen to be caught in a newsworthy contretemps, enterprising snoops will find your worst driver's license photograph. Reputable magazines and newspapers will reprint it endlessly. You will wish you were dead. We call this investigative journalism.

Bad photographs live forever. And even if you have plastic surgery and fix your nose, the media will still use the old photographs. In self-defense, being prepared like the good scout that you are, you should:

- Have a flattering photo ready for your lawyer or PR flack to hand out, which may forestall the hunt for that perfectly dreadful picture. Lazy editors print what they have. Make sure it's good.
- Remember that newspapers really like compromising photos, so I strongly suggest this rule: No Nudes Is Good Nudes. Make sure there are none lurking around on the Internet.
- Never, and I mean never, let a photographer take your picture from below your eye level. You will be sorry. If he's down on his knees angling for a jowls-and-wattle shot, quickly kick him where it counts with your tasteful navy pumps. Be polite as he writhes on the ground. Say, "I'm so sorry! Did I do that?" Then walk briskly away and don't look back. (PS: Don't let this encounter be caught on film.)
- Understand that the smart scandal victim always has a

good pair of sunglasses and a silk scarf handy when photographers are close. The sunglasses hide the bags under your eyes, and the scarf camouflages a double chin from nibbling comfort foods. You'll look mysterious. Could be worse.

- Forget about being comfortable in the privacy of your own home. Ever hear of a telephoto lens? So no sweatpants and sweatshirts and sloppy college T-shirts while you're hiding out. The tabloids will report you're letting yourself go. Or that you are pregnant. Choose sleek tops and black slacks instead, and keep those curtains closed.
- Finally, good luck. You'll need it.

Chapter 12

For the media stakeout on Tuesday, Lacey wore Aunt Mimi's 1939 black dress with matching emerald and black bolero. Shades of Rita Hayworth. Feminine and strong, it suited Lacey perfectly. Besides, no one else in the Washington press corps had anything remotely like it.

The scene outside the E. Barrett Prettyman United States Courthouse bordered on farce. There were media crews reporting on Marcia Robinson and media crews reporting on the media crews reporting on Marcia Robinson. Every known network, including Fox, CNN, BBC and German television, had satellite vans blocking all parking along Constitution Avenue.

Over two hundred reporters, photographers, and technicians were stationed like occupying troops at all three public entrances to the building, as well as the parking lot. *Good thing no real news is happening,* Lacey thought. The network guys all had little tents set up to guard against nasty weather. Many had been covering the developing story for months. Lacey realized it wasn't true that the broadcast media didn't read. Boredom reduced them all to reading the newspapers to stave off the ennui.

The photographers, whether television cameramen or newspaper still photographers, observed their own dress code: jeans, athletic shoes, T-shirts or casual polo shirts, and windbreakers. The print reporters were rumpled, but all wore jackets, as they were required to wear in the congressional press galleries. One young woman had to be a television reporter, one of the ubiquitous horse-faced blondes who pass for attractive in Washington. She wore the mandatory Helmet Head hairdo and an indestructible polyester crepe suit in lilac, a popular color choice for ubiquitous blondes. A young Asian reporter was wearing a slightly longer Helmet Head and the same suit in red. There was also an attractive black television reporter for a third TV station, wearing another Helmet Head and a similar suit in larkspur blue. She ducked back into her tent. Lacey observed that the powdered and color-coordinated news anchors did not wait in the hot sun like a pack of salivating canines. That was for the lackeys.

It was the calm before the storm. Cameras were poised for that special moment—possibly twenty seconds—when Marcia would appear, emerge from the car, waltz up the steps, and disappear into the building. The rest of the day, lovely though it was, would be spent in mind-numbing suspended animation.

Lacey overheard a radio reporter phoning in his advance story. "Marcia Robinson is not expected to talk with reporters on her first day of testimony before the special prosecutor at the U.S. Courthouse." Lacey heard him pause and splutter into the phone. "No, damn it, I don't have anything else to say. There's nobody out here to talk to. Maybe you can pull some wire copy. You want me to just make something up? I can do that."

Draped with Nikons, Todd Hansen, *The Eye*'s photographer, accompanied Lacey. He was a sandy blond who would have looked at home building a log cabin in Maine, but somehow took a wrong turn and wound up in the District of Columbia. He was easygoing and very tall; his height, combined with an autofocus zoom lens, usually came up with just the right photos. Mr. Mellow never griped about assignments, which made him a favorite among the paper's reporters.

Lacey handed him a two-way radio from the office. "Call me if you hear that she's coming. There's something I've got to check on."

Todd assured her that was cool. He put on shades, slapped on some sunscreen, sat on a small fold-up stool he'd brought along, and retrieved a cup of coffee and *The New York Times*.

An intern for *The Eye* was assigned the nasty, boring task of watching Marcia's residence and calling as soon as the star witness left the building. *That'll show her how glamorous the news business is,* Lacey thought. It was probably the kindest thing the paper could do for an intern, to discourage young humans from the bizarre life that is journalism in Washington. Across the street, Lacey felt no guilt as she strolled the quiet halls of the National Gallery of Art. The Renoirs were particularly lovely, the faces of children more delicately colored than the rugrats who were screaming behind her. One chubby little boy about four protested to his mother, "My feet are burning up and killing me! Why do we have to walk?"

As the noon hour neared without a Marcia alert, Lacey figured that Marcia would not arrive till after one. She made some calls and checked her voice mail. She was playing telephone tag with a busy woman named Ruby who had been in charge of the crime-scene cleanup at Stylettos. She left another message, and decided to lunch.

Lacey ordered a salad in the Garden Café and sat next to a fountain. But all good things come to an end. At twenty past one, the radio squawked. Marcia was on her way.

In the ladies' room, Lacey smoothed her skirt, powdered her nose, reapplied her lipstick, and combed her hair. If she wound up on camera by accident she might as well look good. She returned to the sidewalk outside the courthouse.

A thrill shot through the crowd of reporters as a black limousine pulled up. Marcia emerged looking well rested, with a small serene smile that appeared to be glued on. *Maybe it's Valium,* Lacey thought. *Or Prozac.* Marcia was dressed as prim as a pilgrim, in a black silk suit dress that skimmed her knees, accented with crisp white collar and cuffs. Pearls and plain black pumps completed the outfit. *Nice choice. Ten points. The only thing missing is the scarlet letter. Maybe "P" for pornographer?* Her hair was pulled into a shiny chignon at the back of her neck. Makeup understated. Lacey heard the *whir* of autowind cameras, and the reporters surged forward en masse toward poor Marcia.

Marcia had been coached well, but she did not look at the press, nor did she wave. It was sensible, but Lacey would have to dock congeniality points for the Sunday story. If she remembered what the heck she promised Mac she would write. Of course, being the only judge, she could always change the rules. Now she was merely intent on getting close enough to ask a question. Lacey had years of reportorial elbowing experience on her side, and she was petite and fast. She dodged into a tiny opening next to the star witness. Marcia was surrounded by cameras and microphones and people were shrieking questions that she pretended not to hear. *This must be what it feels like to be dinner at the cannibals' feast.*

Lacey had to speak loudly to be heard even though she was close, but she did not bark like the rest of the pack.

"Marcia, when did you last see Angie and why did you cancel your last appointment with her? Angie. You remember." Lacey hoped "Angie" was enough to jog Marcia's memory. She wasn't about to feed this wolf pack the full name. Let them work for it.

Marcia was startled and looked straight at Lacey. A hundred microphones pointed. Cameras whirred. Her composure slipped.

"Angie? I—I—I'm sorry. I didn't think—I had no idea she would kill herself! I didn't mean—"

"No comment! Make way, please. Miss Robinson has no comment." Marcia's lawyer, a sweating, overweight man sporting a graying Capital Comb Over, grabbed her arm, glared daggers at Lacey, and rushed his client into the building without another look at the clamoring crowd.

Marcia's reaction electrified the press. As soon as the name "Angie" was out, the television reporters jumped on it like dogs on raw meat. Lacey heard one of them begin, "ABC has just learned that Marcia Robinson will testify about a mysterious woman known only as 'Angie,' perhaps another figure in the growing congressional pornography scandal." Someone else asked, "Oh my God, did she say 'kill herself'?"

CBS was reporting, "Another presumed congressional staffer, known only as Angie for the purposes of today's hearing, is a new link in this story of pornography and corruption that has spread through the corridors of power on Capitol Hill to the White House. . . ."

Lacey walked calmly away with Todd Hansen in tow, Mona Lisa smile in place. A couple of alert TV reporters trotted after her. "Wait! Who is Angie, and who are you?"

She flipped her press credentials at them. All she said was, "*The Eye Street Observer*. Do your own homework."

* * *

Old Beetle Brows was waiting for her as she strolled through the door of the newsroom.

"Smithsonian."

He crooked his index finger and beckoned her into his office for a peek at a news video. Mac ceremoniously pushed the remote and a thirty-second news bite played. It featured Lacey asking her question, Marcia's stunned reaction, and an anchorwoman trying to puzzle it out. The anchor promised there would be more developments, reported first on ABC. Several more news bites played from different stations, all showing Lacey and Marcia from slightly different angles. All promised they would be first with the developing story of the mysterious "Angie."

Lacey thought she looked pretty good. She didn't think the camera added ten pounds, as everybody claimed. Maybe five. But then she was standing next to the zaftig Marcia. Her black and emerald dress and bolero photographed particularly well. Aunt Mimi would be proud.

All three networks grudgingly reported on the air that a journalist from Washington's *Eye Street Observer* provoked Marcia's stunning revelation. They didn't know what kind of revelation; nevertheless, it was better than nothing. And acknowledging Smithsonian might persuade *The Eye* to share. Two stations had already been on the phone with Mac trying to work a deal to get Lacey on the Sunday morning news shows. When Mac mentioned she was the author of the popular "Crimes of Fashion" column, which appeared every Friday in *The Eye*, they said they would call back.

"Don't hold your breath," she said.

Peter Johnson, *The Eye*'s lead writer on the latest congressional scandal series, yanked open the door and stepped inside Mac's office. Peter was thirty-nine, unmarried, asexual, and possibly de-hormoned. He had a face like a pinched nerve, his lips drawn into a tight, thin line. Peter pushed his owlish glasses up his nose and glared at Lacey. Considered a snappy dresser at the office, he wore khakis, a blue shirt, and a screaming yellow bow tie with olives on it. Somewhere in the vicinity of his desk was a rumpled navy blue sport coat. Peter was obviously steamed, but he just stood there with his skinny arms folded and his pale hands knotted in fists. He let Mac take the lead. Mac cracked his knuckles at Lacey.

"So who is the mysterious Angie, and why is Lacey Smithsonian the only one in Washington who knows her?" He was too calm, like a snake choosing its moment before striking, like a toad waiting for a bug. Like an editor seeking a clue.

"I'm not the only one who knows who she was." Lacey was getting warm in the office, so she removed the bolero jacket and folded it carefully over the back of a chair. "Angela Woods was Marcia's hairstylist, the woman who gave Marcia the celebrated makeover just a month ago. Remember, we—*I*—wrote about it first. Last week, according to D.C.'s boys in blue, Angela Woods committed suicide. But there are others who think she was murdered, and that it's ridiculous to believe she would kill herself."

"What others?"

"Well, the manager of her salon." Mac looked doubtful. "Marcia had an appointment with Angie the day Angie died, but Marcia canceled it. And that's all I know." Lacey decided they didn't need to know about the weird haircut and missing hair. Not yet anyway. "Oh, and on Saturday, Angie's apartment was reported burglarized."

"Just how do you know this, Smithsonian?" Johnson asked.

"Style never sleeps, Peter. Except in your case." She yanked on his shabby ID tag. "Fashion tip: Don't wear your photo ID to bed. Do you shower in it too? Maybe I should address this question in a column and dedicate it to you."

Peter sighed and stuffed his ID in his pocket so only the chain was visible.

"Ah, the stealth ID. Much better."

Mac cleared his throat. Lacey dutifully explained that no one had heard of Angie until she styled Marcia Robinson. Because of Marcia and the whimsy of timing, the young stylist had a brief turn in the sun before dying. Marcia Robinson was a good place to start asking questions, and besides, she had the Sunday front feature all sewn up, so to speak. Mac was still perplexed.

"Is this a fashion story, a scandal, a suicide, a murder, or what?"

"Definitely fashion. Probably scandal. Possibly murder.

Once Angie performed her magic on Marcia, Angie became famous in her own circle, creating a lot of jealousy. So maybe it led to murder, or maybe she had personal problems. But if Marcia Robinson hadn't gone to her in the first place, no one would know about Angie Woods. Marcia's scandal has taken its toll." *What did Brooke say?* "Six Hill staffers have lost their jobs. More to come. Two congressmen have resigned. If Angie's death is related in any way, she's another scandal victim. If not, it's a weird coincidence. Either way, it's human interest. You don't like human interest?"

"And why didn't you tell me?" He stroked his bald head.

'Cause I didn't think about that until just this moment. "Because you don't want to be bothered. You don't care about fashion. I mean, just look at you—"

"Well, I care now, especially if Marcia Robinson, accused pornographer and corrupter of youth, has anything to do with murder." Mac liked the idea of the paper breaking a murder story, if it was a murder story. He also found it amusing that the other media were hotly pursuing a phantom named Angie. "I want us to be buddies, Smithsonian. I want us to talk, to share confidences, nothing much, little things, like what the hell you're working on!" Being buddies with her editor was an intolerable thought to Lacey. "It's okay to make everyone else look like a bunch of monkeys, but not me. Got it?" His face clouded. She nodded, but he continued. "And if this story leads to anything remotely to do with the special prosecutor's investigation, you tell Peter." Mac nodded at Peter. Peter nodded back and left the room, confident that Lacey had been put in her place. "I told you not to step on his toes," Mac said.

Lacey shrugged. "I was nowhere near his toes. They were asleep under his desk."

"And I want you to tell Trujillo what you just told me."

Peter Johnson was just a dweeb prima donna, but Trujillo had cojones. He would either try to take the story away from Lacey, or debunk it. He had the heart and soul of a cop reporter. If murder was involved and *The Eye* could score a point on the District's cops, Trujillo would be sure to grab that feather for his own cap. She couldn't let that happen.

"Like hell! I'm breaking it and I'm not giving Tony squat.

This story is mine, Mac. All mine. I researched it. It's my beat and my sources."

He put his hands up in surrender. "Chill out. Okay, fine, Smithsonian. It's yours." Mac smirked. He thought she was really blossoming on the fashion beat. "So the Sunday piece is a go, right? The scorecard thing?"

She needed to get the proof sheets from Todd to determine exactly what Marcia looked like and how she'd score. "Sure thing. By the way, Mac, 'Crimes of Fashion' will be about Angela Woods this week."

This time Mac smiled. "Sure. You might have a real crime this time. Only *this* story's got to go today."

"My deadline is tomorrow!"

"This is a daily newspaper, Smithsonian. Not a country club. Today, you're the talk of the town. Enjoy it. Your *news* story on Angela Woods and Marcia Robinson goes on the Web in forty minutes. We'll box it on the front page tomorrow. You can elaborate on the fashion angle for your column later. Now go."

Trujillo came nosing around her desk as she was batting out the story on "the mysterious Angela Woods." He turned on the charm, honored her with his one-hundred-watt smile, just like a rattlesnake would if a rattlesnake could smile. Thoughts of gardens and apples crossed her mind.

"I'm on deadline, Tony. So boot-scoot boogie out of here."

He suggested they go for a beer after work. She suggested a rain check. He suggested they chat about what she had. She suggested he take a hike so she could wrap up the story on deadline. He suggested he might be able to help her with the possible criminal angle. She suggested a place he could stick his angle and offered to help. He got the hint. He smiled the killer smile again as he left, but he was down to about sixty watts. Lacey smiled to herself. *He'll be back.*

Chapter 13

There were several messages on her voice mail when she got home. Stella was thrilled to see Lacey on TV. "I knew you wouldn't let me down. And you looked great, kiddo. So what's next in our investigation?"

Brooke was the next to weigh in. "Thought you weren't going to get involved. Call me with a full report. If you've got a phone, you've got a lawyer. Oh yes, beware of men wearing earpieces."

The third message was from the one and only Marcia Robinson. "Lacey Smithsonian? Call me. I want to talk about you-know-who, and for God's sake, don't give out this number."

Lacey started dialing before she had a chance to take off her jacket. She was surprised when Marcia herself answered the phone. "You nearly gave me a heart attack today," Marcia said. Of course Marcia felt terrible about Angie and she wanted to know if Lacey had any more information than she had read in the papers. Marcia remembered Lacey's articles on her makeover. To Lacey's relief, she thought they were funny. "The other papers were just mean," she said.

On the record, Marcia told Lacey Angie was "a styling genius" and she was "terribly saddened by her death." Off the record, Marcia said she would fill her in later. Marcia was in a mood to talk, but she suggested that they meet somewhere interesting in person. "My attorney's got me under house arrest and I'm dying to slip out. I swear he might be tapping my phone."

"Which would be a violation of federal wiretapping laws."

"You don't know my lawyer. He thinks he wrote the loopholes in the federal wiretapping laws. Fortunately, I have a cell phone he doesn't know about." Lacey hadn't expected Marcia to be flip. It struck her that Ms. Robinson was not taking the whole rigamarole all that seriously, but her remorse about Angie seemed genuine.

Marcia suggested that they meet at the Washington National Cathedral the following day. She was an avowed agnostic who had never actually gone to church. She told Lacey, "I don't really believe in God, but I have been through hell."

Washington intrigues almost always require clandestine meetings in places like Deep Throat's parking garage. The majestic Gothic church in Northwest, complete with gargoyles, was equally suitable, and although it was Episcopalian and not Catholic, it suggested to Lacey an atmosphere of sanctuary.

Lacey didn't know what would develop with Marcia or if the young scandal scamp would even show up. Therefore, there was no need to bother her new buddy Mac with superfluous information. She read all *The Eye's* coverage of the scandal, looking for insight. Only one interesting note popped up. Sherri Gold, Angie's last client, was one of the staffers who had lost their jobs. Unwisely, she had appeared in the buff on the now-defunct Web site and placed the blame on Marcia. *Sherri Gold in the buff? Another horrifying thought. All sinew and no sex.*

The Eye's front page story on Wednesday, "Dead Hairstylist Linked to Robinson," created a brief sensation, although the other media sniffed derisively once they found out that the mysterious Angie was a mere hairstylist. One called it "a tempest in a Teapot Dome." But Mac was pleased. He had broken very few stories on this scandal. He also liked the homicide angle on Angie. He loved to razz the D.C. police department and its less-than-sterling homicide record. Mac often pointed out that in D.C. you had a better chance of getting away with murder than with overtime parking. What D.C. really ought to do, he said, was to put the relentlessly efficient meter maids to work on homicide.

Pinched-face Peter ignored her in the most obvious way, which was to be expected. Trujillo approached with what seemed like a compliment. "Way to go, Smithsonian."

"What?"

"You didn't see it? You made the DeadFed Web site." Lacey tossed him her what-are-you-raving-about-now look. Tony took it as an invitation to rearrange her desk, sit down on it, and play professor. "Can't believe you don't know. Check it out. Something dot something slash WashingtonDeadFed dot com."

"Cut to the chase, Trujillo."

"It's a clearinghouse of all the dead, dying, beaten, mugged, or vanished people who are now or ever have been related to a Washington scandal. It reaches back as far as Admiral James Forrestal, who either jumped or was pushed out a window during the Truman administration. Vince Foster is, of course, still the big star. Heck, even Clinton's dead dog, Buddy, made the list. Your Angie Woods story put you in the picture."

Lacey switched screens and Trujillo typed in the Web address. She was horrified and fascinated to see a link to her story with the teaser LATEST VICTIM IN CAPITAL CONTRETEMPS?

"Pretty slim link, I'd say," Lacey commented.

"For now. Stay tuned."

The phone rang. She picked it up, glad for an excuse to be rid of Tony.

"Now you've done it!" It was Brooke.

"What? I really don't have time now."

"DeadFed. WashingtonDeadFed dot com. Don't tell me you didn't see it."

"I saw it. Are you going to go into your Conspiracy Queen mode? Because I'm on deadline," Lacey said.

"Fine." Brooke sounded miffed. "I just called to warn you to be careful. Very careful."

"Thank you. I'm fine."

"You might just check out the Dead Journalists link. And Matt Drudge has it too."

"Yikes! We'll talk later."

"Beware of geeks in trench coats, with bulges under their jackets."

"Very good, Brooke. Maybe we can confer on a fashion column."

"Just remember: I warned you." Brooke hung up.

Drama queen. Unfortunately, Lacey still had her column to write before her secret rendezvous with Marcia Robinson. And it wasn't going to be funny.

On the record, Boyd Radford said that Angie was "a nice girl, a hard worker, and it was too bad she died so young." Radford denied threatening his stylists and said, "Of course they could talk freely about Angela." Off the record he told Lacey it was in poor taste to write a column about "this whole mess" and she should leave it alone. Lacey asked whether he had dated Angela Woods or pressured her for sex, as was rumored. Radford hung up. She hadn't even gotten to her questions about his hasty cleanup of the salon.

On the record, Leonardo, "just Leonardo," said, "Angela had not yet reached her peak as a Stylettos stylist, but she would have grown under my tutelage and been a star." Off the record, he said she was just a "pretentious little wench" who couldn't wait to take over his clientele. He was sorry, of course, but "life goes on, sweetheart." Leonardo said it was mere luck that Angie styled Marcia because he had to go out of town that day on a family emergency. He admitted that he had called in sick because it was easier than explaining. Lacey asked if his family lived on the beach and if they could verify that he was there. He slammed the phone down.

On the record, Stella said Angela was "hardworking and sweet and would never have killed herself." She blamed herself for not being there that night. Stella said she had no idea who would want to harm Angela. There was no off-the-record with Stella. "I think maybe she seemed tense lately. But I figured it was 'cause she needed a guy. Know what I mean? Like you're tense all the time."

"I am not."

"You need a man, Lacey."

Angela's mother wept and rambled on about how sweet her departed daughter was. She said that Angie "loved the city but was too trusting." She added that it would be "a cold day in hell" before her other daughters would go to live in such a sinful place as Washington, D.C.

Sherri Gold, Angie's last client on her last day, could not remember anything on the record, except that Angie was "a sweet girl and a genius with a pair of scissors," as good as any in New York. "Too bad she's dead now." Off the record, Sherri said Angie was in a rush and seemed distracted and maybe it wasn't the best haircut she had ever had. Sherri said someone else could have been in the shop, but she didn't really notice. In the meantime, she had an appointment with Leonardo for highlights, as he came highly recommended. When Lacey brought up Marcia Robinson, Sherri was less forthcoming. "What's that got to do with my hair? I'm not answering any questions about that bitch. It's just too bad that nobody slit her wrists and watched her bleed to death, instead of Angela."

Lacey felt goose bumps. "Did you see something, Sherri?" *Or do something and then watch?* "Do you think it was murder and not suicide like the police say?"

Sherri slammed down the phone.

And things were going so well, Lacey thought.

Lacey put in several calls to Vic with a request to see Stylettos' warehouse. He left a message on her voice mail: "Sorry, Lacey, but there's no way. Radford's got a bug up his ass, warned me not to talk to you. Said you're wacko. Déjà vu all over again."

It had been eleven days since Angie died. Since then, ten more people had been murdered or "suicided" in the District of Columbia. On the record, the D.C. police said Angela Woods was "a clear-cut suicide." No mystery to it. Officer Stanley, a PR flack for the department, told her, strictly off the record, there was no way a nice neat suicide, case closed, would be reopened on some reporter's whim. He reiterated what Trujillo had told her: The medical examiner makes the determination and cops don't overrule the M.E.

Was any evidence collected from the crime scene? Lacey asked. For example, a hank of hair or a straight razor? No, ma'am, she was told. No evidence was in custody and it was not considered a crime scene. If there was new evidence, that would be a different matter and the case could be reopened. But it would have to be real evidence, Stanley said. "If you get real evidence, you bring it on down. We aren't unreasonable."

Lacey had no reason to doubt the officer. And she had no reason to doubt the D.C. cops could mistake a murder for a suicide and misplace the murder weapon. She had to look no farther than a recent case where the District medical examiner and the police department had determined that four women whose bodies were found underneath a porch in Southeast Washington had all died of natural causes. Perfectly reasonable. If you were to believe the cops, the women, all about twenty-five years old, had apparently crawled there to die, like elephants seeking a burial ground. Outraged, the neighborhood was up in arms over what they believed could be nothing but four murders. The investigation was finally reopened—a year later. And a year-old cold case in the District was probably unsolvable.

Ruby from Not-a-Trace, the crime-scene cleanup crew, finally connected with Lacey. Over the phone, Ruby's voice was deep and homey and carried traces of Maryland's Eastern Shore. She revealed that there were Polaroids of the bloody mess. They were given to Boyd Radford, presumably for the insurance company. It was probably pointless to ask Radford if she could take a look at them. He was already so touchy about the whole matter.

According to Ruby, the stylist's station was pretty well cleaned up, even though Radford had instructed her not to waste her time, that it was going into storage anyway. And the chair was set aside to be disposed of, because no one would want to use it again. Lacey glanced over at her late predecessor's Death Chair. It held an oblivious intern.

But Lacey was more interested in whether Ruby had seen any long blond hair. It might have been strewn everywhere like a golden spiderweb or dropped in one thick plait, still wound in blue ribbon. But it would have been there in the salon, Lacey was sure. It was preposterous to think it would have been cut anywhere but the salon.

"No long hair," Ruby said. "Some little snippets someone didn't sweep up. Nothing big. No blue ribbon."

"Are you sure?"

"Honey, I've been in this business for five years, cleaning up more gore than you better hope you never see. Blood spatter is funny. It can fly all over the place. We clean it all. We even look for tiny little specks of blood on plant leaves and the insides of drawers when you pull 'em out, just to make sure there isn't a trace left. If there was a big hank of pretty blond hair with a ribbon, believe you me, I would remember it. We don't do hair salons that often."

"Was it a real messy scene?"

"I've seen worse."

"What about a straight razor, maybe covered with blood?"

"Didn't see any such thing. Anything sharp with blood, we handle real careful. Probably the cops would have bagged something like that for evidence."

"Could you tell if there was some kind of struggle?" Lacey persisted. "If more than one person was there?"

"Oh Lord, lady, I just clean it up. I don't spend my time making up ghoulish stories. I leave that up to the police. By the time I get there, it's not an evidence scene anymore."

"Okay. No hair, you're sure?"

"No hair."

Lacey thanked the woman and hung up. So Rapunzel's hair was missing and that meant murder. She had known all along it must have been murder, but this somehow confirmed it on a deeper, more personal level. *Oh my God. And the cops have the murder weapon and don't know it. Or they tossed it after the M.E. said suicide. What do they care? No crime, no evidence needed.*

After a few moments of deep breathing, a walk around the block to clear her head, and a cappuccino break, Lacey returned to her keyboard.

CRIMES OF FASHION

Who Killed Rapunzel?

by Lacey Smithsonian

Just two weeks ago, Angela Woods was on her way to becoming a star hairstylist and stylist to the stars. This week she is headed home to Atlanta, to the family cemetery, where she will be buried next to her grandparents, her father, and an infant sister.

Angela Woods performed a stylists' sleight of hand with her makeover of Washington scandal figure Marcia Robinson. For that magic act, Angela was profiled in local magazines and newspapers, including *The Eye Street Observer*. She believed she was going places. Everyone said so. She made plans for her life. She wanted her own salon someday.

Nevertheless, the D.C. police say Angela Woods took a straight razor, the kind you might find in any hair salon, hacked off her hair, slit her wrists, and died in Stylettos Salon in Dupont Circle. Case closed. End of story.

Those who knew her say that is impossible. Why?

Because suicide was not her style.

When people talk about Angela Woods, they talk about her hair. That's not uncommon with stylists. Hair is what they notice first. Angela decorated her waist-length locks with ribbons, barrettes, and pearl ornaments. She was justly proud of her long blond hair. But ten days ago, the beautiful young woman with the Pre-Raphaelite hair was found brutally shorn. It was the unkindest cut of all. . . .

The column continued with various tributes from people who knew her. Lacey concluded by agreeing with Stella, that somebody killed Rapunzel. She closed with one last question: *Who took the hair, and why?*

Lacey filed her "Crimes of Fashion" column early for Friday's paper, leaving barely enough time to get to the cathedral and meet Marcia. Lacey waited until Mac was on a phone call, then waved to him on her way out. He put his hand over the phone.

"Hey, how's that column?"

"It's a killer," she said.

chapter 14

Lacey grabbed a bright purple hack just outside the office to take her to the lush Northwest D.C. neighborhood of the National Cathedral. She was treated to the classic lurch-and-zoom style cab drivers in Washington have perfected—one foot on the accelerator, the other on the brake, alternating rhythmically to ensure maximum queasiness in the backseat passenger, while cursing under his breath at every red light, stop sign, bus, pedestrian, and daredevil bike messenger. Her driver, Ishmael, according to his posted taxi permit, was careening merrily from pothole to pothole. Washington streets no doubt reminded him fondly of the goat paths of home, wherever that was.

Lacey preferred the older black cabbies, the D.C. natives who really knew the city and had driven its streets for the last thirty or forty years. They circumnavigated the District with ease and could reminisce about the days when Ella Fitzgerald and Duke Ellington held court on the floating bandstand in the middle of the Tidal Basin. They could describe the crowds of people who would gather on the steps to listen to the free evening jazz concerts in a Washington, D.C., that sounded like a pretty great city.

Ishmael lurched to a stop. His cab needed new shocks, but Lacey was relatively unharmed except for nausea, a reporter's occupational hazard. She paid the fare and he sped off.

The National Cathedral was one of her favorite places. When Lacey had first come to D.C., Mimi had introduced her to classical choral music concerts there. It never lost its majesty or its ability to leave her in a more serene state of mind, but she'd been surprised when Marcia suggested it. However, as

Marcia pointed out, it was the last place anyone would look for her. "Meet me by Woodrow Wilson's tomb tomorrow." After a beat, she'd added, "God, I hope that's not an omen."

It was pleasant and cool inside the thick stone walls in the early afternoon. Lacey stood in the appointed alcove beside Wilson's sarcophagus. Light streaming in from the stained-glass windows played along the stone columns and marble floors.

Sweet-looking white-haired docents wearing identical purple caps steered people into tour groups. The tiny senior tour guides proved both efficient and knowledgeable. Lacey made way for a Northern Virginia garden club, mostly cheerful-looking seniors eager to explore the secrets of the Bishop's Garden and view the rouge-colored blossoms decorating the redbud trees. Following the tour, they would take in a civilized tea at the top of the tower and admire one of the best views of the city.

Lacey had scarcely given a thought to her outfit, but it was serviceable: basic black skirt and hose, and a deep-violet fitted sweater and matching jacket. Comfortable and colorful. She liked to be easy for a source to spot.

Lacey heard approaching heels clicking staccato. The weather was not quite warm enough to merit Marcia Robinson's outfit: a yellow sundress abuzz with a flying-bees pattern, straw hat, and sunglasses. Spring had worked its spell on Marcia, who was straining against the media prison cell she had created for herself. This was not the sober gray-suited New Marcia. This was a woman who, it was said, represented the moral black hole of an entire generation. But if today's garb was any clue, somewhere inside this young woman lurked Rebecca of Sunnybrook Farm.

Maybe Marcia wanted to be anybody but the girl on the front page, the butt of late-night comedians' jokes, the terrible child who corrupted other congressional staffers, as well as some White House interns and a few of the underage pages, both male and female. Congress was eager to use her as a symbol of all that had gone soft in America's core, its very soul rotting. Marcia was a product of Generation Why, as in "Why did we produce these people?"

"I'm supposed to be at the dentist." She smiled the now familiar toothy smile. "Lacey Smithsonian. Is that a real name?" Lacey nodded. "Gee, I thought it was made up, to go with the 'Crimes of Fashion' thing."

"No. Just my luck," Lacey said. She held out her hand, which Marcia shook.

Marcia was delighted by her escape from the legal entourage and the rest of the media circus. "You're the one who wrote 'Never Wear Pink to Testify Before the Special Prosecutor.'"

"Guilty." *She looks younger like this, without all the sophisticated clothing.*

"That prick—my attorney—made me memorize it. He kept yelling, 'Be a grown-up! No pink, no Pollyanna!'"

"He didn't."

"Swear to God. He hands it to me all marked up with Hi-Liter and comments all over the margins. He told me, 'If you can't manage to look innocent, try for a little dignity.' Can you believe it?"

A high-powered Washington lawyer who charged hundreds of dollars an hour was taking Lacey Smithsonian's word for what his clients should wear to court.

"Your lawyer quotes me? I'd get a new lawyer!"

Marcia giggled, a giggle that turned into a snort. Lacey caught the mood and laughed too.

A sharp-eyed docent glared at them. Chastened, they moved out into the warm sunshine near the Herb Cottage and strolled beneath the evergreen bowers. In the Bishop's Garden the tulips burst out in vibrant reds, yellows, and oranges against a stone wall. Grape hyacinth made itself welcome around the base of a statue of the Prodigal Son. It smelled of spring. But the subject was death.

A man in a tan suit wearing sunglasses and a repellent gray and lime-green tie reclined on a bench. Maybe it was Brooke's warning, but Lacey wondered if he could be watching them while appearing to read *The Post*. She told herself not to be paranoid. Nevertheless, she moved Marcia out of hearing distance.

Marcia confided that these days she never read the newspapers without a cocktail, and she had promised her mother not to start drinking until after five. Which meant Marcia hadn't yet seen the latest *Eye Street Observer* story about Angela Woods, the official suicide, suspicion of misdeeds, and her connection to it.

"My lawyer is freaking. He warned me not to read anything at all and to keep my mouth shut."

"So why are you talking to me?"

"I want a new lawyer," Marcia said. "Younger and cuter. Plus he's a publicity pig. I can't talk, but he can talk and talk and talk."

Lacey hated to ruin a few minutes of peace, but she too was a product of the media. "You said you were sorry about Angie."

"I can't believe that she actually killed herself. I am really sorry." Marcia swiftly fell off the cloud she was riding. The plump face lost its vitality. The carefully outlined lips curled into a little girl's pout. "You know, my lawyer, the jerk, says I could go to prison for lying about what I did, for talking, for breathing even. It's not fair. It's not like I hurt anyone. Exactly." Marcia pulled a bottle of Evian from her shoulder bag and took a swig.

"From what I hear, you're the original scarlet woman, and you lead others astray, starting with your coworkers."

"As if. For starters, maybe I did encourage a few people to drop their knickers. So what? It's free enterprise, right?"

The Small Business Committee should be proud.

"But it's not like I went into it with some far-flung goal of undermining democracy or something," Marcia declared. "The porno thing—and it was really mild; it was more like art shots—seemed really exciting and fun at first, like putting one over on your parents. All our Web stuff was light, sexy, funny—nothing heavy or weird. So we sell some videotapes and DVDs. No biggie. And such a no-brainer. It didn't seem so bad. I mean everybody's a liberal, right? Consenting adults, First Amendment, and compared to other stuff on the Web, it was totally kid stuff."

"That's another thing. Apparently some of them are kids. Underage pages."

"Yeah, but kids are really mature these days, Lacey. They all surf the Net. I started out as a White House intern when I was really young, and the stories I could tell . . . I was beginning to make good money, everyone was. And now my lawyer says my phones could be tapped, the apartment could be bugged. The FBI's under the bed—that kind of thing."

It was pretty clear to Lacey why Marcia's attorney was concerned. Marcia really liked to talk.

"You have no idea how weird and horrible it is to see your friends subpoenaed, flown in from all over to tell the grand jury about you. I mean, come on! I keep expecting to see my ID picture flashed on *America's Most Wanted.* Me! Public Enemy Number One. With ancient history from high school, you know, who I slept with, what I did. And the press! It's like having your skin stripped off in little pieces and fed to piranhas."

Wait till the special prosecutor gets through with you.

"What about Sherri Gold?"

Marcia rolled her eyes. "Scary Skeleton? That's what we called her. Talk about piranhas. I ruined her life, she says. Sure, she lost her job, but she's not a joke on *Saturday Night Live.* That's my gig."

"Is she really scary?"

"Definitely. She said she'll get me somehow. I saw her slap an intern silly for opening one of her desk drawers once. Said she was just looking for a pencil, but Scary Skeleton accused her of going through her personal files. It was intense. I mean, Sherri just lost it. I had to break it up."

"What do you think she's capable of doing?"

"I don't know. She's pretty much a liar, but I don't know. I'd rather not think about it."

"Tell me about Angie."

Angie was easy to talk to, too easy, Marcia told Lacey. Marcia found that between the shampoo and the blow-dry she was spilling secrets like a sinner in confession. She talked about the Web-site scheme, the money, the big guys. No real names, she said, but nicknames and euphemisms that made the players clear. But when Lacey asked for more details, Marcia clammed up.

"What made you go for the makeover in the first place?"

"Someone found my driver's license picture and blew it up into an eight-by-ten for the tabloids." Marcia gulped down some more water. "Did you see it? I don't think I ever looked that bad in real life. I mean all driver's license pictures are awful, right? But when they blow it up and put it on the front page with headlines like 'Porky Porn Princess Behind Erotic Web Scandal' and 'Would You Buy a Porno Pinup From This Frump?' It was pretty awful." A tear slid down her cheek. She wiped it away. "My mother said, 'Marcia, you gotta do something.' Do you know what else she said to me? 'They can't send you to prison looking like that, Marcia. You don't look that good in orange.' Good God, nobody looks that good in orange."

"How did you happen to go to Stylettos? It's not the most exclusive salon."

"No, but Josephine has plans to make it that way."

"Josephine Radford?"

"Yeah, she's a friend of my mom's. She's going to make her salons really exclusive."

"What do you mean *her* salons?"

"Oh, there's this big nasty property settlement between her and Boyd, her ex, that's still in court. When she gets her share of the salons, she's going real upscale. Anyway, she recommended this Leonardo guy. Supposed to be hot. Her personal star stylist. But I get there and he's a no-show. One of those temperamental *artistes* who has to be in the mood to cut your hair? Anyway, the manager—she's this punkster, with a crew cut and leather girdle, pretty intense—she suggests Angie. Angie turned out to be real sweet. Not spooky at all. And after we did the hair, she suggested new makeup and shaping my eyebrows. Wow! It was radical. I looked completely different. Angie was totally not judgmental and she seemed so eager to help me look good. She was like a really good friend. She just listened. I guess the more nervous I am, the more I talk, the more people tell me to shut up."

Marcia paused for a breath. "Angie never told me to shut up. And she was so pretty. I used to kid her that she could have had her own photo gallery on the Web site."

Good grief. "What was her reaction?"

"She said only if she could be Lady Godiva, with all her hair and everything. But she wasn't serious, she actually seemed kind of shy."

"Why did you cancel your last appointment that day? The day she died."

"I was scared. I told her too much: names of people and places where things happened. I called her that day to tell her that she might get papers making her go to court. I canceled my hair appointment because they were following me everywhere. You know, guys in gray suits, wearing earpieces and sunglasses."

Lacey looked for the man in the cheap tan suit. He was gone. " 'Just because you're paranoid doesn't mean they aren't out to get you,' " she quoted. "Did you tell Sherri Gold you canceled your appointment that day?"

"No. Why would I do that?"

"She took your appointment after you canceled."

Marcia's eyes opened wide. "That is so creepy."

"What do you mean?"

"Nothing. She's just creepy." Lacey wasn't convinced that was all. "Angie was upset on the phone when I called to cancel," Marcia said. "She'd had some fight with Josephine."

"About what?"

"I don't know." Marcia looked away. "Josephine seemed mad that I hadn't used Leonardo. Maybe it had something to do with that." Marcia's lip quivered. "What if it was my fault? I mean, it's crazy, but what if she killed herself because she couldn't face the whole thing—the FBI, the cameras, the special prosecutor? What if she had some, like, terrible secret or something?"

"What if somebody else killed her?"

Marcia's jaw dropped. "Killed her? Oh my God! But why? She wasn't involved. Not really."

"Who do you think would want to kill her, Marcia?"

"God, I don't know. I mean there are lots of people who want to kill *me*. Starting with my mother. But not Angie."

"Someone cut off all her hair, slashed her wrists, and left her to bleed to death."

"Her hair? They cut off her hair?"

Marcia reached for her own luxuriant locks and the tears started for real, just as the tour group poured into the garden. Lacey guided her to solitude in the stone gazebo overlooking the Bishop's Garden. The green buds ushered in a new season, the stone walls harkened back centuries to another time and place. Eventually Lacey and the garden worked to dry Marcia's tears.

The two women chatted Wednesday afternoon away. Lacey

asked Marcia's permission to publish some of the interview on the record, knowing that once again, this was too hot for the LifeStyle section and would wind up on the front page. Yet another opportunity to piss off that smug Peter Johnson and impress tough guy Trujillo. And baffle Mac.

"Doesn't really matter. I'm already screwed, aren't I?" Marcia's mascara was running down her cheeks.

Lacey handed her a fresh tissue. "With or without me, you've already been tossed to the wolves. This way, at least, I can print your side of the story, how you feel about all this." Marcia found herself nodding. "Of course, your lawyer might object," Lacey said.

"Screw him." Marcia blew her nose. Lacey tried not to think about that.

"By the way, Marcia. I'm writing a style piece for Sunday . . ."

"I'm the victim, aren't I?" Marcia didn't look surprised.

"I wouldn't say victim, exactly," Lacey said.

"But you gotta give me credit for not wearing pink, right?"

"Yeah, Marcia, you get extra points."

Chapter 15

Lacey spent all day Thursday sorting out her notes and writing up the secret interview with Marcia Robinson. She worked diligently without attracting attention. She just hoped she could sneak the story in without having to explain how she got an exclusive interview, something no one else had managed, or why she forgot to tell Mac or Peter Johnson.

There was an unwritten policy for reporters to stick around while an editor read their stories, just in case there were questions or fact checking was needed, but occasionally a reporter slipped out without the final read, particularly if it was a run-of-the-mill effort. Lacey was hoping to move quickly.

She finished the story by late afternoon, moments ahead of deadline: "Robinson Feared Dead Stylist Would Be Subpoenaed; Told Her Too Much, Marcia Says."

Lacey nearly made it out the door before Mac hollered. "Smithsonian!" She turned slowly to see him waving her back to his office. Mac was a fast reader. "We've got to stop meeting this way, Lacey. What the hell have you been up to? An exclusive with Marcia Robinson! Good God Almighty!" Several people turned to stare. He gestured her into his office and slammed the door after her. "I told you to keep me in the loop!"

"And you would have sicced Johnson on me."

"It's his beat."

"Marcia would never have spoken to him. She called me."

"She called you?"

Lacey was offended by his tone. "Yes, at home, after I nailed her at the courthouse. Angela Woods is my story."

"Your beat is fashion."

"My beat is my oyster; that's what you said, Mac. I can cover anything as long as it's fashion related. That's a quote. A dead hairstylist is fashion related."

"Smithsonian—" He sounded dangerous.

"Marcia said she would only meet with me. Woman-to-woman. Her attorney's got her under wraps like she's radioactive. She's feeling suffocated. She'd have talked to Eleanor Roosevelt's ghost before Peter Johnson."

"Do you know how many reporters have been trying to get an interview with her? Holy mackerel." Mac was weakening. "But you have to tell me things, Lacey. You have to trust me."

"There's a concept."

Mac glared at her. "This will not happen again. I'm willing to stand behind you, support you. But I can't if I don't know what in damnation is going on. Do we understand each other?" She nodded. "Good, now get out of here. By the way, Lacey, it's a good story. Page one."

Lacey's front page story on Friday generated unusual excitement at *The Eye*. Word was that the new publisher, Claudia Darnell, liked the story. Mac actually smiled.

Curiosity compelled Lacey to go back to the DeadFed Web site, which she had bookmarked. There was a flashing headline with a link to her story. Her follow-up on Angie had appeared on the "Suspicious Suicides" page. Lacey scrolled down a growing list of names compiled by conspiracy theorists all over the country. The bodies were scattered over different scandals during different administrations, but all dead nonetheless. As if there were one Überconspiracy. *Ridiculous.*

Listed by method, several caught Lacey's eye, including a suicide shot twice in the back of the head. Apparently one of several. Just like Vic said. Numerous victims seemed compelled to throw themselves out of windows or die conveniently in unwitnessed one-car crashes on lonely side roads in the early hours of the morning.

Lacey noticed how many of the suicides seemed to slit their wrists, including a woman who had packed her bags as if for a sudden departure, but was found in her bloody bathtub. A freelance journalist, also found with slit wrists, told friends his story was so hot his life was in danger. His notes for that hot story were still missing, but the official version was suicide. She gave up on the Web site. It was too bloody to continue and it gave her a headache.

Peter Johnson appeared in the newsroom, his lips drawn in a tight line. There was an immediate drop in the ambient temperature. He caught her in the small kitchen where a substance alleged to be coffee brewed.

Lacey struck first. "She called *me*, Peter. Not you. Get over it."

"You're making a mockery of this story."

"Are you serious, Peter? How could anybody make a mockery of a congressional staffer's Internet pornography scandal involving the Speaker of the House, interns, pages, possibly the White House, and the attorney general mud wrestling nude with an alligator? How?"

Johnson spoke through clenched teeth. "Stay. Off. My. Beat. Fashionista." He was sweating, but it might have been the humidity.

"I'm wounded, Peter. Deeply."

She returned to her desk with a cup of bitter black coffee and checked out her other article, in LifeStyle. Lacey's satisfaction with her column on Angie evaporated when she saw the headline. Mac had only to approve the headline and keep his hands off. But he couldn't be happy until he mucked it up somehow.

"Oh Mac, how could you?" Lacey waved the paper at him. Her column—"Who Killed Rapunzel?"—appeared under the new headline: "Hair Today, Gone Tomorrow—Hairstylist Was Fashion Crime Victim."

He was unrepentant. "Needed some pizzazz, Lacey."

"It's tasteless." She hoped Stella wouldn't hold it against her.

"I'm crushed." He obviously was not. Mac was still sore at her. "Everyone in Washington wants to talk to Marcia Robinson. You get her and all you talk about is clothes."

"Clothes and other scandalous things."

"Lucky for you."

"Or what? You'd bust me down to obituaries?"

Mac grumbled, sounding like a panther with indigestion. "So, you finished the Sunday piece, right?"

The Sunday piece. "I'm working on it." *Maybe I should start.*

"Deadline is four. Is it funny?"

He always had to ask. It drove her nuts that he couldn't read something and tell if it was funny, sarcastic, or just plain rude. This was a man who was wearing an orange-and-green-plaid short-sleeved shirt with bright blue pants, topped off with a red-white-and-blue striped tie. He didn't think there was anything funny about that.

"It's a scream." Lacey thought the piece would hold its own, when she got around to actually writing it. At least she had the headline: "Penitent, Prim, and Proper: Scarlet Woman Wows Courthouse Crowd."

Lacey looked at the proof sheets with Todd Hansen. She selected five photos: Each would be a column wide and side by side across the top of the page. At the bottom of each would be a box with a score: Wardrobe, 8.5; Hair and Makeup, 8.0; Congeniality, 6.0; Poise, 7.5; and Visible Contrition, 8.0.

The composite score was 7.6, which was respectable. Actually, it was a great score for a Washington woman. And Lacey threw in a bonus point for not wearing pink, arriving at an 8.6 score on a scale of 9.9. *Only Rosalind Russell gets 10.0,* Lacey thought. She congratulated herself on using the photo spread, as it cut down on the copy she would have to write. A few sparkling paragraphs, including some choice words about the sweaty media mob, and it was done.

Lacey was only a half hour past deadline when she filed her story and shoved the photos at Mac.

"Good. Get out of here." He waved at the half-empty newsroom, which on a Friday afternoon wasn't going to have any more heavy traffic. She didn't need to hear it twice.

"Thanks, I'm all out of vocabulary."

Felicity Pickles appeared out of nowhere and made Lacey's stomach jolt. Lacey hated sitting next to Felicity, *Eye Street* food editor, resident cookie baker, and part-time copy-editing bitch from hell. Felicity wasn't unattractive. She may even have been pretty under the extra forty-five pounds packed on her small frame. She had long, thick, chestnut-colored hair and cold violet eyes. Unaccountably, Felicity had a reputation for being nice.

From the start she and Lacey rubbed each other the wrong way. Felicity secretly wanted to be the fashion editor, but she had never dared broach the subject with Mac. Instead, she watched her dream job handed over to Smithsonian, who didn't want it. She never missed an opportunity to insult Lacey.

Felicity cooked up her frustrations in cakes and other goodies, which she lugged to the office in hopes of fattening up everyone else. When she wasn't trying to force-feed Lacey brownies, she was offering work advice. "If you'd only let me help you, Lacey, maybe someday you could learn to write a good article," she once said.

It's too bad that the music from Jaws *does not swell every time she swims by.* Lacey took one look at the food editor and the thought of poor Angie Woods in her coffin surfaced. *Things like that never happen to people like Felicity.*

It was a horrible thought. Lacey tried instead to imagine Felicity as a gnat to be swatted away. The gnat was wearing a large floral-patterned dress. An enormous fly swatter reached down from the sky and—splat! It didn't help.

"Why, Lacey, you're usually gone by this time on a Friday. Don't tell me you've been working." She said it loud enough for Mac to hear. He looked over the top of his newspaper at them, then turned away, rolling his eyes.

"I'm on my way out." They smiled falsely at each other. Lacey made a show of locking up her desk. She suspected that Felicity went through her things as soon as she left.

As Lacey stood to leave, the phone rang. "Ms. Smithsonian, this is Special Agent Jim Thorn with the FBI. I'd like to discuss your story on Marcia Robinson in today's *Eye Street Observer.*"

"What?" It came out shrill. "Me? Why?"

"Can I come over right now?" he asked.

Her stomach flipped over. "No. Anything you have to say to me you can tell my editor." She rattled off the number.

"You're overreacting, ma'am."

"I don't think so. Call him. Douglas MacArthur Jones. Good-bye." Lacey fled as she heard the phone ring in Mac's office.

* * *

It was the kind of day that made her want to ride a horse named Desperado into the nearest saloon, slam down whiskey shooters and riddle the ceiling with bullets just for fun. It wasn't really her style, but she liked to think it was.

But this was D.C. There were no saloons, six-shooters were outlawed, outlaws had automatics, and anyway, shooting up a bar was antisocial. *And the FBI wants to talk to me.*

A manicure and a pedicure were no solution to Lacey's new problem, but they were a start. Lacey cruised through the doors of Stylettos just as Jamie with the Hair of Many Colors was reading this week's "Crimes of Fashion" column about Angie. The rest of *The Eye Street Observer* had already gone into the trash. Jamie told her it was totally great and didn't mention the headline. Stella pulled her aside.

"The column is perfect. And the headline really says it all." There was no hint of sarcasm in Stella's face. *Go figure,* Lacey thought. "But getting Marcia to spill her guts! Wow, that was incredible, Lacey."

If you only knew.

"How do you do it? How do you get them to open up?"

"Generally, people just won't shut up."

Stella picked up a fresh paper with the column and handed it to Lacey. "Would you autograph it for me?"

"I actually just came for a manicure and a pedicure."

"Sure. Sign first." Stella handed her a pen. Lacey was embarrassed, but she hated it when her stylist whined. She signed. "Thanks, Lacey. You really wrote it. You told the world that Angie didn't kill herself, the cops have it all wrong, and she was murdered."

"But what about the murderer?"

"Even real detectives don't always find the killers. They practically have to stumble over them as they're fleeing the scene. That's what Vic says."

"Oh, he does, does he?"

"Do you think maybe the Feds did it? Like Marcia suggested? It would really be dangerous for you. The Feds, they can make anything look like suicide."

"Have you been reading that DeadFed Web site?"

Stella nodded somberly. "Bobby has a laptop. He's like a Web wizard. That 'Conspiracy Body Count,' it scares the pee out of me. But Angie's on it now, so people all over the world can read about her. I really appreciate it, Lacey."

"Wait a minute. This doesn't sound like the Stella Lake I know. That Stella would be sending me out in the night with a pat on the back and a mission. A suicide mission."

Stella's voice dropped and she pulled Lacey out of the doorway traffic.

"Ratboy is freaking furious. He was here before I got the shop open. He'd already read it. I've never seen him so mad. He threatened to fire me and he nearly broke my arm." She showed Lacey a bruised patch on her upper arm.

"My God, Stella, he really is a brute."

"That's how pissed he was. He's going on and on about Angie and how she's wrecking Stylettos. If Beau hadn't been there, I don't know what he would have done."

"Beau?" Lacey tried to place the name.

"He's trying to talk Ratboy into letting him drop out of college and work in the salon. Ratboy never went to college. So he'll kill Beau if he drops out."

"You think it's Boyd, don't you? You think he killed Angie," Lacey said.

A pair of high heels—very expensive black patent leather stilettos—clicked sharply into the salon. Josephine Radford carried a large bouquet of yellow and red tulips and lavender lilacs, which she dumped in Stella's arms.

"These are an apology from me for the behavior of my *très fou* ex-husband. Beauregard told me all about Boyd's little tantrum and said he felt bad for you. And after I got through with Boyd he felt sorry for himself, I can promise you." Josephine was wearing tight black capri pants and a lemon-yellow sweater with strategically placed strips of black patent leather on the bodice, down the sleeves, and around the collar. "I can't afford to lose my best stylists because of him."

The Frenchwoman glanced at Lacey with dismay, but quickly recovered. "Lacey Smithsonian! *Bonjour*. So nice to see you again. Boyd is hysterical about your little column. The man has no sense. It's just a newspaper."

"Did you read it?" Lacey asked.

Josephine waved her hands in dismissal. "I glanced at it. 'Hair Today, Gone Tomorrow.' A metaphor, no?"

Stella busied herself with the tulips and set them in a vase on the receptionist's desk. "These are beautiful."

Josephine rearranged the shampoo and conditioners displayed near the register. She wiped imaginary dust from her fingers. "*Mon Dieu,* I swear that man takes everything so personally. As if she killed herself over him." Josephine uttered something explosive in French and gestured. "Who knows? He's a man."

Lacey wondered about Josephine's own terrifying reputation. Perhaps she and Boyd deserved each other.

"Do you know where Boyd was the night Angie died?"

"He was with me at a fund-raiser. I like to keep an eye on him when he's spending my money."

"What fund-raiser?"

"I can't remember. It's written down somewhere. Wait. Are you investigating like Stella said? This will really make Boyd crazy." Josephine laughed. "He's a funny man, Lacey. He has special feelings for this salon. I think that's why what Angie did—you know—bothered him so much. We took over this little salon from his uncle Max when Beauregard was just a baby. I would bring him and let him play all day in the corner, in his playpen of course."

They both worked in the salon back then, she continued, and Baby Beau was quite happy to sit and watch them. "He even liked to play barber. So cute."

"I heard that you and Angie had an argument before she died. What was that about?"

"*Dieu!* I can't expect to remember every little disagreement I have with a stylist. It would give me the wrinkles. A fashion tip, no?" Josephine decided she had put enough effort into damage control and stalked out the door. *"Au revoir."*

A relieved Stella stopped holding her breath and led Lacey to the pedicure area. Lacey climbed into the monster chair that vibrated while her toes soaked in a roaring whirlpool. Her feet were scrubbed and massaged with lotion. Lacey looked into the mirrored wall, which reflected the entire shop. Jamie was with a man with shoulder-length locks, applying deep conditioner. Next to her, Michelle was shaving the head of a stunning black woman. *Hair,* Lacey thought. *Can't live with it; can't live without it.*

Too soon, Lacey had to move her bottom out of the relaxing pedicure chair. Her toenails were polished, bright red and festive. She was directed toward the small table where Kim would paint her fingernails.

Lacey was dipping her fingers in a soapy bowl when Polly Parsons, Stylettos' giant promo queen, breathlessly entered the salon and made a beeline for her. Lacey had been avoiding calls from Polly all week. *Good grief. How did she know I was here?* Lacey glared at Stella, who averted her eyes immediately, and she knew.

Lacey was captive to her manicure while her nails were filed, buffed, and polished. Making sure they were dry gave Polly another half hour to pummel her with PR chatter to convince her to write a feature on the Stylettos pros who would style celebrities at the Sizzle in the City fashion show. Polly had been given marching orders from Boyd Radford to elicit positive publicity. By the time her nails were set, Lacey wanted to scream.

Lacey naturally was expected to attend. It would be full of politicians and their wives, dressed to their capped teeth and pandering with abandon. Not only are they incorrigible baby kissers, but they are eager to be photographed wearing everything from cowboy hats and full Indian headdresses to hard hats, baseball hats, top hats, helmets, and clown wigs. They have no shame. They will wear almost anything. Why not ruin a fashion show, too?

The charity event would also feature some of the local news anchors, known for doing anything and everything. Balloon rides? They are set aloft. Circus elephants? They ride them. Charity softball games? They arrive with bats and gloves. The media hounds of Washington television are ready for anything, anytime, anyplace, as long as there are cameras rolling.

Polly pressed on, but Lacey wasn't listening. As far as she was concerned, Stylettos had gotten more than enough publicity already. She turned to Polly and said what she always said.

"Send me a press release."

Finally, Polly left, but not without a terrible suggestion: "Let's have lunch." Luckily, when people in D.C. say that, they usually mean, "Good-bye forever."

Lacey confronted Stella. "How could you do that to me?

That woman gives me hives." *Polly Parsons, the FBI. Who's next? Beelzebub?*

"Orders from Boyd. I'm sorry, Lacey. I hated to turn you over to that bitch, but she's sleeping with him and I've got car payments!"

Friday night. *All painted up and no place to go, except into hiding.* The light on her phone was blinking. The first message was from Mac, who never called her at home.

Mac's voice had the power to blister her, even on tape. "Well, well, well, Smithsonian. This is your editor, yeah, you remember, the one you keep leaving out of your secret life as a reporter. This time, I am letting you in on a little secret of my own. And I want you to worry about it all night."

She felt a pain in the pit of her stomach. Damn it, she thought. He knew she was a worrier.

"We have a command performance upstairs tomorrow at ten a.m. That's Saturday, Smithsonian." Upstairs was where *The Eye* kept the publisher and various bigwigs. "You, me, our publisher, the paper's counsel, and oh yes, the Federal Bureau of Investigation. Working with you, Smithsonian, it's special."

The second call was from Stella, apologizing again for Polly Parsons. Followed by a call from Brooke, of course.

"Marcia Robinson! A scoop and you didn't tell me? I'll be over at eight. Unless you have plans. However, unless I'm misinformed, the pheromone jammers are still firmly in place."

Lacey returned Brooke's call. She couldn't wait to hear what Brooke would have to say about the FBI visit. At least she'd have a theory.

The blond barrister arrived with reinforcements, a pizza and a bag of cookies. Brooke was in her glory, theories of conspiracy dancing in her head. Lacey spilled everything.

"Aha! The FBI doesn't work on Saturdays. They're nine-to-fivers. Marcia must be snarled up in something really big."

"What about me, Brooke? I have to talk to the FBI. I'm trying to be cool, but I'm freaked out. And what in the world do I wear?"

Brooke breezed through the apartment, setting out hot pizza, plates, glasses, and napkins. She retrieved a couple of Vic's

Dos Equis from the fridge and they sat down to eat. Brooke doled out legal advice like a dealer tossing aces.

"First of all, you're a reporter and they have to tread very carefully with you, particularly because you didn't break any laws. You didn't, did you? Good. The Fourth Estate still terrifies Los Federales in this town—okay, maybe not *The Eye*—but let's pretend. Second, they've already interviewed hundreds of people in this probe, so it's no big deal. Strictly routine. Besides, they're following Marcia, not you."

"So far."

"Right. Third, take the offensive. You're the reporter, turn it around on them. You ask the questions. And answer what you want to answer. You're not under oath. You're not in court. And fourth, you wrote the book on what to wear, remember? 'Never Wear Pink.' Besides, we'll play dress up together after the movie."

That was four aces. Lacey felt enormously relieved. Thank God for Brooke. She would make Mac—and the FBI—pay for turning her stomach upside down.

"So let's see how Barbara Stanwyck does it," Lacey said.

"Does what?"

"Conquers the world."

Lacey had picked up a couple of Preston Sturges movies at Video Vault. The perfect antidote to modern American life: Not only were the women smarter than the men, the dialogue was delicious and the costume designer was the legendary Edith Head.

Together they watched Barbara Stanwyck befuddle and entrap Henry Fonda in *The Lady Eve* in less than two hours, giggling like schoolgirls. Sadly, success in life doesn't depend on witty repartee and clever little outfits. *If only.* There were too many successful badly dressed clods proving otherwise, like Ratboy. *But being witty and well dressed is its own reward. In that, I've got the FBI beat without even trying.*

Chapter 16

In the morning, thanks to Brooke's take-no-prisoners advice, Lacey was able to calm her panic down into something resembling mild indigestion. Going to the office on a Saturday to meet the FBI was not something she relished. Nevertheless, she almost convinced herself this was a great opportunity to find out more about the FBI, Marcia, and maybe even Angie's death.

She was also very curious about *The Eye*'s publisher, Claudia Darnell. Lacey had heard tales of the notorious woman who had purchased *The Eye* less than three months before, but there had been only a couple of confirmed sightings in the newsroom. She was a new publisher with an old score to settle with Washington, D.C., which three decades earlier had branded her the scarlet woman in a Capitol Hill scandal.

Lacey met Mac in the lobby next to the elevator. He was waiting for her in a navy suit, white shirt, and subdued striped tie, indicating how seriously he took the matter.

"Planning any surprises today, Lacey? I'd like an idea, just in case it's real good. Or do you think keeping me in the dark is healthy for my blood pressure?"

"I was going to tell you about the FBI, Mac, but you seemed busy. I referred them to you."

"So I gathered." He enjoyed seeing her squirm. "This is not what I call keeping me in the loop, Smithsonian. Could have a bright side, though. Maybe you can spend some time in a D.C. jail cell to prove your love for the First Amendment."

"Hey! There are shield laws for reporters in D.C."

"They can still make your life miserable. You can write a column on those orange jumpsuits they make you wear."

"You've been reading my column. How sweet. Are you enjoying yourself, Mac?"

"Yes, I believe I am." He hummed something to himself.

Lacey wore a dark blue crepe dress, circa 1942, that always made her look good and feel in control. It had a V neck and three-quarter sleeves. A splash of bright embroidered flowers on the left shoulder and right hip took it out of the ordinary. She hoped it worked today.

They ascended to the upper floor, a far more rarefied atmosphere than the proletarian newsroom, where the furniture was propped up on OSHA regulations and copies of the *Federal Register.* Mac and Lacey were ushered into the conference room, which was outfitted with cream-colored Chinese carpets and an impressive Georgian cherry conference table and chairs. The soft peach walls featured framed front pages of *The Eye.* The paper's attorney, Sophia Wong, wore a tan linen suit, looked elegant, said little, and was utterly lacking in humor. Wong sat with two FBI agents, one of whom was wearing a familiar ugly tie.

The guy from the Bishop's Garden. Lacey broke the silence. "Agent Thorn, I presume. I see your tie goes just as badly with your blue suit as with the tan."

Mac's mustache bristled. It was a warning.

Agent Thorn coughed. He looked like the second banana to the hero in a comedy. He had thinning pale hair cut very short, light blue eyes, and a slightly long nose. He seemed terribly earnest and tendered a crooked smile. He introduced his partner. Agent Josiah Watkins was black, stocky, and equally earnest. Everyone shook hands and then sat in uncomfortable silence until the door flung open and Claudia Darnell sashayed in.

She looked as if she had flown in from Palm Beach just for the occasion. Perhaps she had; that was her home base in the winter. All eyes turned toward her. Claudia was a knockout for a woman in her mid-fifties. Her tan was creamy toast, her eyes glittering aquamarine, and her hair a straight platinum pageboy. Her butter-soft chamois suit clung to her well-maintained curves. Claudia Darnell was stunning—a lioness—and Lacey marked the rise in the testosterone level of the tame male house cats in attendance.

Following the introductions with Claudia, Agent Thorn cleared his throat. "I have to say, I really think you're all overreacting. We just wanted to talk informally with Ms. Smithsonian concerning her articles about Marcia Robinson. Of course, if you prefer a group discussion with your lawyer, that is acceptable."

Claudia laughed. "I know that when people say they want a lawyer, the FBI immediately assumes they're guilty of something. But if you knew me, you'd know I should always have my conversations in front of lawyers."

Lacey took silent notes. Wong squirmed perceptibly in her seat and the FBI agents shared a look. Mac played with a pen. Lacey decided she liked Claudia—unless she was about to be fired. The notorious Claudia Darnell had been a secretary in a Capitol Hill office. She had a messy and public affair with a married congressman and became famous for not typing. The obligatory scandal ensued. But she was smart. She got out, got educated, and got rich without posing naked for anyone. Claudia's bright white smile spelled trouble, Lacey thought, for anyone who crossed her. "I put off my flight to Palm Beach to be here, gentlemen. So, let the games begin, shall we?"

Thorn directed his questions to Lacey. "How did you contact Marcia Robinson? And what made you think she knew anything about the hairdresser's suicide?"

"That's pretty obvious, isn't it? She called me. And are you aware that Angie Woods was probably murdered?" Lacey countered.

"I'll ask the questions, Ms. Smithsonian," he said. "Now—"

"Will you at least tell me if the Bureau is investigating Angie's death?"

"It happens to be a simple suicide, according to—"

"Could you define 'simple suicide'?" Lacey asked.

"There was no indication anyone else was involved."

"You've seen the police report?" Thorn was silent. "So this was like so many other simple suicides who simply need a little help?"

"Ms. Smithsonian—"

Mac tapped his pen on the table, another warning. "I thought this was just an informal chat," Lacey said. Everyone glared at her except Claudia, who seemed amused.

Thorn started over. "We are interested in Marcia Robinson, not Angela Woods."

"Even if she killed herself because of something Marcia told her?"

"And that would be?"

"Marcia said she didn't know. But she was suffering from a major case of guilt."

Thorn pressed on. Lacey told him everything he wanted to know—everything, that is, that she had already written in her stories. He probed for more information on Marcia's pornographic Web site, which she was glad she did not know. Nor did she know how Angie's death, suicide or otherwise, might be related. "I cover the fashion beat. I just ask fashion-related questions."

"Come now, Ms. Smithsonian, fashion?"

"Okay, what passes for fashion in D.C. The city that fashion forgot."

Thorn stared her down. "Let me get this straight. You spend your days taunting people in print with your tasteless opinions?"

"Basically, yes."

Claudia broke in. "Whether 'Crimes of Fashion' is tasteless or not, Agent Thorn, it sells papers and it adds an air of levity in a town that takes itself far too seriously."

"But these articles are not levity."

"In this case, my dear agents, an *Eye Street* reporter is shedding light on a suspicious death that would otherwise be swept under the carpet."

Mac cleared his throat. "I ordered her to write the story and conduct the follow-up. We had a unique take on it."

Lacey turned to look at him. *Really, tough guy?*

"Is there anything you discussed with Marcia Robinson that you did not include in the story?" Thorn asked.

"Only her personal philosophy on the wearing of orange apparel when incarcerated. I actually prefer black-and-white stripes, only not horizontal. Is the special prosecutor interested in that?"

Mac broke in. "You ought to see what she has in mind for next week."

"Well, Ms. Smithsonian?"

Lacey looked at Mac. He nodded as if they had already agreed on a column. "I think you've inspired me with your unique neckwear choices, something like 'Too Ugly to Die: My Tie Fights Crime for the FBI.' After all, Elliott Ness was supposed to be a snappy dresser and we all know how J. Edgar Hoover loved his party dresses and tutus. Now there's a real fashion role model for the Bureau."

Agent Watkins coughed into his fist, and Agent Thorn's ears turned red. He sighed deeply and closed his notebook. "I think we're through here. We may need to call on you again as our investigation goes forward."

"One more thing, Agent Thorn," Claudia warned. "*The Eye Street Observer* stands behind our reporters all the way. We know the shield laws. We know the Constitution. You cannot bully us."

"We're just doing a routine investigation, ma'am. We don't care how people live their lives. We aren't the morality police."

She answered him with that dazzling smile and purred, "Of course you are. So nice to meet you."

After the junior G-men left, Claudia grinned at her bemused staff. "I'm not the FBI's biggest fan. If they call again, you call me right away. No matter where I am."

Claudia pulled Lacey aside as they left. "Just remember, Lacey, the center of a scandal is a scary place to live. You have a duty to look for the truth and print the truth. But make sure it is the truth. And always be careful when you're poking the bear."

"I will."

"And if you simply must poke the bear, call me. I love a good bearbaiting." Claudia strode out without further ado, attorney Wong trailing behind.

Lacey nudged Mac. "You lied to the FBI. You didn't order me to write that story."

"I wasn't under oath. Ain't life grand? And by the way, Lacey, there's a moratorium on surprises for the rest of the month. Let's make this 'Be Kind to Mac' month."

* * *

At home that night, she was glad to be spared a blow-by-blow with Brooke, who was working late preparing a brief. And Lacey made sure by leaving a message and then unplugging the telephone. She was too tired to talk, even to Brooke.

She opened a large bag of caramel corn and poured herself the last Dos Equis. She opened Aunt Mimi's treasure trunk and spread some patterns around her while she watched *Sullivan's Travels* and looked for inspiration in Veronica Lake's gorgeous 1941 wardrobe. That is, when Veronica wasn't dressed like a bum.

The caramel corn was too sweet and the beer chaser was not a good idea. However, Lacey was feeling brighter just for watching a smart comedy. And Aunt Mimi's evening-gown pattern would be stunning in a cream-colored crepe with gold insets at the waistband and cuffs. If Lacey could find just the right materials. It would help keep her mind off Vic.

Lacey's thoughts kept drifting back to six feet of testosterone and grass-green eyes. She had always been drawn to Victor Donovan. *Why is my timing always off?* That was the trouble. And if once she had felt she could conquer a man's heart the way a climber scales a peak, she had lost that feeling long ago.

On Sunday, as soon as she plugged in the phone, it rang. Lacey picked it up. "Hello, Brooke."

"Good, you're not dead. I didn't actually think you were. You're not on DeadFed dot com. I checked."

"I can always count on you, Brooke. And you were right. It went okay and I still have my job. And about half my nerves."

"By the way, Lacey, nice piece on Marcia Robinson, the little squealer. Glad you stuck to describing her clothes this time. I think you should consider writing a primer on how to dress and prepare for court. I know someone who knows someone who knows John Grisham's agent."

"Brooke, let's stop thinking for a change. Let's *do* something instead. New York City. Small bite of the Big Apple. What do you say?"

"Keep talking, Lacey."

"An invasion. You and me. Bag some cavemen, drag 'em back to our caves. Make 'em invent fire and cook for us."

"Can't. The pheromone jammers will get them."

"Could we at least go ogle them? We could wear sunglasses."

"Tell me, Lacey. Have you gotten a whiff of testosterone lately?"

"Only on video."

She half hoped that Vic would call, but he didn't. She returned the videos, shopped for fabric but didn't find anything, and took a long walk along a secluded path on the river. She passed a man at an easel who was mixing paints with a palette knife. He appeared innocent enough, no earpiece, but Lacey took another long look and nervously checked her surroundings.

She shook off a feeling of unease and told herself she was being ridiculous. No one was going to take her simple pleasures away from her.

First thing Monday morning, Marcia Robinson's attorney put out a press release that he was severing his professional relationship with his notorious client. He complained of leaks to the media. In the break room, Mac informed Lacey that Peter Johnson was already working on that story.

Mac hovered over Lacey's desk all morning like a tropical depression. Her phone rang and she picked up, a signal for her editor to leave her alone. A chirpy voice was on the other end.

"I'm only calling because something weird happened today. Not that it has anything to do with Angie, but when you wrote about her hair being cut off, it got me thinking," a woman said. "I know Angie would never cut her hair like how you described. She was totally into her hair, you know. I knew Angie. She was my best friend."

"And you are? . . ." Lacey asked.

"Oh, Tammi, Tammi White. I'm the manager of the Stylettos Salon in Virginia Beach. I was at the funeral, but I didn't get to meet you. Stella said I should call you. You know Stella."

Lacey stifled a sigh.

"Um, I kind of thought I should call because Angie used to work here in Virginia Beach before she went to Washington. Stella said you knew all about Angie, you know, how she died."

"I'm listening, Tammi." Lacey picked up her coffee, took a sip and flipped open her daybook to see if anything important was on the schedule. *Slow day in the style biz.* She looked at her e-mail. *Too many messages.*

"But anyway, this guy called the salon this morning and he said he wanted some of us to cut our hair if it was really long and he was willing to pay us for it."

Lacey stopped flipping pages and picked up a pen. "Really? Go on."

"His name was George something. I forget. Anyway, he said he was working on a photo layout of haircuts for his portfolio, as an example of a marketing campaign," Tammi said. "For school or something. I wasn't really listening to that part."

It was pretty exciting to Tammi White that the guy was offering stylists $250 to cut their hair from "very long to very short and very dramatic." George Something was willing to pay $100 more if he could videotape the haircut. Several stylists might be willing, Tammi said, herself included, because they needed the money. "I mean, who doesn't?" George told her he had a great stylist for the cut and he would videotape it himself. He was just looking for models with the right kind of hair. Long. Really long.

"I'm kind of interested myself. I have long, curly black hair, almost to my waist, but I've been thinking of cutting it for a while now. High maintenance, you know."

Lacey asked if there was anything else that struck Tammi about the guy. Tammi had no idea what he looked like, and he sounded "like anyone" on the phone. But one thing bothered her.

"He wants the hair," Tammi said.

Lacey rubbed her neck. She felt a prickle run down her back. "Excuse me, the hair? I'm not getting this."

"He offered five hundred dollars for the haircut, the video, and the hair."

"He wants the hair?"

"Yeah, weird, huh? Nobody wants the hair."

Lacey pointed out that stylists often train with model heads, set with real human hair.

"Yeah, I guess so, but I never heard of anyone paying that much for hair around here," Tammi said. "And then I read your column, 'Hair Today, Gone Tomorrow.' Stella faxed it to me."

Tammi also thought there was something strange about the

mysterious George's request to make a videotape. According to Tammi, Stylettos occasionally videotaped guest stylists who flew in and demonstrated the latest techniques. The tapes were produced at the chain's headquarters, the same training salon where the funeral reception for Angie was held. The studio was equipped with lights and camera equipment. But George said his amateur video would be okay and he'd call back to arrange a meeting with Tammi. He wanted to meet tomorrow night.

"Why spend all that money and not even get a professional video? And he said it would be better to meet somewhere else, not at the salon, like this was a top-secret project."

"If you're really nervous about this guy, maybe you should call the police."

"I don't know. What would I tell them?"

"Good question. Did this George guy leave a number?"

"Nah. He said he'd call back."

"If he does call again, keep me posted. It was probably just a crank call."

"Yeah, it was probably a dumb joke. Five hundred dollars for your hair is way too good to be true," Tammi said.

Lacey hung up and turned her thoughts back to simple tasks, like the mail. There were the obligatory press releases, items still addressed to Mariah, some fan mail, ranting hate mail. The usual stuff.

She absentmindedly opened a puffy business-sized envelope with the address printed in block letters to LACEY SMITHSONIAN, CRIMES OF FASHION. A thick lock of pale blond hair tumbled out on the desk like a furry critter, which she at first thought was a bug or a mouse. It bounced up at her, catching her off guard, and she shrieked. She held her breath and hoped no one noticed. She looked around. Everyone had noticed.

The newsroom was used to yelling, laughing, and cursing. That was merely environmental noise, but shrieking tended to stop traffic. She was acutely aware of the silence and people staring. Tony Trujillo, Dingo boots and all, was by her side in a flash. Mac nearly busted a gut running to Lacey's desk, arriving right behind Trujillo, eyebrows in motion. "Now what the hell is going on?"

"Is that hair?" Trujillo peered at it.

"It's nothing. Fan mail. Go away." Lacey reached for the envelope to see if a note was also enclosed, but Trujillo stopped her hand.

"Hold it, Smithsonian. You got any tweezers?"

Her Swiss Army knife had a pair, which she handed over with a groan. He smiled at her. "You gotta love a woman who was in the Swiss army." Trujillo carefully reached inside the envelope and extracted an anonymous-looking note, obviously from a laser printer. She read it, Mac and Trujillo at each elbow. "YOU WANT TO KNOW WHAT HAPPENED TO THE HAIR? HERE'S A SOUVENIR." There was no signature. Trujillo held it up to the light.

"Are we to assume this is from one of your admirers, Smithsonian?"

"That would be my luck." She stared at the note.

"I know. It's tough being popular. Don't touch that note." Trujillo headed back to his desk and returned carrying a box of plastic Baggies.

It was pointless to tell the small crowd that gathered around to go away and mind their own business. They were, after all, reporters. Being a busybody was everybody's business at *The Eye*. And a shriek in the corner was better than old news releases and an assignment editor's list of boring press events to cover.

"Somebody's idea of a sick joke," Lacey said. "You know. After last week's column. The hair thing."

Trujillo carefully tweezed the hair off the desk. The small lock of hair, curled softly at the ends, was tied with a rubber band and a black ribbon. Some strands looked as if they had been yanked out by the roots. He dropped it in one plastic bag and carefully placed the note in another. It seemed very paranoid to Lacey. "Do this often, Tony?"

"Nope. You're the psycho magnet. But if it was evidence, we don't want to contaminate it. Now, does the hair look familiar?"

She was dumbstruck. Sure, it looked like Angie's hair, but thousands of women—or men—could have hair like that. Besides, Lacey had described Angie's hair in her column. Any crude jokester could be capable of this prank. "You watch too much television," she said. But what if it was Angela's hair and sent to her by the murderer? Tony arched one eyebrow; he obviously thought it was.

"No! That would be too stupid for words, Tony! Not to mention dangerous."

"The beautiful thing about most criminals, Lacey, is that they are not smart," Trujillo informed her. "Prisons are loaded with stupid people."

"Okay, fine, smarty-pants. Why not find out for sure? Let's get it tested for DNA," she said.

"Cool." Trujillo was all for it. Mac grumbled about the cost, but he agreed. Before the morning was over, Lacey had contacted Adrienne Woods in Atlanta to find out if she had a lock of Angie's hair and was willing to part with it for comparison. Lacey had rightly guessed that Mrs. Woods was the type of mother who would save all kinds of mementos. Adrienne had saved curls from Angela's baby hair and her first haircut, as well as from her grade-school braid. She assured Lacey she would send a clipping.

"If you're so sure about this, what about the police? Are we going to tell them?" Lacey asked Tony.

"It's a closed case. We don't want to give away anything too soon, and the police wouldn't want something to mess up a nice closed suicide." He paused for a beat. "Why not call your pals at the FBI?"

"You're right, no one needs to know."

Mac concurred. "If it's not her hair, no one's embarrassed by jumping to conclusions. If it is, then we've got a scoop. Hot stuff, Smithsonian. Why would you ever want to give up the fashion beat?"

Bravado was her only choice in front of the newsroom, but it couldn't stop her frenzied thoughts. *If the hair matches, the actual killer is contacting me. And what about Tammi White? The mysterious George? Marcia Robinson? The FBI? DeadFed? Oh God.*

Suddenly nothing about Tammi's George Something sounded right to Lacey. He wanted to lure Tammi away from the salon, arrange for a mysterious stylist, take an amateur video, and collect the hair. Had this George's path ever crossed Angie's? Maybe he had followed her to Washington. And now he'd found another stylist from Virginia Beach with long hair.

Way too melodramatic, Lacey. He's probably just some wacko who stumbled into a weird coincidence. But at the very least, if Lacey could talk to him, she could find out why he wanted the hair. She picked up the phone and called the Virginia Beach Stylettos.

"Tammi, I don't think you should meet this George guy alone. Has he called back yet?"

"Not yet. Why?"

Lacey made a sudden decision. "Why don't I drive down to Virginia Beach tomorrow? We could talk. You could tell me about Angie. After you get off work, we'll meet this guy together."

It sounded fine to Tammi, especially the part about the lunch that Lacey offered to buy. If she could be mentioned in "Crimes of Fashion," even better.

Getting the next two days off from Mac was much easier than she expected. She left Tammi and George Something out of it; no sense borrowing ridicule if it turned out to be nothing. Lacey pleaded stress.

"Yours or mine?" Mac asked. "Stay out of trouble. Wait, what about your column? At least give me a 'Fashion Bite.'"

Don't tempt me. "I'll write you something tonight and e-mail it." It was time to pull an idea from her fashion notebook, maybe that piece on packing. And the idea of getting away from Washington in the middle of the workweek sounded like heaven.

Lacey had never been to Virginia Beach or anywhere in the southern part of the state. She thought about wandering around, taking in some sights, and strolling down an empty beach without a crowd of roasted and toasted sun worshipers. She'd probably have the whole afternoon to herself and she'd spend the night. Because it was still off-season, a cheap hotel room could be had. A place where no one—Stella or Vic or the FBI—could reach her.

Lacey had the rest of the day to plan her wardrobe. Mac walked by and found her deep in thought. "What are you working on, Lacey?"

"List of murder suspects."

"Who's on it?"

"Everybody. Now you're on it too."

"I like to see my reporters happy."

Felicity offered Lacey a juicy apple tart. Lacey put Felicity on her unwritten suspect list on general principle. She realized that she couldn't put everyone she hated on the list. Nevertheless, Felicity stayed on.

That night Lacey needed to pack and clean up the apartment before she left town. The last thing she wanted was to return to a dirty place. It was a holdover lesson from her childhood. Kill yourself cleaning before you leave home. God forbid burglars should find a dirty dish in the kitchen.

As soon as she let herself into the apartment, the phone started ringing. Brooke had a heavy schedule this week, so Lacey knew it wasn't her. *It better not be Stella.* She picked the receiver up gingerly.

"Hey, Lacey." Stella, of course. "So what's this about Virginia Beach? You talked to Tammi?"

"Obviously. You told her to call me. And obviously she called you."

"Yeah, but I thought you'd call me with an update. You left me out of the loop. Thank God Tammi let me back in. Hey, it's a long drive. Maybe I could go with you and help you investigate. Michelle could cover tomorrow— Wait. Leo's out. I'm stuck."

"I'll be fine, Stella. And keep quiet about my trip, okay? I don't want this on the Stella Broadcasting System."

"Anything else, Your Majesty?"

"There are things people shouldn't know."

"Like who?"

"Like killers, Stella. Killers shouldn't know."

"No way, man! You think the Feds are there?

"There are Feds everywhere."

"But this Virginia Beach guy wants to buy hair."

"Right, and somebody wanted Angela's hair. Only she paid the price."

"You think this is really dangerous?"

"Probably not. If we keep our mouths shut."

"And what if Victor Donovan comes by?"

Lacey did not like the way Stella purred when she said Vic's name. "Don't mention my name. What Vic doesn't know won't hurt him."

"He likes you."

"Shows what you know. He's just trying to suck information out of me. And you. Believe me, Stella, it takes one to know one. Besides, Virginia Beach probably won't lead anywhere. I'll call you when I get back."

As she hung up, she noticed the answering machine was blinking. Lacey sank down on the sofa and hit the Message button. "Lacey, this is Marie Largesse." Lacey tried to place the name. "You know, darlin', your friendly neighborhood psychic? Little Shop of Horus? I got your number from Stella."

Lacey had a clear picture now. She started to rub her temples at the headache that was beginning. Marie continued. "I just called to let y'all know a couple things before y'all head down to Virginia Beach."

Only Stella would consult a psychic about my business.

"Don't be too hard on Stella," the message continued. "She's a little nosy, but she's a good friend. First, I have to warn you, it's going to be a little frustrating. Psychic congestion. I'm feeling that very clearly. Just relax and go with the flow. If y'all just give in and let things take their natural course, things'll go better."

At least the weather's supposed to be nice, Lacey thought.

"Oh, and take a warm raincoat. I don't care what the weatherman says, it's going to rain like Katzenjammers."

A second message was from Vic Donovan, asking her to call. She hesitated for a moment, then lifted the receiver. She put the receiver back.

My own psychic hotline and do I get advice about the guy? The tall, dark, handsome man? No, I get: Take a raincoat.

Lacey Smithsonian's

FASHION BITES

The Getaway: Packing in a Hurry

You need a quick vacation getaway. Or simply to escape those rather large men in dark suits with earpieces who always seem to be crossing your path. So run away. Simply jump in the car and go. Wait! First you have to pack. But if you just toss things in a brown paper bag the way they do in the movies, you won't emerge in the next scene glamorously clad for your hideout on the Riviera. You'll look like a fugitive from reality, or worse, a tourist. That's right. You'll be wearing the plaid shorts, the striped top, the neon T-shirt, and some hideous flowered thing you don't remember buying. And if you can't look like a romantic fugitive from justice, why bother? Here are a few tips on how to avoid that thrown-together-in-a-suitcase-just-ahead-of-the-federal-marshals look.

- Keep your luggage handy. Remember that a wheeled bag is so much easier to run with.
- Bring something comfortable to wear while hiding out in the hotel room, perhaps a cotton shirt and shorts or leggings. However, your choice should also be presentable for those awkward times when you leave to retrieve a bucket of ice and return to your room to find that the magnetic key card no longer works and you're nearly naked and have to call security and wait outside your room like the world's most incompetent cat burglar. It happens.
- Nothing screams "on the run" like a pair of clunky running shoes with flashing reflectors that say "chase me" as they hurdle chain-link fences in back alleys on a reality cop show. Instead, choose chic leather flats, which will allow you to outpace Interpol in style. Carry a sleek

leather bag large enough to stash the essentials: a clean wrinkle-free top and an elegant scarf for an instant change of look—or climate.

- Keep a small bag of toiletries ready. It cuts down on the panic when you find you've forgotten your contact lens case and solution and your guidebook doesn't have the French word for toothpaste. And while many nicer hotels provide shampoo, conditioner, and lotion, some motels, the kind where you might find yourself hiding out until the scandal blows over, have only those cheap little chips of soap that make your skin itch like you have a guilty secret.
- If you're going economy, remember that hair dryers and full-size towels are rare on the run. And do you need that special pillow, sentimental teddy bear, or other security-blanket items you can't sleep without? Pack them.
- And do remember to pack a pair of tailored black slacks or skirt and an attractive blouse or sweater for that unexpected dinner out at an exclusive restaurant. Who knows? Maybe your lawyer will call, the charges have been dropped, all is forgiven, and you're a celebrity! The champagne is on the house, and when the paparazzi arrive, you'll look fabulous.

Chapter 17

Lacey packed light, but her overnight bag still weighed a ton. It could be balmy and pleasant, as forecast by D.C.'s renowned meteorologists; or as a certain psychic predicted, it could rain like Katzenjammers. *Whatever that means.* Lacey packed a heavy sweater, a warm hooded jacket, heavy gloves, and an umbrella. She also tossed in khaki shorts, boat-neck cotton tops, sunscreen, and a visor.

She left the light on and gave the apartment one last look before heading to the car. Her new Ella Fitzgerald tape of Cole Porter songs was waiting for the ride down. It was a dew-kissed Tuesday morning with the scent of cut grass. Her favorite emerald sweater and her most comfortable jeans were a talisman against Marie's warnings.

Her key was in the car door. She heard someone behind her.

"Road trip, Lacey?"

Annoyed, she turned on him. "Are you some kind of vampire, Vic? Do you never sleep?" But this time there were no obvious signs that he had been up all night. He looked suspiciously fresh and showered. The Jeep was idling, blocking her in.

"I left a message on your machine yesterday," he said.

"Yeah, so? It's been nice seeing you, Vic, but I've got things to do, people to see." She yanked open the door, wondering why he bothered her so much.

"That's why I called. I thought we could take my Jeep."

"Back up, cowboy. We?"

"You're going to Virginia Beach. Coincidentally, so am I."

"Coincidentally? You just happen to be going to Virginia Beach on a Tuesday? And I am the Queen of the May."

"Business," he said.

"And you expect me to believe that?"

"Radford's down there at his beach house. Wants me to meet him. There's no reason we can't share the drive."

She slammed the door and turned around. "It was Stella, wasn't it? She knows all, she tells all."

"She's your friend."

"That's what you think. Stella is a barnacle I can't scrape off! I only wish you'd had to beat the information out of her. Some friend, blabbing my business all over town."

He chuckled. "Like a reporter?"

"And why do you care anyway?"

Now he laughed. It was too early in the morning for laughter: The sun was barely up; robins were gossiping. The road awaited. Lacey explained to Vic that she had things to do in Virginia Beach and for that she needed her own car. After all, he must have his own agenda as well.

"Thought I'd tag along with you, Lacey."

"You won't open doors for me, but I'm supposed to open doors for you?"

"I couldn't let you in the warehouse. You know that."

"Too bad. Gotta go. I'm staying over."

"My bag is packed. I'm flexible."

A brazen black squirrel stopped on the sidewalk and stared at them. "I don't care what you do, Vic. Your bag is always packed. If we run into each other, maybe I'll let you buy me dinner. But I'm driving my own car."

Vic shrugged. "All right, already. I try to be friendly and see what I get. See you down there." The squirrel scrambled up the oak tree for a better view. Vic roared off in the Jeep and squealed his tires around the corner.

Lacey threw her bag in the back of her car, climbed in, unlocked and removed the Club from the steering wheel, and turned the key in the ignition. Road ready as it allegedly was, the Z failed to turn over. It merely uttered a futile *click, click, click,* a dead giveaway that the solenoid on the starter was dead. She sighed deeply and rested her head on the steering wheel.

"Damn. Damn. Damn."

She could call AAA. Or she could see if Paul at Asian Engines had a starter in stock. Lacey was a good customer, and she could plead an emergency. Surely, Paul would have mercy on her, but it would set her back at least an hour. Maybe three. Disappointment washed over her. She should have known the Z was running too perfectly. *But why today?* She groaned. *I love this car—I don't think 198,000 miles is too much to ask.* She sat for a full five minutes in disgust. She didn't even hear the Jeep pull up again.

Vic knocked on the window. She rolled it down.

"Thought you were right behind me, Lacey. You change your mind?"

"Got a spare starter?"

"Sorry. And just so you know, I did not sabotage your car. Maybe it's depressed." She said nothing. "The offer still stands. Come on. The Jeep is warmed up," he said.

Lacey hated the Jeep. She glared at the gleaming hulk, uncharacteristically washed and waxed. The Jeep was only two years old. No doubt everything on it was in perfect working order. The thought made her growl audibly.

"Is that a yes?" Vic asked. "It'll probably take you all day to get this thing fixed."

She put the Club back on her steering wheel and locked it, retrieved her bag, slammed the door, and stomped over to the Jeep. "Thank you. You can drop me off at a car-rental place down there. I'll drive a one-way back to National Airport. I don't want to burden you." She caught him grinning at her once again. "Don't you dare laugh at me."

"I'm not laughing *at* you, Lacey. I'm laughing *with* you."

She smiled sweetly. "Someday I'll be laughing with *you*." Eventually, she calmed down, about the time he turned off the Beltway down I-95 South. He didn't say a word while she seethed at her fate. Marie's words came back: "Frustrating weekend. Go with the flow." *Grrr!*

Vic spoke as soon as he sensed she wouldn't bite. "Not so bad, is it?" The Jeep was climate controlled and musically enhanced. "You're really attached to that car, aren't you?"

"I was looking forward to the drive. It was supposed to be road ready. Finally." A bad mood descended, weighing down her shoulders.

"You need a new car, Lacey. You had that Z back in Sagebrush. You gonna keep it forever? Did it save Timmy from the well or something?" She growled again in response. "You're a bear until you've had coffee, aren't you?"

"I'm not the bear. I poke the bear."

"Okay, bear hunter. How about some breakfast, then?"

An alluring aroma was coming from a large white paper bag. Vic indicated that she should open it. Lacey peeked. Fresh rolls, coffee, and orange juice. *He thought of everything. As usual.* Of course, she had planned to pick up something at Sutton Place, the gourmet grocery, on her way out of town. "You planned this," she accused him.

"Just have to be prepared, that's all. It's a long drive."

"Damn Boy Scout."

Everyone says the drive to Virginia Beach is three and a half hours from Washington, D.C. Everyone lies, unless they drive ninety miles an hour without traffic and without troopers. It's more like four and a half to five hours, but Vic split the difference and made it in a little over four. It's too long to drive without talking.

"So, why Virginia Beach today?" Vic finally asked.

"Stella didn't tell you? She must be falling down on the job, the tattletale."

"She said you'd kill her."

"Why exactly are *you* going there?"

Vic said he was going to look at potential Stylettos salon sites with an eye toward security, for Boyd Radford.

"More purloined shampoo?" she asked. It struck Lacey that Boyd was relying on Vic an awful lot and Vic could have gone to Virginia Beach anytime.

"Not so far as I know. I'm crazy enough to think you might be onto something. I'm also supposed to ride herd on you."

"With what, your charm? My bad luck with cars?"

"Whatever it takes. Orders from Radford."

"Ratboy's a worm."

"There goes that eyebrow rising again, Lacey. Tell me, is that an automatic response to me, or do you have conscious control over it?"

"I don't need a baby-sitter, Victor Donovan."

"Is that what you think?"

"I think if Radford's that concerned about one insignificant fashion reporter, he's got something to hide. And maybe I need to find out what that is."

"That's the Lacey Smithsonian I know. Always in the middle of things."

"Not true."

"Then you've changed. You were always in the middle of things in Sagebrush."

"Shucks, cowboy, it was a small town. Besides, your buddies in the sheriff's department used to tip me off. The same way your cops tattled on the deputies."

He grimaced. "Doesn't matter how you got there, you were always there."

"What do you think is going on, Vic?"

"I'm not looking for drama, Lacey. I've had enough drama. I'm just trying to figure out how to do this job as well as my dad does it."

The highway was monotonous, but it improved the closer they got to Virginia Beach. Spring was blossoming in the southern part of the state. The trees were filling in the landscape and petals perfumed the air. Lacey poked her nose out the window and inhaled deeply.

Vic exited the highway and headed down Atlantic Avenue near the beachfront. He parked at the city parking lot. Warm salt air greeted them as they emerged from the Jeep. Lacey stretched her legs and grabbed her backpack. "Okay. I'll call a cab from the salon." She reached for her overnight bag, but Vic assured her he would drop it off later. Lacey gave in; she didn't feel like carrying it to lunch with Tammi.

The salon was a couple of blocks away, between Atlantic and Pacific. As they turned the corner she spotted the hot-pink awning emblazoned with Stylettos' logo: a stylized pair of scissors striding in high heels.

But something was wrong. A crowd was jamming the sidewalk. Police cars and an ambulance were blocking the flow of traffic on the street. Two uniformed officers were turning people away from the salon door.

Dread filled the pit of her stomach as she hurried forward.

Vic put a restraining hand over her arm. "God, Vic. What the hell—" His hand tightened.

They arrived on the sidewalk as the front door swung open and a gurney was wheeled out. On it, strapped in and zipped up, was a body bag. Two women followed the emergency medical technicians to the ambulance, clutching each other, streaks of tears on their faces. Both wore the distinctive black polished cotton Stylettos smock with large patch pockets and Chinese collar. The blonde in a short skirt wore her hair in an "Aries," a haircut designed to look like a ram's head, parted in the middle with long "horns" sweeping back around her ears and up beneath her chin. The back was razored short. Lacey had watched Stella cut one. The brunette wore a short urchin cut and a sundress under her smock.

She overheard one of the women whisper "Suicide."

Lacey froze. "Suicide? Oh my God. Who?"

A uniformed cop pushed past her, his voice efficient. "Excuse me, ma'am." He moved into the salon carrying crime-scene tape.

"We don't know what it is, but suicide and homicide are treated the same until a determination is made," Vic reminded Lacey. "We just need to stay out of their way."

It occurred to Lacey that this wasn't the first time she and Vic had stood by the crime tape at a murder scene—not that there had been many murders in Sagebrush. The difference in Sagebrush was that they were on opposite sides of the tape. There had been one murder in particular, she remembered, a woman's body dumped off the highway, strangled, with no witnesses, no suspects, no real evidence. She felt bad now that she'd needled Vic for not solving it. She knew he had sweated bullets and blood over it.

Vic could tell Lacey wanted to talk with the police. He steered her away from the police tape. "No sense in getting in their way and pissing them off. I know someone on the force." He would. Vic was one of those guys who seemed to know someone wherever he went. "Let me make a call and see if we can talk with the detective later."

Lacey approached the weeping stylists, both in their late twenties. She explained who she was and that she had come to talk with Tammi White, hoping against hope that the manager was still in the salon with the cops and that the body in the bag was merely a victim of a bad perm and a heart attack. But Lacey hadn't seen anyone in the crowd with long, curly black hair.

"You're 'Crimes of Fashion'?" The ram's-head blonde turned out to be named Heidi. "Man. Tammi was so excited to see you, but you can't talk to her now. She's in there. . . ." She motioned to the ambulance.

"She's dead!" The brunette, Nan, blurted out, her eyes wet beneath fringed bangs. "God, I've never known any dead people before." Her voice broke.

The two stylists hugged, sobbing, and Lacey helplessly stood by. Guilt seemed to slap her in the face. She could hardly breathe. Had something she said or wrote initiated a chain of events that ended in a woman's death?

Heidi's eyes squeezed out more tears as she related that she and Tammi, her manager, had closed the salon the night before, and she had come into the salon this morning and found Tammi dead. Heidi saw the message in blood on the mirror: *That's All, Folks.* All the blood was a shock. To Lacey it sounded just like Angie's death—slit wrists, the straight razor, the bloody message. It had the same gruesome flippancy as Angie's alleged farewell: *So Long.*

"Did you see her hair?" Lacey asked. "Tammi said she had long black hair."

"The hair? Oh my God!" Nan shrieked. "It was hacked off. I didn't even recognize her at first." The young manager was slumped over her station and her hair was cut off, savagely, very short. "She wore it braided yesterday with a red ribbon wound through it. I remember 'cause we always remember hair and Angie showed her that style. Angie loved hair ribbons."

Stella had said Angie wore her hair braided with a blue ribbon the day she was killed.

"Where was the hair?" Lacey asked.

Now that Lacey brought it up, Heidi couldn't remember seeing the hair. It wasn't on the floor. "I don't know. Shampoo girls always sweep up the hair, we don't even think about it."

"It doesn't make any sense, killing herself. I mean she was totally juiced that you were coming," Nan added. "Tammi had all the news stories about Marcia and Angie. She even came in here once for a condition."

"Who?"

"Marcia. Her mom's got a condo on the beach and she was hiding out," Nan said.

"Marcia Robinson is in Virginia Beach?"

"It was very hush-hush," Heidi said, "but everybody knew."

Both stylists agreed that Tammi had put in extra effort to make the salon look nice for Lacey's visit. "Why would she kill herself?" Nan asked.

"And why would she do it like Angie? It's so messy, and that wasn't like Tammi. She liked everything to be neat."

A silver-gray Jaguar with smoked windows pulled up to the curb. Boyd Radford emerged, slammed the door shut, and pushed his way through the mob to the salon. Boyd wore blue jeans that looked new and stiff over a pudgy belly. His sky-blue polo shirt revealed pasty white arms and a Rolex watch. A black cap with the Stylettos logo was perched on his head. He started when he saw Lacey with Vic Donovan, but he caught himself. Radford signaled Vic to come talk with him. He glared at Lacey. Vic steered Radford off to the side.

"For God's sake," Radford spat at Vic, "what is *she* doing here?" He turned and charged into the salon.

The window on the passenger side of the Jaguar slid down. Josephine, behind designer sunglasses and a black straw hat, calmly sat and watched the crowd. She nodded to Lacey.

Nan threw her cigarette to the ground and stomped on it. She wrinkled her nose. Lacey sensed the familiar loathing for Radford that many Stylettos' stylists seemed to share.

"He came on to you, didn't he?" she asked Nan.

"Does a redneck drive a truck? Yeah, I wanted to be a manager and the head rat suggested a few ways that could happen. Ratboy's idea of a management position is on your back."

"What happened?"

"You're not looking at a manager, are you?" She shook another unfiltered cancer stick out of a pack and lit it, her hand shielding the match against a slight breeze. "What a pig."

Heidi broke in. "You're not exactly subtle about it, you know." Heidi looked at Lacey. "She's always singing the pink-collar blues."

A beautiful smile lit up Nan's face. "I told him he could suck on a hot curling iron before I'd play slap the monkey with an ugly old ape like him. He's, like, totally gross, and I mean he must be fifty. Doesn't that just make you want to hurl?" She blew a smoke ring.

"Yeah, well, watch out or you'll hurl yourself out of a job," Heidi said.

"What about Tammi? Did she have a relationship with Radford?" Lacey asked.

"She's a manager," Heidi said. "She put up with him. But it was kind of understood that it was over." Heidi offered another tidbit. "Ratboy's scouting locations for a new salon. There are two Stylettos in town now. And he owns a beach house on Ocean Front Avenue so he can combine business with pleasure."

"New manager and assistant manager slots will open up. They say some guy from D.C.'s got the inside track on the manager slot," Nan said. "Leonardo with no last name. How's that for pompous? Apparently, he's Josephine's little protégé."

"Leonardo was supposed to come down this week to meet with Tammi and some of the stylists and look at the possible locations, sort of a job interview." Heidi said. It was hard for Lacey not to stare at her strange Aries haircut, but then attracting attention was the point.

Boyd emerged from the salon and spoke quietly with Vic. He announced that Stylettos would be closed for the rest of the day and next two days. His face was unreadable. Lacey couldn't figure out if he looked angry, sad, or shocked.

There seemed to be a routine that a stylist's death required. Boyd already had it down pat. He tacked a handwritten sign on the door telling clients to visit the other Stylettos salon two miles down the beach. The closed salon would be back in business on Friday. He misspelled "bizness" and "simpathy."

Heidi and Nan were told to go home. Three others were told to report to the other Stylettos to see if they could fill in. On his way back to the car, Radford gave a warm hug to a striking titian-haired stylist. He whispered something in her ear and smiled lewdly. He avoided Lacey's gaze. She looked around, but she didn't see where Vic had gone.

Boyd's next glare of disapproval was for his ex-spouse. He

returned to the Jaguar. "Not a word, Josephine. I don't want one goddamn word out of you." He got in and slammed his door shut. Josephine put her sunglasses back on and spat something in French. Her window slid back up and the Jaguar pulled away.

The crowd started to dwindle and Lacey noticed a woman on the edge of the crowd slipping away. *What is Sherri Gold doing here?* Lacey couldn't be sure if the lanky woman in oversized sunglasses was Sherri Gold. She started after the woman but lost her in the crowd. *No, wait. I must be wrong.*

Heidi and Nan showed no sign of leaving while the police were still there. Lacey stood with them silently and waited until Vic emerged from the salon.

She pulled him aside. "Vic, what's going on?"

"I don't know anything except she's dead and they say it does look like suicide. There's a note in blood on the mirror."

"A snide note. Just like Angie's. And her hair was cut off."

"Says who?"

"The stylists. It was long yesterday. Gone today."

"I hadn't heard that." He let out a long breath. "Cops don't pay much attention to hair, I guess. Tell me, Lacey, can you just hold your horses for now and stay out of trouble?"

Lacey cocked an eyebrow at him and gave him the "Look," that special look women reserve for idiots and men.

"Okay. I'm sorry I said it." He didn't look sorry. "I've got to meet up with Radford."

"What did he say?"

Lines around Vic's eyes crinkled in the sunlight. "Told me to keep you under control. What are the odds?"

"I want to talk with the cops."

"Later, Lacey. I'll call you. You got a cell phone?"

She groaned. "I hate cell phones. I'll call you." They walked back to the Jeep and she retrieved her bag before letting him drive off. "Thanks for the ride down. I do appreciate it. I can take care of myself from here. I'll see you later," she said. "Or not. Let me know what you find out."

He waved. "Aye, aye, Captain."

Chapter 18

Lacey treated Nan and Heidi to lunch. There were tears and regrets at the Sandwash Café. Neither woman knew anything about George, the mystery man who had called Tammi with the hair-for-money offer. Lacey again wondered aloud, casually, where Tammi's hair was. Nan and Heidi just stared at each other and shrugged.

"I didn't think about it," Heidi said. "I didn't really take a long look, you know."

Nan suggested that the cops found it and took it for evidence. They couldn't believe that Angie or Tammi had committed suicide, but neither stylist could fathom the thought of murder. Until Lacey brought it up. *Something else Boyd Radford will thank me for.*

"Oh my God," Heidi said. "Do you think someone is going after stylists? That doesn't make any sense!"

Nan ordered another Coke. "I don't know, some people get really pissed off about their hair."

"Has anything out of the ordinary happened lately at the salon?" Lacey wanted to know. Nan and Heidi shared a look and Heidi shook her head. Lacey felt a jolt. "What? Tell me."

"We kind of agreed not to talk about it after Angie died," Heidi said. She looked down at her plate. Nobody was eating much.

"Come on, guys. Two of your friends are dead, whether it's suicide or something else. Whatever you're avoiding, it's better to get it out in the open. Is there some kind of theft ring operating out of the salons?"

Nan shook her head. "I don't know anything about that. You

know, the occasional bottle of shampoo takes a walk, but something big? No. Is that what you think?"

A tear dripped off the end of Heidi's nose. "Oh God. We thought it was just a joke."

"It could be nothing," Lacey rushed to assure her. "But if you tell me, maybe we can figure something out." *You're a glutton for punishment, Lacey.*

"Come on, Heidi. We might as well tell her. And just for the record, if something weird is going on, I am not feeling like killing myself," Nan said. "Although I've never felt worse." Heidi agreed and wiped her eyes with a napkin.

"It's that damn videotape," Nan said. She reached for a cigarette, but remembered they were in a no-smoking section. "Few weeks ago, Tammi gets a package in the mail from Angie. A videotape with a note that says something like, 'Don't watch this garbage and don't tell anyone. Please just hide it.' "

Heidi broke in. "Tammi figured Angie was just being funny and this was some kind of styling video from the company and it was Angie's way of saying that it sucked."

"Anyway," Nan resumed, "we all think it's gonna be a total hoot, you know, a bunch of you-gotta-be-kidding haircuts, so Tammi schedules a salon meeting to watch it, a half hour before the salon opens. We even pop popcorn in the microwave and get our smokes and sodas ready." She snickered at the memory. "Well, goddamn, if it isn't some funky homemade porno film! It's pretty comical in a gross way. Starring all these Comb Overs and Helmet Heads. As if you want to see naked geezers. Geezers, well, you know, forty-somethings. Geezers with really young chicks, like teenagers. Gross. We're just about ready to turn it off when Ratboy shows up."

"At the salon?" Lacey asked.

"No, on the video," Nan continued. "We see him hand over an envelope to some woman with a blond bubblehead cut, you know, short and puffy. And next thing you know, Ratboy's dropped his drawers and Bubblehead is down to just her pearls, and bingo, bango, they're doing it!"

"Now we call him 'Jackrabbit.' Or 'R.R.' For 'Rapid Rodent,' " Heidi said. "It was so funny I snorted Pepsi out of my nose."

Nan mentioned that they played that part at least ten times. "Now we look at Rapid Rodent in, like, a whole new light."

"Did you recognize anyone else?"

"Oh yeah, Marcia Robinson. She was just walking around the room topless with a plate of hors d'oeuvres like at a cocktail party," Heidi said. "She's kind of chubby to go totally naked. And some of the naked people looked familiar, like you've seen them on television or something, but I couldn't tell you who they were."

Nan helpfully added more details. "And some you couldn't see very well because they'd been digitally altered, like on TV. It seemed to change to a couple of different places. I couldn't say for sure."

Marcia had told Lacey she had been selling tapes on the Web site. Maybe this was the blooper tape—outtakes that were too hot to handle?

"Where is the tape now?"

"I don't know. The next day Angie was dead. The tape didn't seem so funny anymore and we didn't talk about it after that." Heidi glanced at Nan.

"Don't look at me," Nan said. "I don't know what happened to it. What do you think, Lacey?"

Would Radford kill for it? And who were the others on the tape? "I think you should tell the cops."

"What, that we watched a dirty movie with our boss in it? Sounds like a quick trip to the unemployment line to me." Nan and Heidi crossed their arms in unison. "We're not talking to the police," Nan said. "Bad enough they've got videocams on the boardwalk now."

"What if it has something to do with Angie's and Tammie's deaths?" They looked doubtful. "If that video surfaces, I think it should find its way to the police. Anonymously." They still looked unconvinced. "Having that videotape could be lethal."

"Lethal?" Heidi said.

"You just told me Angie sent the tape to Tammi. Now they're both dead. It's a dangerous secret. If I write about the tape in my column, it's no longer a secret. No reason to kill anybody." *I hope.*

Nan wanted to know if Lacey would have to tell the police about it. Lacey assured them that it was only hearsay to the police. "From their point of view, I haven't seen it and I'd need to have more proof that it even exists. I will have to write about it, though. It and Tammi."

"She'd like that," Heidi said.

"That's cool, if you don't mention us," Nan said. "And Rapid Rodent, don't mention that he's on it."

A welter of questions sprang to her mind: *Who knows about the tape? How did Angie get her hands on it in the first place? Was it still in the salon or did Tammi belatedly hide it? And who were those almost-familiar people on the tape?* But the stylists didn't know any more about it.

She asked if they knew Sherri Gold. They said no, and Heidi, who filled in the salon book, claimed no one of that name had made an appointment recently and they didn't remember anyone of her description. "We get more 'beachy' people. You know: tan, blond, pretty," Heidi said.

Lacey wanted to see the other Virginia Beach Stylettos, and Nan offered to drive her to the strip mall where it was located. Ram's-Head Heidi went home after hugs all around. Nan introduced Lacey to the hulking bronze 1960s Ford land yacht she called the "Bronze Bomber." It was battle scarred but feared no one. The muffler and air-conditioning were shot, but the stereo was fine and belted out some retro rock from Heart.

"I love this monster," Nan said. "Nobody gets in my way."

The bronze behemoth delivered them safely, if loudly, to the other salon. Inside the storefront, beauticians were abuzz with the news of Tammi's death. Apparently no one had heard of the mysterious George. But then, all the stylists there had very short hair, from Audrey-Hepburn chic to punkette. Not George's style. They were dying to talk about Tammi's death and knowing nothing wasn't going to stop them.

After exhausting her questions about Tammi, Angie, Leonardo, and George Something, and learning nothing, Lacey turned to Nan. "Do you know where Radford's beach house is?"

"Oh yeah. I've had fantasies about TP-ing it. In my younger days I would have. Want to see it?"

Back in the Bronze Bomber, Nan switched the radio to WCMS, blasting out Toby Keith. They cruised Ocean Front Avenue, past a number of beach homes. Radford's matched its neighbors, a dove-gray exterior with blue-gray trim, an ocean-front view, and a profusion of decks.

More interesting was the collection of cars outside: the Jaguar, Vic's Jeep, and a red Camaro that pulled in the drive beside the Jag while the Bomber was parked across the street. Beauregard Radford emerged after checking his reflection in the rearview mirror, which was cluttered with hanging air fresheners. He looked too slight to be driving that flashy car, but he was making a stab at a more daring look, wearing his thin dark hair in a sleek ponytail that screamed "artiste." The puny ponytail was an improvement on his previous Prince Valiant, Lacey thought.

"Who's that?" Nan asked.

"Beau Radford," Lacey answered. "You don't know him?"

"You're kidding! That's Shampoo Boy?" Nan took a closer look. "Jeez, I haven't seen him in years. Not since he went away to college the first time, maybe six years ago. Ratboy used to make him shampoo clients in the summer when we couldn't get enough help. He was as lazy as you'd expect the heir to the throne to be. But I wouldn't have recognized him!"

Lacey wondered briefly if Beau could suspect his own father in the deaths. An eye-popping yellow Corvette roared in next to the Camaro. The D.C. license plate said LEO 1. Leo paid no attention to the women watching from across the street in the big brown car.

Lacey didn't know what more she could glean from the scene, so Nan chauffeured her back to the hotel. Lacey handed her twenty dollars for gas money.

"Hey, thanks, Lacey. The Bomber loves to guzzle." Nan promised to call if she found the videotape or if the elusive George came sniffing around. She zoomed off in her beloved beast.

It was after six when Lacey checked into her hotel room, crawled into bed, and fell into a sound sleep. She woke, groggy and disoriented, to the sound of pounding on the door.

"It's Vic. Open up."

She let him in and stood unsteadily, rubbing her eyes. The clock said it was seven-thirty. *Is it a.m. or p.m.?* Lacey wondered.

"If you can manage to open up your eyes, sleepyhead, I'll take you to dinner."

She yawned and stumbled into a strategically placed chair. "Shouldn't you be getting back to town?"

"Don't worry about me. Can you believe there was a vacancy? Booked a room. Right here; two floors up. Lucky, huh?"

"Lucky you. Still riding shotgun on me, huh?"

"No sense in driving back now. It's been a hard day." He moved behind her and rubbed her shoulders. It felt very nice.

"What did you find out about Tammi?" she asked, her eyes beginning to open.

He stopped rubbing her shoulders and moved toward the door. "I'm not taking you to dinner to hash this out. Not now."

"Two identical deaths! If that isn't murder, what is?"

"That hasn't been determined yet. I've found someone you can talk to tomorrow, a Virginia Beach detective named Harding. But tonight, no more about this." He folded his arms and leaned against the door. "You have to be able to turn it off. Something like this can eat you up."

"What about Radford? What is he really doing here?"

"Time out, Smithsonian. I just want to go to dinner. I need some down-home cooking. You do too."

Lacey opened her mouth to protest but then changed her mind. As long as Vic wasn't going to cough up any information or listen to her, she wasn't going to tell anyone about the videotape—at least until she talked with Marcia.

She looked in the mirror and saw sheet creases on her face. *How utterly glamorous.* At least her makeup hadn't smeared. *Bedroom eyes are one thing; raccoon eyes are another.* She agreed to meet Vic in the bar in a half hour, which gave her time to wake up.

Bloody mirrors and crying stylists wound through her thoughts while she freshened up. Lacey wished she could puzzle out the day's events while spending the evening waltzing through Aunt Mimi's patterns. She wanted to select a new item for her Forties wardrobe, something fabulous. But she couldn't very well ask Vic to drop her off at a mall so she could wander around looking at fabrics. Silks in wonderful colors might serve as an escape from the day's events, but she suspected Vic wouldn't understand. He was, after all, a man.

She changed into a close-fitting crocheted sweater in violet that had been a gift from Mimi. Though it was more than five years old, it still looked new and it flattered her complexion. She grabbed a black shawl embroidered with colorful flowers and glanced one last time in the mirror.

It made her cranky that she was having dinner with a gorgeous man who wasn't remotely interested in her except as a source of information—or trouble. At least she was hungry. And he, no doubt, was on an expense account.

The hotel bar was full of light wood, blue leather, and sailing paraphernalia. On a Tuesday, only a few souls were worshiping in this dimly lit shrine to naughty weekends at the beach. The air-conditioning was on high and it made her shiver through the sweater. Lacey ordered a club soda and dove into a straw bowl of peanuts on the bar. She suggested a seafood restaurant down the beach. Vic insisted they needed more sustenance than a tourist-trap crab shack could offer and suggested they take the Jeep to look for a "real place, with real food," like a caveman in search of a woolly mammoth. They drove away from the beach town as hunger gnawed and elevated her crankiness quotient.

They finally settled on the required "down-home food" in a funky storefront restaurant, aptly named The Wild Monkey, in the older, quainter Ghent neighborhood of Norfolk. A friendly waitress led them to a tiny Formica-topped table in the crowded dining room. Lacey found the hubbub surprisingly comforting. The menu and wine list were written on a huge chalkboard the length of the wall and the place seemed packed with regulars. It was a good sign. Lacey ordered a chicken caesar salad and Vic demanded the meatloaf.

"Meatloaf?" She made a gagging noise.

"Mmmm, meatloaf," he said.

"Our specialty," the waitress replied. "It's real popular."

Lacey gazed around the room. Nearly every man in The Wild Monkey was chowing down enormous quantities of meatloaf. *Yum. No doubt made with woolly mammoth. Cavemen.*

The waitress returned shortly, weighed down with heaping mounds of meatloaf and potatoes, Lacey's ladylike plate of foliage and poultry, and a delightful basketful of hot bread and butter. The waitress winked at Vic. He had a certain effect on waitresses, Lacey noticed. *So the road to Vic's heart is through his meatloaf,* she thought. *He probably thinks stuffed peppers are gourmet.*

Vic was obviously grooving on some memory of his mom in a kitchen apron. He chomped with pleasure and washed the meatloaf down with Guinness. Her memory dredged up the tasteless stuff that her mother produced, which Lacey could barely choke down with milk. Felicity at the office was always offering her a surefire recipe for "great meatloaf," which Lacey considered a contradiction in terms. It did not exist.

Eventually, the food, the dim roar of the regulars, and several glasses of cabernet sauvignon calmed her nerves. She was content to eavesdrop on strangers. She overheard the words "great meatloaf." The wine was warming and had the effect of loosening her tongue, something she always regretted later.

"Vic, are we friends, or what?"

He looked at her, his eyes glittering like green glass in this light, and with that insufferable smirk.

"Sure we're friends, Lacey. Why?"

She wondered how she could ask him why he was no longer interested in her. "When we were in Sagebrush, things were different."

"Different?" He wasn't making this easy.

She took a deep breath and a sip of wine. *Shut up, Lacey.* "I always thought you were interested in me. Attracted to me." He nodded. "Was it only because there were so few women there? Or you were on the rebound from your wife? Or were you just hazing me because I was the girl reporter and you were the alpha cop?"

He laughed. *Bastard,* she thought. "Oh, forget it." She swilled down more wine.

"Lacey, Lacey. This is a different time and place. I chased after you for two years and you always said no. You said more colorful things than no. I can take a hint."

"You were married!"

"I was in the middle of a divorce, as you know now and knew then. And you were cute."

Cute! Ugh! You're a dead man.

"You were wasting your time with that cowboy," Vic asserted. "Whatever his name was."

"Let's just leave 'whatever his name was' out of it right now. And he wasn't a cowboy. Cowboy indeed. Cattleman," she corrected.

"Hell, as soon as Cowboy wanted to make it permanent you were out of town like a shot."

She choked on her wine. "You knew he proposed?"

"Everybody in town knew. Felt mighty sorry for that boy. It was a nice little ring he got you." Now she remembered another reason why she had left town: Everybody knew everything about everyone. "You're skittish, Lacey."

"Who told you that?"

"Personal observation."

"You kissed me once." *Oh God, why did I say that?*

"I remember. I might like to do it again someday." He could see she was flustered. "You never know," he continued. "I might be waiting for an invitation. I wouldn't turn down an outright offer; it wouldn't be gentlemanly."

You arrogant—ooh—what's the word? Man! Lacey did not like this at all. There were few enough things that men ever took responsibility for. Now he was making her completely responsible for anything that might happen between them. All she'd wanted to know was whether he was attracted to her.

"So you're not interested anymore," she said. "I just wanted to get it straight between us."

"If I were interested, I wouldn't want to hear you say no another ten thousand times."

"It wasn't ten thousand times." *And I didn't want to say no.* He offered her the chance to order a gooey dessert, but she wasn't in the mood. She just wanted to return to her room. Alone.

Chapter 19

Lacey peered out her hotel window Wednesday morning. As Marie had predicted, it appeared to be raining Katzenjammers. A sodden sky hung like misery over the beach town, a wet gray cloak Lacey couldn't shrug off. She had agreed to meet Vic at eight, check out of the hotel, then grab breakfast somewhere. After that, they would meet with the cop in charge of the Tammi White investigation. Donovan had promised, and Lacey wasn't about to let him off the hook.

She finished packing, dressed warmly, and headed for a soggy morning walk on the beach. At seven o'clock the beachfront along the hotels was deserted except for a few hardy joggers.

Lacey was grateful now for Marie's call. *Nothing like a little psychic fashion advice.* The turtleneck sweater and hooded jacket felt good. Lacey often took long walks when she didn't know what else to do. Here she took off north, up the boardwalk toward the fishing pier, which would be closed for a few more weeks. The beach looked like every other beach Lacey had seen on the East Coast. Endless boardwalks, endless sunglass vendors. Tall cement and stucco hotels with endless balconies like human ant farms. Swinging past the salon told her nothing. She looked for the infamous Virginia Beach video surveillance cameras, the city's attempt to stop crime on the boardwalk. She wondered if they had one pointed at Stylettos. She didn't see any cameras. Radford's sign was still in the window and the empty shop was dark, waiting for a cleaning crew to strip away the death of Tammi White.

Lacey was drenched to the bone by the time she returned to

the hotel, but her head finally felt clear. Vic was waiting at the front desk.

"You look like a drowned rat," he said.

"Love those compliments, Donovan. Keep 'em coming." She turned and walked toward the elevators. "I'll be down in a minute." She toweled off in the room and applied a bit of makeup. Her hair went up in a French knot with three pins. The marine blue of the dry sweater was perfect with her eyes. *Forget you, Vic Donovan. I'd be wasted on you.*

At the diner off Pacific Avenue, she ordered a breakfast fit for a warrioress.

"You know what I think?" Vic asked out of the blue.

"What now?"

"You could have low blood sugar."

She raised an eyebrow, but he ignored it. She popped a bit of muffin into her mouth and chewed it like red meat.

"You're always cranky before you eat," he said. She lobbed part of her muffin at him. "See. You haven't eaten enough yet. Have some bacon."

"You're impossible, Vic. Just why on earth did you want to be here with me if all I do is irritate you? It's been one lousy trip all the way around, and I'd rather not be insulted on a regular basis, okay? I am a reporter, after all. I'm reviled all the time. I swallow more than my share of it. Every once in a while, I deserve a break."

He smiled at her. "Just trying to be helpful. Have some grapefruit."

Detective Jason Harding had bags under his eyes that you could pack, Lacey thought. A hound dog who looked tired of the hunt. Harding's pale blue eyes were bloodshot and his jowls sagged, but he looked friendly. All in all, he seemed as approachable as an old beagle.

Harding had agreed to meet with them as a favor to a friend of a friend of Vic's. They huddled over coffee in a nearly empty java shop, steam rising from chocolate brown cups. Harding listened politely as Lacey explained about the phone call from Tammi and the strange man named George Something, who wanted to buy hair after a dramatic cut.

"You say he wanted the hair?"

"And a videotape, and he was willing to pay five hundred dollars for everything. Tammi said that never happens. I planned to meet him with her, but I was too late. The other stylists said they'd never heard anything about him."

Vic looked at her questioningly. It was the first he had heard of George Something.

"You didn't want to discuss it, remember?" she said.

Harding coughed and brought her back to the subject. Lacey drew parallels to Angela Woods' death in D.C. The peculiar alleged suicide notes written in blood on the mirrors, the bad haircuts, the straight razors. She asked Harding if Tammi White's hair was found in the salon, but he wouldn't divulge the answer. He barely confirmed that the hair had been cut off. She asked if Tammi had been sexually assaulted. He told her there was no sign of that. To his credit, he actually jotted down some notes on a small pad. She asked if the razor they recovered was a Colonel Conk. He wouldn't say. She asked whether the surveillance cameras had revealed anything and whether he would investigate the salon's phone records to trace calls from the mysterious George. He was noncommittal.

"Does my being a reporter have anything to do with your reticence?" she asked.

It was the first time Harding the Hound Dog smiled. "Yes, ma'am. But I do appreciate your coming to me with this information. Truly." He looked like he'd rather be anywhere else. And he had bad news for her. Stylettos was one block out of camera range of the notorious beachfront cameras. And Tammi White apparently had a history of suicide attempts.

"I don't know what happened up in D.C., but there are copycat murders and copycat suicides. Young women are particularly susceptible to it. You may have to accept the idea that she wanted to go out with the same kind of attention that your beautician up in Washington got."

Before Harding finished his coffee and shambled off, Lacey mentioned her little visit from the FBI. And the fact that the agents seemed very interested in the Marcia Robinson angle.

Harding's big hound-dog eyes looked up at her. She could feel Vic's hand squeeze her arm meaningfully. Another little detail she hadn't mentioned to him.

"Criminy, Ms. Smithsonian." Harding moaned. "Does this mean I am to expect a visit from the FBI? Lord Almighty."

She shrugged. "I just thought you'd like to know."

"Got to admit, interest from the FBI makes it sound more suspicious." Harding closed his eyes. "Anything else?"

"The agent's name is Thorn."

"In the side, no doubt." Harding said he would withhold judgment until the medical report was in. That was his only concession to Lacey's linked homicide theory.

Talked out, worn out, and irritable, they didn't attempt a conversation on the drive back to Alexandria, just a random statement from time to time. The storm refused to abate and the landscape rolled by like an Impressionist painting as the Jeep slogged back up I-95. Vic finally cut off to Route 1 when the traffic became too snarled, near Fredericksburg.

"She didn't kill herself, Vic," Lacey said. He grunted. "Tammi's hair, the hair she supposedly cut off, was missing, no matter what Harding confirms or denies."

"You could have mentioned this George character or the FBI to me. I thought we were friends."

"You make like the Sphinx and I'm supposed to spill my guts? You gotta play fair, Vic. Tell me something I don't know. What's your take on Radford?"

"Do I think he's a killer? Who knows? He's very freaked out about the deaths. Wants a total information blackout."

"So maybe he did it, or knows who did," Lacey suggested. Vic frowned at her. "What do you think of Beauregard Radford?"

"Mama's boy. Josephine's still combing his hair for him."

"And Josephine?"

His expression softened at her name. "She's a formidable woman. Very formidable."

His answer made her heart sink. Vic was attracted to Josephine and Lacey didn't care to explore that connection.

But a plan of action was forming in the back of Lacey's head. She shut her eyes and leaned back. It might not be the brightest thought in a dark day, but it was a plan and it grew more compelling with each swipe of the windshield wipers.

* * *

"I can't believe you talked me into this." Vic sounded surly, but he had yet to sprout horns and breathe flames, so how mad could he be? Lacey figured. It was hard to tell in the dark.

"Must be my powers of persuasion," she said. They had spent many hours together; none that Lacey could say were romantic, but neither had they gone for the jugular. And she had worked on him relentlessly for the rest of the drive.

"Nah. I've probably just lost my mind," he said.

It was nearly midnight on Wednesday night and the moon was hiding behind a cloud-locked sky. "If Radford finds out that I let you in the warehouse after all, he'll split a gasket."

"Yeah, but what if he turns out to be a killer, Vic?"

"Then he'll split *our* gaskets."

She shouldered her Nikon and tripod. They would have less than a minute to get any photos once the luminol raised the bloodstains. If there were bloodstains.

Lacey had badgered him for the remainder of the day, until he gave in to her plan to view the crime scene—or what was left of it—that night, and spray it with luminol. His first reaction was that she read too many mysteries. Vic thought she was nuts, but crazy or not, the idea began to attain a certain logic. He did have access to luminol, after all. And to the warehouse.

By the time Vic picked her up again at eleven-thirty that night, she had dispatched the dead Z back to Asian Engines, checked out her camera equipment, and pulled together what she thought was a passable burglar outfit. Basic black on black, accessorized in black. She had even mobilized a secret weapon. "I love it when a plan comes together," she mocked herself.

She was almost out the door when the phone rang. It was Stella. "Lacey, I was crazy with worry. I called and called to see how it went in Virginia Beach and there was no answer. I finally got ahold of Heidi and she told me what happened to Tammi. You gotta be careful. Oh my God. He's after stylists with long hair!"

"Calm down, Stella. I gotta go."

"Are you okay? Maybe you should ease off for a little while."

"I'm fine. I'll call you."

"Maybe I can give you a short haircut for a little extra protection."

"I'm not cutting my hair, Stella!"

Vic was waiting when she got downstairs, and they took off without a word for the Stylettos warehouse on Four Mile Run Drive in Arlington. It sat between a used-tire outlet and a tuxedo-rental shop. The squat brick building and small paved parking lot were surrounded by a chain-link fence that had little effect on salon products waltzing out. Vic opened the door and disabled the alarm system so they could enter. She gazed at the muscles in his forearms as he worked the heavy door. She wondered what the rest of his muscles looked like and hated herself for it.

Vic's new, improved video surveillance system was not installed yet, so there would be no visual record of their visit. Vic relieved the guard until the next one came on duty at two. Heading up corporate security had its advantages. No one would question why he was visiting the warehouse in the middle of the night: a security check. Since he had redesigned salon security, theft was way down and Radford was pleased, according to Stella. But there still were holes at the warehouse. Vic wouldn't discuss it.

Vic turned at the sound of footsteps. Lacey followed his gaze to the bustling earth mother figure advancing on them.

"And why on earth are we bringing her?" he asked. Marie Largesse had taken a few minutes to meditate in the passenger seat of her small midnight-blue Toyota, but now she joined the team. Lacey was asking herself the same question. It had seemed like a good idea at the time—a crime scene, a psychic. Just like on TV.

"She's my secret weapon. Don't laugh. Her shoulders twitch when she gets these psychic vibrations," Lacey said. Vic rolled his eyes at her. "At least that's what she tells me."

"If anyone finds out about this—"

"Who's going to tell?"

"I'm talking to a reporter," Vic pointed out. "Remind me to recharge the cells in my brain case, okay Lacey?"

It was partly the reporter factor, she knew, that pushed him away from her. But Lacey resented knowing that Vic would be more willing to share his thoughts with Radio Free Stella, the voice of Dupont Circle, who would tell the whole world, than with her.

Marie bustled up to the door in layers of black and royal purple, like a voluptuous queen of the night. She was wearing gauzy skirts, a flamboyant cape, and a multicolored scarf wound through her curls. And she'd gone very heavy on the eyeliner.

"That's better, darlin'. I'm centered now," she said. "I have to tune my harmonic frequency before I can receive vibrations from the astral plane."

Vic turned quickly so Marie couldn't see his lips quivering in repressed laughter.

Marie's task was receiving vibrations. She told Lacey that her specialty was sensing auras and spiritual vibes. Marie's predictions about the trip to Virginia Beach had been dead-on, so to speak. But weather was one thing, and murder was another. Lacey did not necessarily believe that Marie could finger the killer. She hoped that Marie could intuit a clue or two. Vic had told her solving Angie's death was impossible, Lacey thought. So why not try the impossible?

The motley trio entered quietly. The warehouse was dimly lit with skylights and orange Exit signs. Vic was reluctant to light the place up. They passed the empty security booth and headed toward the back, flashlights stabbing the gloom. Lacey bumped into "Medusa," the ancient permanent-wave machine, its shadow looming huge against the wall, its rods dangling menacingly, grabbing at her. She swallowed a yelp.

Angie's modular station, of chrome and mirrors with lacquered shelves and drawers, was stored in a back corner with a jumble of grungy Stylettos artifacts, including furniture remnants from the Red Poppy Period, the Turquoise Period, and worst of all, the Dye-Stained Beige Period. But Angie's last stand sparkled in the flashlight beams, its chrome gleaming. *So Long* was long gone from the mirror. It looked spotless, courtesy of Miss Ruby and Not-a-Trace Cleaners, revealing no remnant of the bloody scene of Angie's death.

But traces of that night might still be there, and if the luminol did its job, they would rise again, like bloodstains in stories told around campfires.

She whispered to Marie as if in fear of waking the dead. "You don't have to touch anything, do you?"

Marie said she did not. She looked at the station and closed her eyes for a moment while a scowling Vic crossed his arms and leaned against the wall. Marie opened her eyes wide and looked at Lacey, who was expecting startling revelations. "Yes, Marie?" she asked.

"I see— I feel— Oh my God," was all the psychic said before crumpling in a queen-sized swoon.

It took a few moments for Lacey and Vic to react to the large woman at their feet. "Is she okay?" Lacey asked as Vic felt for a pulse. Her pulse was strong; she had only fainted. He balked at trying to move her, however. Lacey rolled up Marie's cape and tucked it under her head. They continued their quest.

Wearing latex gloves, they opened the cabinet drawers and found three pairs of styling scissors, cotton balls, hair sprays, and a curling iron. A few silky strands of hair were woven through a brush, but there were no long hanks of hair. "There's nothing, Vic," she said. He nodded.

Once again, she knew she could be destroying evidence, but she had no choice. She also knew that bleach could affect the results and salons were full of bleach. They worked quickly. Lacey set up the camera and tripod. Vic sprayed the whole station lightly with luminol. It struck her as a bizarre party trick, a scientific sleight of hand. They cut the flashlights, and in the dark, the chemical raised the dead. Lacey heard her own sharp intake of breath and Vic's as the blue light glowed from the bloodstains as if they'd been hit by live electricity. She let her breath out slowly. Blood had been spattered and smeared everywhere. With fast low-light film, she took as many photos as possible from every angle while the stains were illuminated. They began to fade almost immediately.

But what did that prove? With a sudden insight, Lacey lay on the floor and sprayed the luminol underneath the counter. On the underside, more dramatic stains told the rest of the story. In her mind, Lacey could see the scene: Angela gripping the counter as blood gushed from her wrists. A small handprint held on to the edge underneath the counter. But there was a larger bloody handprint under there as well, on the left side, gripping the counter with longer, thicker fingers—proof that Angela Woods was not alone as she bled to death. Ruby and her crew had smeared them, but not erased them. Lacey didn't need a psychic to feel the sick vibrations. She shot the rest of the film.

Vic efficiently accounted for their gloves and all traces of their visit. He demanded the film from the camera. She balked. It was their deal, in exchange for letting her into the warehouse, but she dug in her heels.

"Chain of evidence, Smithsonian," he said.

"No. My film, my camera, my property," she said.

"You're on private property. Courtesy of me."

"Are we really going to fight about this, Vic?"

He paused and rubbed his eyes. "We've been through this. We use a photo lab that deals with this kind of thing and I can secure chain of custody."

She sighed. "I'm trusting you on this, Vic."

"And I know a blood-spatter expert. I don't want anyone else to die, Lacey."

"I want to see the photos as soon as they're ready, I want the negatives, and I want to talk to your expert. Okay?" She handed him the roll and folded her tripod.

He pocketed the film and helped her walk a sluggish but conscious Marie out to her car. Marie had come to as Vic and Lacey finished their task—blank as a new videotape. *How convenient,* Lacey thought.

"Be careful, scoop. I like your hair the way it is," Vic said. He ruffled her hair and gave a tug on a lock. Just like a big brother would.

Marie took the passenger seat and Lacey took the wheel. Marie was in no shape to drive yet. But she did seem to be in shape to eat. Lacey agreed; Marie would drop her at home later. Vic would wait at the warehouse for the next security shift.

Lacey found herself at almost two a.m. ordering an early breakfast at Bob & Edith's diner on Columbia Pike, on a school night with a so-called paranormal seer who was drawing a complete blank. Marie sat alertly at a blue Formica-topped table and appeared much refreshed by her impromptu nap.

"My psychic senses just plain overloaded. It was too intense," she said. "I don't do trauma very well."

"Now you tell me. Do you remember anything?"

Marie said she was sorry and dug into a hot breakfast that smelled delicious. "I probably have it all recorded somewhere inside. I'm like a VCR. We could always try hypnotic regression."

Lacey let go of her last hope of a psychic breakthrough. *I am an idiot.* "Let's sleep on it."

It was after three in the morning when she got home. Before tumbling into bed, Lacey left a message on Mac's voice mail that she wasn't feeling well and she'd be in late. Very late.

chapter 20

Lacey had thought about calling Mac while she was in Virginia Beach, but it seemed too complicated to explain, and he might have ideas of his own that would make her life more difficult, so she let it ride. When she dragged herself into the office at noon on Thursday, he was in a meeting. She hoped it was one of the long boring kinds that Washington specializes in.

Her first call was to Marcia Robinson, but there was no answer, again. She'd been calling since seven. Maybe Marcia was screening her calls. Or maybe her new attorney took away her cell phone. Lacey left another message saying it was urgent.

She wondered what hair fetishes and a cheesy video featuring rich geezers had in common. But to assume that the videotape was not pertinent made it too great a coincidence. She remembered the smashed VCR on Angie's floor. Did the burglar throw it in a fit of anger because the videotape was gone? If Angie and Tammi were killed because of the missing video, maybe the haircuts were a red herring. She checked out the DeadFed Web site to see if any of the suspicious suicides had expired with a really bad haircut. Unfortunately, the answer seemed to be no. Some in fact did have bad haircuts, judging from the photos, but they were bad in an ordinary, Washington-haircut way.

Her mind kept rolling back to stylists, pink-collar workers taken for granted in a self-important white-collar town. Women who labored beneath the radar screen in Washington, women of no importance unless they cut the right head of hair. Finding one dead stylist in Washington was one thing, but the dead stylist in Virginia Beach kept washing across her mental landscape. Virginia Beach is another world from D.C.

What if it wasn't the same guy who killed the stylists; what if it wasn't a guy at all? After all, it was a wicked witch who cut off Rapunzel's hair to keep the prince away. Lacey called Sherri Gold, the closest thing she'd seen lately to a wicked witch. There was no answer, so she left a message.

She groaned to herself. *For God's sake, Lacey, who do you think you are? You can't even get a new beat. Or keep your car running two weeks in a row.*

Mac strolled over and looked at her. "You just took two days off and you look beat. So it was a good vacation?" he insinuated.

"Not exactly." Lacey summed up Tammi White's death in Virginia Beach and her efforts to get some answers. Mac was so thunderstruck he sat right down on Felicity's desk, crushing a plastic-wrapped lemon bar. Luckily Felicity was away from her desk. The sight might have killed her.

"You held out on me," Mac accused. "Another death? What the hell is it with you and dead hairstylists? Why the hell didn't you tell me?"

"Good grief. I just got back to the office," she countered.

"You could have called it in," Mac said. "It is news. This is a newspaper. We do have a phone."

"I don't phone it in, Mac. I'd lose control of it."

"Why'd you go to Virginia Beach in the first place?"

"Working on my tan."

"You were chasing the story and you didn't tell anyone!"

"I wasn't sure there would be a story," she said.

"And it turns out to be another dead hairstylist with a bad haircut? Christ. Anything else?"

"That's all I have now," she said.

"So, another crime of fashion. Write it up."

"But Mac, I already gave you a 'Fashion Bite.' Besides, my deadline was yesterday."

"And now it's today. I've got the power and you've got a column to write." Mac considered her for a long moment, daring her to complain; then he grabbed Trujillo and dragged him into a heated discussion. Lacey decided to ignore them and forge ahead on a little cyber research to see what kind of person would want to take the hair. She soon found herself lost in the kinkier corridors of cyberspace, hunting hair fetishists.

Lacey cruised bald-babe bulletin boards and head-shaving

chat rooms. She found a plethora of personal pages featuring bald and near-bald, naked and near-naked women of every description. Lacey uncovered an abundance of men seeking women who were shaved here, there, and everywhere, from top to toe.

She discovered the existence of "Jack the Clipper" and "Razor Dan the Shaving Man." She watched "Bald-Headed Lena" happily getting her head shaved—three times. She discovered men who were looking for women they could personally shave, anytime, anyplace. She even found confessions from men who popped out of alleys to cut off women's ponytails and braids as they jogged by.

But would they kill for it? she wondered. *What does a video with Marcia Robinson and Boyd Radford have to do with the price of haircuts? Or the price of congressmen?*

She vaguely sensed someone peering over her shoulder. Thankfully, it was not Felicity, who was pointedly ignoring her now that Mac seemed to be Lacey's personal copy editor. Today, the food editor was wearing some sort of plaid flannel sack that looked like a nightgown and reached almost to the floor, obviously caught in the clutches of a *Little House on the Prairie* fantasy. Lacey observed her carrying a cup of coffee and an enormous cookie to her desk. She knew that Felicity would break the cookie into small fragments and nibble delicately until they all vanished, because everyone knows small pieces have fewer calories. *Wait'll she sees that lemon bar,* Lacey thought.

The lingering sensation of being watched made Lacey turn around. Trujillo, resplendent in a new pair of Justin alligator boots, was standing behind her.

"Pretty wild, huh? So what do you think, Smithsonian? Is there a link between your two dead haircutters? Some hardcore hair ball with a lust for curly locks? Your killer got a major hard-on for hair?"

"I hate people who look over my shoulder, Tony."

"That's cool. Slide over." He pulled up a chair—Mariah's Death Chair. Someone had painted a skull and crossbones on the seat back with Wite-Out. "So you think the killer gets off on cutting—"

"I'm just gathering information."

"Level with me, Lacey." His voice was silky, seductive. *He's not getting to me,* Lacey told herself. "We could smoke this lowlife out. Write the Big One together," he said. Tony laughed, showing off his pretty white teeth. The "Big One" was *The Eye's* sarcastic shorthand for the story that would win the Pulitzer. It was self-mocking sarcasm, as no one at *The Eye Street Observer*, Paper Number Three, had a prayer of winning the attention of the hallowed Pulitzer Committee.

"It's my story, Tony."

"We'll tag team it."

"Yeah, right. You'll take out everything I write and give it the old Trujillo treatment, a little spin here, a little stretch there."

"I'm hurt." He sounded offended, but she knew it was an act. His hide was thick. "It's more than a fashion story, you know. It's got cultural impact, social significance, and all that. Maybe even sex."

"And I am more than a fashion reporter." She exited the screen. "Abuse your own Internet privileges."

"Protecting your turf is cool, Smithsonian. I respect that, Just remember: We'd make a great team. Think about it." He stood up.

Lacey smiled at him. "You remember: If we do, Smithsonian comes before Trujillo."

"You *would* use the alphabet against me."

"Aren't those boots made for walking?"

He socked her in the arm and strutted off. Her phone rang. It was Marcia calling, from a pay phone in Virginia Beach, too freaked out, she said, to use a cell phone now. The Feds could intercept them, she pointed out.

"What's your connection to Tammi White?" Lacey asked.

"Nothing, really. I hardly knew her. And I've been *so* warned not to talk with you anymore."

"Agent Thorn?"

"Among others. Many others."

"Are you sorry you talked to me?"

"Well, I do have a cute new lawyer. Who also told me not to talk to you."

Lacey was counting on Marcia's deep-seated desire to talk. "Tell me about the videotape."

"How do you know about the videotape? Do you have it?" Marcia's voice rose.

"No. I haven't seen it."

"Oh. Well then, what videotape do you mean?"

"Don't be cute, Marcia. The one with Boyd Radford romping nude with a celebrity blonde wearing pearls. Older guys in suits and teenage pages in birthday suits. You made a guest appearance in an outfit you probably don't want to see in 'Crimes of Fashion.' Talk to me, Marcia."

"I can't."

"How many women do you want to die?"

"I don't want anyone to die!"

"Tell me why you gave Angie the tape in the first place." Lacey was reaching. She hoped she was right. There was a long pause.

Marcia sighed. "I asked her to hide it. People were following me. I had it with me, and I was desperate to stash it somewhere. My lawyer refused to take it. Said he might have to produce it in court. We figured there'd be a search warrant. My mother wouldn't take it. She said we had to get it to a safe place and no one would guess my hairstylist. She said the videotape was my only insurance in this whole mess, but it was just too hot to handle."

"You have an unusual relationship with your mother."

"We're more like girlfriends."

More like delinquents.

The tape, Marcia admitted, contained material that had been intended for her now-defunct Web site, but was deemed too dangerous, too weird, or too creepy.

"So I guess it was the blooper tape?"

"Worse." It was a compilation of hidden video of the high and mighty doing the down and dirty at various times and places. And there might have been some politicians. Marcia wouldn't say who made it or name names of anyone on the tape, but she admitted that Boyd Radford was one of the unsuspecting players. She wasn't sure he even knew the tape existed. However, Marcia's mother had told her close friend Josephine Radford about the tape, because Josephine was concerned about where Stylettos' profits were going. Boyd Radford was a big contributor—to politicians and to women. Too big, Josephine thought.

"Marcia, who helped you with the video? Who shot it?" No answer. "Are there more videos? Other copies?"

"No. Everything else got subpoenaed."

"Are you sure you don't have another insurance policy? Who were you going to blackmail with this stuff?"

"Nobody! It was just for protection, you know? Anyway, it isn't really blackmail if you don't ask for money. Everyone knows that."

"Trading other people's secrets for favors or protection isn't blackmail?" Lacey was aghast. "What the hell do you call it?"

"Negotiation! I hide your little secret, you hide mine. I spill his little secret, you let me off the hook. This *is* Washington, you know. Everyone does it. You should get out more."

"So after your mother counseled you to obstruct justice, what did you do?"

Marcia ignored the dig. "After things calmed down, I wanted it back, but Angie said she'd mailed it to a safe place. I didn't expect her to *mail* it to somebody! I was so pissed, I canceled my appointment."

"Do you know who she sent it to?"

"I wish. Just to someone in Virginia Beach. I'd kill to get it back. Sorry, bad choice of words. I was crazy to let my mother talk me into dumping it on Angie."

"Maybe you were so angry you went to the salon after it closed and confronted her and things got out of hand."

"What are you saying? I didn't kill her!"

"Why are you in Virginia Beach?"

"I needed a break. My mom has a place at the beach. But I never went to the salon."

"Did you see Sherri Gold?"

"No! I hate Sherri Gold. God, Lacey, I thought you understood." Marcia hung up.

Lacey decided there was no more putting it off. It was time to write about Dead Hair Day Number Two. She owed it to Tammi White to write a fair and accurate story. Since she didn't have enough facts to make it accurate, she'd have to settle for sensationalistic and inflammatory.

Lacey glanced over at Mac. He was leaning back in his chair, feet on his desk, wearing a wrinkled plaid shirt, loosened Jerry Garcia tie, and rumpled khakis that bore stains from this morning's coffee, upset during an editorial meeting. Mac was reading *The Wall Street Journal*, dreaming of the career he might have had.

The late afternoon brought an air of quiet melancholy that drifted through the newsroom. Spring lay in wait outside, bursting with blossoms and the curious ability to wring despair in newshounds who had ignored too many beautiful afternoons. The azaleas abounded in passionate colors, and roses were exploding up and down climbing vines. But in their accursed climate-controlled cubicles, *The Eye's* reporters could not even open a window to breathe in the warm air, redolent with the aroma of new grass. Soon keyboards started clicking again. Deadlines. Even in springtime there were deadlines.

Lacey tried Sherri Gold's number again. To her surprise the woman picked up. "I have nothing to say to you," Sherri said. *Caller ID strikes again,* Lacey thought. "And just so you know, this conversation is off the record. It isn't background, or deep background. In fact, we're not even having it."

We would have to play this game. Washingtonians! "How about I call you a source and leave out any identifying information, if I happen to use any information I may get from you?"

"Yeah, whatever."

"What were you doing in Virginia Beach?"

"I don't know what you're talking about."

"Sure you do. I saw you. You saw me."

"You're wrong," Sherri insisted. Lacey felt she was stonewalling.

"Outside of Stylettos, the one near the boardwalk."

"You don't know anything."

"You were wearing sunglasses and split as soon as you saw me. Really, Sherri, two women are dead and you're the last person to see at least one of them alive."

"What are you insinuating? Maybe I was there looking for a job. Maybe I have to go somewhere they don't know me."

"Maybe you went to confront Marcia Robinson about the videotape." Lacey heard Sherri suck in her breath.

"You think you're smart, don't you? You're not so clever, Lacey. Besides, the person who should die is Marcia."

"Haven't enough people died already?"

"She wrecked my life! She said I'd be important, I'd make money. Then I got fired!"

"Marcia's not in such a good position herself."

"Are you kidding? She's famous! That's what you did, you and all the bloodsuckers in the media. You made her a star!"

"She's the butt of jokes. It'll never go away."

"Yeah, so what? Everyone knows who she is. And she even got a great makeover. She looks better than she ever did in her life. I went to Angie and I didn't come out looking like Ms. American Pop Star."

"More like Ms. American Porn Star. Is that what you want, Sherri, a makeover?" Even though she said it facetiously, Lacey knew it wouldn't help. The woman was irrational. Sherri ignored her.

"Next thing, she'll be getting paid to be interviewed. Barbara Walters will be moaning about her hard luck and her great hair," she yelled in a high staccato voice. Lacey could imagine the veins popping in Sherri's neck as her face got redder and redder and her voice got tighter and tighter. "Marcia will probably write a book! Marcia will have a talk show! She'll have a future. And I'm a nobody. She ought to be dead, and I mean that sincerely!" Sherri slammed down the phone.

Lacey looked at the receiver before putting it down. The woman had issues, major issues. Could she kill a hairstylist? Lacey had no doubt. Sherri made her skin crawl.

Lacey felt she was getting nowhere and her deadline was pressing in on her. She thought of another approach. *Egging a killer on—dangerous, stupid, or both? Both.* Maybe he, or she, would give her more to go on. "Okay, Hair Ball, here goes."

CRIMES OF FASHION

It Was a Hostile Makeover

by Lacey Smithsonian

The worst haircutter in the area has just doubled his clientele. By one. This razor-cut specialist may look like anyone else, but he's got a dirty little secret: His clients don't leave

> the salon alive. "Suicide" is the usual ruling. But these suicides are assisted. Brutally.
>
> He thinks his secret is safe. He thinks nobody knows. But I know and others know. This sleazy slasher has killed two women in the beauty trade. He's made their deaths look like suicides, and he thinks he's pretty clever. But he's not. He wants to brag about it. He's stolen their hair. And he sent me a message care of this newspaper.
>
> But now I've found out the killer may really be interested in something else the victims had. A videotape that may or may not be linked to the ongoing congressional follies. . . .

Lacey was way over the line on this one. She didn't care. She added a note at the bottom:

> Confidential to "George." You wanted the hair. You got it. What else were you looking for? Contact "Crimes of Fashion," *The Eye Street Observer.*

Mac read it. He rubbed his eyes, held his chin in his hands the way he did when he thought about the reaction from publisher Claudia Darnell, and studied Lacey.

"A hot videotape? Got a couple predictions for you, Smithsonian. I see another visit from the FBI in your future. And we're going to have another little chat about telling your editor the whole story."

It turned out to be a long evening. Later, she got an e-mail from Trujillo, who did a second read for Mac.

Let me know when the Demon Barber of Dupont Circle comes calling, was all he wrote.

Chapter 21

She wasn't surprised to see FBI Agent Jim Thorn sitting by her desk Friday morning when she arrived at work. But she couldn't stop herself from sighing deeply. *Call Claudia, or Mac, or just wing it?*

"Sorry to wring so much pathos out of you this morning." He had a copy of the day's column in his lap. *Agent of Doom* passed through her mind. He looked very clean and neat, as if his mother had dressed him. "Can we just chat without turning it into a summit conference?"

Wing it. "What can I do for you?" Lacey asked.

"Nice decor you have here." He was sipping a cup of coffee, no doubt supplied by Felicity, who was making cow eyes at him.

They had a polite discussion that didn't last long. The column had told Thorn most of what he wanted to know: that a scandalous videotape did indeed exist and it was traveling.

"And your sources are? . . ." Thorn inquired.

"My sources are unnamed and shall remain so."

"It was worth a try." Thorn smiled. "I'll be in touch." On his way out he turned. "You seem to have a knack for encouraging people to talk."

"Just lucky, I guess."

"Maybe you could give me some pointers." She laughed at that. "Lots of people just clam up when they meet me," he said.

"Imagine that."

"How about dinner?"

"I don't think so. Thanks."

"Perhaps some other time." He left. Lacey gave him points for not pushing it.

She checked DeadFed dot com. Sure enough, there was a flashy headline: "Sex, Death and Videotape: Fashion Reporter Traces Pattern," and a link to her "Hostile Makeover" column.

Her voice mail carried a message from Detective Harding in Virginia Beach. He reported that Tammi White's death had not yet been ruled suspicious, but her column allowed him to get a search warrant for the salon. "One step ahead of the FBI," Harding said. He also mentioned that he had lectured the stylists at Stylettos on taking extra security measures. "Just so you'd know we do care about crime down here in Virginia Beach." Harding sighed. "I wish you'd leave that nasty scandal of yours up north."

Another message came from Nan, the spunky stylist with the big Bronze Bomber. "Lots of excitement today. Cops showed up with a search warrant and snatched all our videotapes. A little bird says they aren't going to find what they're looking for." *So Nan knows the videotape isn't in the salon.* No doubt, she had already searched for it. Maybe Tammi White destroyed it? Or maybe the killer had it? "I'll see what I can find out," Nan promised.

Stella also weighed in with a plea to be careful, and she swore she knew nothing about a sleazy videotape: "I must be slipping. Usually I'd know all about stuff like that."

Brooke's message was comforting. "Lacey, what on earth do you think you're doing? Call me, I know where you can get a Kevlar vest."

Kevlar: Bulletproof, but is it style proof?

It was still early when Lacey left the office that afternoon with a copy of the latest "Crimes of Fashion" column in her hand. She crossed the alley to reach the parking garage where her car sat, finally fitted with new battery, starter, and alternator. She did not notice the silver-gray Jaguar waiting for her. The Jag's engine roared and she caught sight of Boyd Radford. She groaned. She was sick of everything about him. If she never wrote another word about a hair salon or hair or dead stylists, it was okay with her.

Radford stepped out of the Jag and waved a copy of the paper as if it were a cudgel. "I told you not to write about this!"

"You can't tell me what to write."

"You don't know anything about it."

"About what? The deaths or the videotape? You should be thankful I left out your starring role."

"You can't write this shit! I don't know anything about a videotape!" he screamed.

Radford looked bad. His eyes bugged out and a vein throbbed over his right eye. His hair was slick with sweat and stuck down over his shiny forehead. He waved the paper; her column had been circled with a big black pen.

"Those women did not kill themselves and you know it."

"I don't know why they're dead! It's not my fault." His voice was hoarse.

"What are you hiding, Boyd?"

He grabbed her arm roughly. "You keep your nose out of it. Or you'll get it cut off."

"Are you threatening me, Radford?" At this close range she smelled alcohol on his breath. Lacey pulled away, but she stood her ground.

"I'm promising you trouble." She pushed past him. He threw the paper at her. "You mention my salons in this piece of garbage again, and there'll be hell to pay. Do you understand me? Hell to pay!" He slid back into the gleaming Jag and shot away, his tires squealing.

She was shaking. She had to sit in her car for fifteen minutes listening to Mozart and breathing deeply before she trusted herself to drive. She thought about telling Vic. Maybe Vic could joke about it, make her forget her troubles. Or deck Ratboy. After all, that's what friends are for, right? Maybe Tony, but he'd already left for the day. She had other friends, but they would only freak out and tell her useless things, like to remember to lock her doors or complain to the Better Business Bureau. Brooke would suggest a restraining order. Anyone at *The Eye* would tell her to grow up. You're not a real reporter if you don't piss people off, she reasoned.

When she got home, there were four messages on her machine, three hang-ups and one call from Vic Donovan, from whom she had not heard more than a grunt since their amateur science project with luminol. Of course that was only a little more than a day ago. It just seemed like a lifetime had passed since then.

"Lacey, just what the hell do you think you're doing with that column?" Donovan sounded pissed off, like he was chief of police again.

Wow. I can't believe men read my column. First Radford, now Vic. How embarrassing.

"You're setting yourself up as a target for this nut, and it's a damn stupid thing to do. Did you really do this on purpose? We've got to talk. Now. It's Vic. I mean it, Lacey. Call me."

She needed to get out of the apartment. It felt stuffy and confining. She needed to be somewhere without a phone. She changed her clothes, hurling what she'd worn that day onto the bed. She threw on some comfortable light blue cotton slacks and a soft white V-neck sweater, and new white sneakers that she hoped would not blister her feet.

She headed down the bike path alongside the George Washington Memorial Parkway toward Mount Vernon, heart pumping. All her disjointed thoughts settled while she marched at a steady pace. The rhythm of her footsteps put a comforting distance between her familiar surroundings and the world of Stylettos, full of possible killers.

She strode through Belle Haven Park, past the marina, and turned off the main path into Dyke Marsh, a wetland wildlife preserve. Small waterways wound through the marsh, opening up vistas on the Potomac, where trim sailboats were anchored waiting for their absent owners. The path was green and quiet. The panic that had set in with Ratboy's rant was easing. Damp earth smells tickled her nose and she felt lighter and lighter the more she walked.

Farther down into the green woods, signs of the last storm were still evident. Nature had waged a small war on itself. Two huge oaks were uprooted and they lay angled across the path, their roots splayed out in sunbursts reaching heights of eight and ten feet, their trunks three feet and more across. Park rangers had yet to clear the path with chain saws, forcing walkers and joggers to climb over or go around them. Lacey could see rough new trails, but she chose to climb over the first of several large limbs. In spite of the damage, blossoms still clung to some of the bushes, scenting the air with honeysuckle. Lacey drank it in, ignoring everything else in her need to forget the menace of Radford's angry threat.

She heard a twig snap behind her as she climbed over the damaged tree. A leather-gloved hand abruptly closed over her mouth and another, the right, grabbed her around the waist. Lacey struggled as she was dragged backwards toward the dense woods. She assumed it was a man, but not a huge man. Her first thought was that it was Boyd Radford, but she didn't think he had the courage. Maybe he had sent a henchman? The stranger spoke in a raspy growl, obviously trying to disguise his or her voice.

"Careful. I have a straight razor. Wouldn't want to bleed all over that white sweater, now would we? Wouldn't want a hostile makeover, would we?" She kept her hands wrapped around his arms. Her assailant forced the razor up to her level of vision. She froze. He flicked it open with a quick flash of the wrist. The blade riveted her attention. Lacey tucked her head down so he couldn't get at her throat.

"You wrote about me."

Lacey tried to scream into the glove.

"Remember? I sent you a souvenir."

With a surge of adrenaline, Lacey bit down hard into his wrist above the glove. He yelped and reached for her hair, grabbed a hank in front and pulled. The razor flashed past her eyes. "A souvenir for me," the stranger said. Lacey shrieked. She formed a fist with her right hand and slammed her elbow back into his solar plexus. He grunted and let go. "Bitch!"

Loud barking somewhere close on the trail startled them both. A large yellow dog bounded toward them, stopped, and growled. Her assailant pushed her face-forward into a mud puddle. She turned over and slid in the slimy muck, catching a glimpse of a figure clad in black, wearing a black ski mask, backing away from the growling dog. Lacey grabbed a rock and threw it at him, glancing it off his shoulder. The dog barked again and Lacey screamed at the top of her lungs.

"Bastard!" The figure in black vaulted over the tree trunk and disappeared into the bushes. "Good girl," she said to the mutt. The dog licked her face and sat down, panting at her until its unseen owner whistled it away.

Shaking, she ran her hand through her hair. The creep in black had sliced off a lock right in front. The spiky edge he had left was no more than half an inch long. Slowly, she rose to her feet, not hurt, but shaken and trembling. She was covered with sticky brown muck. *Perfect day to wear white, Lacey.* It was only later that she realized someone had tried to kill her.

Reporters do occasionally receive death threats, usually in the course of doing something brave, like covering a war zone, or exposing a crime boss. But not LifeStyle reporters. Not Lacey.

"Good God, I cover fashion!" She said it aloud to the cardinals, who had not yet shown her their red coats. She gave up trying to brush off the mud and walked to a pay phone at the marina to call the police. "The assailant wore basic black and I look like the Swamp Thing," she lamented.

It was difficult enough for Lacey to make the report to the Park Police without having the officer question every word she said. He was young, tall, clean-cut, and earnest, with a spray of freckles across his nose and cheeks and clear celadon eyes. His hair was close-cropped, military style.

Lacey was acutely aware that she was covered with brown slime and had a ragged edge of hair angled across her forehead. Her makeup was smeared and she had visions of how she looked to this six-foot-two, solidly muscled officer who was wearing his professional cool-and-detached face. She tried to explain that her articles had apparently provoked the attack. The words seemed to stick in her throat.

"I write a column on fashion for *The Eye Street Observer*. 'Crimes of Fashion.' "

"Fashion, ma'am?" His eyes measured her. He stopped writing and folded his arms. Lacey grabbed her savaged forelock.

"You don't think I did this to myself, do you?"

He turned his attention to his report.

The Park Police looked for the assailant, but found only broken branches and smeared footprints that disappeared at the paved bike trail. Lacey called a taxi to take her home from the marina, all of a mile. The charm had gone out of the afternoon.

* * *

Once the hot water and shower steam hit her and the music of Joan Armatrading was loud in the background, Lacey let the tears fly. She sobbed, she screamed, she swore. She scrubbed her skin till it glowed lobster red. Finally, exhausted but purged, she knew the tears were over, though she was still muttering "bastard, filthy bastard, filthy bastard pig," and variations on that theme. Her eyes still stung and they were as puffy as golf balls, but she was in one piece. She wrapped herself in a soft turquoise dress, long and gauzy.

She switched on the bathroom light and peered again at the short chunk of hair the bastard's razor had left. She looked like a mental patient. She considered calling Brooke, but at the moment she didn't need her friend to ratchet up her anxiety and paranoia. She marched into the living room, picked up the phone, and dialed the only person who could help.

"Whoever this is, it better be good." Stella giggled. She sounded otherwise occupied, but Lacey didn't give her a chance to explain.

"Stella, this is Lacey. I'm really sorry to call you at home but this is an emergency."

Her stylist was now at full attention, concern and curiosity in her voice. "Lacey? You sound funny. Are you okay? What kind of emergency?"

"A deeply personal stylistic emergency. Can you come over right now and bring your scissors? I wouldn't ask if it weren't a crisis."

There was a slight pause. "Okay, but you gotta tell me *everything!*"

Within a half hour Stella, the midget car, and Bad Boy Bobby arrived at the apartment. Stella took one look at Lacey's locks and yelped. "Oh my God! Bangs!"

"I can't wear bangs! Besides, these aren't bangs; they're an aggravated assault. Attempted homicide!"

"I think it looks sort of cool. Punk, but not quite there yet," Bobby said. "You know?" Both women stared at him.

Stella explained, "But it's not her own personal style, Bobby. She's not a 'bangs' kind of girl."

Lacey told him there was fresh beer in the fridge and he could help himself, which he did. He carried a couple of Dos

Equis out to the balcony and let the screen door slam. "Hey, you can see the river out here. Cool. You got a telescope?"

Stella steered Lacey toward the bathroom. "Nice place you got. Kind of a time warp. Looks like you."

"*I* don't even look like me," Lacey said. "Not bangs. Please, anything but bangs."

"Sorry, Lacey. Unless you want a buzz cut like mine, all I can do is bangs or one of those short-on-top, long-in-back things. Not exactly a feminine look, if you get my drift."

"A Mullet! Oh God, the haircut that dare not speak its name. Never!"

"Come on. Sooner or later, it'll grow, but until then that means bangs. And if you got some tea bags, put 'em on your eyes to take the puffiness away."

"I look bad, don't I?" Lacey asked.

"Not bad, exactly." Subtlety was never Stella's strong suit, but she tried. "More like you had a rough day, a really rough day. At least you didn't wind up with slit wrists. Do you want to talk about it?"

Lacey glanced again at the short fringe her assailant had left. "That dirty bastard is going to pay!" She didn't know how and she didn't know when, but she knew someday she'd unmask him and pay him back, double or nothing. She only hoped he wasn't already bald. "If he's bald, I'll scalp him. To the bone."

"I can give you decent bangs. They'll be feathery and reach your eyebrows. They'll cover the damage as the shorter hair grows, and I can make that look less chunky. I promise I won't give you that first-day-in-kindergarten look." Stella again quoted the unofficial Stylettos motto: "It'll grow. Now, which dirty bastard would this be?"

Lacey recounted the attack as Stella fashioned her new bangs, camouflaging the vicious razor cut. Stella also "shaped up" the style, meaning that Lacey lost another inch and a half on the bathroom floor.

"Give me the hair, Stella. I want to save it."

"What for?" She looked skeptical.

"I don't know. DNA testing. So I can discover my true identity. Just humor me, okay?"

Stella pressed the trimmings into Lacey's hand. "If you used that deep-conditioning treatment I recommended, it wouldn't be so dry on the ends," Stella scolded.

"I do use it!"

Stella gave her a pointed look over her head in the bathroom mirror. "Dry ends. Okay. You're flat on your face in the mud, then what?"

Her stylist was relishing this tale a bit too much, Lacey thought. "It was the killer. It had to be."

"You're lucky you're not dead in a ditch. And bald. Not even bangs could save you then."

"This is not for Saturday-morning broadcasting."

"My lips are sealed."

"I mean it, Stella." Lacey pointed out that the killer could be in the salon working right next to Stella, or even a client. Or the boss.

"Lucky for me, my hair's too short for this pervert." Stella ruffled her short spiky 'do in the mirror and grinned. "I attract my own kind of pervert."

Bangs and a shorter, fluffier hairstyle reflected back at Lacey from the mirror. It was now more Betty Hutton than Lauren Bacall, more *Incendiary Blonde* than *The Big Sleep*.

"I know it's a little more screwball comedy than film noir, like you like," Stella said. "But it's nice. Really."

It's too cute, but not that bad, Lacey thought. Stella was amazing. This woman, who somehow had accidentally become one of her closest confidantes, never questioned that a sudden hair crisis was not the most important thing in the world. She dropped everything, packed her styling tools and boyfriend, and flew to Lacey's aid. Lacey felt humbled. And all Stella wanted in return was a beer and every single, excruciating detail.

"And Freckles, the park ranger, your little Mountie, was he, like, totally cute?"

The phone rang and Lacey let the machine pick up. It was a worried Brooke. "I have to be out for the evening, but have your machine call my machine. I want to know that you haven't been snatched by a Man in Black or something equally dastardly."

"She's a little spooky," Stella said. "But you should call her anyway, so she won't worry. She might just pop on over, you know. I would."

Lacey did as Stella suggested, leaving Brooke a message that they would talk tomorrow. Stella made herself at home with the fridge and passed cold beers around. They opened the olives, sliced some cheese, and found the crackers. Then they retired to the balcony with Bobby, who was peering down the river with a pair of binoculars out of his backpack. "You really need a telescope, Lacey. I could help you buy one. I was an astronomy major once."

Before Lacey could ask what on earth he had switched to, Stella scolded her. "Stop playing with your hair; you look fine. Did you call Vic yet?"

After Vic's gruff phone message, Lacey wasn't up to talking to him. She had egged the hair ball on, as he had warned her, and it had worked rather too well. Now she was shorn of both her hair and her dignity.

"I-told-you-so's are too hard to take right now."

"The power of the press. But still, Vic ought to know."

Lacey warned Stella not to call him, either, and not to blab about her adventure in Dyke Marsh, noting that it was a police matter. Stella reluctantly agreed; Lacey realized the spirit was willing, but the mouth was weak. She knew the whole story would get out. It was just a matter of time. Vic would find out. She wondered if she should tell Mac or if he would hear it from someone else. He would alert Tony, the whole newsroom would know, and he would take the story away from her. It would be a huge embarrassment and all they would say is, "Lousy fashion beat gets a death threat! Can you imagine that?"

Stella was dying to tell Lacey her own secret. "Vic's not home tonight, anyway."

"Are you keeping his social calendar these days, Stella?" Lacey's appetite suddenly abated.

"No, but for your information, the ex–Mrs. Radford dropped by the salon and mentioned seeing Mr. Victor Donovan tonight. Business, I'm sure. Business that required a facial, a French braid, and a fresh manicure: Man-eating Magenta. If you don't make a move on him, Lacey, he's a goner. I've seen her work before."

"He's not interested in me anyway. So what if he prefers that raven-haired vixen?" Lacey ran her fingers through her hair.

After Stella and Bobby left, Lacey actually dialed Vic's number, her need to tell the story was so strong, but she got his machine and hung up. *Go to bed, Lacey. It'll grow,* she told herself. She didn't think she would sleep, but she had not counted on the Dos Equis and the sheer exhaustion that overtook her. Within minutes, she was out.

Lacey Smithsonian's

FASHION BITES

It's Your Hair. Stand Up for It.

Why would a seemingly intelligent woman walk into a hair salon, throw up her hands in despair, and tell an eighteen-year-old stylist with rainbow-striped hair and multiple facial piercings to "Just do what you like"? I have no idea. But it happens often enough to merit comment. Maybe it's because she thinks vanity is wrong, but public humiliation is good for the soul. Maybe she has no spine, or maybe she's too darn optimistic about what mere scissors and styling implements can do in the hands of an adolescent sociopath. The result: a hair disaster that only Medusa could laugh off. Remember, once you're the victim of a bad haircut, it's too late. All you can do is wait. It'll grow.

The first—and last—rule of getting what you want is this. Be clear, very clear, about what you want, and stick to it. Discuss the look you really want, not the one your stylist wants to experiment with. Bring photos, use hand gestures if necessary, and don't be afraid to say STOP if the haircut is turning too scary. If you want to have it your way, also beware of:

- Excessive flattery that can only be false: "Honey, you are so gorgeous. All you need is a change. Let me free your inner vixen."
- Insults to show stylistic superiority: "What shampoo do you use? Janitor in a Drum?"
- Occupational hazards: brain damage from hair spray, dyes, and perm fumes; carpal tunnel syndrome from rolling perms and holding vibrating hair dryers; and of course, delusions of artistic grandeur.

Follow these tips and you can improve your odds of getting what you asked for. But even if you get what you want, it may be sending a message you don't want. Have you ever wondered what your hairdo is telling others even while your lips are sealed? Here's a small sample:

- The Rainbow Mane—Behold, I am a peacock, strangely proud and proudly strange!
- The Haystack—Conditioner? I don't need no stinking conditioner!
- The Layered Rat-Chewed Shag—My stylist said this would look, like, totally cool.
- Frosted Streaks, Dark Hair—I think zebras are pretty. Don't you?
- The Daily Ponytail—My hair in its full glory is too wondrous to waste on you.
- The Perfect Sleek Blond Tigress—I'm so high-maintenance you couldn't afford me.
- The Washington Helmet Head—Control. It's all about control. Mine.

So, what is your hair saying about you behind your back? Are you listening?

chapter 22

Incessant pounding on her apartment door woke her up. It was nine a.m., according to the clock next to her bed. Saturday morning. She staggered to the tiny foyer wrapped up in her white satin robe, grabbed a pair of sunglasses to cover her puffy, bloodshot eyes, and peered out the peephole in the door. It occurred to her that maybe it was Vic, who was known for his early-morning forays into her life. But it never crossed her mind that Tony Trujillo would show up. He obviously had eluded the highly effective building security system, like every other visitor she'd had lately.

"I know you're in there, Smithsonian. Open up. I come in peace."

She unchained, unlocked, and slowly opened the door, her eyebrows quizzical above the tinted lenses.

"This isn't exactly your neck of the woods, Trujillo. I didn't think you ever left the District."

"I crossed the Big Water just to see you."

"No doubt you saddled up your Mustang?" Lacey had heard about, but had never seen, his new wheels, a special-order black convertible with a white ragtop.

"Exactly." He appraised her attire. "Very glamorous. Do you always do the movie-star routine around the house?"

"Always. You're not even in the door and you're already irritating me." She smoothed her hair, trying to calm it down. Trujillo wore tight blue jeans, black snakeskin boots, a blue work shirt, and a black leather jacket. He looked terrific and he knew it.

"Invite me in. I can be even more irritating." He entered the apartment, wandered through the kitchen and around the living room. "Fascinating police report this morning."

"Any particular jurisdiction?" *Oh God, he knows.* But after all, there were the U.S. Park Police, any number of city police, Virginia and Maryland state police, District police, federal police, Metro transit police, and more. *No, he knows.*

"Park Police, Dyke Marsh," he said. She sighed. Someone had called him. Trujillo would not be perusing a Park Police blotter ("Man Chases Duck") without a tip-off. "I guess you really got to the guy," Tony said. He suggested she get dressed and they go out for coffee. "And wear something casual, Smithsonian. It's Saturday. No need to dazzle your adoring fans."

The bedroom door slammed, leaving him in the living room while she dressed. Her mud-soaked clothes were in the laundry basket, a filthy reminder. She felt dangerous and on edge. No one from her office had ever been in her place before. Trujillo was an intruder into her territory. At least he cared—about what? The damn story? She set out a pair of clean jeans and a light blue sweater that hugged her curves.

"I'll just make myself at home," Trujillo yelled as she dashed from bedroom to bathroom for a quick shower.

"Don't you dare," she yelled back before closing and locking the door. She gritted her teeth as she stepped gingerly into the spray, which wasn't yet hot.

Only after she put on makeup to camouflage her tired eyes and scrunched some waves in her hair did she feel like facing him. The hair came out tousled, the eyes smoky. Satisfied that she looked as dangerous as she felt, she emerged from her steamy sanctuary to find him poking into Aunt Mimi's trunk.

"Hey, get out of there!"

"There's cool stuff in here. Your own 'way-back' machine, like in the cartoons. Now I know where you get that kooky Smithsonian style."

"Out. Now."

He shrugged and gave her a smile and a wink. "I'm a snoop. It's my nature. It's my job."

"That's enough, Newsboy," she said.

"Don't worry. Your secret is safe with me." Reluctantly, Trujillo put the lid down. He looked her over and she thought she saw something like concern in his expression. "New hairdo, Lacey? Good job. You can't even tell where he cut it."

"So, that's in the report?"

"Cop logs are a unique literary form, you know. Sort of a minimalist, stream-of-consciousness style, but I got the gist of it: Masked assailant snipped off chunk of hair, was interrupted by barking dog, and ran off."

"Hey, I bit the bastard and elbowed him in the gut too. It wasn't just the barking dog."

"That wasn't in there. They gave the dog all the credit."

Where on earth does Trujillo get sources who call him at home? She was suddenly aware that her body ached all over. Her shoulders sagged. She leaned against her sofa.

"I bet you need something to eat. I'm buying. By the way, your hair, it looks nice. Sexy." Trujillo seemed to be one of the few men in Washington unafraid of a volatile word like "sexy."

"Razor cut," she said. "The latest thing."

Lacey wanted to walk into Old Town—it would be faster than parking—but Tony insisted on driving his Mustang so she could lust after it. They decided on Bread & Chocolate, a bakery and café on King Street, for breakfast. Lots of bread and sweets under glass up front and tables in the back. The aroma of fresh coffee filled the air. *There must be something about me that makes men want to buy me food.* They ordered cappuccinos, baskets of bread, and plates of cheese. It was destined to be a comfort-food weekend.

"Lacey." Tony used her first name only when he wanted something or when he was contrite. "I'm really sorry. I had no idea the guy would go after you physically."

She savored her coffee, both hands wrapped around the mug. "It wasn't your fault. It was my column. My idea." She was a grown-up; she took her own licks. She made a mental note to pick up some muscle rub.

"But I told you that you should write it."

"It was my idea before you suggested it. No use blaming anyone else." Lacey was not going to let Tony take credit for it. She grabbed the last piece of olive bread away from him as he reached for it.

"I just thought he'd write you another love letter. I never thought this would happen." Tony pulled out his card and wrote his home phone number and address on the back and slid it over to her side of the table.

In a loud voice, someone said, "Lacey Smithsonian! God, you're *everywhere*. Do you live around here?" Leonardo advanced on her table, eyeing Trujillo, who sat casually against the wall. "Quite the spunky column you wrote. Got everybody all excited. Let me know if you find that hot videotape. I'd love to see it."

"Did you see me in Virginia Beach?"

"No, I was supposed to interview for a management spot, but that plan just got put on hold."

"Well, Tammi did die."

"And it is ever so tragic, Lacey, my dear. I know that, but we must bear up and go on."

"Maybe you should try another salon, Leo."

Leonardo leaned in close to her, conspiratorially. "Actually, and this is just between you and me, and not for 'Crimes of Fashion,' there are plans in the works. If Josephine's property settlement ever comes through, I'll have my own salon. My own name on the awning."

"What's the problem?"

"Boyd. He's stalling."

"So, she's your backer."

"I'll give you an exclusive when it happens."

"You're a peach. Do *you* live around here?"

"No, but Eric does. This is Eric. Say hello, Eric." Eric said hello. He was smaller than Leonardo and delicate-looking. He wore tiny wire-framed glasses, a fresh crew cut, and a beige fisherman-knit sweater. Leonardo, as usual, wore black to set off the dramatic auburn sweep of his hair. He looked inquiringly at Lacey's companion. Lacey obliged his curiosity, up to a point.

"Anthony Trujillo. Friend of mine. Tony, this is Leonardo. Just Leonardo." Tony nodded and sipped his cappuccino while Leonardo peered at Lacey's hair, making her squirm.

"Oh my God. Bangs?" Leonardo waggled his finger at her. "I told you to come see me! What on earth were you thinking?" Leonardo stepped closer and fingered her bangs, sweeping them away from the shorter fringe underneath. Lacey slapped his hand away. He arched an eyebrow, but said nothing. She noticed an Ace bandage peeking out of his left sleeve. She felt a chill despite the hot coffee.

"Hurt yourself, Leo?" *Bite marks? Mine?*

"Nothing so exciting, my dear. Carpal tunnel. Occupational hazard from rolling too many perms. And not nearly enough rolling in the hay." He reached for her hair again. She stopped his hand. "Are we to assume the person who did this doesn't like you? It wasn't Stella, was it? Next time, Lacey, see me for a real haircut. Come in next week. I'll cancel someone for you."

"It's not that bad!"

"I didn't say it was bad, exactly."

"She looks great," Trujillo said, half rising. His tone was enough to shove Leonardo right back to his table. Leonardo sat, picked up his menu, and ignored them, although Eric couldn't seem to take his eyes off Tony.

Lacey grinned at Trujillo. "Thanks, pal."

"So, was the guy who attacked you that tall? For example, exactly that tall?"

"I don't know. He was behind me. I was on the ground and I only saw him run away. But I suspect everyone. Including you." She gave Tony the *look.* He picked his card off the table and tucked it into her coat pocket.

"Don't lose this, Lacey. Call me if anyone messes with you. I can be there in twenty minutes."

"Swell. If anyone 'messes' with me, you'll be there in time for the crime-scene photos. 'Hair Ball Claims Third Victim.' "

That afternoon, Lacey finally felt strong enough to face Brooke, new haircut and all. Only this time *she* had the plan.

An incredulous Brooke stared at Lacey's hair. "Bangs, huh? It looks . . . good. It's just so different. Fluffy."

"You hate it." Lacey smoothed it back.

"No. Actually, I'm just glad you still have hair after that little adventure yesterday."

"Are you coming with me?"

"Definitely. I'm in. You want to pull a surveillance on Boyd Radford?"

"I wouldn't call it a surveillance, I just want to know where he lives, are the lights on, are the drapes drawn, what cars are in the driveway. That's all for now."

"Absolutely. He threatened you. Then you were attacked. We just need to collect information on potential suspects. Now, why do you want to take my car?"

"You have a pavement-gray Acura with smoked windows. Sorry, Brooke, but it's totally anonymous. In this town, you could be looking straight at it and still not see it."

"Exactly why I ordered it that way."

For all his money, Radford's house in Falls Church, Virginia, was not all that flashy, with the exception of a grand Southern touch in the Tara-like pillars defining the front porch. The lot was small and the house sat fairly close to the street, which made it easier to watch. Brooke parked between a couple of Hondas and an older Volvo, all gray. It was still light when Brooke and Lacey, both in basic black, arrived there, but night was falling. At dusk, the preset lights at Chez Radford turned on. The house was quiet with no sign of activity. Brooke handed Lacey a pair of compact ten-power binoculars.

"These are adorable. Where'd you get them?" Lacey asked.

"The Counter Spy Shop on Connecticut."

"You're kidding."

"I have an account there."

"And what are those?" She pointed to the large pair of binoculars that Brooke kept to herself.

"Night vision. Second generation. Totally cool and indispensable. But why should I tell you? You won't even carry a cell phone."

"Well, I don't travel with a treasure trove of techie spy toys, no." A movement outside Radford's house caught their attention. Lacey raised the binoculars and focused on a woman at the door, a woman dressed in black. "It's Josephine."

"Who?"

"Radford's ex. She's trying the door with her key. Uh-oh."

"What?" Brooke trained the night-vision binos on the front door.

"Looks like her key won't work. Maybe Radford changed the locks. Hey, I think she just said something bad in French, and I think she made a couple of French gestures. Rude French gestures."

"She looks like a French movie star playing a burglar. And if she's his ex, why does she have a key in the first place?"

"I gather that it's very complicated." Failing to get in, Josephine signaled to someone. Leonardo emerged from the shadows, and at her signal, jimmied the lock like a pro. The door had a sliver of glass on either side, through which Lacey saw Josephine disarm a burglar-alarm system. "I guess he didn't change the code."

"Cool. And I thought this was going to be another lost Saturday night. Where's my cell phone?"

"Why?"

"To call the police."

"You can't do that."

"Lacey, I am an officer of the court. I cannot stand by and witness a crime being committed." Brooke rummaged around for her phone.

"Wait. We don't know whether or not Radford just forgot to give her a key. Besides, they'd hang together if the police got involved."

"You're right. We haven't seen the whole show anyway." Brooke put her cell phone away and picked up her binoculars. An upstairs light went on. They caught glimpses of Josephine tearing through the drawers of a huge antique oak roll-top desk and tossing papers all around. Leo helped, but he was not quite so messy or enthusiastic. "I can't understand people who never shut their drapes, especially when they're tossing the place. Don't they realize that anybody could be out here with binoculars?"

"It would be a shame to cover up those Palladian windows though. Man, she looks really irritated."

"Guess she didn't find what she was looking for."

The lights switched off, and a few minutes later Josephine and her protégé left. Leo's yellow Corvette pulled out of an alley behind the house.

"Well, for what it's worth, I don't think we were spotted," Brooke said. "Want to hang out some more? See who breaks in next?"

"No." Lacey thought that they had probably witnessed the main event, and if Josephine felt safe enough to rummage through the place with the lights on, she probably knew that Boyd was out for the evening. "Let's go."

They decided to visit Josephine's digs, a pricey new town house at Evans Farm in McLean. Josephine beat them there, but she'd been chauffeured home in a screaming yellow 'Vette. Brooke took a circuitous route in the anonymous Acura to be sure they weren't followed. "You may be taking this spy stuff a little too seriously, Brooke."

"That may be true, Lacey, but you'll notice my hair is still untouched."

"You hate my hair."

"I don't hate it. It's . . . nice." Brooke parked where she had a view of the town house's front door. The lights were on and a figure moved behind filmy white drapes. Twenty minutes later, a green Jeep with Colorado plates drove past and Lacey recognized the driver. That familiar sinking feeling hit her. Moments later Vic knocked on Josephine's door.

"Wow, he's a babe," Brooke said. "Any idea who he is?"

Lacey bit her tongue. It was too complicated to explain.

"Just Stylettos' new security guy."

"He could keep me secure anytime."

Josephine, lovely and freshly changed into sleek purple pants and a hot-pink sweater, opened the door. She smiled and kissed Vic on both cheeks, then drew him in and shut the door. Stella's warning about Josephine's man-eating ways came back to Lacey. "Let's get out of here. I need a drink."

"Okay, but just one."

Lacey didn't know yet what value this night's surveillance had, but she knew one thing: She could never tell Vic.

Chapter 23

Like a penitent nun pondering her sins the next morning, Lacey decided to return Vic's call from Friday. She hoped he wouldn't be home so she could just leave a message on the machine; something like, "Hi, Vic. It's Lacey. Got your message. Also got messages from Radford and some guy with a straight razor. Just thought you should know. Bye." Nothing about Josephine's rampage at Radford's. Nothing about Vic's nocturnal visit to Josephine's.

It was ten o'clock Sunday morning, so if he had spent Saturday night with Josephine, as she assumed, he wouldn't be home yet. The thought of Vic with the ex–Mrs. Radford made Lacey clench her teeth. However, it was more likely than imagining Vic Donovan in church, where Lacey had gone that morning, to an early Mass at nearby St. Mary's to light a candle of thanks for letting her live. And another candle for letting her keep most of her hair, too. And a third to be prepared for any more surprises.

She dialed and heard him pick up the receiver and bark. "Yeah!" She was on the verge of hanging up. He barked again. "Talk to me, Lacey."

"Damn it. You have Caller ID. Boy, that figures."

"Of course I do." Now he sounded exasperated. Lacey hated Caller ID. Most of her sources had caller identification. Even pizza-delivery joints had Caller ID, but *The Eye* was too cheap and she refused to have it at home.

"I'm just calling you back," she said.

"You took your sweet time about it."

"Me? You never got back to me about the photos. What's the

rush? You were out gallivanting with the remarkably well preserved Mrs. Radford all weekend."

"We weren't gallivanting. It was work."

"I'm sure it was," Lacey purred.

"Where did you get your information?"

"Stella is an equal-opportunity songbird," she said. Vic emitted some guttural sound. "Besides, you only called me to yell at me."

"And I'd throttle you over the phone if I could. Two women are dead and you invite some slasher to call anytime? Isn't life dangerous enough?"

"Yeah, it's dangerous enough!" On the verge of tears, Lacey gulped a breath of air. She was going to hang up on him. *Damn it, you are not going to make me cry.* "And what about the photos?"

"I've got them."

"How do they look?"

Vic caught a note of desperation. "What aren't you telling me, Lacey?"

Screw you!

"Lacey?"

"I was going to tell you that your pal Boyd Radford warned me not to write any more stories about Stylettos. He said there'd be hell to pay. He threatened me after work on Friday." She rushed it out, then stopped. Damn if she was going to tell him about the incident at Dyke Marsh. There was a moment of dead air.

"We have to talk in person," Vic said.

"Bring the photos."

"I can't. I left them with the blood-spatter guy."

After wrangling about it, they compromised on lunch and a trip to a firing range for a self-defense lesson. That was Vic's idea, or rather his demand, in exchange for his information.

She assumed it would be dirty at the range. She decided on khaki slacks and a safari jacket. The jungle motif prepared her mentally for battle and she was tired of her black burglar outfit. Vic picked her up at noon in the Jeep, and took one long, close look at her, which gave her goose bumps. His face darkened, but his voice was quiet.

"What happened to your hair, Lacey?"

"Don't you like it?" He glared at her. "Stella shaped it up a little, that's all. Friday night."

"Stella wasn't working Friday night."

"My stylist makes house calls. I hear yours does too."

Vic slammed on the brakes and pulled over to the curb. He turned off the engine and set the emergency brake.

"Damn it, Lacey. What happened?" She had never actually seen him really angry before. At least not with her. His eyes burned right through her. Notwithstanding being a journalist, lying effectively was not one of her skills, so she looked out the window.

"I was . . . He . . . There was an incident, in Dyke Marsh. With the Hair Ball. He took a little souvenir with him. . . ."

"He cut your hair?" She nodded. He reached over and touched it, sending chills through her. The moment passed quickly.

Donovan wanted everything: the time, the place, the name of the park policeman, the breed of mutt that interrupted the attack. The wind direction, the color of the mud. Then he wanted to hear it again. She also spilled the tale of the lock of hair and the terse message.

"And you didn't tell me? Or the police?"

"The police couldn't care less and you didn't want to know. Remember? It was 'suicide.' "

He lectured her on the dangers of inciting madmen to foolish actions. "I am not on trial here, Vic," she said. Lacey refused to look at him and only afterwards wondered why she just stayed there and took it, why she didn't get out of the blasted Jeep, slam the door, and walk out of his life. Probably because he would have hunted her down to finish his manly dissertation.

"It was a stupid-ass thing to do, Lacey." Finally, after more insights on her foolish behavior, he turned the key.

"And I thought you didn't care," was all she could manage.

They drove in silence. She suspected that he couldn't find words descriptive enough to explain just how pissed he was. His mouth was set in a tight line and he tuned the radio to a country station so they could fill the silence with songs about busted love, faithless women, and good old American trucks.

He took her to lunch at Anita's, a Mexican restaurant not far from the firing range out in Fairfax County. Finally, it was his turn to talk. But none of it was for publication.

"Radford's really rattled by these deaths, and someone broke into his house last night."

Lacey almost choked on her enchiladas. "Really?"

"He doesn't know what they're after.

"Any suspects?"

He shrugged. "Radford's been spooked lately. Told me he even changed the locks at his house. Should have let me do it. I'd have changed the alarm code too. Anyway, nothing seems to be missing. Whoever it was made a heck of a mess though."

"I need to talk to him and clear this up. I will not be threatened."

"I don't think he was seriously threatening you."

"You weren't there. I'm going to talk with him. Soon."

"Wait a minute."

"I mean it, Vic."

"In that case, I'll go with you."

"You don't trust him?"

"Maybe I don't trust you."

"Very funny."

Vic didn't linger over lunch. He insisted that she learn to shoot a gun in self-defense. She argued that she didn't have a gun and if she did, she couldn't take it into the District of Columbia, where handguns were outlawed, even though every other kid on the street carried one. If Lacey had possessed a gun, she couldn't drag it along in her purse in Virginia because she didn't have a concealed-weapons permit. He produced an application for one. In Virginia, he elaborated, the right to bear arms was considered one of the more important rights, and concealed-weapons permits were available to the average citizen with the proper training in firearms. He recommended it.

Vic didn't need to point out that she had already been assaulted. But he did. The least she could do was protect herself in her own home. And though it was understood, he reminded her that the slimeball knew where to find her: He had followed her to Dyke Marsh.

Lacey asked about stun guns, but Vic sneered. Would she really want to let the killer get that close? She then suggested that a derringer would be small and handy, not to mention adorable.

"Only if you promise to wear it in your garter, Annie Oakley," he said.

The firing range was located in a large, nondescript warehouse complex in the suburban wilds of Fairfax County. It featured a store in front that sold guns and ammo and various accessories. The pleasant aroma of gunpowder perfumed the air, smelling like fireworks, she thought. They signed releases, paid for their time and an extra box of .38 wadcutter target cartridges, and stopped at the door to the indoor target range.

Vic opened his black leather bag and pulled out ear and eye protectors. They weren't allowed on the range without them. Vic had an extra set for Lacey.

"Two of everything, huh? So how many other women do you take out to the range, Vic?"

"Just be good and put them on, Lacey."

Vic was serious. She wondered briefly if he might actually care about her. More likely, he simply didn't trust her not to jump in front of the killer, hollering "Murder me!" They put on their protective gear and passed through to the range. She found the sound deafening even with the ear protectors on, so she added a pair of soft foam plugs, also courtesy of Vic, underneath the earmuffs.

Vic had explained over lunch the essential points of handgun etiquette, which she was already fuzzy about. He reviewed them. They started with a Smith & Wesson .38 revolver, a diminutive Model 60. Lacey was relieved: Revolvers looked more like real guns to her. She was less fond of automatics. He showed her how to open the cylinder, load the cartridges, and click it shut. The abstractions of firearms protocol were coming into focus.

"Treat every gun as loaded. Know your target. Know what's behind it. Know what you'll hit if you miss or shoot through it. Don't point a gun at anything you're not willing to kill. Keep your finger off the trigger till you're ready to shoot." Vic made her repeat it like a mantra.

Her biggest fear was that she would embarrass herself in front of him. After all, she had a history. He clipped a target to a wire and sent it down the lane about seven yards, a "social distance," he called it. She aimed at the silhouette of a man with a red dot in the center of his head and one in the middle of his chest. She prayed she wouldn't hit the floor, the ceiling or her foot. Or Vic. *Well . . .*

He put his arms around her shoulders, cradling her arms and hands around the gun to demonstrate the proper isosceles triangle position. Their earmuffs bumped. Lacey concentrated, lined up the sights, focused on the upper red dot, held her breath, and squeezed the trigger. The recoil startled her, jerking her hands and arms up and back. *Nobody ever has recoil on television!*

"How'd I do?" She had to shout.

"You pierced his ear."

"All right!" She had hit the target and almost hit Mr. Red Dot's head. By the end of the .38 session, they'd shot up all the wadcutters and she was clustering her shots more or less where she intended. Lacey had decoratively pierced various sensitive body parts on Mr. Red Dot.

They advanced to shooting with his customized Colt .45 semiautomatic, which practically knocked her on her butt at first. It had serious recoil, but it was smooth and consistent. Finally Vic brought out his 9mm Glock. She didn't like its grim black plastic looks. But she could shoot with it.

"Damn, Lacey. I think you've got a knack for this kind of thing," Vic said. "You've got good rhythm and you don't flinch. What do you think?"

"I think if the guy with the red dot on his head comes after me, he's a dead man. Problem is, what if he's not wearing the red dot?"

He handed her the .38 Smith & Wesson and watched her clean it, reload it, and unload it to demonstrate her new knowledge. He gave her the gun and carrying case despite her protests. It was hers on loan for as long as she wanted it..

Afterwards, they stopped for chili at Hard Times Café in Old Town. They both ordered the Texas with everything and a couple of Lone Star beers. Marty Robbins was on the jukebox singing about El Paso and Vic was reading the label on the Lone Star.

"What's on your mind, Vic?"

"I think you ought to try to stay out of trouble."

"You're still mad about the column."

"It was a cheap stunt and dangerous, to boot," he said.

"Angie is dead. Tammi is dead. Radford warns me not to

write any more columns about them, after which I get attacked. Am I not supposed to tell the world there's a killer out there?"

"Excuse me, folks. Anything else?" The waitress flashed a friendly smile at the handsome Donovan, who asked for the check. "Be right back with that for you, sir." She was obviously a pro, unfazed by talk of killers over chili.

"I give up. How are we supposed to push this investigation further?" Lacey asked.

"Do you want to push it till you're dead too?"

"I was hoping to avoid that possibility."

"This isn't Dodge City, Lacey. It's not even Sagebrush. Look, you made a police report, and once I get the blood-spatter report on the photos I'll contact the proper authorities."

"Ooh, the proper authorities! That'll take a bite out of crime. So when are you going to unleash the Keystone Kops?"

"After I take you home. But you're going to stay out of it. Got it?"

"Oh no, I'm going to see Radford. His address is in the phone book."

"Still intent on that nonsense?" She didn't budge. "Okay. I'll make a call."

"You think he's dangerous?"

"No. I'm afraid you'll tear his head off."

"Flatterer."

Vic had arranged to take Lacey to meet Radford later that night, at eight o'clock at Stylettos' headquarters. As he pulled into the company parking lot, he warned her, "Now, play nice. And I don't want to see any of this in the paper."

"Ha! Then you'd better read *The Post*." She didn't want to tell him how sick she was of writing stories on Stylettos. Lacey stepped out of the Jeep slowly. It had been a long, exhausting day, and the picture of Josephine greeting Vic played over and over in her head. Never mind the scenes her imagination supplied after the ex–Mrs. Radford shut the door. Not asking him about it was becoming to be harder than asking.

Vic unlocked the front door of the office building. They had just started up the stairs when they heard a woman scream. Vic took the stairs two steps at a time. Lacey followed on his heels. They rounded a corner through a lavishly decorated reception area into Boyd's office, where Josephine was screaming hysterically. Boyd Radford lay face-up across a coffee table, his hand clutching a bronze sculpture of a blow-dryer. His throat was cut. Blood drained onto the floor. Lacey noticed that his hair was neatly slicked back, not even a lock out of place. His eyes were open and Lacey stifled a scream and willed her stomach to calm down. She was not about to be sick, especially with Josephine caterwauling like a wounded banshee.

Although it seemed useless, Vic took Radford's pulse. He looked at Lacey and shook his head. He reached for the cell phone in his pocket. "Can't you do something with her?" He indicated Josephine.

"I thought that was your job." Nevertheless, Lacey grabbed Josephine by the shoulders and shook her. Josephine wouldn't focus. She was surprised to see the imperious Frenchwoman in such a state, her makeup smeared, her hair flying out of her chignon.

"Get her out of here. And don't touch anything," Vic barked at her.

"You think I don't watch television?"

Josephine, noticing Vic for the first time, snatched her purse from the floor where it had fallen before Lacey could safely steer her out into the reception area. "*Mon Dieu,* what a mess. An unholy mess," Josephine muttered. "*Merde, merde, merde.*" She retrieved a mirror and gasped at her reflection. Then she sat down on a leather sofa and went to work repairing the damage. Lacey watched as Josephine used a delicate handkerchief to wipe away the tears. She took a small vial of cream and patted it gently on her face, following that with a dab of concealer. She freshened her lipstick and blush and expertly combed and restyled her hair. Her eyes still glittered from her crying jag. All the while she chattered.

"I just came here to check up on Boyd. He has been so not himself lately. So hard to pin down. I wanted to talk to him about family matters. Our property settlement. He wasn't home, so I came here, went through that door, and found him like that. So horrible."

"Did you touch him?"

"Touch him?" Josephine shivered. "With him looking like that?"

Lacey had to agree the thought was pretty unappetizing. "To see if he was still alive?"

"No. I didn't think he could be alive. His throat . . ." Josephine stopped speaking and looked at Lacey for the first time. "What are you doing here?"

"I had an appointment to talk with Boyd."

"And you came with Victor?" Josephine caressed his name, but her eyes narrowed.

"That's right." Lacey wasn't convinced that Josephine was telling the truth, but police sirens interrupted her thoughts. First the officers came, then the ambulance and the detectives. They took Josephine to a conference room and closed the door. That was the last Lacey saw of her that night.

Lacey's part in the police investigation was relegated to a short statement and a long wait for Vic, during which she made a phone call from an outside pay phone to Tony "Be there in twenty minutes" Trujillo, who wasn't answering his cell phone. She didn't leave a message, but instead called the night desk at *The Eye* with a tip. She knew that she wouldn't be writing the cop story on Radford's murder. She would save her own observations for a later column.

Several hours later, Vic drove her home. They had nothing to say beyond a few polite words of good night. Lacey was almost certain it wasn't her fault that every time she and Vic were together lately, someone ended up dead. But she had a feeling Vic didn't see it that way.

chapter 24

When three people you know turn up dead in a short period of time, others are bound to notice. Even reporters.

Someone had fashioned a large warning sign above Lacey's desk. Bright orange letters outlined in black declared: WARNING: FASHION MAY BE HAZARDOUS TO YOUR HEALTH. Sitting in the Death Chair was a skull wearing a beret with a rhinestone clip and the legend THIS BEAT KILLED ME! YOU MAY BE NEXT! –MARIAH.

Felicity popped up in an oversized red plaid jumper, a white shirt with a Peter Pan collar, knee socks, and loafers. It was a cute outfit for a second-grader. She giggled at Lacey.

"When you walk by, Lacey, bodies fall."

If looks could kill . . . "Well, step right up. Who's next?"

"You're so funny, Lacey. We all thought it was just awful about the attack, the haircut, and all, but your hair is so cute now," she gushed. "I like it so much better this way."

Trujillo must have spilled his guts. He even told them about her hair. Lacey knew coming into the office would be tough, and there was nothing she could do but take it. To fortify herself, she wore a sapphire-blue suit that had been a favorite of Mimi's. The jacket had full shoulders and a nipped-in waist with pearl buttons. The slim-fitting skirt reached just below the knees and featured side kick pleats. She'd pulled her hair back with tortoiseshell combs. The total look had an early Brenda Starr/Lois Lane don't-mess-with-me effect. She hoped.

"You could be some kind of walking occupational hazard," Felicity pointed out. "A carrier, you know? Like Typhoid Mary."

"Oh, Felicity, you witty thing." Lacey wished she felt a little more dangerous, to give her courage. Her comrades in the newsroom all wanted journalism's five Ws: who, what, where, when, and why. And they wanted them "now, now, now." She shouldn't begrudge them their curiosity. But she did.

She glared at Trujillo across the room. He squirmed. "I had nothing to do with the decorating, Lacey, I swear." He had, however, already written the story on Radford's homicide, as well as one on her attack in Dyke Marsh. Thankfully, the story on her haircut was tucked inside the news section at the bottom of the page, next to a tire ad.

"What's this?" she asked, holding up the Radford story.

"I grabbed some background from your columns and the story on the Dupont Circle and Virginia Beach deaths, to make the connection to Radford. Two dead women. Their boss winds up dead. Coincidence? I credit you in the third 'graph."

"Thanks, Tony." She knew she wouldn't have been allowed to write about Radford's death and get it into print. It was Trujillo's beat, but it still rankled. She went looking for her editor.

"Mac, you gotta take me off this fashion beat. It's bad luck. Did you see my desk? Even the reporters think I'm a public menace."

"Nice try, Smithsonian," Mac said. She noticed he wasn't even wearing anything funny today. He looked pretty good. Dark blue slacks, white shirt, muted tie. *His wife must have dressed him.* Mac invited Lacey and Trujillo into his office. He refrained from making cracks about her bangs. Trujillo looked uncommonly solemn, dressed ominously in black T-shirt, black leather jacket, black jeans, black boots.

Mac shut the door. *Now what did I do?* Lacey thought. *Am I being fired?* "Sit down, Lacey." It was an order, but she remained standing. "First of all, I want you to know that *The Eye Street Observer* asks a lot of its reporters, but it does not ask them to risk their lives for a story."

Unless it's a really big story, Lacey thought.

"If you were expecting trouble you should have told someone, me or Tony," Mac said. He drummed a pencil on his desk.

Lacey shrugged. "How could I anticipate an ambush on the bike path? The only threats came here at the paper."

"Threats? As in threats plural?"

"The hair and the letter, you know." She hadn't told him about the Radford threat, which happened after work on Friday. Now it seemed pointless to mention it. Suspicion clouded his face, but he let it go.

"After the guy attacked you, why didn't you call me first thing?"

"Trujillo had the story in hand. Hell, he knew about it almost before I did."

"I'm not talking about the story, damn it! Did it never cross your mind that I might care whether one of my reporters lives or dies?"

It never had crossed her mind. She was a reporter, he was an editor, and never the twain shall meet.

"No," she said. He rubbed the back of his neck and glared at her. She wondered what his angle was on this. "I guess it would be embarrassing to lose another fashion reporter, after Mariah. But you could always take a hook and grab one off the street."

Mac growled and smacked his fist on the desk. "That's not funny, Smithsonian. I am very concerned about this! About you! Two women die. You are attacked. Then this Radford character gets himself killed in his own office. Somewhere in the mix is a missing videotape and a federal witness. The police are saying he may have interrupted a burglary, but we all know that's a lot of coincidence for a lousy hair salon."

"But not for Washington," Lacey said. "And what burglary?" She had seen only the headline. Vic hadn't mentioned a burglary. But of course, Josephine had been there, so who really knew? Mac shoved over a copy of the latest edition.

"There's something else you should know," Mac said. "We got the DNA results back. Tony tells me the lab broke its own speed record for him. It's a match." Mac fingered a piece of paper. He slid it to Lacey.

She whistled. "So it *was* Angela Woods' hair." *Of course it was Angie's. Duh.* It seemed like she'd had no rest at all since Friday. The weekend had been packed: an assault, a makeover, Radford's death, and a lecture and a lesson at the gun range. *Several lessons,* Lacey reflected. But this would be one hell of a front-page story over the byline Lacey Smithsonian.

"That's what they say."

Lacey sank down into a chair. "Stupid. Sending the hair. Doesn't this guy even watch TV?"

"The cops will say it doesn't prove anything, in and of itself," Tony said. "And it doesn't. It could be years old. No way to trace the jerk who sent it."

"Of course we'll inform the Metropolitan P.D. what we've got. Courtesy call," Mac said. "They'll thank us and pay no more attention to it. The police response, or lack thereof, ought to be played high in the story. We'll box it on the front page."

"What about the FBI?" Lacey asked.

Mac snorted. "Let them call us." The magnitude of the story was beginning to dawn on her. There was a moment of silence.

Lacey stood up. "Well, thanks for the information, guys. I've got work to do." Her mind was racing, starting with the calls she needed to make. "What's my deadline on this one?"

Mac cleared his throat. "Not your deadline. This one is Tony's. You've got fashion, Lacey, not cops and robbers. Not murders." Tony looked away when she glanced at him. This was exactly what she had been afraid of. They were going to pull the rug out from under her. *The rats,* she thought. *I already paid the price of admission on this story.* "And if anything further develops on the hair killer, or Boyd Radford, Tony gets it. He's the police reporter, after all."

"That's completely unfair, Mac. I'm the one who got the death threat! I should get the story," Lacey protested. "I'm the one who got the hair."

"Yes, you're the one who got the death threat!" Mac seemed ready to jump over the desk at her. "That's why you're off the story. I want you out of the line of fire."

"Don't be ridiculous. I am a reporter."

"Sing me no sad songs, Smithsonian. Life is unfair. I mean it. Stick to fashion and stay out of trouble."

"Boyd Radford's memorial service is tomorrow. I have to be there." Stella had already called her with a full report to go with her breakfast.

Mac was adamant. "Cool your jets. It's Tony's."

"But I know all the players. The stylists trust me. I can put things together." *With a little help, a lot of luck, and maybe divine revelation.*

"Then tell Tony all about it," Mac said. She shot poisonous

looks at each man. "Take it easy, Lacey. You're probably in shock or something. Just write your column, something funny, something light." Something light. As if she could whip up humor like a soufflé, light, frothy, insubstantial. *Is that still what you think of me?*

She glared at him. "It'll be about Big Head Ted, the senior senator from Massachusetts," Lacey said, seizing on one of her most reliable whipping boys. "You might not know it, but Kennedy's tailor must be the cleverest man in Washington and he deserves some credit. For anyone to get that fat head of Ted's to look human is some kind of miracle." Slamming the venerable senator was a sure way to get Mac to spark and Lacey was spoiling for a fight. "If Ted rummaged his suits off the rack at Men's Wearhouse, he'd look just like Bob's Big Boy. With white hair."

Mac loved the Kennedys the way he loved his old corduroy jackets. No matter how frayed around the edges, no matter what dirt was lurking deep in the pockets, he believed that they were always right. He didn't think there was anything funny about either. Often he would let Lacey rant on, but he drew the line at her making sport of the Kennedys.

"Good Lord, Lacey, haven't the poor Kennedys suffered enough?"

"I'm being unfair. Ted Kennedy's tailor deserves a Nobel prize. Anybody who can hide Teddy's tubby torso should tackle the national debt."

"Leave poor Teddy alone. I'm talking about that sizzle-city charity thing on Wednesday. I've had several calls about it. That's right up your alley." What Mac neglected to mention was that the calls were futile requests that *The Eye Street Observer* send anyone but "that Smithsonian woman" who wrote "Crimes of Fashion." Mac didn't care. "You're pissed off. Good. Take it out on them. Give 'em hell."

Lacey stomped back to her desk in a black cloud. Making things worse was a phone message from Vic informing her she was explicitly banned from Radford's service. But he was wrong. This was one service she would attend, one way or another. Being banned from an event made her feel like a real Washington reporter. And better yet to get kicked out.

The last thing she wanted to think about was the stupid fashion show. She'd been dreading it for weeks, ever since Polly Parsons began badgering her to write about the Stylettos angle. She had been writing about little else but Stylettos since mid April, almost three weeks before. *And now I've lost the one story I've sunk my teeth into—and I hope the bastard needs a tetanus shot.*

The charity fashion show was being billed as "Capital Style–Sizzle in the City." *People should know better than to use a word that rhymes with fizzle and drizzle.* Stylettos was still on board to provide hairstyling, but Polly Parsons had mysteriously stopped talking to Lacey and apparently had dropped "Crimes of Fashion" from her mailing list.

The pleading phone calls had come from various underlings of Beth Ann Woodward, the chairman of the Capital Style show. She was determined that nothing would mar her charity event, her moment in the sun, including negative publicity about some insignificant suicidal stylists and now the demise of Stylettos' sleazy owner. It was even stickier because Mrs. Woodward was a friends with Josephine Radford, who seemed to have friends everywhere.

Lacey was familiar with Beth Ann Woodward. She was one of those Washington blondes that people insist on calling beautiful. Many of them marry well, to senators or even secretaries of state. Without the puffy blond helmet hair, the Chanel suits and St. John's knits, Beth Ann could have doubled as a Cabbage Patch doll.

But Beth Ann Woodward was nobody's fool. Only that morning, she had picked up her gold-and-white French-style phone and dialed Lacey's editor herself. The underlings hadn't gotten the job done. She was charming and solicitous and earnest. Her special request was that *The Observer* send some other reporter, any other reporter, to the fashion show. Someone more sympathetic. This tickled Mac's funny bone. He imagined sending Trujillo, or one of the sports writers, or one of the prima donnas on the Hill beat, to slap out some haute couture copy. Perhaps Felicity Pickles could critique the hors d'oeuvres.

"It's a charity benefit, Mr. Jones. Mac," the chairwoman pleaded. "You could be charitable, too."

Mac laughed. There's no charity for the rich—everyone

knows that—especially from the Fourth Estate, the self-appointed champion of the common man.

Mac told Beth Ann she was free to ban Smithsonian from the fashion show, in which case Lacey would be free to write about being barred by the Washington cave dwellers and would undoubtedly savage the show anyway. Beth Ann backed off gracefully.

"Never pick a fight with folks who buy paper by the ton and ink by the barrel," he muttered to himself. It was his favorite saying. He had it framed on the wall.

"But, Lacey, there are strict orders from Josephine. About you and the memorial service. She'd skin me alive!"

"I have to be there, Stella." Lacey cupped the phone closer.

"Lacey, I'm on really thin ice here."

"The killer is on the move. He got Angie. He got Tammi. He got Ratboy. He almost got me. You could be next."

"But that's no fair. I got short hair!"

"Ratboy had a bald spot. Didn't save him." Lacey paused for effect. "Look. No one will even know I'm there—with your help, of course. You're such a magician, Stella."

"What are you suggesting?" Stella stopped cracking her gum.

"Your big chance to really make me over." Lacey hung up, satisfied. The sky, like Mac's face, looked threatening. Mac was a veritable storm center. He was bawling out Peter Johnson for something or other. Lacey grabbed her dark green raincoat and black-watch-plaid umbrella and waited for her moment.

Playing peacemaker, Felicity offered Mac and Peter double-chocolate-chip cookies from an enormous platter she had brought from home. Mac took three, tasted one, and grabbed another. Felicity was so pleased, she took another one for herself. Mac's head turned as Lacey strode swiftly across the office. But she was gone before he could swallow his cookie.

Lacey dodged the smokers littering up the building's entry and tried to hold her breath through Cancer Alley. Passing through this toxic corridor was a group of children from the day-care center next door. Twelve toddlers hung on to two ropes with both hands, walking in a straight line guided by three adult women. One curly-haired lad was screaming in indignation. She didn't blame the little guy. Lacey imagined a headline: "I Was a Prisoner on a Baby Chain Gang!"

An hour later, Lacey gazed in the mirror at a woman in a short chestnut-brown wig, looking a lot like Claudette Colbert in *It Happened One Night.* The new dark red lipstick and sultry eye makeup gave her a distinctly foreign flavor. She also talked Stella into giving her a black Stylettos smock. She added a beret and sunglasses. *Not bad,* she thought.

"My own mother wouldn't know me. Not that she does anyway."

"I wouldn't know you myself. We could cut your hair that way. I like it. Very rich-girl-on-the-run, you know?" Mondays were slow, the salon was empty, and Stella and Michelle, who aided and abetted the makeover, were alone until one.

"No cutting! I'm very nervous about the whole concept of cutting right now."

"Showing up at the funeral like this could be risky. What if Josephine figures out it's you?"

"Stella, there'll be at least a hundred stylists from all over the company there," Michelle pointed out. "And Josephine doesn't waste her time looking at other women. She's what they call a man's woman."

"Yeah, she's a Vic Donovan kind of woman."

Lacey refused to take the bait. "I've been thrown out of better places than this. Goes with the territory."

"Well, don't say nothing while you're there. I can't disguise your voice. And promise to tell me everything, Lacey, all the clues, when you figure it out. You really think the Hair Ball will be there, don't you?"

Stella was so hopeful, Lacey didn't have the heart to express her deep, depressing doubts.

"Stella, you told me yourself that killers always go to funerals. Maybe we'll get lucky."

"As long as we don't get dead."

chapter 25

There was an air of anticipation about Boyd Radford's memorial service. The little black dress was out in abundance on the sunny Tuesday morning at eleven a.m., creating a surrealistic cocktail-party atmosphere. Whether the stylists thought it was appropriate mourning attire or they simply were celebrating Radford's demise, Lacey didn't know, but she enjoyed the not-quite-Washington ambience.

It certainly felt like old home week at Evergreens Mortuary, the place of Lacey's last sighting of Angela Woods a few short weeks before. Unlike Angela, Boyd Radford was not on display. His body had been released from the medical examiner's office and cremated as soon as possible, per the request of his heirs. Approximately seven pounds of his lingering earthly remains occupied a plastic sack in an empty shampoo carton until Josephine could select a tasteful silver urn. For now, he resided in the trunk of his ex-Jaguar, next to his ex-golf clubs.

Many of the stylists were disappointed at this turn of events. They wanted to see him dead, or at least to witness the reassuring testimony of a coffin. Instead, the mourners were all handed a brochure titled *In Memoriam* featuring Radford's last professional photograph, which unfortunately emphasized his rodentlike features, a tally of accomplishments, personal testimonials, and a listing of all twenty-five salons with phone numbers, presumably to keep on the refrigerator as a handy reference. Lacey was surprised it didn't include a Stylettos magnet for the refrigerator door in the shape of the high-heeled scissors logo.

Lacey stood in the back of the chapel with Stella on one side and Michelle on the other. The wig felt like a hot bathing cap with hair. In her somber outfit of black beret, Stylettos smock, black skirt, tights, and sunglasses, she looked identical to at least half a dozen other stylists. Stella and Michelle shepherded Lacey like a lost lamb. Their cover story was that Stella's new stylist, "Claudette," had laryngitis and was under strict doctor's orders not to speak. Every time they said it, "Claudette" rolled her eyes, which, of course, were covered.

No one questioned why "Claudette" wore sunglasses. Stella also wore shades and had encouraged others to wear them as a special sign of respect for Ratboy. "They'll think we've been crying," she explained. "With joy," added Michelle, behind her Ray-Bans.

The widow Radford was so grief stricken she had to employ Vic Donovan as a bodyguard. At least until Boyd's killer was caught. That's what she told Donovan, and that's what Donovan had told Lacey when he called Monday to reemphasize that she was not wanted, invited, or expected at the service. *When will he learn I cannot be ordered around?*

As Vic escorted Josephine up the aisle, he stared at Lacey hard and long, making her nervous. He looked slightly puzzled and she was glad for the sunglasses. Vic shrugged as Josephine's hand closed over his arm with a gentle squeeze of ownership. They took their seats in the front row.

The raven-haired mistress of Stylettos wore a plain black silk dress with a square neckline outlined in magenta piping. The matching princess coat had a band of magenta around the bottom of wide bell sleeves. Josephine also chose a close-fitting hat, worn on the crown of her head above the sleek black chignon. Large diamond earrings and the simple wedding band, retrieved from the bottom of her jewelry box for the occasion, were her only jewelry. She accessorized with black patent leather pumps. Josephine's face bore no obvious signs of tears or lamentations, only a stately solemnity. She played the part of the bereaved widow so well that to mention the divorce would be gauche. Her demeanor suggested a queen in full command of the whole royal shebang.

"She really knows how to dress for a funeral," Lacey admitted grudgingly.

"She's been planning that outfit ever since the divorce," Stella said. "Maybe since the wedding."

On Josephine's right arm she wore Donovan, the perfect accessory. The sorrow of losing her ex-husband evidently required the tall, handsome Vic to console her. Lacey felt a pang seeing them together. *The fox and the hound.*

They made a stunning couple, and Vic even wore a beautifully tailored navy suit, a pale blue shirt, and a subdued striped tie. It was a look Lacey had never seen him in.

Nevertheless, Lacey had to appreciate Josephine's knack for keeping Vic under her control. Other women might lack the financial upper hand, but Josephine was not embarrassed to use that strategy. *Shouldn't take too long,* Lacey thought, and it made her sadder than she expected. Josephine was older than Vic, but still a striking woman. And for all his fine law-enforcement skills, he was a dope about the fairer sex. After all, he knew nothing when it came to Lacey.

She also spotted Tony Trujillo, who was representing *The Eye Street Observer.* He knew Lacey without a moment's hesitation, smiled and gave her a thumbs-up sign. She looked away.

The crowd milled around for half an hour. Then the organist began playing "Somewhere Over the Rainbow," which saved the day. People took seats and the program began. The head accountant for Stylettos, a small, wizened man in oversized spectacles with age spots on his bald head, opened the event with an account of Radford's little-known charity work.

"Tax dodge," Stella said.

Josephine apparently was too overwrought to address the multitudes of little people who kept the cash registers full. But Beau Radford was scheduled to speak. He stood to Josephine's left, and he had also spruced up for the occasion, in an oversized black suit, which must have belonged to Boyd. The white shirt was likewise too large; the French cuffs, fastened with gaudy gold cuff links, fell to his knuckles. His only personal affectation was a blazing blue tie, featuring the cartoon emblem of Superman. He was still wearing the ponytail.

"His hair looks darker and thicker," Lacey whispered.

"Yeah, he must be dyeing it. Thickens the hair shaft," Stella said.

"Looks like he curled it."

"Maybe Josephine permed it," Michelle added.

Josephine fussed with Beau's suit before he got up to speak. She glared at his tie. She whispered in French, but it didn't seem to faze him.

Mild-mannered Beau informed the crowd he would be running the company, along with his mother, as stipulated by the will. He promised to make his old man proud. Beau quietly stepped away from the podium just as Leonardo flew into the hall, looking like a wild man. He was puffy faced, red eyed, and disheveled, his hair matted and sweaty. He had thrown on a dirty black trench coat over a black T-shirt and wrinkled black jeans. Stella shot him a dirty look as he threw himself down next to them.

"Leo, you're late and you're a mess!" Stella whispered. Leo glanced blankly at Lacey. "Hey, what's wrong with you?"

"What's wrong? I've just spent four hours being interrogated by the goddamn cops!" His voice was piercing and several rows of mourners turned to look at him. "They think *I* did it. They think I killed Boyd!" Leonardo's voice soared higher and louder. His diction had slipped back into his old neighborhood. This was no longer the smooth, professional Leonardo, star stylist, but a desperate Leonard Karpinski from Queens, New York. He had everyone's attention, and people began to stand and crane their necks to get a better view.

"But why do they think that?" Claudette asked, forgetting her laryngitis.

"How the hell do I know? 'Cause the cops are idiots!"

Donovan crossed the room like a freight train. He locked an arm around Leo's bicep and lifted him out of his loafers.

"You were told not to come." Two plainclothes Arlington cops were right behind him, and two of Vic's employees moved to screen Josephine.

"You can't keep me out! I belong here."

"Do you want everyone to know you were fired yesterday?" Vic's voice was low and dangerous. A ripple of excitement pulsed through the crowd.

"Fired?" Stella blurted. "Leo, but why?"

"Leo knows why," Vic said.

"I can explain about that shampoo warehouse shit. Josephine! I have to talk to Josephine. She knows what was going down there. Josephine, you gotta give me my job back!" Leo tried to escape Vic's grasp, but Vic marched him out of the room in an armlock.

"This is insane. I'll sue! You'll be sorry. Josephine, you gotta tell them!" The Arlington cops pulled the chapel door shut behind them, but Leo had succeeded in stopping the proceedings in their tracks. Vic returned alone and the organ began again. It was too late. The crowd was on its feet. Nothing was going to get them back in their chairs now.

"So Leo was the shampoo bandit?" Lacey whispered to Stella through the excited buzz of the crowd. "Vic must have caught him and Radford fired him. But what's Josephine got to do with it?"

"What *doesn't* she have to do with? You think Leo killed Boyd for her?" Stella said. "Jeez, I never had Leo as Suspect Number One."

The mysterious "George" had failed to appear, at least under that name. Stella had checked the signatures in the book at the door. *Could Leonardo be "George"?* Lacey wondered. *But why would Leonardo want to buy long hair? And what about the videotape?*

As the service broke up prematurely, Lacey kept her eye on Vic and Josephine, who in turn had her big imploring eyes on Vic. Lacey could only guess what she was saying to him in that mellifluous French-accented voice. Something like: "You cannot leave me alone, you big handsome American man, I am so afraid. Make love to me."

Sex is always the answer in French movies, Lacey lamented. She lost sight of them as she and Stella drifted with the crowd out of the chapel into the lobby, which had doors leading to viewing rooms. The smell of flowers mingled with waxen death while large fans kept the air circulating.

"You coming to the reception, 'Claudette'?" Stella asked. "You still up for it?"

"So far, so good. I'll just get my car and meet you—"

"Could I see your invitation, 'Claudette'?" From behind her, Vic clamped a hand on Lacey's arm and very firmly steered her away from the others.

"Oh, man!" Stella squeaked. "Busted!"

Vic dragged Lacey into one of the Colonial viewing rooms.

It was empty except for the lone occupant, an elderly man in his coffin. She shook Vic's hand off and rubbed her arm.

"Oww. You bully. Save your armlocks for Leo."

"I don't believe you'd pull a stunt like this! After I expressly told you not to come, at the specific request of the family."

"Ex-family. I'm sure she has lots of special requests for you, Vic. Just how many gatecrashers will you toss out?"

"As many as I have to, Lacey."

"It's 'Claudette.'"

"Whatever your name is, you're not welcome here."

"Vic, is it true? Leo killed Radford? And what about Tammi and Angie? What about the scandal angle? Boyd was on the missing tape."

"Lacey, stop playing detective. Please."

"I'm not playing anything, Vic Donovan," she snapped. "I am a reporter and my life was threatened."

His eyes narrowed. He looked dangerous. "Unless you want to be threatened again, I suggest you stay away from that reception. It's a private affair."

Affair being the operative word. "I bet."

"If I so much as suspect you are on the premises, I'll find you, handcuff you, and throw you in the Jeep until Labor Day."

Promises, promises. Lacey backed up and nearly fell into the open casket, catching herself just in time to avoid the cold embrace of a very dead octogenarian. She glared at Vic. She noted the faintest hint of amusement in his eyes.

"Don't flatter yourself. I'm not going. I hope you're happy."

He took one long look at her, lifted an eyebrow, turned on his heel, and left.

"I still want those photos, Donovan!"

He kept walking. She adjusted her beret and returned to the hall in time to see Vic lecturing a defiant Stella and a sullen Michelle. The crowd was thinning. Lacey noticed Beau standing in an alcove with his mother. Josephine reached out her hand to straighten a flyaway strand of her son's hair. Beau slapped her hand and laughed. Josephine sighed and looked away.

Lacey had had enough of Vic, Josephine, Beau, and "Claudette." She needed the safety of her Z. But first she had to make it past the line of photographers outside the funeral home. The media apparently had caught up with the connection between dead stylists and Boyd Radford. She spotted Todd Hansen, who had been sent by Mac. With sunglasses in place, she walked briskly past them. If only she could get away without anyone else unmasking her or ripping her wig off, or making her feel even smaller.

Too late. Trujillo caught up with her just outside the door. "Pretty good show, don't you think? How do you like your friend Leonardo as a suspect? By the way, Mac told me you called in sick. You're not fooling anyone."

She strode past Radford's silver Jaguar and wondered if Vic was chauffeuring Josephine in it now. She didn't want to wait to see. Next to the Jag was Beau's red Camaro, cluttered with air fresheners instead of dice. She watched four men climb into a van across the street, black with smoked windows. They had attended the service and all wore black suits and sunglasses. *Could that be Agent Thorn?* Marcia hadn't shown up, but apparently the special prosecutor was still on the job.

Trujillo was at her heels. "So, what's your angle?"

She whirled on him. "I'm researching what a story-stealing snake wears to a rat's funeral." She took in his choice of wardrobe. "Apparently the snake wears a charcoal-gray silk-blend suit with a black linen shirt and a black-and-turquoise silk tie." She had to admit that Trujillo looked very hot. "And snakeskin boots, perfect for a snake."

"Glad you like them." He was not offended. "By the way, great disguise. Very exotic."

"If it's so great, how on earth did you know me?"

"I've seen those movie-star specs before. I'm your biggest fan. Can I have your autograph?"

chapter 26

In her Z, she ditched the beret, wig, and black smock, leaving the black turtleneck underneath, which made her look, she thought, like an art student. Okay, an aging art student. It occurred to her that a real detective would go to the reception anyway and stake out the parking lot, but the thought of it made her feel like a stalker. Not in the mood to go home, Lacey wanted to be in a crowd that did not include any Donovans, Radfords, Trujillos, or killers.

Overlooking the Potomac, the Jefferson Memorial almost glittered. The air was crisp; the sky was blue. She turned off Fifteenth Street and circled the Tidal Basin. She felt restless.

Why not wander around that new exhibit she'd read about: "The Pursuit of Beauty in America"? Jamie, the stylist, had mentioned that the notorious permanent wave machine, "just like Medusa," was on display. Perhaps she could pick up an idea for her column, now that she was officially off the dead-body beat. She headed back toward the Mall. *So Trujillo gets the story. Fine. Hope it bores him to death. Or maybe he'll be mobbed by stylists. Or smothered by Polly Parsons.*

In the National Museum of American History she was happily undisguised and anonymous. First she dropped in on her favorite display—the First Ladies' gowns.

Low lights illuminated the display cases to protect the ancient gowns from further deterioration. Tiny mannequins represented the diminutive early grande dames of the Capital. Most of the older dresses were muted with age, rendered into barely discernable pastels.

Lacey admired the heroic Dolley Madison, First Lady from

1809 to 1817, and her simple Empire Period gown, delicately hand-embroidered with flowers, butterflies, and dragonflies. She paused briefly to gaze at the exquisite creations worn by Frances Folsom Cleveland, who reigned in the White House from 1885 to 1889. Judging from her laced and beaded confections from Paris and Baltimore, Frances was quite the clotheshorse.

Poor Mamie Eisenhower had been relegated to the distant past. Her famous "Mamie pink" dress was missing, replaced by a claret-red gown of silk damask in a classic Fifties style, cinched-in waist and full skirt.

The last glass case held the gowns of the recent first wives, from Jackie Kennedy on. This display was Lacey's favorite, because the viewing public seemed to feel free to comment as if they were all intimate friends.

"Oh here's Barbara, in royal-blue velvet and taffeta. I just love her," Lacey overheard one woman say. "She wore Scaasi, you know." Women who could never dream of a designer gown of their own were surprisingly familiar with the artists who had fashioned garments for the women of the White House. And all without the help of the notes provided by the museum.

"James Galanos designed that for Nancy Reagan," one woman wearing cat-eye glasses and a bright yellow jogging suit commented. "I didn't like her politics, but I love that white beaded dress." Her companion nodded. "But can you see me in a one-shoulder gown?"

Some fashion statements become untranslatable. Jackie Kennedy's white inaugural gown with its sheer overblouse clearly stumped one teenager in enormous blue jeans and a fringed leather jacket. "What's up with that?" Her friend with a nose ring grimaced. "Clueless. I'm totally clueless." A fiftyish woman gazed at the turquoise dress and full-length overvest of Rosalynn Carter. "She was very frugal, you know," she said to no one in particular. "She wore that dress everywhere."

Laura Bush's sparkling red gown was on display upstairs, in another exhibit on "The American Presidency." Lacey thought maybe she'd catch that later.

Two sturdy Midwestern matrons, one in a baby-pink running suit, the other in baby blue, were dissecting Hillary Clinton's deep violet beaded inaugural gown.

"I can't believe her waist is really that small," Pink said.

"I know. She's got those stumpy legs and she's tried every hairstyle in the book," Blue said. "And have you seen her lately? Good heavens."

"It must be harder than hell to get a good haircut in Washington," Pink said.

"If you only knew," Lacey muttered. Whether it was the hard museum floor or her failure to connect the dots on the Stylettos murders or the debacle at the memorial service, she felt weighed down as by an anchor. She sought out the museum café. She hunched over a cup of coffee, breathing in its aromatic steam.

You let yourself down. You let Stella down. Stella had such faith in fashion clues, style nuances, and the "brilliant" Lacey Smithsonian. Misplaced faith, Lacey concluded. She was no closer to collaring the killer than when she first saw Angela's horrible haircut.

But were there two killers? If Boyd killed the stylists, who was the vigilante who stopped him? Or did he know who the real killer was and get killed for it? Then who killed Radford? *Good God, who wouldn't?*

Lacey tossed her empty cup in a trash can and headed to "The Pursuit of Beauty in America in the Twentieth Century and Beyond." As the exhibit would demonstrate, from Gibson Girls and flappers to hippies, punks, the MTV Generation, and Generations X, Y, and Z, American women had found myriad ways to be attractive and self-confident.

At the entrance, a black-and-white film clip greeted visitors. Suffragettes marched for women's right to vote. Flappers danced the Charleston. And Rosie the Riveter was taking a break at the airplane factory to apply fresh lipstick. Tucking her compact and lipstick back in her overalls, she lowered her goggles and proceeded to rivet those B-29 wings with a smile on her face. At the end of the exhibit, a mirrored wall reflected the viewer's own pursuit of beauty into the twenty-first century. The displays combined both humor and pathos, hitting the highlights and the lengths (short and long) to which women were willing to go to achieve an ever-evolving ideal of beauty.

In the early years of the twentieth century, according to the first display, American beauties relied only on rose water and glycerine and the lightest touch of rouge to help them in their quest. The next display was a replica vintage beauty salon where a Twenties' flapper was defiantly bobbing her hair. The mannequin was happily appraising her new look in a hand mirror. Next to her stood the famous permanent-wave machine, Medusa's sister.

Lacey's view was blocked by a young mother and a chubby little blond boy in the throes of his terrible twos, grabbing at his mother's hair. Lacey heard the exasperated woman say, "Leave Mommy's hair alone." As the woman secured it in a ponytail, she sighed. "I'm just going to have to cut it all off." She scolded and he laughed. She smoothed his hair and he slapped her hands away, giggling.

As they moved aside, Lacey's eye was caught by the long braid that had belonged to the freshly bobbed flapper in the display. It lay on the counter of the replica salon next to a comb, brush, and scissors. The braid was a rich dark auburn, about eighteen inches long, and tied with a pink brocade ribbon.

Saving hair was nothing new, she thought, even the Victorians did it. They made jewelry with it. They used it to add fullness to their own hair in the form of a long braid or fall. A memory clicked in: Josephine reaching out to smooth Beau's hair, a ponytail that was suddenly looking much thicker and darker. And longer. And beautifully curled. Something else tickled her brain. The air fresheners in Beau's car were also tied with ribbons, one red, another blue. *Oh my God. He was wearing hair extensions!* And she knew where he'd gotten the hair.

The mother and her little monster moved on, still fussing at each other. But Lacey stood as still as the mannequins. She knew who killed Boyd Radford and Angie and Tammi. It was as clear as the exhibit in the museum.

Take a neglected two-year-old, raise him in a hair salon, the high temple of hair, watch him grow into an arrested-development geeky teenager, force him to work as a shampoo boy, let him fail at all normal pursuits, like college, and somehow you get Hair Ball Boy, a killer who thinks that women's hair is everything that's sexy and powerful in the world. And if he takes it away from them, then he becomes sexy and powerful too.

The cops who said that Angie and Tammi weren't sexually

assaulted were wrong. They were, but in a different way. For this killer, sexual assault meant cutting off his victim's hair and making it his own.

But he had left clues. *Hell, he had mailed them.* No doubt he also squirreled away the ribbons and combs from the burglary at Angie's, more trophies to wear and admire. He attacked Lacey at Dyke Marsh and took a souvenir. He was saying, "Catch me if you can." He was the mysterious George Something.

He was Beauregard Radford: Oedipus with a straight razor.

She wasn't sure how Marcia's videotape fit in, but it did somehow. Maybe he was on it, or maybe he wanted to put the screws to Ratboy? Perhaps Boyd discovered his son's murderous pastime; he would have been eager to cover it up, to take care of it the way he had taken care of all of Beau's problems. As simple as sending him to another college. That's why he was so frantic to stop Lacey from writing about the women's "suicides." Did Josephine know? Who knew if Beau even had an alibi? But then, no one even considered him a suspect.

Lacey stroked her bangs and the shorter hair underneath. It had to be Beau, but who would believe her? After this morning, Vic would probably never speak to her again. Cops everywhere were apparently blind to stylists being scalped. She could see the glazed looks her half-baked tale of hair extensions and pretty blue ribbons would get from the police. "Is 'Smithsonian' the name on your drug prescription, ma'am?"

She could not share this crackpot theory. No one would believe her. Except Stella. But it was too risky to tell Stella, perhaps even fatal. She might have to tell Mac, but not until she had a better story, not until she had proof. She would just have to find a way to trap Beau and prove he did it.

Yeah, right, she thought. *In what mad universe?*

But first there was the fashion show.

Chapter 27

Like some ancient Celt or an Indian warrior, Lacey decorated her face for battle. War means war paint, and war paint means war. The better she looked, the less anyone would suspect how vulnerable she felt. Bestowing the magical power of war paint on makeup justified her cosmetic rituals. In the eternal war between the sexes, it was necessary to have some advantage, even if it was just the psychic boost of foundation, blush, shadow, liner, and the all-important mascara.

"I gotta go slap on some war paint." It was one of Great-aunt Mimi's phrases that Lacey always loved. It smacked of doing battle with the world at large. The way Aunt Mimi said it made being a woman sound brave and exhilarating. Being a great dame like Mimi meant you looked life in the face and punched it in the nose if you had to. That was why you needed broad shoulders, a straight back, and a little war paint. You put on a smile (with fresh lipstick) and stood up for yourself, by heaven. You went out and fought life's battles and won a few.

Even as a gray-haired old lady, Mimi never gave up her coral lipstick and face powder. At Mimi's funeral, Lacey tucked a brand-new tube of "Hot Sunset" lipstick and a compact of translucent corn-silk powder into Mimi's pocket for her final journey—just in case—so the old dear could have her "face on" to meet the angels.

Her mother caught her. "Is that makeup you're putting in her coffin? Good Lord! Sometimes I think you're as nutty as she was, Lacey."

"I certainly hope so, Mother." Then she leaned down and

whispered to Mimi, "Good-bye, sweetheart, I gotta go slap on some war paint."

She examined her face in the mirror. Mimi would be proud.

On Marie's psychic advice she wore her new wine-colored suit. Actually, Marie had left one of her cryptic messages. She specified red. "I think you'll just be more comfortable wearing red today. Don't ask me why. It just came to me. Red. Talk to y'all later." *What the hell. It couldn't hurt.* The suit, which she had just picked up from Alma Lopez, fit fabulously—nipped in at the waist, with lots of give in the shoulders. She particularly liked the navy accents and plenty of pockets. She anchored a navy hanky in one pocket with a decorative pin of a red cardinal with wings of ruby rhinestones. Mimi had given her the pin years ago. Cardinals were good luck, according to Mimi.

Spread out on her bed were her evening's accessories: navy leather bag, a small notepad and fountain pen, voice-activated tape recorder, Aunt Mimi's opera glasses to view the fashion details on the runway. And Vic's .38, which seemed bigger and bigger every time she picked it up. It was too big for her pockets. She had no shoulder holster, which in any case would have ruined the line of the jacket, and sticking it in her waistband was not an option. The weapon made an unattractive bulge in her purse next to the tape recorder and fell out on the bed when she opened it. *I told Vic a derringer would be the way to go, but no . . .* Anyway, the handgun was also illegal in the District of Columbia, but that didn't stop the murders committed almost daily with guns. And with celebrities in attendance, there would be security and the ubiquitous metal detectors.

Figuring she would be perfectly safe with hundreds of people there, Lacey gave up on taking the gun. Brooke had been badgering her to get a cell phone, but Lacey couldn't stand the idea of people like Mac being able to call her anywhere and everywhere. Besides, she had formulated a battle plan that didn't involve guns or phones. She wasn't sure it would work, or if it was smart, but it was her plan and she was sticking with it.

Beau Radford would almost certainly be seated at Stylettos' table, along with his mother, Vic, some company bigwigs, and Polly Parsons. Without missing a beat, Polly apparently had switched her romantic loyalties from Ratboy to Shampoo Boy,

Stella had informed Lacey the previous evening. She had phoned with an exhaustive post-reception briefing. "You shoulda seen it, Lacey. They were all over each other at the reception, and Ratboy not even cold yet."

"Not cold? Hell, he was cremated, Stella. He was toast."

Lacey had prepared a special note for Beau, which mimicked the hair mailer's anonymous note to her; she had handled it only with gloves, just to add that paranoid Washington touch. *What are you worried about? Your prints aren't on file. Not yet.* To the plain white sheet of paper, she taped a lock of her hair, the hair she had gathered up and saved following her emergency haircut by Stella, and tied it with a ribbon. The note said, "STICK THIS UP YOUR PONYTAIL, SHAMPOO BOY." She tucked the note in an envelope, sealed it, and dropped it in her purse.

One last glance in the full-length mirror told her she was ready.

The Lee Wood Park Hotel in Northwest Washington was the host for Sizzle in the City. Near the National Zoo, it was a grande dame, a monument to travel in a kinder age. Its tall towers overlooked the city, and its lovingly tended gardens exploded with roses and irises in multicolored hues. Lacey took a few moments to enjoy the floral display in the sunset. The delicately scented irises floated on the landscape in stripes of color, from the softest pale yellows to the boldest gold. White and timid pink gave way to vibrant purples. It was a shame to have to go inside.

The proceeds of the show would benefit culture in the District's schools, and apparently culture was a wise choice, judging by the turnout. "Culture in the classroom" had no downside. It was upbeat and positive, no ugliness, death, or wasting disease attached to it.

Lacey passed through the ever-present metal detectors and the scrutiny of two security guards at the entry to the ballroom. The only glitch was that the guard with the clipboard couldn't find her name on the approved media list. Lacey was left to cool her heels for ten minutes while someone on the show committee was retrieved to authorize her entry. *No doubt Beth Ann Woodward's idea of a little joke,* she thought.

At that moment, Beth Ann was praying there would be no important business on the Hill to detain any of her prized models. It was a Washington hostess's worst nightmare to unexpectedly find the guest of honor on the floor of the House condemning some postage-stamp country or voting for a phony tax cut, instead of adorning her exclusive soirée.

Inside the gates, Washington celebrities and fashion-biz insiders could mingle in a secure, guard-free environment. The Cherry Blossom Grand Ballroom was decorated with large murals of graceful flowers and Washington landscapes. Hundreds of pink azaleas in gilded pots supplemented the floral motif. High-priced tables flanked the models' runway.

Surrounding the ballroom was a labyrinth of rooms where the preshow pandemonium was contained. Flipping her press ID out so it showed, Lacey wandered down the hall to get an idea of the layout and say a quick hello to Stella.

Models were prepped first with hairstyling and makeup before being herded into connecting rooms, which had makeshift dressing rooms for men and women and racks and racks of designer fashions.

Lacey peeked into a backstage madhouse where more than a dozen Stylettos stylists were furiously twisting and pinning hair, moussing and fluffing, and generally asphyxiating everyone with hair spray. She caught sight of Stella French-braiding Marcia Robinson's sleek dark hair. Stella waved. Marcia saw Lacey in the mirror and waggled her fingers. Marcia didn't seem to hold a grudge.

"Of course," Lacey said. "You're the surprise celebrity."

"Guess what they're making me wear?"

"Pink?" Somehow Lacey knew.

Marcia nodded. "Hot-pink. Too funny, right? I think it's an editorial comment."

"No doubt." Lacey just smiled. *I will never write about pink again.*

Apparently it was too late to fire Leonardo from the fashion show, or maybe he had talked to Josephine after all, because there he was, cajoling a blond anchorwoman to sweep her hair off her forehead. Jamie, now wearing green braids held in place by multiple butterfly pins, was brushing out a chubby District city councilwoman, who looked alarmed. Assistant Manager

Michelle was performing a last-minute check on the celebrity models as they were ushered into the wardrobe rooms where their dressers were waiting. Designers, fitters, stylists, models, staff, and hangers-on were flitting everywhere.

It was too much. Lacey ducked out and returned to the ballroom. She smiled and waved at Beth Ann Woodward, who curled one lip in response, an attempt at a smile that got stuck on sneer.

Lacey located the Stylettos table and casually dropped her note in the chair reserved for Beau. She found her seat across the room, from which vantage point she could observe the young heir opening her note. If she were completely wrong about Beau, he would merely think it was from some loon insulting his new hairstyle. But if he were the killer, he would subtly betray himself somehow by his reaction, and Lacey would pick it up with her ultrasensitive nose for nuance and write a searing exposé. *Well, it's a theory.* She sighed.

She took her seat and waited and watched, opera glasses at the ready. Beau soon arrived. He still wore his newly luxurious ponytail. He also had on yesterday's suit, now worn with a black T-shirt. *How hip.* He picked up the note, opened it, and read it. Lacey's stomach lurched. He gazed around the room and spotted her. He laughed and sniffed the lock of hair. Then he licked it.

Gross! Not the subtle revelation she had anticipated. She was nauseous. That was much too easy, she thought, her head spinning. *Now what was the rest of my brilliant plan?*

Lacey watched Polly Parsons switch place cards so she could sit next to him. He folded the note and put it in his breast pocket. He looked pleased with himself and kissed Polly on the mouth. Although Lacey couldn't hear what Polly was saying, she recognized the familiar hand gestures, pulling at her hair, playing for his attention. *Whatever you do, Polly, don't ask him what to do with your hair.* The lights dimmed and the music heralded the show. Vic and Josephine slipped in just before the narration began. Vic looked tired and grumpy. *Hah. Suffer. Tough duty. And please keep your eye on Beau. Maybe I should have told you my theory, after all.*

Lacey tried to watch the show. Even though it was billed as "Sizzle in the City," implying a summer theme, it naturally featured clothes for fall. Collections draped on actual skinny fashion models would alternate with the more well-padded local celebs in Donna Karan and Ralph Lauren.

The show began with Neil Isaacs, a hot young designer whose presence was a coup for Beth Ann. Isaacs' collection was described in the program as featuring "liquid fabrics," which were supposed to hug curves. But there were no curves to hug. The clothes hung like sackcloth over a parade of hollow-eyed fashion martyrs with dour faces and painted purple lips. Hip bones jutted out of the "liquid" fabrics like chicken bones out of soup. Electronic music thudded. She made notes for use in her column.

Everything was offered in "the new neutrals," which looked like the same old dreary Washington pavement palette, as if the designer had washed the rainbow of colors, mixing them in the tannic waters of the Great Dismal Swamp. Pink became dead mauve, light blue became battleship bilge, green became dirty khaki. And "crisp gray" was simply a contradiction in terms. The whole collection could be called "The Death of Summer." In fact, it might be Lacey's headline.

The second wave on the catwalk ushered in the first celebrity model, who was greeted with a gasp from the audience and a wave of laughter. Marcia Robinson waltzed out under the spotlights in her pink suit, carrying Bo Peep's staff, and followed by three handsome men in skimpy lamb costumes. Applause and laughter erupted. Marcia pranced down the runway and winked at the crowd. Lacey surveyed the audience's delighted reaction, and her eyes landed on the Stylettos table. Beau's seat was empty and so was Polly's. A wave of sheer panic shot through her. She had never liked Polly, but she had to warn her somehow that a haircut from Beau would be the wrong 'do to die for.

Escaping from the ballroom as unobtrusively as possible, she fought her way through the backstage crowd. A newsman from Channel Nine was combing over his thin spot and adjusting an egregious gray tie with a geometric pattern. So many reporters *in* the show, so few covering it. The event would score perhaps a paragraph or two from the "Reliable Source" in *The Post* Style section and a half page in the "Party Line" gossip section of *The Times*. A pretty anchorwoman from Fox stopped

Lacey. "Great suit! I love it. Which designer? Are you in the next segment?"

Lacey pressed on. When she ducked back into the styling area, no one was there. No guards. No stylists. No models. She tried to tell herself that Beau and Polly had left for a quick romantic rendezvous. The stone in her stomach said otherwise.

The makeshift styling stations were concocted from conference tables and standing mirrors, lining two sides of the room. Burgundy brocade hotel chairs were scattered everywhere at odd angles, left just as they were when the last models were herded out. Bottles of gels, cans of hair spray, combs, brushes, curling irons, and scissors littered the tables. Towels were casually flung over every surface. And the stylists must have dropped everything to sneak in the back to see the show. They all wanted to see Marcia, Stylettos' star client. They might not be back until the intermission.

Lacey thought she heard a noise in the dressing area and she headed there. She couldn't see anyone; she headed farther back. It resembled an enormous walk-in closet. Racks of clothes nearly lined the walls, blocking the exits. Street clothes were carelessly thrown on hangers and chairs, along with alternate fashion choices that had been discarded. Even the department stores' staffs had abandoned their posts to get a glimpse of naughty Marcia in her pink suit with her lost lambs.

The lights were dim and it seemed too quiet, much too quiet. The hair rose on the back of Lacey's neck, as if a cold wind had picked up and tickled her spine. She checked her tape recorder in her purse, wishing it were Vic's gun.

This is the moment, Lacey, where the stupid heroine goes into the basement even though she knows that the monster is lurking there. The movie music swells— Oh, don't be silly!

She shrugged off her fears and continued, compelled by sheer journalistic idiocy, curiosity, the need to find Polly. Lacey tiptoed to the back of the room. No one was there.

They must have left the ballroom as soon as the lights went down. Before that, the area would have been crawling with models, stylists, dressers, and assistants.

Suddenly, the smell of blood stung her nostrils and made her eyes water. Slumped against the wall, between two clothes racks, half sitting, half leaning over on one knee, was Polly Parsons. Freshly dead. Still warm. Her eyes were wide open in shock and her mouth sagged. A thin cut ran along her throat and made a necklace of blood. Lacey stifled a scream and gagged.

Polly's hair had been hacked off nearly to the scalp. Lacey didn't touch her. It was obviously too late. *So much for my no-gun, no-phone plan. A phone. Got to find a phone. Or a guard. Or Vic.*

chapter 28

Beau could still be there. Anywhere. She bent down to see if he was hiding in the hanging garments, like a little boy playing in a closet. She didn't see anyone. She crept back to the salon, senses tingling.

The makeshift styling salon also looked empty. If she could cross the room, there were phones down the hall and people milling around, even security guards. But then she heard a clinking sound. Someone had thrown a comb against the closest mirror. Lacey turned to glance into it. He was behind her.

Stupid move, Lacey. You're in the basement now. And here's the monster.

Beauregard Radford was waiting for her with a grin on his face. He was holding a bloody straight razor, his weapon of choice, and a hank of hair, muddy brown with silvery blond highlights.

He waited for her to turn around. He was playing with her and it made her mad. "Damn."

His laugh had an unpleasant high-pitched ring to it. She looked around for the nearest exit. It was behind Beau Radford.

"Damn, damn, damn."

Beau laughed again. "I got your note. It was sweet."

"You're a pervert, Shampoo Boy!"

"Don't call me that." He said it pleasantly enough.

"Which? Pervert or Shampoo Boy?" Beau blocked her way to the door, which he had taken the precaution of closing. In the other room was the dead Polly and doors blocked by clothes. She did not want to see Polly's blank eyes again—or walk into a trap. Beau looked amused.

"How about Razor Boy?" she said. "You like that better?"

"You have such beautiful hair, Lacey."

"What's left of it, you freak! Look at these bangs. I can't wear bangs!" she said. *That's right. Poke the bear. Think for a change.*

He lunged at her. She dodged behind a chair and backed into a table. "I like your hair. It's prettier than Polly's," he said. He threw the bloody hank at her. The mess hit her in the chest and slid to the floor. It occurred to her that the dark streaks it made would have been even worse on a lighter suit. Marie had told her to wear red.

"You son of a bitch. This is new."

"I thought it was funny when you slid into the mud."

"Where are all the stylists?" she asked. She was frightened, but she gathered steam from pure adrenaline. Her face was burning.

"Watching the show. Now it's time for a little fashion show of our own." Beau seemed very calm, almost as if he'd taken a tranquilizer.

A salon is full of weapons, Jamie had told her at Angie's funeral, describing their game, Salon of Death. On the right side of the nearest table was some rebellious stylist's cigarette lighter, on the left was a hot curling iron, still plugged in, a hand mirror, mousses, gels, hair spray. She whirled around and grabbed the hair spray and reached for the lighter. Beau advanced on her. She turned back to face him.

"Stop right there, Shampoo Boy."

"I don't like it when you call me that, Lacey."

"I don't like my haircut." She flicked the lighter with her right hand and aimed the spray can with her left.

"What's that supposed to be?"

"It's a blowtorch, college boy."

He laughed. "Come here. I'll be your stylist today. A little off the top?"

"Wait a minute, Beau. Don't you want to talk to me, tell me why you're doing this?"

"Like on some lame TV cop show? Oh please. It would take hours, sweetheart, not that I couldn't get into that. Maybe with you all tied up." He stood still, imagining the scene. "Maybe in one of the salons at midnight. My salons."

"Your salons? That's why you killed your father?"

"It was his fault. Get help, he says. Get help. Hell with that. I help myself. So Lacey, should I tell you I love hair, or did you figure that out already?" He took one step toward her. Lacey flicked the lighter again. He stopped.

"Why Angie? Why Tammi? And your father?"

"Let me cut your hair. I'll tell you all about it," he purred.

Keep him talking, Lacey. "So it is the hair and not the videotape? What about the videotape?"

He sighed. "The stupid videotape. It was for Mother. I tried to track it down for her. Angie didn't have it. Tammi didn't have it. And there were other things I wanted. Things they did have. Their hair was so beautiful."

"Why did Josephine want it?" *Don't tell me they died because Josephine asked this idiot to get the video for her!*

"Who knows, who cares? Some scheme to get to Dad. But Angie and Tammi wouldn't let me touch their hair. They kept saying no to me, and nobody says no to me. I just wanted a lock of hair. They wouldn't let me cut a simple lock of hair."

"What about Polly?"

"Polly was different. Polly wanted me to do something with her hair."

"Where is the videotape now?"

"I don't have the freaking videotape! If she wants it, she'll just have to find it herself. I only want your hair. I already have a lover's lock of it." Lacey flashed back to the attack at Dyke Marsh. "I want more. I want to razor off your hair and take it home with me. But this time no biting. Never bite your stylist."

"Did it hurt?"

"Not like this will." He swished his razor at her. Lacey took a step back. Beau didn't like talking as much as she had hoped.

"Scared you, didn't I? Gee, this is fun. Wish we had all night."

"It's been swell for me too, Beau."

Lacey prayed that she had her finger on the right side of the hairspray nozzle. She flicked the lighter and sprayed into the small flame, creating a huge ball of fire. Beau was singed and jumped back, but so did Lacey, and she dropped the lighter.

Beau kicked it out of the way. Lacey still hung on to the hair spray. He moved toward her and she sprayed again. This time she scored a direct hit to Beau's eyes. He yelled. She grabbed a hand mirror to throw at him. It bounced off his forehead and clattered across the floor. He lurched toward her, blinking his eyes.

She yanked a hot curling iron out of the wall socket and lashed out with it. He reached for her and she burned his left hand. He screeched in pain. *Sizzle in the city*, she thought. But his right hand still held on to the razor.

"Bitch! Now I'm really going to make it hurt." He peered through swollen red slits, tears running down his face.

"Drop the blade, crybaby." Lacey backed away, holding the curling iron like a sword, and sprayed him again in the eyes with the hairspray. He howled. She threw the curling iron at his face and turned around to grab something, anything. There: a pair of long-bladed dressmaker's shears. She saw him rush toward her in the mirror and she twisted around just in time to dodge the edge of his razor. He was swinging wildly with his right hand, clawing at his eyes with his burned left hand.

"You're going to pay, you bitch. You're mine. I'm going to put your hair inside my pillow, so at night I'll smell you, you and your sweet dead hair. Mine forever."

She sprayed his eyes again. The can sputtered out and she threw it in his face. An enraged Beau blindly threw his razor at her. She ducked. She heard it bounce off a mirror. He dove at her with outstretched hands, roaring. Lacey crouched and held the shears straight out with both arms locked, just as if she were aiming Vic's gun. She held her breath. As his hands reached her hair and pulled, she felt the blades go in just above his belt buckle. It wasn't easy. He pulled harder. She gave the shears an extra push. He let go of her hair. He backed away.

Beau shrieked like a kamikaze going down. He waved his arms at her, then grabbed his stomach. He looked at the blades in his guts and the wet spot beginning to form on his black T-shirt. He turned over a chair as he crumpled, sliding down on his back, the long shears sticking up from his belly, his chest heaving.

Lacey's legs felt like rubber, but she stood up in spite of feeling shaky and light-headed. She stared down at Beau.

Absurdly, Lacey remembered her high-school first-aid class, where she was warned never to pull out a sharp implement from a puncture wound, whether an arrow, a stick, or a pair of scissors, which of course she was warned never to run with. Leave the pulling out to an expert. Lacey was more than willing to wait, even though her fingerprints were on the weapon.

First aid, my ass, she thought. She retrieved her note and her hair from Beau's jacket pocket. She gazed at him twisted on the floor like so much dirty laundry. *This is the bastard who killed Angie and butchered your hair.* He was still alive. The shears moved up and down with the rhythm of his breathing.

Styling debris was everywhere. Her reflection in a dozen mirrors was disheveled from every angle and dark stains marred her crimson suit. A box of tissues and a small shiny pair of styling scissors caught her eye. With the scissors, she bent over the now-quiet Shampoo Boy, grabbed a hunk of his hair, and swiftly cut it off at a ridiculous angle. It was a horrible yet satisfying feeling. She had no idea how long the whole episode had lasted. It seemed like hours.

She became aware of a commotion in the hall. There were sounds of footsteps and shouting. She wrapped the lock of black hair in a tissue and wiped the styling scissors free of fingerprints and hair. She replaced the scissors on the shelf and stuffed the tissue-wrapped hair in her pocket, her heart still pounding, her breath ragged.

Welcome to the Salon of Death.

The door burst open and people poured through it.

Vic Donovan was the first one in, followed by two guys who seemed to be taking his orders. They were followed by a chicly attired Josephine Radford, who screamed and had to be restrained by Vic's people from pulling the bloody shears out of her son's midsection. Lacey noticed that Josephine was looking rattled yet impeccable in a deep lilac Chanel suit.

Vic took one look, flew over to Lacey, who was shaking, and moved her safely out of the way of Beau's hysterical mother.

"I can't leave you alone for a minute, can I?"

She looked at him. She felt as if she were wrapped in cotton. Her voice sounded strange.

"Where the hell have you been? You are never there for me, Vic Donovan, so just what the hell damn good are you?"

"Whoa, calm down, Lacey. I'm here now."

"Easy for you to say. I have to face Razor Boy, here, all alone. By the way, he's the killer. In case anyone was wondering." Her voice rose. "The killer. Times three. No, four. Almost five."

"It's under control, Lacey." Vic's guys were talking into cell phones.

"Now it is! No thanks to you! I told you they weren't suicides. But do *you* do anything? No! I have to subdue the goddamn killer all by myself."

"Lacey, you're a little hysterical."

"What do you mean, a little? I deserve to be hysterical! A lot hysterical." She laughed. "I have to defend myself with hair spray and a curling iron! Damn! Damn! Damn!" To her complete horror, her eyes filled with tears. She turned around so he wouldn't see them. Vic put his hands on her shoulders.

She cleared her throat. "I was trying to find a phone to call nine-one-one, but he blocked the door. Polly Parsons is dead. Beau killed her. She's in the other room. Poor Polly. She should never have asked him about her hair." She heard someone run in there and scream. It might have been Josephine. "I think I'll sit down now."

Someone got her a chair; she didn't notice who it was.

Vic was afraid she would cry for real. "Dueling with scissors, Lacey. That's real commando stuff. We didn't cover that at the range."

"A woman's gotta do what a woman's gotta do."

Security guards burst in and took over the door. Then emergency personnel flooded the area. They put Beau, still unconscious, on an IV and strapped him to a gurney. They left the shears in place. *They must've taken the same first-aid class.* The guards blocked the room where Polly Parsons fell.

"I'm sorry I wasn't here." Vic knelt next to her. "Okay, Dragon Slayer. It's all over now."

She knew it wasn't. It was a big mess. Stella appeared out of nowhere and wrapped Lacey up in a ferocious hug. The story had spilled out of the room as if on tom-toms. Vic left them alone to help secure the scene.

"You did it, Lacey!" Stella squealed. "You are totally *grrrr!* But holy cow, honey, how did you know it was Beau?"

Lacey found herself babbling. "Hair. Hair. His hair. Hair extensions."

"Hair extensions? What hair extensions?" Stella looked puzzled; then it dawned on her. "Oh my God! That's where their hair went? Hair extensions? That's disgusting!"

More Stylettos hairstylists arrived and formed a protective wall around Lacey. When the D.C. cops finally arrived, Stella and her stylists sang out a deafening chorus in defense of the woman who had won the title round of Salon of Death against a killer.

The aftermath developed into a ready-made media mob scene, with so many broadcast personalities unexpectedly all dressed up at the actual scene of a crime. They called in their camera crews and broke into regularly scheduled programming with innumerable updates to show off their fabulously fashionable new looks, courtesy of Sizzle in the City and Stylettos. *Polly would have been proud.*

Lacey Smithsonian of *The Eye Street Observer* was hauled off for questioning and the story led the news on four stations and CNN. Claudia called from Paris, thrilled. The paper might not have the respect of its peers, but it could poke them in the eye with a world-class scoop once in a while. Mac was strutting like his namesake, General MacArthur.

Unfortunately, Lacey's last view of Vic was with Josephine draped all over him as he was propping her up and helping her to be strong. The cops took Lacey to a secure, undisclosed location. She immediately lawyered up and waited until Brooke Barton, Esquire, of Barton, Barton & Barton, arrived to guide her though the process and help bully the cops.

By midnight, Lacey was hoarse from endless explanations to the D.C. police and Agent Thorn of the FBI. But the tide of their questioning turned from hostile to accommodating when she remembered the voice-activated tape recorder in her purse, with Beau's admissions and his plans to save her hair after she was dead. Brooke practically glowed with pride. She loved clandestine tape recordings. Lacey also told them about Angie's blood-spattered styling station and the luminol photos, which Vic later turned over.

The question she found hardest to answer was this: "If you

had suspicions, Ms. Smithsonian, why didn't you tell the police?" She finally had to remind them that she had told the world, or at least her readers, that the two suicides were really murders. And the cops hadn't believed her.

At one a.m., Brooke had had enough and demanded they either press charges or back off. When they finally turned Lacey loose, Brooke took her back to her town house in Alexandria, where they ate hot-fudge sundaes and drank whiskey shooters until three.

Mac had told her to take the rest of the week off, which she rejected. She knew that she could never gain back the newsroom's hard-won respect if she wimped out. She would have to put on her war paint and storm right back into the newsroom tomorrow morning, fashionably late, but back. To Mariah's Desk of Doom. To Mac's bad ties and plaid shirts. To Felicity's tart lemon bars.

To the fashion beat.

CRIMES OF FASHION

Ask Not for Whom the Scandal Tolls—Get that Makeover Now!

by Lacey Smithsonian

Right now, somewhere in Washington, D.C., a scandal is brewing. It hasn't happened yet, but it will. Tomorrow or the next day or the next. Somewhere, a hapless victim is on the precipice of a fashion disaster. An unsuspecting woman will have her unsavory secrets exposed to the harsh light of day, the hot lights of television news, and the wisecracks of stand-up comedians everywhere.

When the scandal comes—and it will—this woman will be targeted for a full-scale assault on the way she acts, dresses, and looks, in addition to the salient details of her particular mess. Remember Linda, Paula, Monica, and Marcia. And now you.

Take it from a reporter. Whoever you are, we, the media, will excoriate you. Your old friends will rat on you. And it will be worse if your face isn't ready to face the music.

It is of appearance we speak here. Because how you are treated by the press depends greatly on how you look. It's not fair, but that's life. And it's worse for women. Generally, the media does not bother to humiliate men for their flab, their droopy jowls, their comb overs. Photographers do not waste film trying to get the best angle on their double chins and imperfect orthodontia. No, it is the modern-day Jezebel who is always dragged through the tabloid mud.

You know who you are—or maybe you don't, and you'll find out the same way we all will, by opening the morning newspaper. But if you wait to have that makeover until after the scandal breaks, it's too late—your image is already set in black-and-white and color. The lesson learned from past scandals is that you must look your best at all times. In the interest of fairness, I'm suggesting a few tips.

Your attention, class: Smithsonian's School for Scandal.

Washington Fashion Rules for the Scandal-Scorched

First, be clear about the look you're going for as you prepare to testify before the special prosecutor or chat with your friends in the Federal Bureau of Investigation. You want to appear attractive, demure, innocent, and thin. You do not want to look guilty, like a femme fatale, or, heaven forbid, fat.

Now, let's take it from the top, shall we? What about your hair? Short, sleek, shiny hair is a popular look for court. It is also acceptable to pull back long hair and secure it with a subtle tie. Try a chignon or a sophisticated French twist à la Hitchcock heroines. Hair can be any almost any color, but please avoid overprocessed, overpermed blond hair. That cotton candy look does not sell in our Nation's Capital. And for heaven's sake, use a comb! Bed head is dead. Remember that in humidity-drenched Washington, most women need gel, hair spray, or mousse to keep their hair under control. If you simply must sport Pre-Raphaelite masses of curls, or wear oversized hair ornaments like bows or scrunchies, throw yourself on the mercy of the court.

Crying jags make skin splotchy, and this looks bad, which we all know means you're guilty. Make friends with makeup—with a well-blended foundation. Use concealer for those dark circles from sleepless nights, and use mascara and subdued shadow to emphasize your eyes. Don't forget blush and lipstick. Nails should be neatly manicured. It should go without saying that green, blue, purple, and black polish will send the wrong message to the legal system.

For those panicky public encounters, do consider wearing:

- Pearl earrings and necklace, which say you're really very cultured in spite of your scandalous behavior. A small tasteful pin for the lapel is also appropriate.
- Subdued well-tailored suits, in flattering though reserved colors, when you testify. Navy, brown, and black may be boring, but boring is good, the opposite

of scandalous. A sharply tailored coatdress is also a winner and easy to wear. Bright colors and pastels will send a weak impression. In Washington, red is the exception to the bright-color rule. It is a power color. But be careful: Power corrupts. And remember, sleeves are never supposed to reach the second knuckle.

- Purses that are neat, tailored, and in good shape. A sleek shoulder bag is fine. Anything approaching the size of a grocery bag is too large. But they should be practical, large enough to carry a comb, lipstick, and a small compact for a quick touch-up in the ladies' room. And while you would probably like to carry a stun gun for those pesky journalists, I have to counsel against it.
- Black pumps, navy if necessary, medium heels, and no whining. Stockings, of course. The look should be well polished and neat.

Things to avoid like a visit from *60 Minutes*:

- Loud prints, polka dots, or plaids. They draw the wrong kind of attention.
- Dresses with puff sleeves and little ties in the back. You are not five.
- Odd garments such as overalls, unless you are a farmer or have a reasonable explanation, such as building houses for the poor.
- Stretched-out sweaters, which look particularly desperate. Desperation equals guilt.
- High hooker heels, unless you are in that business and not even then. In Washington, if your shoes scream guilty as sin, you're doomed.

Finally, take time to plan what you'll wear to court, to Congress, or to the press conference. Make sure everything fits well and is pressed and clean, the buttons are secure, the hem is stitched. If you're going to be in the media spotlight, you can at least look like a star, not a fashon felon. And when your tawdry little scandal finally fades—and it will—you'll still have those tabloid clippings to remind you of the good old days when you were the hottest thing inside the Beltway.

Chapter 29

On Thursday, Beauregard Radford was charged in the District of Columbia with the murder of Polly Parsons and the attempted murder of Lacey Smithsonian. Shampoo Boy was in intensive care, but expected to recover fully. Other charges were pending against him in Northern Virginia for the murder of Boyd Radford. Investigations into the deaths of Angie Woods and Tammi White were being reopened and murder charges were expected. Leo was telling everyone from the Arlington police to Tony Trujillo that he was just a fall guy. Josephine Radford wasn't responding to the media. Beth Ann Woodward had gone to her summer place in Maine, a little early in the season.

Mac announced he would put Lacey's picture at the head of her "Crimes of Fashion" column. She was horrified, and they were still wrangling over it weeks later. DeadFed dot com dedicated an editorial to "Scissor-Hand Smithsonian" and opined that she might be the target of a congressional conspiracy. Trujillo wrote the Thursday breaking story—"Eye Reporter Defends Herself with Shear Genius"—on the shocking events at what *The Eye* called "Slaughter in the City."

Marcia's videotape, her "insurance policy," had yet to be found, even though the FBI was very interested now. Angie's mother called to thank Lacey, but Lacey pointed out that she should really thank Stella, who had urged her on every step of the way. *Nudged, cajoled, and badgered, to be exact.*

Trujillo threw her an impromptu party at the newsroom late Friday afternoon. Claudia flew in from Paris. Brooke brought her entire law firm, including her father and uncle, both retired federal prosecutors, and danced with every man in the newsroom. She was delighted to find Tony Trujillo's pheromones apparently unjammed. Stella arrived with Michelle, Jamie, Bobby, and Marie the psychic, who gave everyone a free reading and told Mac his aura was "plaid." Mac supplied the food and liquor at company expense, and best of all, Felicity had to leave early and missed the party altogether.

Vic did not attend the party. Stella offered to invite him, and Lacey offered to find another stylist. She didn't want him there. When asked why, she was ironic about it. "It never fails. There I am alone with a madman and where's Prince Charming? Out feeding his horse, polishing his guns at the tavern with some serving wench on his lap."

"Hardly a serving wench, Lacey. She's the grieving widow."

"The point is, Stella, my dear, we don't need knights in shining armor as long as we have our own weapons, whether they're hot curling irons, a full can of hair spray, or sharp shears."

Sometime after midnight, in Farragut Square, across from *The Eye*'s headquarters, Lacey, Brooke, and Tony toasted the statue of Admiral David "Damn the torpedoes; full speed ahead!" Farragut with the paper's champagne. They agreed that "full speed ahead" was the only way to run a newspaper.

She went home, unplugged the phone, slept late, took naps, and indulged herself in picking out a vintage pattern of Aunt Mimi's and shopping for materials all weekend.

By the following Friday, the story on the Stylettos slayings was as dead as health-care reform. There would be more to come later, and Lacey might get to write about what to wear to testify, but for now her notoriety had faded like the cherry blossoms, downgraded to an old link on the DeadFed Web site. Mail was piling up in her box. Other reporters no longer demonstrated any interest in her fan mail. They had their own piles of press releases to wade through.

Lacey attacked her inbox after lunch and ripped open a puffy manila mailer. It held a videotape. No identification. No note. She checked the postmark: Virginia Beach. She glanced around. Johnson was on the Hill. Trujillo was on a story. Mac was at a meeting. Felicity was covering a Bake-Off. She was as good as invisible, so she headed to *The Eye*'s library, where a private room held a television and VCR, for news purposes only. Pleading deadline, she kicked out a couple of soap opera fans and shut the door. As she expected, the videotape quality was poor—it would never be a Sundance Film Festival finalist. But the players were there: Marcia Robinson, Boyd Radford, and a motley assortment of politicians, lobbyists, staffers, and teenage pages. And some surprises: Josephine Radford with some handsome boytoys, the attorney general dancing topless in a pink tutu while the "Waltz of the Hours" played in the background. No doubt, many people would want to see this. But who would be first?

Mac always says, 'Trust your editor.' Lacey smiled. She strolled past Mac's desk and dropped the videotape on top with a note: *Thought you'd know what to do with this. Watch for the pink tutu. I'm taking the afternoon off. Lacey.*

She canceled her date with Stella and went home. It was a perfect day for a walk, if your last Friday-afternoon stroll in the park hadn't ended up with a death threat, a dip in a mud bath, and an unwanted change in hairstyle, Lacey thought. She ran her hands through her hair, mentally encouraging the shorter fringe in front to grow faster. She breathed in the blue sky, the slight dampness in the air from an overnight spring shower, and the hint of wood smoke. Her legs felt rubbery, but she forced one foot in front of the other, down the path that led to the trail into Dyke Marsh.

Don't be crazy. He's locked up now. It's been two weeks since he attacked me here, Lacey told herself. And the simple law of averages would rule out another such attack for ages, years, maybe forever. How many people could she really piss off to the degree that they would want to kill her? Again? Even writing "Crimes of Fashion"? After all, it was only fashion. As she walked, Lacey concentrated on the things that gave her pleasure: a great blue heron swallowing a fish and snowy egrets standing like royalty among the commoners, the flocks of lowly ducks and gulls. She slowed her pace and let others pass her.

Her legs complained, but this was something she had to do, or else Beau would succeed in stealing far more than that lock of hair, which was now in a pillowcase full of various hair samples in a police evidence locker somewhere in the District of Columbia.

She couldn't tolerate the thought of being a victim. Once she completed this walk down the George Washington Memorial Parkway to the marsh, it would be easier to do it again. Someday she would reclaim the peace she had always found there.

The bulletin board at the entrance to Dyke Marsh still announced the early-morning bird walks in the wildlife preserve. Little had changed. It was quiet, with the occasional bird chirping its complaints. As always, it was comforting in its sameness. The sun sifted through the trees, creating a perfect blend of green light and golden haze. She hoped she would see a cardinal, Aunt Mimi's omen of good fortune.

She knew why it was more important that she make peace with the incident in Dyke Marsh than with the bloody mess behind the scenes at the fashion show. In the Salon of Death, she had been the winner. But walking down the trail meant returning to the scene of a skirmish she had lost, lost on her own turf, and it might easily have been much worse.

She began at a slow stroll, but her heart started pounding and her throat went dry. She felt a chill and realized that she was shaking. That made her angry, angry at the infamous Shampoo Boy, angry at herself for being such a wimp. She gained speed.

Now she moved faster and faster, walking with purpose. Her arms were swinging and her fists were clenched. The fallen trees had been cleared off the main path, huge trunks had been sawn into logs and piled off to the sides, and Lacey walked right past the place where Beau Radford attacked her, pausing only a moment to look behind her and take a deep breath. It was important, she thought, to get past it. To reach the end of the trail.

She turned left at the bend up to a small footbridge and realized she wasn't alone. He was sitting on a post, his face warmed by the sun. Blue work shirt and cowboy hat. Blue jeans that fit like temptation. His eyes seemed to be closed. She decided just to walk on by. He had left a few messages, but she hadn't returned them. *Probably just wanted his gun back.*

"Nice day for a walk, Lacey."

She stopped. "Walk? Vic, you never walk! Where'd you hide the damn Jeep?"

"Thought I might catch up with you here. You know, not everyone would come back here after a tussle in the woods."

"I had to. And I'll do it again and again, till it doesn't scare me anymore."

"That's what I figured. You never were a sissy. Crazy, but no sissy."

"Thanks. Same to you." Vic smiled at her. Heat spread through her limbs. "How did you know I would come here?"

"Little bird said you might be by. Said you canceled on her and took the afternoon off."

"A little Stella-bird?"

"That was a wicked-looking wound you gave Shampoo Boy."

"I should have aimed lower. They'd be calling him Soprano Boy."

"And it looked like someone took a chunk out of young Radford's hair. Like a souvenir. Sliced it off with a razor blade or something like that. Beau swears he can't remember. You wouldn't know anything about that, would you?"

Ignoring the question, she leaned against one post of the planked bridge.

"Why are you here, Vic? Your client Ratboy is dead. Shampoo Boy is locked up until he can go to trial or the nuthouse." Young Radford—who threatened to commit suicide when the cops took his hair extensions for evidence—had been "MOd" for a thirty-day mental observation. "And the grieving ex-widow . . . Well, what about the widow? Doesn't she require your personal services anymore?"

Josephine was in seclusion. The widow was torn, it seemed. She loved her son and had hated her ex-husband, but couldn't reconcile herself to the entire nightmare. All because she had asked Beau to retrieve Marcia's videotape from Angie. And when Beau failed, she put Leo on the job. Josephine had given him carte blanche to find the tapes. She told him to do whatever it took, including burglary. And now Lacey knew why.

"She wanted me to join Beau's defense team as lead investigator. I passed. Besides, I'm on your side. We're friends. Aren't we friends, Lacey?"

Lacey stared at him, not trusting herself to speak, although of course she would. She would probably stick her foot in her mouth at the same time.

"The truth is, Vic, I don't want to be your friend. It's too hard. I can't deal with just being your friend and watching you waltz off with that barracuda, Josephine."

"We aren't waltzing off anywhere. We aren't even waltzing. And we've never waltzed."

"You're sure? Not even a quick two-step?"

"I swear. Not even once."

"Not that you've ever asked me for a dance. Or anything."

"I see," Vic said.

"Is that all you can say? 'I see'? That's it. Fine. I am done with humiliating myself." She took a step backward. "I have swallowed a boatload of humiliation lately, including unburdening my soul to you. Thanks for everything, Vic, but I don't need a baby-sitter. I can take this walk by myself, okay?" She straightened up, took a deep breath, and turned toward the end of the marsh. "Go away."

He slid off his post and stood in front of her.

"I was just waiting for you to say it, Lacey. That's all."

"Say what?"

"That you want to waltz off with me."

"I want to waltz off with you?"

"Well, I guess that'll do." He held her, kissed her hard and long. Here was a man who knew what he was doing. He was just the right height and his arms felt damn good around her. She melted a little, not that she'd let it show. He pulled her into a slow waltz right there on the bridge.

"You're going to drive me crazy, Victor Donovan."

"Don't worry, honey. It's a short drive."

A **Crime of Fashion** Mystery

by Ellen Byerrum

Designer Knockoff

When fashion columnist Lacey Smithsonian learns that a new fashion museum will soon grace decidedly unfashionable D.C., it's more than a good story—it's a chance to show off her vintage Hugh Bentley suit. And when the designer, himself, notices her at the opening, Lacey gets the scoop on his past—which includes a long-unsolved mystery about a missing employee. When a Washington intern disappears, Lacey gets suspicious and sets out to unravel the murderous details in a fabric of lies, greed, and (gasp!) very bad taste.

0-451-21268-1